PENGUIN BOOKS

*Tender is the Night*

*worked for a short time in Hollywood as a screen-writer.*

F. Scott Fitzgerald was born in 1896 in St Paul, Minnesota, and went
to Princeton University, which he left in 1917 to join the army. He
was said to have epitomized the Jazz Age, which he himself defined as
'a generation grown up to find all Gods dead, all wars fought, all faiths
in man shaken'. In 1920 he married Zelda Sayre. Their traumatic
marriage and her subsequent breakdowns became the leading influ-
ence on his writing. Among his publications were five novels, *This Side
of Paradise*, *The Great Gatsby*, *The Beautiful and Damned*, *Tender is the Night*
and *The Last Tycoon* (his last and unfinished work); six volumes of short
stories and *The Crack-Up*, a selection of autobiographical pieces.
Fitzgerald died suddenly in 1940. After his death *The New York Times*
said of him that 'He was better than he knew, for in fact and in the
literary sense he invented a "generation" ... he might have interpreted
and even guided them, as in their middle years they saw a different and
nobler freedom threatened with destruction.'

*hospitalized in psychiatric hospitals*

*1934*

*alcoholic*

Richard Godden is Professor of American Literature in the Department of American Studies at the University of Keele. His interest in
how economic structures may be read as the generative source of
fictional forms is reflected in his critical studies *Fictions of Capital* (1990)
and *Fictions of Labour* (1997).

*Jazz Age 1919–1929*

*corresponds w/ Diver's marriage*
*married in 1919*
*divorced 1929/1930-ish*

*Nicole's sickness spans the involvement of the Americans in WWI*

# F. SCOTT FITZGERALD

## Tender is the Night

### A ROMANCE

*Edited by* ARNOLD GOLDMAN
*With an Introduction and Notes by* RICHARD GODDEN

PENGUIN BOOKS

**PENGUIN BOOKS**

Published by the Penguin Group
Penguin Books Ltd, 80 Strand, London WC2R 0RL, England
Penguin Putnam Inc., 375 Hudson Street, New York, New York 10014, USA
Penguin Books Australia Ltd, 250 Camberwell Road, Camberwell, Victoria 3124, Australia
Penguin Books Canada Ltd, 10 Alcorn Avenue, Toronto, Ontario, Canada M4V 3B2
Penguin Books India (P) Ltd, 11 Community Centre, Panchsheel Park, New Delhi – 110 017, India
Penguin Books (NZ) Ltd, Cnr Rosedale and Airborne Roads, Albany, Auckland, New Zealand
Penguin Books (South Africa) (Pty) Ltd, 24 Sturdee Avenue, Rosebank 2196, South Africa

Penguin Books Ltd, Registered Offices: 80 Strand, London WC2R 0RL, England

www.penguin.com

First published 1934
Revised version published 1951
Revised version published in Penguin Books 1955
First edition, with emendations, published in Penguin Books 1982
First edition, with further emendations, reprinted 1986
Reprinted with a new Introduction and Notes 1998
Reprinted in Penguin Classics 2000

5

Copyright 1934 © F. Scott Fitzgerald
Editorial matter copyright © Arnold Goldman, 1982, 1986
Introduction and Notes copyright © Richard Godden, 1998
All rights reserved

Made and printed in Great Britain by
Clays Ltd, St Ives plc
Set in Monotype Baskerville

TO
GERALD AND SARA
MANY FÊTES

# CONTENTS

*in medias res*
→ *in the middle of things*

*"Already with thee! tender is the night,*
*. . . But here there is no light,*
*Save what from heaven is with the breezes blown*
*Through verdurous glooms and winding mossy ways."*
"Ode to a Nightingale"

# INTRODUCTION

## I

At the close of Book I, Dick Diver is a skilled socialite; at the close of the first sentence of Book II, he is Doctor Richard Diver, his professional education following in rapid paraphrase. In Book I there have been intimations of a proper job, a 'work house' glimpsed (35), a 'scientific treatise' abandoned (72), a medical practice discontinued (73) ... but nothing to undermine the prevalent impression of Dick as a man who can spot a beach, talk to hoteliers; organize a party, borrow the Shah of Persia's car, gloss a battlefield – in short, make it 'all right' (125) for expatriate Americans, 'promenading insouciantly upon the national prosperity' (85). As such, Dick does the dollar's work.

A demobbed American in Paris, making a living by selling American newspapers to English speakers at inflated prices, shows Dick a cartoon featuring 'a stream of Americans pouring from the gangplank of a liner freighted with gold'. The salesman offers an estimate of 'two hundred thousand' passengers, spending 'ten million a summer' (105). Arguably, his guess is conservative: the economic historian Herbert Feis speaks of a decade in which the dollar, operating as 'the universal balm' engaged in 'exuberant tours of the world [looking] for something to do' (Feis 48), while Emily Rosenberg notes that 'the United States flooded the world with products, branch plants and investment capital ... making the decade one of the most economically expansive in the nation's history' (Rosenberg 122). Baby Warren follows suit, investing capital from the sale of Chicago property in a Swiss psychiatric 'plant' (Fitzgerald's noun (192)). In 1919 direct US investment abroad ran at $38 million, the amount rising to $7.9 billion by 1924. During the summer of 1925, Nicole Warren litters the beach at Tarmes with parasols, portable bath houses and inflatable horses, items which for Fitzgerald exemplify 'the first burst of luxury manufacturing after the War' (27). Given Nicole's spending spree in Paris (65), there is every chance that these are of European manufacture. But, since the US government encouraged private overseas loans in the post-war period, European manufacturers are likely to be operating thanks to the exuberancy of the dollar. To schematize: the US emerged from the war with a great capital surplus and owning much of the world's gold; in order to sell abroad it had to transfer wealth to potential buyers. Dick's liner becomes the ship of state offloading gold on behalf of 'a global expansion of American property holding' (Rosenberg 157).

On the evidence of Book I *alone* Dick might pass as the dollar's diplomat and agent of a 'promotional state' (Rosenberg 63). During June and July of 1925 he is quite literally immersed in liquidities: he swims well and drinks much. The foundation of these activities is itself an act of mutation, care of the Warren fortune: we are told that the Villa Diana owes its site in 'the ancient hill village of Tarmes' to the combination of 'five small houses', four more being 'destroyed to make the gardens' (35–6). The mere presence of the Divers during the summer transforms Gausse's year, persuading him to extend the season of the Hôtel des Étrangers, a decision which modifies the economy of the coast (11). The subsequent removal of Dick and Nicole to Paris, indicative of the general mobility of those who 'follow the dollar' (Cowley 82), provides more evidence of violent transformations promoted by wealth and attendant upon Dick. Two incidents are typical. First, a party in 'a house hewn from the frame of Cardinal de Retz's palace', the 'outer shell' of which 'seemed ... to enclose the future so that it was an electric-like shock' (82). Second, the case of Jules Peterson, 'a small manufacturer of shoe polish' from Stockholm (119), who approaches 'the entirely liquid Mr. North' (84) with a request that he invest in a business in Versailles. Peterson receives two hundred francs on account and is next seen dead on Rosemary Hoyt's bed in a Paris hotel room. Dick tidies up, observing that Peterson's remains are removed 'with a celerity that ... as a businessman, [he] would have quite understood' (125).

Yet a reading of Dick as a function of America's post-war economic liquidity is partial because in the midst of what, from the viewpoint of exchange, might be termed creative destruction, he remains 'hard'. Synonyms for Dick's hardness litter Book I, but tend to gather around the issue of his manners. Rosemary variously notes a 'layer of hardness', stemming from 'self-control', which renders him 'complete' (28); a 'hard, neat brightness' that generates 'surety' (40); and a 'tensile strength' (76), appearing at times 'fixed and Godlike' (117). Dick's fixity is purposive. He exists, at least in Book I, to be the 'organizer of private gaiety, curator of a richly incrusted happiness' (87) at the centre of which stands Nicole – the wife who, from her first appearance, shares her husband's epithet, being 'hard' (14), with a 'hardness' (64), 'mean [and] hard' (29), which does not detract from her loveliness.

The couple's joint impermeability includes elements of the archaic. Curatorship involves preservation, most typically in a museum. Incrustation suggests a layering which is best understood through Fitzgerald's sense that a Diver day on the Riviera is organized 'like the day of the older civilizations to yield the utmost from the materials at hand, and to give all the transitions their full value' (30). The civilizations in question are mannered and Victorian. I hesitate to compare the beach at Tarmes to a late-nineteenth-century interior, but I take the risk because both places share 'transitions' and 'materials' which are 'full' to the 'utmost' (or 'hard') with and through the cumulative niceties of a particular system of manners; besides, Dick's beach boasts three British nannies knitting 'the slow pattern of Victorian England . . . into sweaters and socks' (12). By way of comparison, I offer an 1870s interior from Wharton's *The Age of Innocence* (1920):

There was something about the luxury of the Welland house and the density of the Welland atmosphere, so charged with minute observances and exactions, that always stole into his system like a narcotic. The heavy carpets, the watchful servants, the perpetually reminding tick of disciplined clocks, the perpetually renewed stack of cards and invitations on the hall table, the whole chain of tyrannical trifles binding one hour to the next, and each member of the household to all the others, made any less systematized and affluent existence seem unreal and precarious. (Wharton 190)

Time and the air are created by the latent law of manners made plain through decoration. Time is retrospective; a clock *reminds* the present that the past is its measure and corrective. Each social season in Wharton's New York repeats the events of the previous season. Received manners give form and protect that form from change. Not surprisingly, the carpet is 'heavy', the atmosphere 'narcotic' and the stack of cards, though it changes, remains the same. Taste in the 1870s must encourage inertia in order to proclaim the stability of the accumulated wealth from which it arises.

To move through such spaces requires cumulative knowledge, dependent upon leisure time and deriving from a secure property base. As Thorstein Veblen put it in 1899, 'the pervading principle and abiding test of good breeding is the requirement of a substantial and patent waste of time' (Veblen 51). *The Theory of the Leisure Class* introduces the phrases 'conspicuous leisure' and 'conspicuous consumption' as it makes the case that leisure, far from being indolent, requires persistent and 'useless' labour in the cultivation of artifacts whose values mount in exact proportion to the number of discriminations sedimented within them. For example, Veblen's leisure class expends great energy breeding pedigree dogs, while the van der Luydens, first among Wharton's New York families, tend orchids; the acme of each form is an exemplar that perishes almost as it is conceived – the perfect pug has a face so flat that an operation is required at birth to free its nasal passages, the finest orchid is but a brief flower. Such objects are useless but dense with fine distinctions. Dick's raking of the beach is similarly useless but equally productive of discrimination: the white do not sit with the tanned, they sit among 'pebbles and dead sea-weed' (14), nor do they swim as well; and although they appreciate Dick's 'plot', both social and territorial, they 'don't know who's in [it] . . . and who isn't' (16).

The beach is merely one of the densely patterned 'sureties' created by Dick. Whether these involve a café table, a railway terminal or, eventually, in Book II, a clinic, each is an exclusive and integrative environment, organized to posit a wealth of information where, perhaps, there was none before. Dick's manner can transform any object or person into a set of signs, while convincing those around him that his signs are wonders belonging only to them. Witness Dick's achievement during an inauspicious party at the Villa Diana:

Rosemary, as dewy with belief as a child from one of Mrs. Burnett's vicious tracts, had a conviction of home-coming, of a return from the derisive and salacious improvisations of the frontier . . . The table seemed to have risen a little toward the sky like a mechanical dancing platform, giving the people around it a sense of being alone with each other in the dark universe, nourished by its only food, warmed by its only lights. And . . . the two Divers began suddenly to warm and glow and expand, as if to make up to their guests, already so subtly assured of their importance, so flattered with politeness, for anything they might still miss from that country well left behind. Just for a moment they seemed to speak to every one at the table, singly and together, assuring them of their friendliness, their affection. And for a moment the faces turned up toward them were like the faces of poor children at a Christmas tree. Then abruptly the table broke up—(43–4)

The aura is one of return; expatriate Americans recover the USA as the essence of one leisure class. The period, for a moment, is 'the golden nineties' (191), Dick's phrase for a time of new 'landfall' (191) and 'innocent expectation' (192). Cap D'Antibes is not quite recast, care of *The Great Gatsby*, as the 'green breast of the new world' (*The Great Gatsby* 182); but the 'frontier' of 'the dark universe' is momentarily still out there, and ripe for appropriation. These people rest assured, their identities provided for by earlier appropriations – theirs is the 'only food', the 'only light'. Where selfhood resides in private property, privately improvised, mutuality takes form as mutual appreciation and emulation; consequently, the guests feel at once 'alone' and 'with each other', even as their hosts speak to them 'singly' and 'together'. Flattery and politeness create a unifying sentiment, at once integrational and territorial. The Christmas-tree allusion marks it as a sentimentality, while 'the mechanical dancing platform' underscores contrivance. None the less, Diver's manner has transformed a disintegrating group into an archaic leisure-class. The effect cannot long withstand the degree of its fabrication. The Villa Diana is as detached from the world of 1925 as Mrs Burnett's *Secret Garden* (1911), and it is only a matter of time before its proprietor's manners seem as mannered as those of her *Little Lord Fauntleroy* (1881). But for most of the long moment of Book I, the various places that Dick makes retain solidity.

Symptomatically, their 'curator' learned his manners from his father, a master of the Victorian drawing-room:

"Once in a strange town when I was first ordained, I went into a crowded room and was confused as to who was my hostess. Several people I knew came toward me, but I disregarded them because I had seen a gray-haired woman sitting by a window far across the room. I went over to her and introduced myself. After that I made many friends in that town." (223)

The Reverend Diver is a clerical dandy more given to taste than to theology: his 'good heart' derives from 'good instincts' which are the creatures of his 'honor' and 'courtesy' and 'beautifully cut clerical clothes' (223). Dick throughout his life 'referred judgments to what his father would probably have thought or done' (222), again an indication of an archaic inclination. This element of preservation in Dick's character brings us back to Veblen, for whom the leisured are characterized by 'arrested spiritual development' in so far as they resist change by indulging in 'survival and reversion' (Veblen 145).

## II

I have undertaken two partial readings, each in itself misguided. In the former Dick embodies the flow of a globalizing capital. In the latter he epitomizes an archaic manner which rigidifies that flux. My readings are apparently contradictory, yet their conjunction may be explored since they meet in Nicole, who is the recipient both of Warren's disruptive fortune and of Dick's surety of manner. As such, she is the site of an untenable disturbance: taught to be 'hard', she is the conduit of all that softens. Fitzgerald locates the origin of her instability within the act of paternal incest.

Early in Book II we learn that Dick is a psychiatrist who has taken on, nominally for life, the damaged child of 'feudal' monies

(142), under a 'ducal' name (175); in other words, the spoiled daughter of accumulated capital, spoiled by her father. For Nicole Dick creates his sureties, displacing her 'bad' father by means of the manners of his 'good' father. Before discussing the narrative implications of the incest trauma, it is necessary to recognize both its centrality and its pervasiveness. Devereux Warren's sexual pathology keeps cropping up. *Tender is the Night* is beset by ill-disguised fathers and under-aged girls. In Rome (city of papal fathers), on his way to court to be tried for striking a plain-clothed policeman, Dick learns that a native of Frascati has been arrested for raping and killing a child: in court Dick cries out, 'I want to explain to these people how I raped a five-year-old girl. Maybe I did—' (256). Disturbed by the recent death of his own father, Dick perceives himself as a child molester because, by transference, he may be, in Nicole's eyes, the molesting father. In which case, Dick is two fathers: the good reverend father and the bad Devereux Warren. Paternity becomes him but is always liable to become something else. He meets Rosemary on the eve of her eighteenth birthday, objects that he has no intention of marrying his daughter Topsy (278) and threatens his son Lanier with divorce (285). As though enough were enough, Fitzgerald cut from the last page of the manuscript the suggestion that Dr Diver of Lockport is 'entangled' not simply with 'a girl who worked in a grocery store', but with a sixteen-year-old.

Not all the paternal duplicities relate directly to Dick. The Chilean aristocrat who begs treatment for his homosexual and alcoholic son is called Señor Pardo Y Cuidad Real – I offer in my own defence Dick's warning to Abe North, 'You can come if you want to play anagrams' (121) – transposed, the Spanish might read, 'Senior, sorry, I see you Dad for real.' Once witnessed, the indirect exposure of culpable fathers and consenting children proliferates and permutates. *Baby* Warren and *Daddy's* Girl are simply surface clues to an associative network capable of determining interpretation. Both casual and condensed usage contributes to an emergent, if occult, pattern which ghosts characters and modifies action. For example, Dick's cry as he assaults his policeman – 'first I'll fix this baby' (246) – could pass as coincidence, were it not that within a page, Fitzgerald notes, across from Baby Warren's hotel, two carabinieri 'grotesque in swaddling capes', one of them a 'tall member of a short race' (247). Sustained innuendo triggers a sub-plot pregnant with infantile desire. The same occult design probably prompts Dick to recall Fatty Arbuckle as he relieves Rosemary of her stained Parisian bed linen – Arbuckle's career was cut short by charges of murderous attention to a child below the age of consent. Sexually poisonous adults achieve their nadir in the father of the American artist treated at Zugersee for nervous eczema: she dies 'imprisoned' in an 'Iron Maiden' of scab (202) as a result of neuro-syphilis, possibly contracted from her father at conception. Under-aged girls come no younger. The diagnosis is Dohmler's; Dick does not want to hear it, insisting, 'If she cared enough about her secret to take it away with her, let it go at that' (263). Why is he so secretive? During the patient's decline, Dick 'went out to her unreservedly, almost sexually. He wanted to gather her up in his arms, as he so often had Nicole, and cherish even her mistakes, so deeply were they part of her' (204). The doctor would 'cherish' the deep 'mistake' of incest, containing the 'secret' with the therapeutic advice, 'We must all try to be good' (204). As an 'Iron Maiden' his patient is profanely pure and quite beyond sexual exchange; Dick's role as a surrogate good father is consequently eased. To conclude any account of what I would call the incest constellation with this example is to psychologize a sub-plot whose implications are far broader. The associative network should not be hidden within the psychology of one character, or indeed of the author, since Fitzgerald's preoccupation with the social and financial status of the father (good or bad) requires that incest be understood as a trauma within which the sexual and the economic semanticize one another.

The father, according to the incest taboo, must release his daugh-ter into marriage outside the family. Warren's greed is such that he fails in this exchange; he keeps his daughter for himself. The logic of accumulation transgresses the incest taboo, and Dick is hired to make good that transgression. The word 'cure' would be inappropriate. Dick as the good father supplants the bad father, restoring Nicole to integrity: she is made 'complete' and 'hard', terms carrying a Jamesian freightage. However, restoration involves blocking the trauma. Nicole is denied access to her father's offence. Secret keys proliferate on Dick's person: plainly he is the key to the case, but during Dohmler's clinical report Dick remembers 'a scene in his childhood when everyone in the house was looking for the lost key to the silver closet', a key he had hidden in his mother's top drawer (154). Janitorial duties started young. At some level Nicole recognizes Dick as her keeper: she bars Mrs McKisco from the troubled bathroom in the Villa Diana 'because the key was thrown down the well' (185), and Nicole knows who did it. Her allusion, redolent of nursery rhyme, chimes in with her own earlier letter in which she described Dick as 'wise behind your face like a white cat' (139). The wise 'pussy' who joins the key at the bottom of the well presumably sees the solution as incarceration. When – with 'verbal inhumanity' seeping through the keyholes – the reader finally enters 'the horror' in the bathroom it is to witness Dick shutting doors:

Nicole knelt beside the tub swaying sidewise and sidewise. 'It's you!' she cried, '—it's you come to intrude on the only privacy I have in the world —with your spread with red blood on it. I'll wear it for you—I'm not ashamed, though it was such a pity. On All Fools Day we had a party on the Zürichsee, and all the fools were there, and I wanted to come dressed in a spread but they wouldn't let me——'

'Control yourself!'

'—so I sat in the bathroom and they brought me a domino and said wear that. I did. What else could I do?'

'Control yourself, Nicole!'

'I never expected you to love me—it was too late—only don't come in the bathroom, the only place I can go for privacy, dragging spreads with red blood on them and asking me to fix them.'

'Control yourself. Get up——'

Rosemary, back in the salon, heard the bathroom door bang, and stood trembling: now she knew what Violet McKisco had seen in the bathroom at Villa Diana. (125–6)

In a room designed for purgation Dick insists on repression. Nicole resists as she has resisted before. Her memory of procedures at the

Zürichsee might be glossed, 'While at the clinic, among the foolish and the mad, I wished to wear a spread but was given a domino.' 'Spread' condenses a plot; prompted by stained bed-linen, the word recalls the sheet marked with the blood of Nicole's hymen. Despite 'spread[s]' declarative openness, the clinical staff gave her a 'domino' – an elaborate and often sequined mask. When Nicole tried to understand her trauma, her doctors sought to disguise it with the artifacts of mannered wealth. Dick is of their party. He holds the key to her case and keeps the door locked. None the less, the stain and the domino are complementary; if they were not, Dick's therapy could not work. The mask typifies the affluence of a particular class, even as its occasion and incrustation embody those discriminating principles which condense leisure objects into systems of 'invidious difference' (Henry James). The stain too is a surface dense with comparative information: beneath it lies the father/phallus, but before he can be seen he is displaced by the hotel linen, the clinicians, the domino, Dick, Mcbeth . . . Though the associative list can be extended, my point remains a simple one – items in both the bourgeois drawing-room and the unconscious solidify through cumulative nicety. The furnishing of each privacy depends upon an absent father; the Victorian interior expresses his consolidating aggression in the market-place, while in the unconscious, according to Fitzgerald, images solicit over-interpretation and designate at the core of their wealth the missing and threatening father.

Dick's task, as a psychiatrist and socialite, is to reduce the paternal threat while maintaining the father's good name. He is therefore an agent who extends the logic and imperatives of bourgeois privacy. Nicole is Devereux Warren's continuity: his first daughter is 'wooden and onanistic' (168) and will possibly not marry; rebuilt by Dick, the damaged younger child will exchange with her proper mate, that is to say, with a male who can ensure the 'ducal' group's exclusivity and privilege. Warren's 'feudal' monies will be safe with Tommy Barban, mercenary in royal causes, opponent of socialism and trainee stock-speculator. Oddly, by preparing Nicole for the right marriage, Dick preserves the fount of his own gifts – the accumulations that foster and give purpose to his manners. As the Reverend Diver's child, nostalgic for 'religion and years of plenty and tremendous sureties and the exact relation that existed between the classes' (67), he cannot afford to acknowledge that the monies of the *haute bourgeoisie* were corrupt, even at their head and point of distribution. He knows, better than most, how 'a century of middle-class love' finally 'spent' itself: he could doubtless map 'the last love battle' and measure to the inch the 'great gust of high explosive love' (68); incest is very much his Western Front and the end of 'all [his] beautiful lovely safe world' (68). He says as much on a visit to the trenches around Amiens; however, by globalizing incest Dick gnomically and unanalytically extends the power of the father.

The case obliges him to find paternity everywhere and to encourage the reader and Nicole to make and fear such revelations. At a late stage in their marriage Nicole objects, 'Am I going through the rest of life flinching at the word "father"?' (311). Her rebuke is a measure of her renewal: she ceases to be a child of two fathers and becomes instead her grandfather reincarnate – her voice and 'white crook's eyes' encourage her to believe that she has 'gone back to [her] true self' (314). There is, however, nothing regressive about her return, since, in this instance, the displacement of both fathers ensures the viability of the Warren monies. The whole point about crooked grandfathers is that they know how to invest. Nicole, as her grandfather's spirit *circa* 1929, would take his money to Hollywood: symptomatically, she marries a man who likens himself to Ronald Colman and who, in her eyes, resembles 'all the adventurers in the movies' (290).

But I run ahead of myself. To recap: I have argued that, for Fitzgerald, the central sexual act of *Tender is the Night* operates as an economic metaphor, transposing Devereux Warren's sexual greed, in all its irresponsibility, into a symptom of compulsive accumulation. Dick by 'transference' (134) is associated with the values of a pre-war leisure class. His sureties grant miraculous longevity to the Father (after a brief interview with Dick in Lausanne the apparently dying Warren takes up his bed and walks (271)). None the less, it is important to recognize that the incest motif can be read in another and seemingly opposed way. Seen from within a longer economic perspective, the act contains a second impacted narrative: it embodies accumulation but simultaneously transgresses limits. By penetrating Nicole, Warren becomes father *and* lover, even as he makes his child into daughter *and* mistress. Incest creates *dis*integral selves through a multiplication of roles which, by analogy, I would liken to a shift in economic emphasis. An intersection between sexual and economic trauma registers precisely how a change in the history of capital changes the history of bourgeois selfhood. For the full and Janus-faced significance of incest in *Tender is the Night* to be recognized some account of a crucial shift in the history of capital is necessary.

### III

The interlude which follows is premised on the belief that the foundation of manners is economic, and that as economic structures change, so manners are modified. From the close of the Civil War to 1900 the story of American capital is largely one of expansion and accumulation of resource. Alan Trachtenberg dubs the gilded age the age of incorporation; however, it is clear that during the opening three decades of the new century the very form of capital was seen to change. But first some facts and figures. While a worker's income increased by an average of 14 per cent between 1923 and 1929, corporate profit rose in the same period by 62 per cent, and corporate dividends by 65 per cent. The reason for this may be glossed in two terms, 'centralization' and 'standardization'. Mergers were endemic, particularly in the fields of electricity and banking. Even as the energy that drove industrial capital centralized, so the credit that financed expansion passed into fewer and fewer hands; by 1929, 1 per cent of the banking facilities of the country controlled over 46 per cent of the nation's banking resources.

The net effect of centralization was an increasing rationalization of resources, and with it fresh fears of an excess capacity. To ensure continuous and full use of their accumulations firms had to move into new markets and develop new lines. Each expansion put greater strain on the running of production, and a managerial revolution, coupled with the multiplication of national distribution systems, simply fuelled the cause of standardized and efficient administration.

By the 1920s 'administration' was gargantuan in ambition: as scientific management and technological innovation guaranteed that expanding and incorporating capital could produce cheaply, advertising sought to monitor and create market needs. Indeed, as early as 1843 one New York copywriter claimed:

Advertising has to deal with the greatest principles underlying the relation of man to man . . . It is the medium of communication between the world's greatest forces – demand and supply. It is a more powerful element in human progress than steam or electricity. (Quoted by Frank Presbrey 341).

By 1920 it was plain that only by controlling desire could corporate capital reproduce itself. As Stuart Ewen puts it, the 'captain of industry' had to become the 'captain of consciousness' if his accumulations were to survive; between 1900 and 1930 national advertising revenues increased thirteenfold.

Statistics can indicate the quantity of change but miss the qualitative shift. What one witnesses between 1900 and 1930 is a shift in economic emphasis from 'accumulation' to 'reproduction' characteristic of the age of late capitalism (Mandel 245). By 1900 the accumulated capital existed; the real issue was reproduction – how to produce sufficient profit to support that accumulation. Neither Taylor's time and motion studies nor Ford's flow production in and of themselves offer adequate protection, because high productivity can yield the necessary profit only if the markets are primed to consume what has been produced.

Arguably, consumers are the most important product of late capitalism: they are the primary machine without which 'the very play time of the people' could not be 'run . . . into certain moulds' (Lynd 491):

Consumption is the name given to the new doctrine; and it is admitted today to be the greatest idea that America has given to the world; the idea that the workmen and masses be looked upon not simply as workers and producers, but as consumers . . . Pay them more, sell them more, prosper more is the equation. (Christine Frederick, *Selling Mrs Consumer* (1929), quoted by Ewen 22)

In the words of Paula Fass, analysing collegiate youth in the twenties, 'the big sell had become synonymous with America's contribution to Western Civilization' (Fass 257). Selling required high levels of advertising and credit.

All this may seem some distance from the 'richly incrusted' niceties of Dick Diver's mannered spaces. Although his quasi Victorian interiors at the Villa Diana and the clinic certainly manifest conspicuous leisure and conspicuous consumption, they cannot guarantee a high turn-over in consumption, and positively militate against a truly mass market for the items that they contain. Those items are 'solid', even as the manners that surround them are 'solid' (so scrupulously learned as to appear innate). What capital increasingly needs after 1900 is a highly mobile, highly reproducible and highly controllable system of manners. That is to say, fashion must supplant manners: where taste once stood, style must stand.

Manners and taste are cumulative and integrative; indeed the selfhood that they realize is its own ultimate possession. Fashions and styles are equally an extension of capital, but of capital focused on the sphere of reproduction. Fashion is always disintegrative; it aims to give us several selves, thereby providing capital with a diversification of markets.

The new 'science' of advertising invested heavily in social insecurity. Consumers of the twenties were taught to denigrate their own bodies: in 1920 Listerene was just another general antiseptic – with the help of 'halitosis' (exhumed from an old medical dictionary) and a story line ('He never knew why') the copywriters Feasley and Seagrove invented a new anxiety and with it a new habit. Between 1921 and 1929 Listerene's 'virtues' spread panic through pore and orifice: the public learned of its capacities as a dandruff, cold and sore-throat cure, astringent, deodorant and douche. 'Bromodosis' (sweaty feet), 'office hips', 'accelerator toe', 'vacation knees', 'ashtray breath', and 'spoon-fed face' may be dated diseases, but the sustained economic assault on the consumer's 'integrity' is far from over, and its direction is ever inwards – witness vaginal deodorants and suppository selling. The problem lies in the finances of the corporate body and not in the sweetness of the bodies on the street. Likewise, the solution is corporate: consumers must forget their deficient 'self' and purchase the selves made available by the business community.

One way of focusing the interconnected histories of self and capital is to present their liaison in schematic form:

| *Sphere of accumulation* | *Sphere of reproduction* |
|---|---|
| Inertia of capital ('emulation') | High turn-over of capital (mass market) |
| Leisure class | Culture industry |
| Manners | Fashion |
| Integrative selfhood | Disintegrative selfhood |
| (A drawing-room) | (Hollywood) |

*Tender is the Night* straddles the transition from classical imperialism to late capitalism largely by way of the incest that lies at its narrative core. Witness how the incest victim is 'cured': her cure is unconventional, she simply moves towards an alternative mode of selfhood, lodged in a modified economic reality. She negates the incest trauma by ignoring it. The 'cord' can be 'cut ... forever' (324) because Nicole appreciates herself as a new species of consumer, one to whom accumulations are no longer of primary relevance. Consequently, her interior and its old environs – cumulative, private, dense and supported by an etiquette equally weighted with 'interpretation or qualification' (320) – can be forgotten. Indeed, amnesia is obligatory. The father-centred world must give way to brand name and movie still if grandfather's capital (the capital of classical imperialism) is to adapt and counter the inertia of excess capacity. For Barban she crosses herself with Chanel Sixteen and hopes to resemble 'the moving pictures with their myriad faces of girl-children' (312); with Barban she stands 'black and white and metallic against the [Mediterranean] sky' (336), an apt study for the movies. Fitzgerald names brands to point to a transition that was merely latent in Nicole's life with Dick. The brand name and the tourist spot – no matter how exclusive – prompt rapid translation from word to material image, the better to speed consumption. Any associative pattern latent in the name has been pre-arrayed there by advertising. In contradistinction, the psychiatrist's phrase or any item beneath the Divers' beach umbrella emanates density and stasis. Gausse's beach is a commodity, but it is a commodity manufactured by Dick, during the early twenties, which might have been modelled on an orchid. Veblen would have understood the doctor's tireless application of the rake (302); like any rare hybrid, Gausse's sand denotes that key to 'good breeding', 'a substantial and patent waste of time'. However, by 1928 the leisured devotions due to 'a bright tan prayer rug of a beach' (11) are no longer observed. The sand serves a different expenditure and signals an alternative form of wealth. When Dick and Nicole bought 'sailor trunks and sweaters' in Nice backstreets (302), they did not intend to create fashion. Paris couturiers copied the style: Fitzgerald does not need to tell us that *haute couture* pirated from *Vogue* or *Vanity Fair* became a market leader – the busy presence of an Associated Press photographer on the steps of Gausse's hotel indicates that the new users are more interested in image and spectacle than in etiquette. With beach umbrellas and pneumatic rubber horses, those 'new things' purchased 'from the first burst of luxury manufacturing after the War' (27), the Divers make their version of a Victorian resort and so manage temporarily to deny the very purpose of that wave of manufacture. They achieve 'absolute immobility' (27) on the sand, where the future health of their capital stipulates absolute mobility. The adroit instillation of cumulative nuance into necessarily transitory luxury items is an archaic trait that the Warrens cannot afford. Equine inflatables are not and should not be Jamesian porcelains. At the novel's close Dick quits the beach that is no longer his kind of artifact. Nicole, for all her recognition that it now serves 'the tastes of the tasteless' (301), stays, presumably to be photographed by the Associated Press.

Each Diver accessory is a potential meeting-point between the two forms of economic authority which I have allegorized in shorthand as accumulation and reproduction. The meaning of the sweater or the umbrella depends upon who is economic master. Mastery involves a conflict whose history constitutes the texture of the object. Fitzgerald has an eye for the detail that retains the tracery of this struggle; he registers the economic latencies which divide objects as an archaeology lying at the very surface of things. At first glance Gausse's beach is easily consumable, but the image is fissured: as a 'prayer rug', it summons ceremonies whose form Veblen might have declared typical of leisure in the 1890s; as a tanning mat, it services the body beautiful – that curious site of narcissism and self-denigration that encourages tourists to replace their own bodies with commodity selves.

What passes on the beach (30), like the beach itself, is a struggle between forms of power. One incident may be treated as typical: Dick emerges from the dressing tent in transparent black lace drawers, *pour épater la nouvelle bourgeoisie.* His impulse is territorially effective; McKisco (one of the untanned among the pebbles) asserts his gender and insults the gender of his companions, while the knowing joke affirms the unity of the Diver entourage by releasing 'a nursery-like peace and good will'. In fairy stories frogs turn into princes at the drop of a kiss; Dick's transformation is only slightly less spectacular. Fitzgerald marks its importance by insisting, 'At that moment the Divers represented externally the exact further-most evolution of a class.' As with incest, so with homosexuality: sexual preference in *Tender is the Night* should be read within an economic context. Dick, the keeper of accumulation's daughter, appears to reveal his own phallus (the drawers *seem* transparent) by performing the absence of that member (the drawers *are* opaque). At one level the genital logic accords with Dick's phallic subordi-nation to the bad father. The daughter approves the emasculation, since it is she who sews the trick costume. Her needlework – in all probability Dick's conception – is part of a treatment which enables her to assure Rosemary that she is 'a mean, hard woman'. As a bonus, this particularly 'invidious comparison' captures the child whose Hollywood credentials commit her economically to the sphere of reproduction. With a 'bubble' of 'delight' Rosemary is initiated into the group and into Dick's love. Accumulation rules. However, 'in reality a qualitative change had already set in that was not at all apparent to Rosemary.' It *is* apparent to Fitzgerald, for whom the 'pansy's trick' is capable of double articulation as two plots. Read from within the imperatives of reproduction, Dick transgresses the bounds of phallic sexuality through a stage-managed and 'spectacular' multiplication of his own gender. He woos and wins a very different Daddy's girl by establishing a disintegrative selfhood. Fitzgerald's point about the 'furthermost evolution of a class' refers to the moment at which a class becomes conscious of the need to assume alternative forms of behaviour, sexuality, spending and finance. Their 'bargain with the gods' is 'desperate' because transition is awkward. In this instance Nicole will make it, Dick won't. For Dr Diver 'gods' will always, in the last analysis, wear 'finely cut clerical clothes'. For Nicole the 'gods' will increasingly become the mass audience in the cheaper seats whose desires her fashions and her monies will seek to renew and control.

Though the demise of a father-centred phallocentrism – with its attendant etiquette and economics – looks complete, it is neither easy nor radical. What Fitzgerald bears witness to via his semantic sub-plot or sub-articulation is a shift in the administration of power rather than the overthrow of that power. Dick's homosexual play leads, through the pun on 'gods' (theological and theatrical), to the world of the spectacle. Fitzgerald explores what is in effect a major economic transition. Since in market terms so much of that transition focuses on the redistribution of the human body (particularly the body of the female), it is perhaps unsurprising that Fitzgerald should approach the economic through the sexual.

I would reiterate that the body in question belongs to a Daddy's girl. Incest is the constellation of difficulty upon which *Tender is the Night* turns. Devereux Warren's crime comprises a plot of considerable complexity and precipitates particular character groupings in order to realize the fullness of that complexity. Fitzgerald marries Dick to Nicole to explore accumulation and supplies him with Rosemary as an entrée to the sphere of reproduction. Dick's affections shift between Daddys' girls to externalize the contradictory nature of Warren's incest. At one level the father refuses to exchange his child beyond the family; at another and opposed level he denies both the differentiation of social roles and the familial organization deriving from the incest prohibition – that is to say, Warren's sexual energy seeks unrealized relations and forms. The plot latent in the sexual/economic overlap thickens. Accumulation stores money; reproduction must create new needs and discover new markets. Late capitalism builds into each of us its own realm of desires lacking adequate objects, the better to pre-sell those objects.

Rosemary markets desire. A product of the culture industry, she has at least two fathers, too many selves and absolutely no trauma about it. By responding, Dr Diver shifts allegiance from the integrating interior (the last territory of the private, bourgeois self) to a disintegrative and global image (Rosemary films in Rome and Hollywood, and screenings of her work seem available almost anywhere). Rosemary is publicity, and the changing pattern of desire which she instigates makes a comparison with Nicole obligatory. The two women, one 'hard' (dense) and the other transparent, stand at different moments in the history of desire. Veblen's terms still apply to Nicole, or at least to Mrs Diver, but Rosemary requires a new vocabulary. When Nicole's dress and manners provoke others to 'invidious comparison' or emulation, she can afford to ignore it because her 'ducal' wealth, though regulative of others, protects her from being regulated back. Rosemary, as publicity, stimulates envy but is inextricably tied to the gaze of those who envy her. Under Dick's tuition Nicole achieved self-possession, she grew 'hard', 'whole', 'complete' and anachronistic. Rosemary's self is a number of styles which exist to be alienated from her; like fashion, she is created to earn envy so that her style(s) may be purchased by others.

Walter Benjamin, in his essay 'The Work of Art in the Age of Mechanical Reproduction', clarifies my distinction between density and transparency, through the distinction he draws between 'person' and 'personality'. While an actor in a theatre may regulate gesture in response to audience reaction, building a 'complete' performance over the span of the play, film actors are subjected to camera shifts and editorial decisions which fragment their role. The film industry responds to this shrivelling of the actor's 'person' with an artificial build up of the 'personality' outside the studio: 'The cult of the movie star, fostered by the money of the film industry, preserves not the unique aura of the person but the "spell of the personality", the phoney spell of a commodity' (Benjamin 233). I have my doubts about 'unique aura[s]': the Jamesian possessive individual *is* denser than Benjamin's cinematic personality, but both should be set within that anthology of selves which constitutes a history of the identities that culture has recommended. Rosemary is a 'star' in Benjamin's terms. The disintegrative requirements of cinematic capital are as immediate to her as the solidities of accumulated wealth are natural to Mrs Diver.

Rosemary's greatest compliment to Dick is the offer of a screen test, even as 'the most sincere thing' she says to him is 'we're such *actors*—you and I' (118; italics in source). Her 'love' is gestural and involves careful self-direction, a dance of camera angles culminating in the ultimate movie still. Scene: Paris, a hotel. Enter two lovers, who are to walk up five flights of stairs. 'At the first landing they stopped and kissed.' Each landing is the site of variously careful kisses, until the final 'good-by with their hands stretching to touch along the diagonal of the banister and then the fingers slipping apart' (87). Freeze frame. The example is unfortunate in so far as it implies a degree of manipulation by Rosemary. What I am trying to suggest is rather different: that at spontaneous, intuitive, instinctive levels the system of production within which she works modifies her desire. Take her response to the director, Brady, in Monte Carlo: the director 'looked her over completely': he desires her, and in 'so far as her virginal emotions went', she 'contemplate[s] surrender'; 'It was a click . . . Yet she knew she would forget him half an hour after she left him—like an actor kissed in a picture' (33). Brady desires the image of her that he might produce; she, in his looks as in a mirror, admires the image of herself remade: 'It was a click.' He has made her; she has bought it. Fitzgerald's terse noun is richly physiological *and* mechanical. Camera (lens) meets body (orifice) in a metaphor whose impertinence resides in the suggestion that desire is a machine. Fetishized and fetishistic, Rosemary is passive; she is pleasured by becoming an image in the directorial eye – an image which may be varied according to market requirements. In her manifestation as screen virgin she should be both penetrable and impenetrable, because to maximize profits she must, like the fetish, be available to all and possessed by none.

Therefore, in Paris, when Collis Clay mentions her 'indiscretion' in a locked compartment of the Chicago train, Dick is agonized by 'the image of a third person' coming between himself and Rosemary. However, his obsessionally recurrent question, 'Do you mind if I pull down the curtain?' (100) casts him in two roles: as the lover who pulls down the blind and as the intruder requesting blindness. His duplicity conforms to the structure of the fetish within which violation is inextricable from innocence:

The vividly pictured hand on Rosemary's cheek, the quicker breath, the white excitement of the event viewed from outside, the inviolable secret warmth within.

'—Do you mind if I pull down the curtain?(100)

Repression succeeds only in generating phrases that censor as they sensualize: 'white excitement' and 'inviolable secret warmth' point two ways, offering double-sensed messages which dramatize the mental musculature of the recipient of commodified sex. Since the viewer of pictures is stimulated by what he cannot have, innocence fuses with semen ('white'), while, like a hymen within a hymen, Rosemary's virginity (?), locked in a compartment, enfolds the mind's eye of the voyeur in its 'warmth'. Nathanael West was to present the contradiction with cartoon clarity in *The Day of the Locust* (1939); his would-be starlet, Faye Greener, though a part-time prostitute, is most typically described as an egg, a cork, a tree and as having legs like scissors – all to underline her impenetrability. When we finally witness her penetration, two-thirds of the way through the novel, she raises a sheet in front of her face and vanishes. It is her last appearance because, possessed and thoroughly witnessed as possessed, she is no longer in the market.

Rosemary lives her body as a series of takes: in love she makes 'an exit that she had learned young, and on which no director had ever tried to improve' (122), while 'a sort of ballet step' carries her clear of a dead black on her bed (122). Neither move is artificial; hers is simply a physicality keyed to the emergent forms of economic reality. Dick, appearing at the onset of her stardom, offers a brief regression to an earlier though still active social form – an affair of nostalgia for the world of archaic fathers. Though technically the child of two fathers – military and medical – Rosemary is really the adopted daughter of the new fathers, anonymous, corporate figures who work to establish different modes of authority, protected and indeed naturalized by consumer desires, or rather by consumer frustrations. Possessed, Rosemary is no longer a star. During the final, protracted consummation of the affair in Rome, Dick wonders whether he is first or six hundred and forty-first; Rosemary's assurance that her previous sexual experience has been 'abortive' (231) hardly reassures. Dick will never know nor will he need to know, since consummation cancels his desire.

## IV

Dick's interest in Daddys' girls is ruinous but revealing. Named for a phallus, Dick as a Diver may only detumesce. The deep structure of the nominal joke contains an absolute impasse. Dick marries Nicole and renders her 'complete' (166) by way of the solid manners of his 'good' father. But, by standing in place of the 'bad' father, he risks repeating the incestuous offence. Dick's answer is to remain hard but not to spend, which returns me to my point of departure. In Book I, Dick the socialite organizes expenditure in highly liquid forms while stringently budgeting his own outgoings; Fitzgerald stresses that Dick draws a line between a limited scientific income and the expanding Warren fortune. Both sexually and economically, Dick is split by his desire. Seeking to be the 'good' father inside the 'bad' father's girl, he condemns himself to the psychic equivalent of coitus interruptus. I risk riddling, but offer in clarification the curious patterns of articulation ghosting Dick's sexuality.

When Rosemary discovers Jules Peterson's corpse on her hotel bed, Dick immediately thinks of Fatty Arbuckle: his analogy sexualizes a potential scandal which is at that point merely murderous. However, since Peterson lies where Dick, earlier on the same day, all but lay, his blood is for Dick a necessary and scandalous sign of the deathly consequences of his own desired emission. Certainly, Nicole reads the stained bed-linen as evidence of an incestuous release. Scandal is avoided, and the disconcerting sheets suppressed, only because Dick exhibits control. My associative path is tangled, though not untypical of the novel. Peterson's blood is Arbuckle's semen, and since, by association, it first 'smear[s]' Dick and then Devereux, their emissions too are 'paint[ed]' black and marked for death (124).

A similar pattern occurs when Dick encounters Tommy Barban in a Munich bar (Book II, Ch. XVII). Dick has taken leave of absence from the clinic; Barban has returned from fighting for the White Russians. Among Barban's companions is a Mr Hannan, who, in shaking hands, accuses Dick of 'fooling around' with his aunt, before changing tack and demanding to know why Dick, a stranger, has approached him with a 'cock-and-bull' story about aunts. The non-sequitur is sustained when, from the piano, Hannan insists that he didn't say 'aunts' but 'pants' (216). His wordplay links sex-inside-the-family to the sartorial elegance of Barban and the Russian prince with whom he sits; both wear suits 'of a cut and pattern fantastic enough to have sauntered down Beale Street on a Sunday' (216). The suits, although made by a Polish tailor, are all but zoot suits, fashionable among African Americans in Memphis and elsewhere. At which point, Hannan's quick 'black eyes' have created a design sufficient to release Ham from Hannan and to darken all this inauspicious talk of 'cock' and 'bull'. (The sons of Ham were blackened in punishment for Ham's offence against his father Noah.) None of which might matter much were it not that similar semi-occult linkages surface in the next chapter.

Dick has removed from Zurich to Innsbruck for the climbing: in his hotel garden, in the evening, a woman's figure 'detached itself from the black shape of a tree' (220), breaking the 'black frieze' she made 'with the foliage'. Dick is attracted, wondering whether 'strange children' should say 'Let's play' (221). The markers are in place: arousal; a woman rendered a child; ethnic stains among the shadows, with intimations of Genesis as a bonus. Nothing happens. But the next night, after dinner, 'he felt excited, without knowing why, until he began thinking of the garden' (221). Back in his room, and 'still excited', he opens a cablegram from America, which reads, 'Your father died peacefully tonight      HOLMES' (222). The conjunction of a persistent and textually ill-concealed erection and the death of the 'good' father would be striking even without the appearance of a Holmes on the scene. The rector's name is a pun on the 'home' that Dick has finally lost, but summons 'Sherlock', already present in the text via an account of Professor Dohmler's head, which resembled 'some fine old house' (155) and nodded in the style of that arch-protector of Victorian domiciles, Sherlock Holmes (142). Little detection is required to spot a patricidal and poisonous emission, particularly since Dick's physical reaction substitutes grief for semen in an act of controlled purgation, mirroring the very emission that it interrupts: 'He felt a sharp wince at the shock, a gathering of the forces of resistance; then it rolled up through his loins and stomach and throat' (222). It seems barely necessary to point out that during a relapse, associated with the birth of Topsy, Nicole should toy with the notion that her doctors told her that her baby was black (178). Or that Barban, Dick's rampant substitute, should be repeatedly referred to as sunburnt to the point of blackness, becoming a 'Co[a]leman' (290), though 'without attaining the blue beauty of negroes' (289).

Emission and its consequences are, for Dick, dark. He seeks therefore to avoid release while remaining 'hard'. Since his position is barely tenable and scarcely tellable, it emerges as a whisper forming among apparently coincidental items whose repeated proximity, one to another, infer a disruptive excitement, an excitement both sexual and semantic. The best gloss I can find for Dick's desire, as it prompts Fitzgerald to occluded exposure, is an observation of Nicole's, given in Book III as she measures her growing distance from Dick:

She guessed that something was developing behind the silence, behind the hard, blue eyes, the almost unnatural interest in the children. Uncharacteristic bursts of temper surprised her . . . It was as though an incalculable story was telling itself inside him, about which she could only guess at in the moments when it broke through the surface (288).

# V

I have tried to 'calculate'the hidden narrative shaping Dick's desire for Daddys' girls. Fitzgerald provides two – Nicole and Rosemary – each of whom may be read as embodying a tendency within the history of capital. As Dick shifts his romantic allegiance from wife to mistress, so, in my markedly parabolic terms, he achieves emission, loses hardness and comes apart in the very flows that he has always contained. Two events are symptomatic of what is generally read as Dick Diver's decline, the death of the Reverend Diver and the beating in Rome. His father's death discontinues Dick's ties with the 'sureties' of the nineteenth century; more importantly, the funeral allows him to recognize that severance: 'Good-by, my father—good-by, all my fathers' (224). The reader may find in the ensuing return to Europe several clues to fallen paternity. McKisco shares Dick's passage: Fitzgerald notes that he has made a literary name from pastiche, and adds, tellingly, the 'feat . . . [is] not to be disparaged' (225). Misrepresentation of an original authority can, it seems, be the basis for 'new self-respect'. On the train to Rome, Dick discovers 'a miserable family of two girls and their mother' at a loss for a father; Dick immediately stands in – his 'pleasure' at enabling them 'to regain their proper egotism' is brief and based, he now knows, on 'plot' and 'illusion' (226). The 'ego', as underwritten by the father, suffers further damage as Dick books into the Hotel Quirinal in Rome and consummates his affair with Rosemary (only to feel like the Black Death (239)). Quirinus is a god of war identified with the deified Romulus. Fitzgerald's taste in Hotels is less than casual: Dick beds the daughter of the new economic fathers in a room dedicated to a founding classical paternity. As if sacrilege against one deity were not enough, Dick finds the city of papal fathers 'dirty', liable to 'Victorian dust' (241) and to the 'sweat of exhausted cultures' (244), a setting well suited to disaffiliation and to the guilty self-dismemberment which succeeds it. The imbroglio with the taxi drivers results directly from Dick's disappointment at failing to contact a girl in a night club:

She was a young English girl, with blonde hair and a healthy, pretty English face and she smiled at him again with an invitation he understood, that denied the flesh even in the act of tendering it . . . 'She looks like somebody in the movies,' he said. (242-3)

The pick-up – a commercial extension of Rosemary – is not picked up (though, predictably, there is an 'unpleasant' 'Bahama Negro' at the edge of the scene (242)). Dick punishes himself for his desire by provoking a fight: 'He felt his nose break like a shingle and his eyes jerk as if they had snapped back on a rubber band into his head. A rib splintered under a stamping heel' (246). Dick asks for it, as though to prove to himself the evacuation of his own 'integrity'. In the shadow play of allegory he has cast down multiple fathers and has responded to the delights of the sphere of reproduction; he can, therefore, no longer experience selfhood as an entity. In court he has no option other than to insist that *he* raped the five-year-old girl. By straining to bury the 'bad' father and to resurrect the 'good' so that Nicole may be made 'whole' again, Dick's entire professional and domestic life up to this seemingly ludicrous protestation may have served only to repeat the 'bad' father's crime. Hasn't Rome, and Dick's commitment to a Daddy's girl whose very existence is wealth's new experiment with untraced channels of expenditure, *proved* that at one level he raped Nicole? My question is at once gnomic and dogmatic.

To clarify: read retrospectively, incest embodies accumulation; read as a projection having a different economic emphasis, Warren's act and Dick's complicity become expressions of accumulation's new problematic – the problematic of self-transgression – whereby energy (in this case sexual) needs to try untried combinations and to multiply selves as a multiplication of markets. Having acknowledged incest, Dick can only come apart multitudinously. The logic of reproduction has it that self-destruction, or rather a systematic revision of selfhood, is integral to the continuity of capital. The bourgeoisie of this phase are ever their own best barbarians; only by putting themselves to the sword, in the form of the advertising-copywriter's pen, can they ensure class longevity. Breakage becomes a structural principle of the bourgeoisie during the twenties and therefore informs the latent plots and available personalities of that class.

The affair with Rosemary intensifies Dick's dawning sense of his own theatricality. In Rome he assures her 'gently' that his own social gifts are a 'trick' (236); earlier on the Riviera, he made a similar declaration to her mother, but then cheered himself up with the phrase 'a trick of the heart' (181). The integrative capacity of that iconic organ will not, however, withstand his later, careful distinction between manner and morale. Discussing his own transformation, he tells Rosemary at their final meeting, 'The change came a long way back—but at first it didn't show. The manner remains intact for some time after the morale cracks' (307). His moral would seem to be: where manners are experienced as mannerisms, 'whole soul[s]' can no longer crystallize from their systematic application.

The degree of Dick's self-knowledge belies the critical consensus which deprives him of an active place in his own fall. The very vocabulary of decline charges an external force with responsibility: critics generally name alcohol, money or authorial autobiography as the prime suspects. However, Dick's knowledge of his own position within a sexual and economic trauma makes the term 'failure' a critical whitewash. Dick neither declines nor falls – he jumps or, more specifically, takes a dive. His repeated failure to raise a man on his shoulders while riding an aquaplane can be taken as an expression of middle-aged vanity or as the nostalgia of a dissolute athlete; however, such readings ignore the pervasive vocabulary of theatre running through the incident. Arguably, Dick's manner of parting company with the Baby Gar is the last act in his release from and of Nicole. Immediately after the event, on the beach with Rosemary and Nicole, Dick discusses acting in what is effectively a gloss on his own recent performance. He promotes a style of 'burlesque' arising from the actor's compulsive need to retain audience attention, arguing that, since the audience can 'do the "responding" for themselves', the duty of the performer is to 'do something unexpected': 'If the audience thinks the character is hard she goes soft on them—if they think she's soft she goes hard. You go all *out* of character—you understand?' (309–10; italics in source). Dick outlines his own method on the board. He too went 'all *out* of character'. Where the audience thinks him adroit (hard), he is inept (soft). Where the audience hopes for direction, he mismanages. A performance of decline is undertaken at some distance from the facts of decline – almost in the style of one of Brecht's Chinese actors:

The performer portrays incidents of utmost passion, but without his delivery becoming heated. At those points where the character portrayed is deeply excited the performer takes a lock of hair between his lips and chews it. But this is like a ritual, there is nothing eruptive about it. It is quite clearly somebody else's repetition of the incident: a representation. (Brecht, 'Alienation Effects in Chinese Acting' 93)

Dick's 'alienation effect' entails the representation of dissolution so that Nicole may be released to the new forms of money. Earlier, and with intimations of another dive, it had involved a tacit mutual suicide from the deck of Golding's yacht:

his eyes focussed upon her gradually as upon a chessman to be moved; in the same slow manner he caught her wrist and drew her near.

'You ruined me, did you?' he inquired blandly. 'Then we're both ruined. So——'

Cold with terror she put her other wrist into his grip. All right, she would go with him—again she felt the beauty of the night vividly in one moment of complete response and abnegation—all right, then——

—But now she was unexpectedly free and Dick turned his back sighing: 'Tch! tch!' (294)

Dick 'portrays' the suicide pact, delivering this trope from the genre of romance with the detachment of a chess player, and terminating his exposition on two brief expulsions of breath, which caption both the scene and Nicole's absorption in it as childish nonsense. Barban approaches and Dick demonstrates the appropriateness of Nicole's new partner with the pointed question, 'Are you rich, Tommy?' (295).

To return, briefly, to Dick's beach workshop on theatre technique – although addressing Rosemary, he simultaneously talks to Nicole:

let's suppose that somebody told you, 'Your lover is dead.' In life you'd probably go to pieces. But on the stage you're trying to entertain—the audience can do the responding for themselves. First the actress has lines to follow, then she has to get the audience's attention back on herself, away from the murdered Chinese or whatever the thing is. (309)

Given that everyone involved has been party to the murder of Peterson, Dick's example is calculated. In effect, Nicole is told that her lover is dead, and that in order to retain her class position (perceived as a relationship with a mass audience) she must avoid response and pursue gesture. Significantly, Dick casts himself as the 'murdered Chinese': his choice of figure is complex, perhaps involving an ironic reflection on his status as disposable servant; it also makes cryptic allusion to his own ethnically stained emissions, while, for Rosemary, hinting that what went on in Parisian and Roman hotel rooms was little more than the hiring and firing of a foreign body. These layers remain peripheral to the main direction of his lesson which, as the culmination of his language of fabrication, reflects his conviction that the social arena has become a stage where audience demand is paramount. In such circumstances, 'charm' and 'grace' give way to mere lying, as the mass market requires of its market leaders only that they surprise and so, through provision of the 'new', continue to lead. Nicole obeys instructions: she turns directly to Barban and to brand name, going 'all *out* of character' in order to retain the characteristics of a changing class. She leaves the beach feeling 'new and happy' (310), and 'knowing vaguely that Dick had planned for her to have [her freedom]' (311), she writes a letter propositioning her next husband.

Book III charts Dick's sustained performance of decline, during which he declares himself no longer effective; no longer a centre, an author or indeed a responsible agent of action. All is lethargy, parody and scorn: witness the sustained metaphors of vampirism, Dick's bouts of interior laughter (337) and his final act –'with a papal cross he blessed the beach from the high terrace' (337). Dick abdicates comprehensively from what he has made, from his familial and professional tasks and, more disturbingly, from what he has been made – a 'whole-souled' (67), integral being.

Nor can he be put together again. Poised above contrary movements within the capital which provides his foundation, he quits the sites which his adoptive class prefers. In no particular order, and virtually all at once, he deserts the psychiatric armchair, the surrogate drawing-rooms, the phallus and even (projecting) the sound-stage. Dick's dive is complete and outdistances the critics. Perhaps 'the old interior laughter' prompted the selection of an aquaplane from which to parody his surname. To push the pun (maybe no further than Fitzgerald intended) Dick does not resurface: without fixed abode or declared destination, his movements after his return to America are quite literally mapped by Nicole, but they are not understood. Symptomatically, he rejects her offer of money and no longer 'ask[s] for the children to be sent' (338), capital and the family being two of the mediations through which he made himself what he was and has chosen no longer to be.

The problem remains: if Dick decides to quit, and money, alcohol, general dissolution or Fitzgerald's autobiography cannot in any emphatic sense be 'blamed', why does he quit? At no point in the novel is his decision directly addressed, an omission that should not produce charges of slack construction or inadequate characterization. The question raises the broader issue of Fitzgerald's narrative technique. Cause passes from persons into objects viewed as metaphors or, more properly, as plot miniatures and encapsulated narratives. Fitzgerald's nine-year struggle with the construction of *Tender is the Night* reflects his fear that story no longer issues from voice, even as action no longer resides in he who acts. Commodity, perceived as having a particular history, becomes the new narrative centre. Things, and characters as their carriers, determine action. Such a view is focused by Marx in his definition of the commodity form: 'It is nothing but the definite social relation between men themselves which assumes here, for them, the fantastic form of a relation between things' (Marx 165). 'Things' grow positively hydra-headed as they register a marked shift in the system of production and so in relations between men.

*Tender is the Night* establishes that a beach umbrella casts the 'shadow of the fantastic phallus', (Deleuze and Guattari 97), which as it falls assumes the restless forms of changing accumulation and modified manners. The umbrella is typical of the Divers' belongings in that it comes to mean through various human processes. If the meaning of an object is not an idea but a petrifaction of action, things are always and necessarily human: it follows that action may recognize itself in those objects of which it is a part. I have been reading Fitzgerald's perceptual habits through Sartre's *practico inert*; further quotation may help: 'The idea of a thing is in the thing, that is to say, it is the thing itself revealing its reality through the practice which constitutes it, and through the instruments and institutions which define it' (Sartre 50). The *practico inert* is a large constituent of our subjectivity, since it makes up what surrounds us *ad nauseam*, in whose worked matter we learn, almost without learning, how to work. Things so defined operate as a strict but scarcely felt necessity at the heart of human relations: 'Materialized practices, poured into the exteriority of things, impose a common destiny on men who know nothing of one another' (Sartre 179). Sartre would surely concede Marx's point that under capital 'destiny' cannot finally be 'common' because the interests and actions of those who labour and those who invest are not necessarily at one. Within commodity production, matter is not fully coherent, since it bears contradictory inscriptions and contending futures. Fitzgerald knows that 'folding beach cushions' and 'miniatures for a doll's house' are products 'of much ingenuity and toil' (65), not the least of it going on in chicle factories and canneries and that consequently, if 'toil' changes, the future latent in cushions and dolls must change. Again Sartre clarifies: '[things] possess an inert future within which we have to determine our own future. The future comes to man through things insofar as it previously came to things through man' (Sartre 178).

For 'future' it is tempting to say 'futures', particularly of 1929, and still more particularly of 1929 viewed from 1934. It should be remembered that *Tender is the Night* was published in 1934, and spans the period from 1917 to the summer of 1929. It would be gratifying to see the Crash as *annus mirabilis*/the time of changes when 'destiny' shifted from the manifest to the several. What is striking is that, having timed Dick's dive for the summer of 1929 and having provided a glimpse of flame on Wall Street, Fitzgerald implies calmly that capital survives through structural transformation and that futures, though they should be legion, may not even number two. In a much-quoted passage describing Nicole's shopping, Fitzgerald sets global capital aboard a fast train running anarchically from Chicago to a Parisian shop window; his extended metaphor implies a crash the better to avert it:

as the whole system swayed and thundered onward it lent a feverish bloom to such processes of hers as wholesale buying . . . She illustrated very simple principles, containing in herself her own doom, but illustrated them so accurately that there was grace in the procedure, and presently Rosemary would try to imitate it. (65)

Nicole illustrates capital's tendency to recurrent crisis. Her family money 'contain[s] its own doom' because, by investing in the massive expansion of production during the post-war decade, the Warrens promote overproduction and the attendant dramatic fall in their own profit. The plot has a twist (as incest has two faces): Nicole's graceful buying mirrors capital's self-correcting concern for consumers and consumption. So, standing at 'the exact furthermost evolution of [her] class' (30), Accumulation's child may yet give a lesson to the daughter of Reproduction and eventually find her 'grace' in the procedure imitated in the movies. By such indirections do the imperatives of accumulation metamorphose into the necessities of reproduction. The moral is as simple as the story: the market's narrative is self-healing and absolute.

What is initially odd about this passage is that it ignores one of its own fiercest insights: that things are the loci of more or less antagonistic connections between classes. Fitzgerald could at this point be charged with wilful amnesia, except that what he leaves out he points to. Fitzgerald indicates that if 'love-birds' come tagged 'chicle factory' then labour makes leisure. There is no need for the critic to slip an unsolicited economic sub-text into *Tender is the Night*, since the novel's dating ensures that 1929 shadows all events; the fact that it has so little final effect is neither ambiguous nor evasive, it is merely decisive. Fitzgerald's muffled Crash implies the continuity of capital. Labour has no future beyond consumerism because capital ensures its own vitality by switching plots.

Once again I return to my two available master-stories – Accumulation and Reproduction. The one archaic, the other curative, each implies different kinds of subject and object. Dick's decisive dive, though less dramatic, is rather more telling than suicides from tall corporate premises. His career involves a long marination in the realm of carefully considered objects, be they beach cushions or words from a couch. His problem in 1929 is that the objects are changing as market practice and the instruments and institutions of capital change. Dick appreciates, but will not make, that particular transition. Instead he disengages himself from his marriage and from the *haute bourgeoisie*, old and new.

Initially the facts of the new life do not support an act of severance and self-revision; indeed, the final chapter repeats the pattern of the larger narrative. Repatriation and return to Buffalo, the last parish of the good father, suggest a ghostly reversion to 'whole soul[s]', while Dick's choice of subsequent domicile (Geneva), allied to a disruptive association with a 'girl', indicates that disintegral elements persist. However, several details carry hints of Dick's 'interior laughter'. The choice of Lockport, given that Dick viewed himself as both key and janitor, is a striking revision of autobiography: the name splits – Nicole's keeper is now a creature of passage between several ports of call. His unfinished manuscript, whose title 'would look monumental in German' (162) (a taxonomic work, preoccupied with '*Uniform . . . Classification*'), is carried with him as a sexual come-on: the proximity between 'much admired by the ladies' and the 'big stack of papers on his desk' (338) is more than suggestive, it is a comic recapitulation of Dick's first love – after all, if his profession got him a wife, why should it not make him a less orderly ladies' man? Just as a Shakespearean sub-plot will often re-perform high doings among the lower orders, so the last chapter of *Tender is the Night* repeats the novel from an entirely different perspective. Dick is no longer a psychiatrist but a general practitioner, and his 'girl' is now culled from a 'grocery store' (I am reminded of the girls who 'worked rudely at the Five-and-Tens on Christmas Eve' to pay their 'tithe' to Nicole (65).) Once puns are recognized as a route to social inversion, other terms become loopholes, issuing covert glances towards another class. Dick stops for a time in Geneva, a town which Nicole locates with an atlas as being in 'the Finger Lakes' section of New York: since Dick has quit his adoptive class and wanders from town to smaller town to 'very small town', he doubtless practises or will practise among manual workers. Perhaps her session with the atlas reminded Nicole that she was 'born hating the smell of a nurse's fingers dressing her' (260); maybe the name even triggers Frau Gregorovious' body-odour, 'less a smell than an ammoniacal reminder of the eternity of toil and decay' (260)?

Such speculation has less to do with Nicole's psychology than with the novel's tendency to promote the reading of its persons and things from divided and antagonistic social perspectives. Words like 'Lockport' and 'Finger,' once set within their associative networks, tend maliciously to distort themselves, hinting at diversity and implying that their diversity rises from social conflict.

However, the double articulation which characterizes the last chapter of the novel is different from that into which the reader is elsewhere invited. The conflicting semantic determinants of 'Finger' and 'Lockport' may be traced to a suppressed dispute between voices, each possibility deriving its intention from a markedly different class position. In contradistinction, the broader duplicities of the incest story depend upon and express the changing dynamic of a single class. It is tempting to read Book III, chapter XIII as a return of the repressed, and therefore as Fitzgerald's exoneration of Lukàcs' judgement that the proletariat (though hidden in puns and masked in simile) is the only radical class, because it sees the entirety of the system from the base (and so must murmur threats through the established meaning of dominant groups). It *is* striking that Book III draws attention to servants and features refusals and uprisings amongst underlings, most notably Dick's, but also Frau Kaethe's complaint against Nicole (Ch. I); the cook Augustine's assault with a butcher knife, accompanied by the charge that her employer drinks like 'a day-laborer' (286); prostitutes 'thin and barbaric' in Nicole and Tommy's hotel room (Ch. VIII), and Gausse's kick to Lady Caroline Sibley Biers' backside (Ch. X). However, to overemphasize subversion would be to carry reading against the grain towards a pet pathology. For all his sensitivity to double-directed words and fissured referents, Fitzgerald recognizes that capital – albeit capital in transition – determines semantic collisions. Labour, even in 1934, has to his ear only sufficient voice to whisper from the depths of concluding puns.

It might be objected that my reading of Fitzgerald has made far too much of ambivalence, that multiple meaning has been induced and puns provoked by reference to associative networks that may look all very well in this essay but bear little relation to the pages of *Tender is the Night*. I can only appeal again to Fitzgerald's perception of economic history to explain his proclivity if not for puns then for internally polemical terms. In 1922 Fitzgerald described himself as 'a socialist' nervous about 'the people' (Fitzgerald, *Letters* 173); in 1932 he described Dick Diver as 'a communist-liberal-idealist, a moralist in revolt', adding, 'the hero . . . is a man like myself brought up in a family sunk from haute bourgeoise to petite bourgeoise' (Fitzgerald, quoted by Bruccoli, *Grandeur* 335–6). A reading of the letters suggests that to combine any and all of these terms would be to approximate to the vagaries of Fitzgerald's political position(s). What is clear is that he read some Marx, advocated the reading of Marx and by the late thirties believed that 'most questions in life have an economic base (at least according to us Marxians)' (*Letters* 347). The throw-away parentheses are typical: writing to his cousin Ceci Taylor in 1934 he appends a confidential postscript to a letter preoccupied with the problems of making money from scripts and stories:

P.S. Apropos of our conversation it will interest you to know that I've given up politics. For two years I've gone half haywire trying to reconcile my double allegiance to the class I am part of, and the Great Change I believe in . . . I have become disgusted with the party leadership and have only health enough for my literary work, so I'm on the sidelines . . . This is confidential, of course. (*Letters* 437)

The two-year period in question (1932–4) spans his most concentrated work on *Tender is the Night*. A *Ledger* note of November 1932 reads, 'Political worries, almost neurosis' (Bruccoli, *Grandeur* 347). Just as in the last chapter of the novel Fitzgerald alludes to a class dispute that is contained within a semantic dispute, so, in his letters, those aspects of his life that threatened the social fabric to which he is committed are bracketed or set to one side. None the less, while writing *Tender is the Night*, Fitzgerald experienced 'double allegiance' with troubling intensity; his decision to bracket the political, and to interdict family talk about that decision, suggests that a certain leakage of anxiety into the manuscript was inevitable. In this case, the divided semantics which I have been tracing within the novel's language may be said to arise from Fitzgerald's acute, awkward and partially prohibited sense of the interrelations of class and change.

Fitzgerald is not a punster in any simple sense of the word: the valency of his language is the product of significant quibbles within capital. Capital changes, particularly during the merger wave of the twenties and the early Depression years, dividing the bourgeoisie: social planes collide within a class, yielding divided objects, subjects and meanings. As capital perfects its translation from the monopoly form to what has been designated 'late' or 'multinational' capital, so its objects and subjects stabilize, at least for a time. The fissured owning-class heals itself and continues (Nicole is 'cured'). Fitzgerald's quibbling registers a revolution within a class. The instability of his text (also realized in its nine-year multiform gestation, and in its preoccupation with wounds, scars and surface 'completeness') is a response to a revolution within capital. Because, during the twenties, capital contained pronouncedly different kinds of capital, 'emergent' and 'residual' forms necessarily clashed within social and semantic relations. Read historically, Fitzgerald's puns are not playful; behind them, as with so much else in *Tender is the Night*, lie voices arguing for different ways of life.

Benjamin, Walter, 'The Work of Art in the Age of Mechanical Reproduction', *Illuminations*, London: Cape, 1970: 219–53.

Brecht, Bertolt, *Brecht on Theatre*, John Willet (ed.), London: Methuen, 1974.

Bruccoli, Matthew J., *The Composition of 'Tender is the Night'*, Pittsburgh: University of Pittsburgh, 1963.

Bruccoli, Matthew J., *Some Sort of Epic Grandeur: The Life of F. Scott Fitzgerald*, New York: Harcourt Brace, 1981.

Cowley, Malcolm, *Exile's Return*, New York: Viking Press, 1974.

Cummings, Katherine, *Telling Tales: The Hysteric's Seduction in Fiction and Theory*, Stanford: Stanford U.P., 1991.

Deleuze, Giles and Guattari, Felix, *Anti-Oedipus*, New York: Viking Press, 1982.

Doherty, William E., '*Tender is the Night* and the "Ode to a Nightingale" in *Critical Essays on F. Scott Fitzgerald's 'Tender is the Night'*, Milton R. Stern (ed.), Boston: Hall, 1986: 147–59.

Ewen, Stuart, *Captains of Consciousness*, New York: McGraw-Hill, 1976.

Fass, Paula, *The Damned and the Beautiful*, Oxford: Oxford U.P., 1977.

Feis, Herbert, *The Diplomacy of the Dollar*, Baltimore: Johns Hopkins Press, 1950.

Fitzgerald, F. Scott, *The Great Gatsby*, New York: Scribners, 1925.

Fitzgerald, F. Scott, *The Letters of F. Scott Fitzgerald*, Andrew Turnbull (ed.), Harmondsworth: Penguin, 1968.

Fitzgerald, F. Scott, 'One Trip Abroad', *The Short Stories of F. Scott Fitzgerald*, Matthew Bruccoli (ed.), New York: Scribners, 1989: 577–97.

Fussell, Paul, *The Great War and Modern Memory*, Oxford: Oxford U.P., 1975.

Lynd, Helen and Robert, *Middletown*, New York: Harcourt and Brace, 1929.

Mandel, Ernst, *Late Capitalism*, London: Verso, 1980.

Marx, Karl, *Capital*, vol. 1, Harmondsworth: Penguin, 1976.

Natterman, Udo, 'Nicole Diver's Monologue', *Massachusetts Studies in English*, vol. 10, no. 4 (Fall 1986): 213–28.

Parkinson, Kathleen, *Tender is the Night: A Critical Study*, Harmondsworth: Penguin, 1986.

Piper, Henry Dan, *F. Scott Fitzgerald: A Critical Portrait*, New York: Rinehart and Winston, 1965.

Presbrey, Frank, *The History and Development of Advertising*, New York: Doubleday, 1929.

Prigozy, Ruth, 'From Griffith's Girls to Daddy's Girl: The Masks of Innocence in *Tender is the Night*', *Twentieth-Century Literature*, vol. 26, no. 2 (Summer 1980): 189–221.

Rosenberg, Emily, *Spreading the American Dream*, New York: Hill and Wang, 1982.

Sartre, Jean-Paul, *Critique of Dialectical Reason*, vol. 1, London: Verso, 1982.

Stern, Milton R., *Tender is the Night: The Broken Universe*, New York: Twayne, 1994.

Swann, Charles, 'A Fitzgerald Debt to Keats', *Notes and Queries*, vol. 235, no. 4 (Dec. 1990): 437–8.

Trachtenberg, Alan, *The Incorporation of America: Culture and Society in the Gilded Age*, New York: Hill and Wang, 1982.

Veblen, Thorstein, *The Theory of the Leisure Class*, London: Unwin, 1970 (first published 1899).

Vot, André le, *F. Scott Fitzgerald: A Biography*, New York: Doubleday, 1983.

Wexelblatt, Robert, 'Doctor Diver and General Grant in F. Scott Fitzgerald's *Tender is the Night*', *Notes on Modern Literature*, vol. 8, no. 3 (Winter 1984): Item 16.

Wexelblatt, Robert, 'F. Scott Fitzgerald and D. H. Lawrence: Bicycles and Incest', *American Literature*, vol. 59, no. 3, 1987: 377–88.

Wharton, Edith, *The Age of Innocence*, London: Constable, 1960 (first published 1920).

*Tender is the Night*

**BOOK I** Rosemary's
point of view
priveleged

Mr. McKisco - writer (arriviste)
Abe North - composer, hasn't written
        anything for years.
        - in love w/ Nicole for many years.


Nicole = Nightingale
        - a muse for Abe + Dick, leads to
        destruction
        - hair the colour of a 'chow' (bred for
                                    fighting)

        [ stasis ]

illusion/reality
night     day
•party    •duel
p.44      p59

Barban - protector of the Divers
        - French man
        - 'gun for hire'
        - younger than Dick
    → Barbarrian (not Greek)

ON the pleasant shore of the French Riviera, about half way between Marseilles and the Italian border, stands a large, proud, rose-colored hotel. Deferential palms cool its flushed façade, and before it stretches a short dazzling beach. Lately it has become a summer resort of notable and fashionable people; a decade ago it was almost deserted after its English clientele went north in April. Now, many bungalows cluster near it, but when this story begins only the cupolas of a dozen old villas rotted like water lilies among the massed pines between Gausse's Hôtel des Étrangers and Cannes, five miles away.[1]

The hotel and its bright tan prayer rug of a beach were one. In the early morning the distant image of Cannes, the pink and cream of old fortifications, the purple Alp that bounded Italy, were cast across the water and lay quavering in the ripples and rings sent up by sea-plants through the clear shallows. Before eight a man came down to the beach in a blue bathrobe and with much preliminary application to his person of the chilly water, and much grunting and loud breathing, floundered a minute in the sea. When he had gone, beach and bay were quiet for an hour. Merchantmen crawled westward on the horizon; bus boys shouted in the hotel court; the dew dried upon the pines. In another hour the horns of motors began to blow down from the winding road along the low range of the Maures, which separates the littoral from true Provençal France.

A mile from the sea, where pines give way to dusty poplars, is an isolated railroad stop, whence one June morning in 1925 a victoria brought a woman and her daughter down to Gausse's Hôtel. The mother's face was of a fading prettiness that would soon be patted with broken veins; her expression was both tranquil and aware in a pleasant way. However, one's eyes moved on quickly to her daughter, who had magic in her pink palms and her cheeks lit to a lovely flame, like the thrilling flush of children after their cold baths in the evening. Her fine high forehead sloped gently up to where her hair, bordering it like an armorial shield, burst into lovelocks and waves and curlicues of ash blonde and gold. Her eyes were bright, big, clear, wet, and shining, the color of her cheeks was real, breaking close to the surface from the strong young pump of her heart. Her body hovered delicately on the last edge of childhood—she was almost eighteen, nearly complete, but the dew was still on her.

As sea and sky appeared below them in a thin, hot line the mother said:

"Something tells me we're not going to like this place."

"I want to go home anyhow," the girl answered.

They both spoke cheerfully but were obviously without direction and bored by the fact—moreover, just any direction would not do. They wanted high excitement, not from the necessity of stimulating jaded nerves but with the avidity of prize-winning schoolchildren who deserved their vacations.

"We'll stay three days and then go home. I'll wire right away for steamer tickets."

At the hotel the girl made the reservation in idiomatic but rather flat French, like something remembered. When they were installed on the ground floor she walked into the glare of the French windows and out a few steps onto the stone veranda that ran the length of the hotel. When she walked she carried herself like a ballet-dancer, not slumped down on her hips but held up in the small of her back. Out there the hot light clipped close her shadow and she retreated—it was too bright to see. Fifty yards away the Mediterranean yielded up its pigments, moment by moment, to the brutal sunshine; below the balustrade a faded Buick cooked on the hotel drive.

Indeed, of all the region only the beach stirred with activity. Three British nannies sat knitting the slow pattern of Victorian England, the pattern of the forties, the sixties, and the eighties, into sweaters and socks, to the tune of gossip as formalized as incantation; closer to the sea a dozen persons kept house under striped umbrellas, while their dozen children pursued unintimidated fish through the shallows or lay naked and glistening with cocoanut oil out in the sun.

As Rosemary came onto the beach a boy of twelve ran past her and dashed into the sea with exultant cries. Feeling the impactive scrutiny of strange faces, she took off her bathrobe and followed. She floated face down for a few yards and finding it shallow staggered to her feet and plodded forward, dragging slim legs like weights against the resistance of the water. When it was about breast high, she glanced back toward shore: a bald man in a monocle and a pair of tights, his tufted chest thrown out, his brash navel sucked in, was regarding her attentively. As Rosemary returned the gaze the man dislodged the monocle, which went into hiding amid the facetious whiskers of his chest, and poured himself a glass of something from a bottle in his hand.

Rosemary laid her face on the water and swam a choppy little four-beat crawl out to the raft. The water reached up for her, pulled her down tenderly out of the heat, seeped in her hair and ran into the corners of her body. She turned round and round in it, embracing it, wallowing in it. Reaching the raft she was out of breath, but a tanned woman with very white teeth looked down at her, and Rosemary, suddenly conscious of the raw whiteness of her own body, turned on her back and drifted toward shore. The hairy man holding the bottle spoke to her as she came out.

"I say—they have sharks out behind the raft." He was of indeterminate nationality, but spoke English with a slow Oxford drawl. "Yesterday they devoured two British sailors from the flotte at Golfe-Juan."

"Heavens!" exclaimed Rosemary.

"They come in for the refuse from the flotte."

Glazing his eyes to indicate that he had only spoken in order to warn her, he minced off two steps and poured himself another drink.

Not unpleasantly self-conscious, since there had been a slight sway of attention toward her during this conversation, Rosemary looked for a place to sit. Obviously each family possessed the strip of sand immediately in front of its umbrella; besides there was much visiting and talking back and forth—the atmosphere of a community upon which it would be presumptuous to intrude. Farther up, where the beach was strewn with pebbles and dead sea-weed, sat a group with flesh as white as her own. They lay under small hand-parasols instead of beach umbrellas and were obviously less indigenous to the place. Between the dark people and the light, Rosemary found room and spread out her peignoir on the sand.

*[handwritten margin note: between petite + haute bourgeoisie (literally + metaphorically)]*

Lying so, she first heard their voices and felt their feet skirt her body and their shapes pass between the sun and herself. The breath of an inquisitive dog blew warm and nervous on her neck; she could feel her skin broiling a little in the heat and hear the small exhausted wa-*waa* of the expiring waves. Presently her ear distinguished individual voices and she became aware that some one referred to scornfully as "that North guy" had kidnapped a waiter from a café in Cannes last night in order to saw him in two. The sponsor of the story was a white-haired woman in full evening dress, obviously a relic of the previous evening, for a tiara still clung to her head and a discouraged orchid expired from her shoulder. Rosemary, forming a vague antipathy to her and her companions, turned away.

Nearest her, on the other side, a young woman lay under a roof of umbrellas making out a list of things from a book open on the sand. Her bathing suit was pulled off her shoulders and her back, a ruddy, orange brown, set off by a string of creamy pearls, shone in the sun. Her face was hard and lovely and pitiful. Her eyes met Rosemary's but did not see her. Beyond her was a fine man in a jockey cap and red-striped tights; then the woman Rosemary had seen on the raft, and who looked back at her, seeing her; then a man with a long face and a golden, leonine head, with blue tights and no hat, talking very seriously to an unmistakably Latin young man in black tights, both of them picking at little pieces of sea-weed in the sand. She thought they were mostly Americans, but something made them unlike the Americans she had known of late.

After a while she realized that the man in the jockey cap

was giving a quiet little performance for this group; he moved gravely about with a rake, ostensibly removing gravel and meanwhile developing some esoteric burlesque held in suspension by his grave face. Its faintest ramification had become hilarious, until whatever he said released a burst of laughter. Even those who, like herself, were too far away to hear, sent out antennæ of attention until the only person on the beach not caught up in it was the young woman with the string of pearls. Perhaps from modesty of possession she responded to each salvo of amusement by bending closer over her list.

The man of the monocle and bottle spoke suddenly out of the sky above Rosemary.

"You are a ripping swimmer."

She demurred.

"Jolly good. My name is Campion. Here is a lady who says she saw you in Sorrento last week and knows who you are and would so like to meet you."

Glancing around with concealed annoyance Rosemary saw the untanned people were waiting. Reluctantly she got up and went over to them.

"Mrs. Abrams—Mrs. McKisco—Mr. McKisco—Mr. Dumphry——"

"We know who you are," spoke up the woman in evening dress. "You're Rosemary Hoyt and I recognized you in Sorrento and asked the hotel clerk and we all think you're perfectly marvellous and we want to know why you're not back in America making another marvellous moving picture."

They made a superfluous gesture of moving over for her. The woman who had recognized her was not a Jewess, despite her name. She was one of those elderly "good sports" preserved by an imperviousness to experience and a good digestion into another generation.

"We wanted to warn you about getting burned the first day," she continued cheerily, "because *your* skin is important, but there seems to be so darn much formality on this beach that we didn't know whether you'd mind."

## II

"We thought maybe you were in the plot," said Mrs. McKisco. She was a shabby-eyed, pretty young woman with a disheartening intensity. "We don't know who's in the plot and who isn't. One man my husband had been particularly nice to turned out to be a chief character— practically the assistant hero."

"The plot?" inquired Rosemary, half understanding. "Is there a plot?"

"My dear, we don't *know*," said Mrs. Abrams, with a convulsive, stout woman's chuckle. "We're not in it. We're the gallery."

Mr. Dumphry, a tow-headed, effeminate young man, remarked: "Mama Abrams is a plot in herself," and Campion shook his monocle at him, saying: "Now, Royal, don't be too ghastly for words." Rosemary looked at them all uncomfortably, wishing her mother had come down here with her. She did not like these people, especially in her immediate comparison of them with those who had interested her at the other end of the beach. Her mother's modest but compact social gift got them out of unwelcome situations swiftly and firmly. But Rosemary had been a celebrity for only six months, and sometimes the French manners of her early adolescence and the democratic manners of America, these latter superimposed, made a certain confusion and let her in for just such things.

Mr. McKisco, a scrawny, freckle-and-red man of thirty, did not find the topic of the "plot" amusing. He had been staring at the sea—now after a swift glance at his wife he turned to Rosemary and demanded aggressively:

"Been here long?"

"Only a day."

"Oh."

Evidently feeling that the subject had been thoroughly changed, he looked in turn at the others.

"Going to stay all summer?" asked Mrs. McKisco, innocently. "If you do you can watch the plot unfold."

"For God's sake, Violet, drop the subject!" exploded her husband. "Get a new joke, for God's sake!"

Mrs. McKisco swayed toward Mrs. Abrams and breathed audibly:

"He's nervous."

"I'm not nervous," disagreed McKisco. "It just happens I'm not nervous at all."

He was burning visibly—a grayish flush had spread over his face, dissolving all his expressions into a vast ineffectuality. Suddenly remotely conscious of his condition he got up to go in the water, followed by his wife, and seizing the opportunity Rosemary followed.

Mr. McKisco drew a long breath, flung himself into the shallows and began a stiff-armed batting of the Mediterranean, obviously intended to suggest a crawl—his breath exhausted he arose and looked around with an expression of surprise that he was still in sight of shore.

"I haven't learned to breathe yet. I never quite understood how they breathed." He looked at Rosemary inquiringly.

"I think you breathe out under water," she explained. "And every fourth beat you roll your head over for air."

"The breathing's the hardest part for me. Shall we go to the raft?"

The man with the leonine head lay stretched out upon the raft, which tipped back and forth with the motion of the water. As Mrs. McKisco reached for it a sudden tilt struck her arm up roughly, whereupon the man started up and pulled her on board.

"I was afraid it hit you." His voice was slow and shy; he had one of the saddest faces Rosemary had ever seen, the high cheek-bones of an Indian, a long upper lip, and enormous deep-set dark golden eyes. He had spoken out of the side of his mouth, as if he hoped his words would reach Mrs. McKisco by a circuitous and unobtrusive route; in a minute he had shoved off into the water and his long body lay motionless toward shore.

Rosemary and Mrs. McKisco watched him. When he had exhausted his momentum he abruptly bent double, his thin thighs rose above the surface, and he disappeared totally, leaving scarcely a fleck of foam behind.

"He's a good swimmer," Rosemary said.

Mrs. McKisco's answer came with surprising violence.

"Well, he's a rotten musician." She turned to her husband, who after two unsuccessful attempts had managed to climb on the raft, and having attained his balance was trying to make some kind of compensatory flourish, achieving only an extra stagger. "I was just saying that Abe North may be a good swimmer but he's a rotten musician."

"Yes," agreed McKisco, grudgingly. Obviously he had created his wife's world, and allowed her few liberties in it.

"Antheil's my man."[2] Mrs. McKisco turned challengingly to Rosemary, "Antheil and Joyce. I don't suppose you ever hear much about those sort of people in Hollywood, but my husband wrote the first criticism of *Ulysses* that ever appeared in America."

"I wish I had a cigarette," said McKisco calmly. "That's more important to me just now."

"He's got insides—don't you think so, Albert?"

Her voice faded off suddenly. The woman of the pearls had joined her two children in the water, and now Abe North came up under one of them like a volcanic island, raising him on his shoulders. The child yelled with fear and delight and the woman watched with a lovely peace, without a smile.

"Is that his wife?" Rosemary asked.

"No, that's Mrs. Diver. They're not at the hotel." Her eyes, photographic, did not move from the woman's face. After a moment she turned vehemently to Rosemary.

"Have you been abroad before?"

"Yes—I went to school in Paris."

"Oh! Well then you probably know that if you want to enjoy yourself here the thing is to get to know some real French families. What do these people get out of it?" She pointed her left shoulder toward shore. "They just stick around with each other in little cliques. Of course, we had letters of introduction and met all the best French artists and writers in Paris. That made it very nice."

"I should think so."

"My husband is finishing his first novel, you see."

Rosemary said: "Oh, he is?" She was not thinking anything special, except wondering whether her mother had got to sleep in this heat.

"It's on the idea of *Ulysses*," continued (Mrs. McKisco. *always speaks for her husband* "Only instead of taking twenty-four hours my husband takes a hundred years. He takes a decayed old French aristocrat and puts him in contrast with the mechanical age——"

"Oh, for God's sake, Violet, don't go telling everybody the idea," protested McKisco. "I don't want it to get all around before the book's published."

Rosemary swam back to the shore, where she threw her peignoir over her already sore shoulders and lay down again in the sun. The man with the jockey cap was now going from umbrella to umbrella carrying a bottle and little glasses in his hands; presently he and his friends grew livelier and closer together and now they were all under a single assemblage of umbrellas—she gathered that some one was leaving and that this was a last drink on the beach. Even the children knew that excitement was generating under that umbrella and turned toward it—and it seemed to Rosemary that it all came from the man in the jockey cap.

Noon dominated sea and sky—even the white line of Cannes, five miles off, had faded to a mirage of what was fresh and cool; a robin-breasted sailing boat pulled in behind it a strand from the outer, darker sea. It seemed that there was no life anywhere in all this expanse of coast except under the filtered sunlight of those umbrellas, where something went on amid the color and the murmur.

Campion walked near her, stood a few feet away and Rosemary closed her eyes, pretending to be asleep; then she half-opened them and watched two dim, blurred pillars that were legs. The man tried to edge his way into a sand-colored cloud, but the cloud floated off into the vast hot sky. Rosemary fell really asleep.

She awoke drenched with sweat to find the beach deserted save for the man in the jockey cap, who was folding a last umbrella. As Rosemary lay blinking, he walked nearer and said:

"I was going to wake you before I left. It's not good to get too burned right away."

"Thank you." Rosemary looked down at her crimson legs. "Heavens!"

She laughed cheerfully, inviting him to talk, but Dick Diver was already carrying a tent and a beach umbrella up to a waiting car, so she went into the water to wash off the sweat. He came back and gathering up a rake, a shovel, and a sieve, stowed them in a crevice of a rock. He glanced up and down the beach to see if he had left anything.

"Do you know what time it is?" Rosemary asked.

"It's about half-past one."

They faced the seascape together momentarily.

"It's not a bad time," said Dick Diver. "It's not one of the worst times of the day."

He looked at her and for a moment she lived in the bright blue worlds of his eyes, eagerly and confidently. Then he shouldered his last piece of junk and went up to his car, and Rosemary came out of the water, shook out her peignoir and walked up to the hotel.

## III

IT was almost two when they went into the dining-room. Back and forth over the deserted tables a heavy pattern of beams and shadows swayed with the motion of the pines outside. Two waiters, piling plates and talking loud Italian, fell silent when they came in and brought them a tired version of the table d'hôte luncheon.

"I fell in love on the beach," said Rosemary.

"Who with?"

"First with a whole lot of people who looked nice. Then with one man."

"Did you talk to him?"

"Just a little. Very handsome. With reddish hair." She

was eating, ravenously. "He's married though—it's usually the way."

Her mother was her best friend and had put every last possibility into the guiding of her, not so rare a thing in the theatrical profession, but rather special in that Mrs. Elsie Speers was not recompensing herself for a defeat of her own. She had no personal bitterness or resentments about life—twice satisfactorily married and twice widowed, her cheerful stoicism had each time deepened. One of her husbands had been a cavalry officer and one an army doctor, and they both left something to her that she tried to present intact to Rosemary. By not sparing Rosemary she had made her hard—by not sparing her own labor and devotion she had cultivated an idealism in Rosemary, which at present was directed toward herself and saw the world through her eyes. So that while Rosemary was a "simple" child she was protected by a double sheath of her mother's armor and her own—she had a mature distrust of the trivial, the facile and the vulgar. However, with Rosemary's sudden success in pictures Mrs. Speers felt that it was time she was spiritually weaned; it would please rather than pain her if this somewhat bouncing, breathless and exigent idealism would focus on something except herself.

"Then you like it here?" she asked.

"It might be fun if we knew those people. There were some other people, but they weren't nice. They recognized me—no matter where we go everybody's seen 'Daddy's Girl.'"

Mrs. Speers waited for the glow of egotism to subside; then she said in a matter-of-fact way: "That reminds me, when are you going to see Earl Brady?"

"I thought we might go this afternoon—if you're rested."

"You go—I'm not going."

"We'll wait till to-morrow then."

"I want you to go alone. It's only a short way—it isn't as if you didn't speak French."

"Mother—aren't there some things I don't have to do?"

"Oh, well then go later—but some day before we leave."

"All right, Mother."

After lunch they were both overwhelmed by the sudden flatness that comes over American travellers in quiet foreign places. No stimuli worked upon them, no voices called them from without, no fragments of their own thoughts came suddenly from the minds of others, and missing the clamor of Empire they felt that life was not continuing here.

"Let's only stay three days, Mother," Rosemary said when they were back in their rooms. Outside a light wind blew the heat around, straining it through the trees and sending little hot gusts through the shutters.

"How about the man you fell in love with on the beach?"

"I don't love anybody but you, Mother, darling."

Rosemary stopped in the lobby and spoke to Gausse père about trains. The concierge, lounging in light-brown khaki by the desk, stared at her rigidly, then suddenly remembered the manners of his métier. She took the bus and rode with a pair of obsequious waiters to the station, embarrassed by their deferential silence, wanting to urge them: "Go on, talk, enjoy yourselves. It doesn't bother me."

The first-class compartment was stifling; the vivid advertising cards of the railroad companies—the Pont du Gard at Arles, the Amphitheatre at Orange, winter sports at Chamonix—were fresher than the long motionless sea outside. Unlike American trains that were absorbed in an intense destiny of their own, and scornful of people on another world less swift and breathless, this train was part of the country through which it passed. Its breath stirred the dust from the palm leaves, the cinders mingled with the dry dung in the gardens. Rosemary was sure she could lean from the window and pull flowers with her hand.

A dozen cabbies slept in their hacks outside the Cannes station. Over on the promenade the Casino, the smart shops, and the great hotels turned blank iron masks to the summer sea. It was unbelievable that there could ever have been a "season," and Rosemary, half in the grip of fashion, became a little self-conscious, as though she were displaying an unhealthy taste for the moribund; as though people were wondering why she was here in the lull between the gaiety of last winter and next winter, while up north the true world thundered by.

As she came out of a drug store with a bottle of cocoanut oil, a woman, whom she recognized as Mrs. Diver, crossed her path with arms full of sofa cushions, and went to a car parked down the street. A long, low black dog barked at her, a dozing chauffeur woke with a start. She sat in the car, her lovely face set, controlled, her eyes brave and watchful, looking straight ahead toward nothing. Her dress was bright red and her brown legs were bare. She had thick, dark, gold hair like a chow's.

With half an hour to wait for her train Rosemary sat down in the Café des Alliés on the Croisette, where the trees made a green twilight over the tables and an orchestra wooed an imaginary public of cosmopolites with the "Nice Carnival Song" and last year's American tune. She had bought Le Temps and The Saturday Evening Post for her mother, and as she drank her citronnade she opened the latter at the memoirs of a Russian princess, finding the dim conventions of the nineties realer and nearer than the head-lines of the French paper. It was the same feeling that had oppressed her at the hotel—accustomed to seeing the starkest grotesqueries of a continent heavily underlined as comedy or tragedy, untrained to the task of separating out the essential for herself, she now began to feel that French life was empty and stale. This feeling was surcharged by listening to the sad tunes of the orchestra, reminiscent of the melancholy music played for acrobats in vaudeville. She was glad to go back to Gausse's Hôtel.

Her shoulders were too burned to swim with the next day, so she and her mother hired a car—after much haggling, for Rosemary had formed her valuation of money in France— and drove along the Riviera, the delta of many rivers. The chauffeur, a Russian czar of the period of Ivan the Terrible, was a self-appointed guide, and the resplendent names— Cannes, Nice, Monte Carlo—began to glow through their torpid camouflage, whispering of old kings come here to dine or die, of rajahs tossing Buddha's eyes to English

23

ballerinas, of Russian princes turning the weeks into Baltic twilights in the lost caviare days. Most of all, there was the scent of the Russians along the coast—their closed bookshops and grocery stores. Ten years ago, when the season ended in April, the doors of the Orthodox Church were locked, and the sweet champagnes they favored were put away until their return. "We'll be back next season," they said, but this was premature, for they were never coming back any more.

It was pleasant to drive back to the hotel in the late afternoon, above a sea as mysteriously colored as the agates and cornelians of childhood, green as green milk, blue as laundry water, wine dark. It was pleasant to pass people eating outside their doors, and to hear the fierce mechanical pianos behind the vines of country estaminets. When they turned off the Corniche d'Or and down to Gausse's Hôtel through the darkening banks of trees, set one behind another in many greens, the moon already hovered over the ruins of the aqueducts. . . .

Somewhere in the hills behind the hotel there was a dance, and Rosemary listened to the music through the ghostly moonshine of her mosquito net, realizing that there was gaiety too somewhere about, and she thought of the nice people on the beach. She thought she might meet them in the morning, but they obviously formed a self-sufficient little group, and once their umbrellas, bamboo rugs, dogs, and children were set out in place that part of the plage was literally fenced in. She resolved in any case not to spend her last two mornings with the other ones.

## IV

THE matter was solved for her. The McKiscos were not yet there and she had scarcely spread her peignoir when two men—the man with the jockey cap and the tall blonde man, given to sawing waiters in two—left the group and came down toward her.

"Good morning," said Dick Diver. He broke down. "Look—sunburn or no sunburn, why did you stay away yesterday? We worried about you."

She sat up and her happy little laugh welcomed their intrusion.

"We wondered," Dick Diver said, "if you wouldn't come over this morning. We go in, we take food and drink, so it's a substantial invitation."

*but not really* He seemed kind and charming—his voice promised that he would take care of her, and that a little later he would open up whole new worlds for her, unroll an endless succession of magnificent possibilities. He managed the introduction so that her name wasn't mentioned and then let her know easily that everyone knew who she was but was respecting the completeness of her private life—a courtesy that Rosemary had not met with save from professional people since her success.

Nicole Diver, her brown back hanging from her pearls, was looking through a recipe book for chicken Maryland. She was about twenty-four, Rosemary guessed—her face could have been described in terms of conventional prettiness, but the effect was that it had been made first on the heroic scale with strong structure and marking, as if the features and vividness of brow and coloring, everything we associate with temperament and character, had been molded with a Rodinesque intention, and then chiselled away in the direction of prettiness to a point where a single slip would have irreparably diminished its force and quality. With the mouth the sculptor had taken desperate chances—it was the cupid's bow of a magazine cover, yet it shared the distinction of the rest.

"Are you here for a long time?" Nicole asked. Her voice was low, almost harsh.

Suddenly Rosemary let the possibility enter her mind that they might stay another week.

"Not very long," she answered vaguely. "We've been abroad a long time—we landed in Sicily in March and we've been slowly working our way north. I got pneumonia making a picture last January and I've been recuperating."

"Mercy! How did that happen?"

"Well, it was from swimming." Rosemary was rather reluctant at embarking upon personal revelations. "One day I happened to have the grippe and didn't know it, and they were taking a scene where I dove into a canal in Venice. It was a very expensive set, so I had to dive and dive and dive all morning. Mother had a doctor right there, but it was no use—I got pneumonia." She changed the subject determinedly before they could speak. "Do you like it here—this place?"

"They have to like it," said Abe North slowly. "They invented it." He turned his noble head slowly so that his eyes rested with tenderness and affection on the two Divers.

"Oh, did you?"

"This is only the second season that the hotel's been open in summer," Nicole explained. "We persuaded Gausse to keep on a cook and a garçon and a chasseur—it paid its way and this year it's doing even better."

"But you're not in the hotel."

"We built a house, up at Tarmes."

"The theory is," said Dick, arranging an umbrella to clip a square of sunlight off Rosemary's shoulder, "that all the northern places, like Deauville, were picked out by Russians and English who don't mind the cold, while half of us Americans come from tropical climates—that's why we're beginning to come here."

The young man of Latin aspect had been turning the pages of The New York Herald.

"Well, what nationality are these people?" he demanded, suddenly, and read with a slight French intonation, " 'Registered at the Hotel Palace at Vevey are Mr. Pandely Vlasco, Mme. Bonneasse'—I don't exaggerate—'Corinna Medonca, Mme. Pasche, Seraphim Tullio, Maria Amalia Roto Mais, Moises Teubel, Mme. Paragoris, Apostle Alexandre, Yolanda Yosfuglu and Geneveva de Momus!' She attracts me most—Geneveva de Momus. Almost worth running up to Vevey to take a look at Geneveva de Momus."

He stood up with sudden restlessness, stretching himself with one sharp movement. He was a few years younger than

26

Diver or North. He was tall and his body was hard but overspare save for the bunched force gathered in his shoulders and upper arms. At first glance he seemed conventionally handsome—but there was a faint disgust always in his face which marred the full fierce lustre of his brown eyes. Yet one remembered them afterward, when one had forgotten the inability of the mouth to endure boredom and the young forehead with its furrows of fretful and unprofitable pain.

barbant (fr.)

"We found some fine ones in the news of Americans last week," said Nicole. "Mrs. Evelyn Oyster and—what were the others?"

"There was Mr. S. Flesh," said Diver, getting up also. He took his rake and began to work seriously at getting small stones out of the sand.

"Oh, yes—S. Flesh—doesn't he give you the creeps?"

It was quiet alone with Nicole—Rosemary found it even quieter than with her mother. Abe North and Barban, the Frenchman, were talking about Morocco, and Nicole having copied her recipe picked up a piece of sewing. Rosemary examined their appurtenances—four large parasols that made a canopy of shade, a portable bath house for dressing, a pneumatic rubber horse, new things that Rosemary had never seen, from the first burst of luxury manufacturing after the War, and probably in the hands of the first of purchasers. She had gathered that they were fashionable people, but though her mother had brought her up to beware such people as drones, she did not feel that way here. Even in their absolute immobility, complete as that of the morning, she felt a purpose, a working over something, a direction, an act of creation different from any she had known. Her immature mind made no speculations upon the nature of their relation to each other, she was only concerned with their attitude toward herself—but she perceived the web of some pleasant inter-relation, which she expressed with the thought that they seemed to have a very good time.

She looked in turn at the three men, temporarily expropriating them. All three were personable in different ways; all were of a special gentleness that she felt was part of their lives, past and future, not circumstanced by events, not at all like the company manners of actors, and she detected also a far-reaching delicacy that was different from the rough and ready good fellowship of directors, who represented the intellectuals in her life. Actors and directors —those were the only men she had ever known, those and the heterogeneous, indistinguishable mass of college boys, interested only in love at first sight, whom she had met at the Yale prom last fall.

These three were different. Barban was less civilized, more skeptical and scoffing, his manners were formal, even perfunctory. Abe North had, under his shyness, a desperate humor that amused but puzzled her. Her serious nature distrusted its ability to make a supreme impression on him. But Dick Diver—he was all complete there. Silently she admired him. His complexion was reddish and weather-burned, so was his short hair—a light growth of it rolled down his arms and hands. His eyes were of a bright, hard blue. His nose was somewhat pointed and there was never any doubt at whom he was looking or talking—and this is a flattering attention, for who looks at us?—glances fall upon us, curious or disinterested, nothing more. His voice, with some faint Irish melody running through it, wooed the world, yet she felt the layer of hardness in him, of self-control and of self-discipline, her own virtues. Oh, she chose him, and Nicole, lifting her head, saw her choose him, heard the little sigh at the fact that he was already possessed.

Toward noon the McKiscos, Mrs. Abrams, Mr. Dumphry, and Señor Campion came on the beach. They had brought a new umbrella that they set up with side glances toward the Divers, and crept under with satisfied expressions—all save Mr. McKisco, who remained derisively without. In his raking Dick had passed near them and now he returned to the umbrellas.

"The two young men are reading the Book of Etiquette together," he said in a low voice.

"Planning to mix wit de quality," said Abe.

Mary North, the very tanned young woman whom Rose-

28

mary had encountered the first day on the raft, came in from swimming and said with a smile that was a rakish gleam:

"So Mr. and Mrs. Neverquiver have arrived."

"They're this man's friends," Nicole reminded her, indicating Abe. "Why doesn't he go and speak to them? Don't you think they're attractive?"

"I think they're very attractive," Abe agreed. "I just don't think they're attractive, that's all."

"Well, I *have* felt there were too many people on the beach this summer," Nicole admitted. "*Our* beach that Dick made out of a pebble pile." She considered, and then lowering her voice out of the range of the trio of nannies who sat back under another umbrella, "Still they're preferable to those British last summer who kept shouting about: 'Isn't the sea blue? Isn't the sky white? Isn't little Nellie's nose red?' "

Rosemary thought she would not like to have Nicole for an enemy.

"But you didn't see the fight," Nicole continued. "The day before you came, the married man, the one with the name that sounds like a substitute for gasoline or butter——"

"McKisco?"[3]

"Yes—well they were having words and she tossed some sand in his face. So naturally he sat on top of her and rubbed her face in the sand. We were—electrified. I wanted Dick to interfere."

"I think," said Dick Diver, staring down abstractedly at the straw mat, "that I'll go over and invite them to dinner."

"No, you won't," Nicole told him quickly.

"I think it would be a very good thing. They're here— let's adjust ourselves."

"We're very well adjusted," she insisted, laughing. "I'm not going to have *my* nose rubbed in the sand. I'm a mean, hard woman," she explained to Rosemary, and then raising her voice, "Children, put on your bathing suits!"

Rosemary felt that this swim would become the typical one of her life, the one that would always pop up in her memory at the mention of swimming. Simultaneously the whole party moved toward the water, super-ready from the long, forced inaction, passing from the heat to the cool with the gourmandise of a tingling curry eaten with chilled white wine. The Divers' day was spaced like the day of the older civilizations to yield the utmost from the materials at hand, and to give all the transitions their full value, and she did not know that there would be another transition presently from the utter absorption of the swim to the garrulity of the Provençal lunch hour. But again she had the sense that Dick was taking care of her, and she delighted in responding to the eventual movement as if it had been an order.

Nicole handed her husband the curious garment on which she had been working. He went into the dressing tent and inspired a commotion by appearing in a moment clad in transparent black lace drawers. Close inspection revealed that actually they were lined with flesh-colored cloth.

"Well, if that isn't a pansy's trick!" exclaimed Mr. McKisco contemptuously—then turning quickly to Mr. Dumphry and Mr. Campion, he added, "Oh, I beg your pardon."

Rosemary bubbled with delight at the trunks. Her naïveté responded whole-heartedly to the expensive simplicity of the Divers, unaware of its complexity and its lack of innocence, unaware that it was all a selection of quality rather than quantity from the run of the world's bazaar; and that the simplicity of behavior also, the nursery-like peace and good will, the emphasis on the simpler virtues, was part of a desperate bargain with the gods and had been attained through struggles she could not have guessed at. At that moment the Divers represented externally the exact furthermost evolution of a class, so that most people seemed awkward beside them—in reality a qualitative change had already set in that was not at all apparent to Rosemary.

She stood with them as they took sherry and ate crackers. Dick Diver looked at her with cold blue eyes; his kind, strong mouth said thoughtfully and deliberately:

"You're the only girl I've seen for a long time that actually did look like something blooming."

In her mother's lap afterward Rosemary cried and cried.

"I love him, Mother. I'm desperately in love with him—
I never knew I could feel that way about anybody. And he's
married and I like her too—it's just hopeless. Oh, I love
him so!"

"I'm curious to meet him."

"She's invited us to dinner Friday."

"If you're in love it ought to make you happy. You ought
to laugh."

Rosemary looked up and gave a beautiful little shiver of
her face and laughed. Her mother always had a great in-
fluence on her.

## V

ROSEMARY went to Monte Carlo as nearly sulky as it was
possible for her to be. She rode up the rugged hill to la
Turbie, to an old Gaumont lot in process of reconstruction,
and as she stood by the grilled entrance waiting for an
answer to the message on her card, she might have been
looking into Hollywood. The bizarre débris of some recent
picture, a decayed street scene in India, a great cardboard
whale, a monstrous tree bearing cherries large as basket-
balls, bloomed there by exotic dispensation, autochthonous
as the pale amaranth, mimosa, cork oak or dwarf pine.
There were a quick-lunch shack and two barnlike stages
and everywhere about the lot, groups of waiting, hopeful,
painted faces.

After ten minutes a young man with hair the color of
canary feathers hurried down to the gate.

"Come in, Miss Hoyt. Mr. Brady's on the set, but he's
very anxious to see you. I'm sorry you were kept waiting,
but you know some of these French dames are worse about
pushing themselves in——"

The studio manager opened a small door in the blank
wall of stage building and with sudden glad familiarity
Rosemary followed him into half darkness. Here and there

figures spotted the twilight, turning up ashen faces to her like souls in purgatory watching the passage of a mortal through. There were whispers and soft voices and, apparently from afar, the gentle tremolo of a small organ. Turning the corner made by some flats, they came upon the white crackling glow of a stage, where a French actor—his shirt front, collar, and cuffs tinted a brilliant pink—and an American actress stood motionless face to face. They stared at each other with dogged eyes, as though they had been in the same position for hours; and still for a long time nothing happened, no one moved. A bank of lights went off with a savage hiss, went on again; the plaintive tap of a hammer begged admission to nowhere in the distance; a blue face appeared among the blinding lights above, called something unintelligible into the upper blackness. Then the silence was broken by a voice in front of Rosemary.

"Baby, you don't take off the stockings, you can spoil ten more pairs. That dress is fifteen pounds."

Stepping backward the speaker ran against Rosemary, whereupon the studio manager said, "Hey, Earl—Miss Hoyt."

They were meeting for the first time. Brady was quick and strenuous. As he took her hand she saw him look her over from head to foot, a gesture she recognized and that made her feel at home, but gave her always a faint feeling of superiority to whoever made it. If her person was property she could exercise whatever advantage was inherent in its ownership.

"I thought you'd be along any day now," Brady said, in a voice that was just a little too compelling for private life, and that trailed with it a faintly defiant cockney accent. "Have a good trip?"

"Yes, but we're glad to be going home."

"No-o-o!" he protested. "Stay awhile—I want to talk to you. Let me tell you that was some picture of yours—that 'Daddy's Girl.' I saw it in Paris. I wired the coast right away to see if you were signed."

"I just had—I'm sorry."

"God, what a picture!"

Not wanting to smile in silly agreement Rosemary frowned.

"Nobody wants to be thought of forever for just one picture," she said.

"Sure—that's right. What're your plans?"

"Mother thought I needed a rest. When I get back we'll probably either sign up with First National or keep on with Famous."

"Who's we?"

"My mother. She decides business matters. I couldn't do without her."

Again he looked her over completely, and, as he did, something in Rosemary went out to him. It was not liking, not at all the spontaneous admiration she had felt for the man on the beach this morning. It was a click. He desired her and, so far as her virginal emotions went, she contemplated a surrender with equanimity. Yet she knew she would forget him half an hour after she left him—like an actor kissed in a picture.

"Where are you staying?" Brady asked. "Oh, yes, at Gausse's. Well, my plans are made for this year, too, but that letter I wrote you still stands. Rather make a picture with you than any girl since Connie Talmadge was a kid."

"I feel the same way. Why don't you come back to Hollywood?"

"I can't stand the damn place. I'm fine here. Wait till after this shot and I'll show you around."

Walking onto the set he began to talk to the French actor in a low, quiet voice.

Five minutes passed—Brady talked on, while from time to time the Frenchman shifted his feet and nodded. Abruptly, Brady broke off, calling something to the lights that startled them into a humming glare. Los Angeles was loud about Rosemary now. Unappalled she moved once more through the city of thin partitions, wanting to be back there. But she did not want to see Brady in the mood she sensed he would be in after he had finished and she left the lot with a spell still upon her. The Mediterranean world was less silent now that she knew the studio was there. She liked the people on the streets and bought herself a pair of espadrilles on the way to the train.

Her mother was pleased that she had done so accurately what she was told to do, but she still wanted to launch her out and away. Mrs. Speers was fresh in appearance but she was tired; death beds make people tired indeed and she had watched beside a couple.

## VI

FEELING good from the rosy wine at lunch, Nicole Diver folded her arms high enough for the artificial camellia on her shoulder to touch her cheek, and went out into her lovely grassless garden. The garden was bounded on one side by the house, from which it flowed and into which it ran, on two sides by the old village, and on the last by the cliff falling by ledges to the sea.

Along the walls on the village side all was dusty, the wriggling vines, the lemon and eucalyptus trees, the casual wheel-barrow, left only a moment since, but already grown into the path, atrophied and faintly rotten. Nicole was invariably somewhat surprised that by turning in the other direction past a bed of peonies she walked into an area so green and cool that the leaves and petals were curled with tender damp.

Knotted at her throat she wore a lilac scarf that even in the achromatic sunshine cast its color up to her face and down around her moving feet in a lilac shadow. Her face was hard, almost stern, save for the soft gleam of piteous doubt that looked from her green eyes. Her once fair hair had darkened, but she was lovelier now at twenty-four than she had been at eighteen, when her hair was brighter than she.

Following a walk marked by an intangible mist of bloom that followed the white border stones she came to a space overlooking the sea where there were lanterns asleep in the fig trees and a big table and wicker chairs and a great market umbrella from Siena, all gathered about an enormous pine, the biggest tree in the garden. She paused there a moment, looking absently at a growth of nasturtiums and iris tangled at its foot, as though sprung from a careless handful of seeds, listening to the plaints and accusations of some nursery squabble in the house. When this died away on the summer air, she walked on, between kaleidoscopic peonies massed in pink clouds, black and brown tulips and fragile mauve-stemmed roses, transparent like sugar flowers in a confectioner's window—until, as if the scherzo of color could reach no further intensity, it broke off suddenly in mid-air, and moist steps went down to a level five feet below.

Here there was a well with the boarding around it dank and slippery even on the brightest days. She went up the stairs on the other side and into the vegetable garden; she walked rather quickly; she liked to be active, though at times she gave an impression of repose that was at once static and evocative. This was because she knew few words and believed in none, and in the world she was rather silent, contributing just her share of urbane humor with a precision that approached meagreness. But at the moment when strangers tended to grow uncomfortable in the presence of this economy she would seize the topic and rush off with it, feverishly surprised with herself—then bring it back and relinquish it abruptly, almost timidly, like an obedient retriever, having been adequate and something more.

As she stood in the fuzzy green light of the vegetable garden, Dick crossed the path ahead of her going to his work house. Nicole waited silently till he had passed; then she went on through lines of prospective salads to a little menagerie where pigeons and rabbits and a parrot made a medley of insolent noises at her. Descending to another ledge she reached a low, curved wall and looked down seven hundred feet to the Mediterranean Sea.

She stood in the ancient hill village of Tarmes. The villa and its grounds were made out of a row of peasant dwellings that abutted on the cliff—five small houses had been combined to make the house and four destroyed to make the garden. The exterior walls were untouched so that from the road far below it was indistinguishable from the violet gray mass of the town.

For a moment Nicole stood looking down at the Mediterranean but there was nothing to do with that, even with her tireless hands. Presently Dick came out of his one-room house carrying a telescope and looked east toward Cannes. In a moment Nicole swam into his field of vision, whereupon he disappeared into his house and came out with a megaphone. He had many light mechanical devices.

"Nicole," he shouted, "I forgot to tell you that as a final apostolic gesture[5] I invited Mrs. Abrams, the woman with the white hair."

"I suspected it. It's an outrage."

The ease with which her reply reached him seemed to belittle his megaphone, so she raised her voice and called, "Can you hear me?"

"Yes." He lowered the megaphone and then raised it stubbornly. "I'm going to invite some more people too. I'm going to invite the two young men."

"All right," she agreed placidly.

"I want to give a really *bad* party. I mean it. I want to give a party where there's a brawl and seductions and people going home with their feelings hurt and women passed out in the cabinet de toilette. You wait and see."

He went back into his house and Nicole saw that one of his most characteristic moods was upon him, the excitement that swept everyone up into it and was inevitably followed by his own form of melancholy, which he never displayed but at which she guessed. This excitement about things reached an intensity out of proportion to their importance, generating a really extraordinary virtuosity with people. Save among a few of the tough-minded and perennially suspicious, he had the power of arousing a fascinated and uncritical love. The reaction came when he realized the waste and extravagance involved. He sometimes looked back with awe at the carnivals of affection he had given

36

as a general might gaze upon a massacre he had ordered to satisfy an impersonal blood lust.

But to be included in Dick Diver's world for a while was a remarkable experience: people believed he made special reservations about them, recognizing the proud uniqueness of their destinies, buried under the compromises of how many years. He won everyone quickly with an exquisite consideration and a politeness that moved so fast and intuitively that it could be examined only in its effect. Then, without caution, lest the first bloom of the relation wither, he opened the gate to his amusing world. So long as they subscribed to it completely, their happiness was his preoccupation, but at the first flicker of doubt as to its all-inclusiveness he evaporated before their eyes, leaving little communicable memory of what he had said or done.

At eight-thirty that evening he came out to meet his first guests, his coat carried rather ceremoniously, rather promisingly, in his hand, like a toreador's cape. It was characteristic that after greeting Rosemary and her mother he waited for them to speak first, as if to allow them the reassurance of their own voices in new surroundings.

To resume Rosemary's point of view it should be said that, under the spell of the climb to Tarmes and the fresher air, she and her mother looked about appreciatively. Just as the personal qualities of extraordinary people can make themselves plain in an unaccustomed change of expression, so the intensely calculated perfection of Villa Diana[6] transpired all at once through such minute failures as the chance apparition of a maid in the background or the perversity of a cork. While the first guests arrived bringing with them the excitement of the night, the domestic activity of the day receded past them gently, symbolized by the Diver children and their governess still at supper on the terrace.

"What a beautiful garden!" Mrs. Speers exclaimed.

"Nicole's garden," said Dick. "She won't let it alone— she nags it all the time, worries about its diseases. Any day now I expect to have her come down with Powdery Mildew or Fly Speck, or Late Blight." He pointed his forefinger decisively at Rosemary, saying with a lightness seeming to conceal a paternal interest, "I'm going to save your reason—I'm going to give you a hat to wear on the beach."

He turned them from the garden to the terrace, where he poured a cocktail. Earl Brady arrived, discovering Rosemary with surprise. His manner was softer than at the studio, as if his differentness had been put on at the gate, and Rosemary, comparing him instantly with Dick Diver, swung sharply toward the latter. In comparison Earl Brady seemed faintly gross, faintly ill-bred; once more, though, she felt an electric response to his person.

He spoke familiarly to the children who were getting up from their outdoor supper.

"Hello, Lanier, how about a song? Will you and Topsy sing me a song?"

"What shall we sing?" agreed the little boy, with the odd chanting accent of American children brought up in France.

"That song about 'Mon Ami Pierrot.'"

Brother and sister stood side by side without self-consciousness and their voices soared sweet and shrill upon the evening air.

> "Au clair de la lune
> Mon Ami Pierrot
> Prête-moi ta plume
> Pour écrire un mot
> Ma chandelle est morte
> Je n'ai plus de feu
> Ouvre-moi ta porte
> Pour l'amour de Dieu."

The singing ceased and the children, their faces aglow with the late sunshine, stood smiling calmly at their success. Rosemary was thinking that the Villa Diana was the centre of the world. On such a stage some memorable thing was sure to happen. She lighted up higher as the gate tinkled open and the rest of the guests arrived in a body—the McKiscos, Mrs. Abrams, Mr. Dumphry, and Mr. Campion came up to the terrace.

Rosemary had a sharp feeling of disappointment—she looked quickly at Dick, as though to ask an explanation of this incongruous mingling. But there was nothing unusual

38

in his expression. He greeted his new guests with a proud bearing and an obvious deference to their infinite and unknown possibilities. She believed in him so much that presently she accepted the rightness of the McKiscos' presence as if she had expected to meet them all along.

"I've met you in Paris," McKisco said to Abe North, who with his wife had arrived on their heels, "in fact I've met you twice."

"Yes, I remember," Abe said.

"Then where was it?" demanded McKisco, not content to let well enough alone.

"Why, I think—" Abe got tired of the game, "I can't remember."

The interchange filled a pause and Rosemary's instinct was that something tactful should be said by somebody, but Dick made no attempt to break up the grouping formed by these late arrivals, not even to disarm Mrs. McKisco of her air of supercilious amusement. He did not solve this social problem because he knew it was not of importance at the moment and would solve itself. He was saving his newness for a larger effort, waiting a more significant moment for his guests to be conscious of a good time.

Rosemary stood beside Tommy Barban—he was in a particularly scornful mood and there seemed to be some special stimulus working upon him. He was leaving in the morning.

"Going home?"

"Home? I have no home. I am going to a war."

"What war?"

"What war? Any war. I haven't seen a paper lately but I suppose there's a war—there always is."

"Don't you care what you fight for?"

"Not at all—so long as I'm well treated. When I'm in a rut I come to see the Divers, because then I know that in a few weeks I'll want to go to war."

Rosemary stiffened.

"You like the Divers," she reminded him.

"Of course—especially her—but they make me want to go to war."

39

She considered this, to no avail. The Divers made her want to stay near them forever.

"You're half American," she said, as if that should solve the problem.

"Also I'm half French, and I was educated in England and since I was eighteen I've worn the uniforms of eight countries. But I hope I did not give you the impression that I am not fond of the Divers—I am, especially of Nicole."

"How could any one help it?" she said simply.

She felt far from him. The undertone of his words repelled her and she withdrew her adoration for the Divers from the profanity of his bitterness. She was glad he was not next to her at dinner and she was still thinking of his words "especially her" as they moved toward the table in the garden.

For a moment now she was beside Dick Diver on the path. Alongside his hard, neat brightness everything faded into the surety that he knew everything. For a year, which was forever, she had had money and a certain celebrity and contact with the celebrated, and these latter had presented themselves merely as powerful enlargements of the people with whom the doctor's widow and her daughter had associated in a hôtel-pension in Paris. Rosemary was a romantic and her career had not provided many satisfactory opportunities on that score. Her mother, with the idea of a career for Rosemary, would not tolerate any such spurious substitutes as the excitations available on all sides, and indeed Rosemary was already beyond that—she was In the movies but not at all At them. So when she had seen approval of Dick Diver in her mother's face it meant that he was "the real thing"; it meant permission to go as far as she could.

"I was watching you," he said, and she knew he meant it. "We've grown very fond of you."

"I fell in love with you the first time I saw you," she said quietly.

He pretended not to have heard, as if the compliment were purely formal.

"New friends," he said, as if it were an important point, "can often have a better time together than old friends."

40

With that remark, which she did not understand precisely, she found herself at the table, picked out by slowly emerging lights against the dark dusk. A chord of delight struck inside her when she saw that Dick had taken her mother on his right hand; for herself she was between Luis Campion and Brady.

Surcharged with her emotion she turned to Brady with the intention of confiding in him, but at her first mention of Dick a hard-boiled sparkle in his eyes gave her to understand that he refused the fatherly office. In turn she was equally firm when he tried to monopolize her hand, so they talked shop or rather she listened while he talked shop, her polite eyes never leaving his face, but her mind was so definitely elsewhere that she felt he must guess the fact. Intermittently she caught the gist of his sentences and supplied the rest from her subconscious, as one picks up the striking of a clock in the middle with only the rhythm of the first uncounted strokes lingering in the mind.

# VII

IN a pause Rosemary looked away and up the table where Nicole sat between Tommy Barban and Abe North, her chow's hair foaming and frothing in the candlelight. Rosemary listened, caught sharply by the rich clipped voice in infrequent speech:

"The poor man," Nicole exclaimed. "Why did you want to saw him in two?"

"*Naturally* I wanted to see what was inside a waiter. Wouldn't you like to know what was inside a waiter?"

"Old menus," suggested Nicole with a short laugh. "Pieces of broken china and tips and pencil stubs."

"Exactly—but the thing was to prove it scientifically. And of course doing it with that musical saw would have eliminated any sordidness."

"Did you intend to play the saw while you performed the operation?" Tommy inquired.

"We didn't get quite that far. We were alarmed by the screams. We thought he might rupture something."

"All sounds very peculiar to me," said Nicole. "Any musician that'll use another musician's saw to——"

They had been at table half an hour and a perceptible change had set in—person by person had given up something, a preoccupation, an anxiety, a suspicion, and now they were only their best selves and the Divers' guests. Not to have been friendly and interested would have seemed to reflect on the Divers, so now they were all trying, and seeing this, Rosemary liked everyone—except McKisco, who had contrived to be the unassimilated member of the party. This was less from ill will than from his determination to sustain with wine the good spirits he had enjoyed on his arrival. Lying back in his place between Earl Brady, to whom he had addressed several withering remarks about the movies, and Mrs. Abrams, to whom he said nothing, he stared at Dick Diver with an expression of devastating irony, the effect being occasionally interrupted by his attempts to engage Dick in a catercornered conversation across the table.

"Aren't you a friend of Van Buren Denby?" he would say.

"I don't believe I know him."

"I thought you were a friend of his," he persisted irritably.

When the subject of Mr. Denby fell of its own weight, he essayed other equally irrelative themes, but each time the very deference of Dick's attention seemed to paralyze him, and after a moment's stark pause the conversation that he had interrupted would go on without him. He tried breaking into other dialogues, but it was like continually shaking hands with a glove from which the hand had been withdrawn—so finally, with a resigned air of being among children, he devoted his attention entirely to the champagne.

Rosemary's glance moved at intervals around the table, eager for the others' enjoyment, as if they were her future stepchildren. A gracious table light, emanating from a bowl of spicy pinks, fell upon Mrs. Abrams' face, cooked to a turn in Veuve Cliquot, full of vigor, tolerance, adolescent good will; next to her sat Mr. Royal Dumphry, his girl's comeliness less startling in the pleasure world of evening. Then Violet McKisco, whose prettiness had been piped to the surface of her, so that she ceased her struggle to make tangible to herself her shadowy position as the wife of an arriviste who had not arrived.

Then came Dick, with his arms full of the slack he had taken up from others, deeply merged in his own party.

Then her mother, forever perfect.

Then Barban talking to her mother with an urbane fluency that made Rosemary like him again. Then Nicole. Rosemary saw her suddenly in a new way and found her one of the most beautiful people she had ever known. Her face, the face of a saint, a Viking madonna, shone through the faint motes that snowed across the candlelight, drew down its flush from the wine-colored lanterns in the pine. She was still as still.

Abe North was talking to her about his moral code: "Of course I've got one," he insisted, "—a man can't live without a moral code. Mine is that I'm against the burning of witches. Whenever they burn a witch I get all hot under the collar." Rosemary knew from Brady that he was a musician who after a brilliant and precocious start had composed nothing for seven years.

gay?

Next was Campion, managing somehow to restrain his most blatant effeminacy, and even to visit upon those near him a certain disinterested motherliness. Then Mary North with a face so merry that it was impossible not to smile back into the white mirrors of her teeth—the whole area around her parted lips was a lovely little circle of delight.

Finally Brady, whose heartiness became, moment by moment, a social thing instead of a crude assertion and reassertion of his own mental health, and his preservation of it by a detachment from the frailties of others.

Rosemary, as dewy with belief as a child from one of Mrs. Burnett's[7] vicious tracts, had a conviction of homecoming, of a return from the derisive and salacious

43

illusion / reality
night   day

improvisations of the frontier. There were fireflies riding on the dark air and a dog baying on some low and far-away ledge of the cliff. The table seemed to have risen a little toward the sky like a mechanical dancing platform, giving the people around it a sense of being alone with each other in the dark universe, nourished by its only food, warmed by its only lights. And, as if a curious hushed laugh from Mrs. McKisco were a signal that such a detachment from the world had been attained, the two Divers began suddenly to warm and glow and expand, as if to make up to their guests, already so subtly assured of their importance, so flattered with politeness, for anything they might still miss from that country well left behind. Just for a moment they seemed to speak to every one at the table, singly and together, assuring them of their friendliness, their affection. And for a moment the faces turned up toward them were like the faces of poor children at a Christmas tree. Then abruptly the table broke up—the moment when the guests had been daringly lifted above conviviality into the rarer atmosphere of sentiment was over before it could be irreverently breathed, before they had half realized it was there.

But the diffused magic of the hot sweet South had withdrawn into them—the soft-pawed night and the ghostly wash of the Mediterranean far below—the magic left these things and melted into the two Divers and became part of them. Rosemary watched Nicole pressing upon her mother a yellow evening bag she had admired, saying, "I think things ought to belong to the people that like them"—and then sweeping into it all the yellow articles she could find, a pencil, a lipstick, a little note book, "because they all go together."

Nicole disappeared and presently Rosemary noticed that Dick was no longer there; the guests distributed themselves in the garden or drifted in toward the terrace.

"Do you want," Violet McKisco asked Rosemary, "to go to the bathroom?"

Not at that precise moment.

"I want," insisted Mrs. McKisco, "to go to the bathroom." As a frank outspoken woman she walked toward the house, dragging her secret after her, while Rosemary looked after with reprobation. Earl Brady proposed that they walk down to the sea wall but she felt that this was her time to have a share of Dick Diver when he reappeared, so she stalled, listening to McKisco quarrel with Barban.

"Why do you want to fight the Soviets?" McKisco said. "The greatest experiment ever made by humanity? And the Riff?[8] It seems to me it would be more heroic to fight on the just side."

"How do you find out which it is?" asked Barban dryly.

"Why—usually everybody intelligent knows."

"Are you a Communist?"

"I'm a Socialist," said McKisco, "I sympathize with Russia."

"Well, I'm a soldier," Barban answered pleasantly. "My business is to kill people. I fought against the Riff because I am a European, and I have fought the Communists because they want to take my property from me."

"Of all the narrow-minded excuses," McKisco looked around to establish a derisive liaison with some one else, but without success. He had no idea what he was up against in Barban, neither of the simplicity of the other man's bag of ideas nor of the complexity of his training. McKisco knew what ideas were, and as his mind grew he was able to recognize and sort an increasing number of them—but faced by a man whom he considered "dumb," one in whom he found no ideas he could recognize as such, and yet to whom he could not feel personally superior, he jumped at the conclusion that Barban was the end product of an archaic world, and as such, worthless. McKisco's contacts with the princely classes in America had impressed upon him their uncertain and fumbling snobbery, their delight in ignorance and their deliberate rudeness, all lifted from the English with no regard paid to factors that make English philistinism and rudeness purposeful, and applied in a land where a little knowledge and civility buy more than they do anywhere else—an attitude which reached its apogee in the "Harvard manner" of about 1900. He thought that this Barban was of that type, and being drunk rashly forgot that he was in awe of him—this led up to the trouble in which he presently found himself.

Feeling vaguely ashamed for McKisco, Rosemary waited, placid but inwardly on fire, for Dick Diver's return. From her chair at the deserted table with Barban, McKisco, and Abe she looked up along the path edged with shadowy myrtle and fern to the stone terrace, and falling in love with her mother's profile against a lighted door, was about to go there when Mrs. McKisco came hurrying down from the house.

She exuded excitement. In the very silence with which she pulled out a chair and sat down, her eyes staring, her mouth working a little, they all recognized a person crop-full of news, and her husband's "What's the matter, Vi?" came naturally, as all eyes turned toward her.

"My dear—" she said at large, and then addressed Rosemary, "my dear—it's nothing. I really can't say a word."

"You're among friends," said Abe.

"Well, upstairs I came upon a scene, my dears——"

Shaking her head cryptically she broke off just in time, for Tommy arose and addressed her politely but sharply:

"It's inadvisable to comment on what goes on in this house."

# VIII

VIOLET breathed loud and hard once and with an effort brought another expression into her face.

Dick came finally and with a sure instinct he separated Barban and the McKiscos and became excessively ignorant and inquisitive about literature with McKisco—thus giving the latter the moment of superiority which he required. The others helped him carry lamps up—who would not be pleased at carrying lamps helpfully through the darkness?[9] Rosemary helped, meanwhile responding patiently to Royal Dumphry's inexhaustible curiosity about Hollywood.

Now—she was thinking—I've earned a time alone with

him. He must know that because his laws are like the laws Mother taught me.

Rosemary was right—presently he detached her from the company on the terrace, and they were alone together, borne away from the house toward the seaside wall with what were less steps than irregularly spaced intervals through some of which she was pulled, through others blown.

They looked out over the Mediterranean. Far below, the last excursion boat from the Iles de Lérins floated across the bay like a Fourth-of-July balloon foot-loose in the heavens. Between the black isles it floated, softly parting the dark tide.

"I understand why you speak as you do of your mother," he said. "Her attitude toward you is very fine, I think. She has a sort of wisdom that's rare in America."

"Mother is perfect," she prayed.

"I was talking to her about a plan I have—she told me that how long you both stayed in France depended on you."

On *you*, Rosemary all but said aloud.

"So since things are over down here——"

"Over?" she inquired.

"Well, this is over—this part of the summer is over. Last week Nicole's sister left, to-morrow Tommy Barban leaves, Monday Abe and Mary North are leaving. Maybe we'll have more fun this summer but this particular fun is over. I want it to die violently instead of fading out sentimentally—that's why I gave this party. What I'm coming to is—Nicole and I are going up to Paris to see Abe North off for America—I wonder if you'd like to go with us."

"What did Mother say?"

"She seemed to think it would be fine. She doesn't want to go herself. She wants you to go alone."

"I haven't seen Paris since I've been grown," said Rosemary. "I'd love to see it with you."

"That's nice of you." Did she imagine that his voice was suddenly metallic? "Of course we've been excited about you from the moment you came on the beach. That vitality, we were sure it was professsional—especially Nicole was. It'd never use itself up on any one person or group."

Her instinct cried out to her that he was passing her along slowly toward Nicole and she put her own brakes on, saying with an equal hardness:

"I wanted to know all of you too—especially you. I told you I fell in love with you the first time I saw you."

She was right going at it that way. But the space between heaven and earth had cooled his mind, destroyed the impulsiveness that had led him to bring her here, and made him aware of the too obvious appeal, the struggle with an unrehearsed scene and unfamiliar words.

He tried now to make her want to go back to the house and it was difficult, and he did not quite want to lose her. She felt only the draft blowing as he joked with her good-humoredly.

"You don't know what you want. You go and ask your mother what you want."

She was stricken. She touched him, feeling the smooth cloth of his dark coat like a chasuble. She seemed about to fall to her knees—from that position she delivered her last shot.

"I think you're the most wonderful person I ever met—except my mother."

"You have romantic eyes."

His laughter swept them on up toward the terrace where he delivered her to Nicole. . . .

Too soon it had become time to go and the Divers helped them all to go quickly. In the Divers' big Isotta there would be Tommy Barban and his baggage—he was spending the night at the hotel to catch an early train—with Mrs. Abrams, the McKiscos and Campion. Earl Brady was going to drop Rosemary and her mother on his way to Monte Carlo, and Royal Dumphry rode with them because the Divers' car was crowded. Down in the garden lanterns still glowed over the table where they had dined, as the Divers stood side by side in the gate, Nicole blooming away and filling the night with graciousness, and Dick bidding good-by to everyone by name. To Rosemary it seemed very poignant to drive away and leave them in their house. Again she wondered what Mrs. McKisco had seen in the bathroom.

## IX

It was a limpid black night, hung as in a basket from a single dull star. The horn of the car ahead was muffled by the resistance of the thick air. Brady's chauffeur drove slowly; the tail-light of the other car appeared from time to time at turnings—then not at all. But after ten minutes it came into sight again, drawn up at the side of the road. Brady's chauffeur slowed up behind but immediately it began to roll forward slowly and they passed it. In the instant they passed it they heard a blur of voices from behind the reticence of the limousine and saw that the Divers' chauffeur was grinning. Then they went on, going fast through the alternating banks of darkness and thin night, descending at last in a series of roller-coaster swoops, to the great bulk of Gausse's Hôtel.

Rosemary dozed for three hours and then lay awake, suspended in the moonshine. Cloaked by the erotic darkness she exhausted the future quickly, with all the eventualities that might lead up to a kiss, but with the kiss itself as blurred as a kiss in pictures. She changed position in bed deliberately, the first sign of insomnia she had ever had, and tried to think with her mother's mind about the question. In this process she was often acute beyond her experience, with remembered things from old conversations that had gone into her half-heard.

Rosemary had been brought up with the idea of work.  Mrs. Speers had spent the slim leavings of the men who had widowed her on her daughter's education, and when she blossomed out at sixteen with that extraordinary hair, rushed her to Aix-les-Bains and marched her unannounced into the suite of an American producer who was recuperating there. When the producer went to New York they went too. Thus Rosemary had passed her entrance examinations. With the ensuing success and the promise of comparative stability that followed, Mrs. Speers had felt free to tacitly imply tonight:

"You were brought up to work—not especially to marry. Now you've found your first nut to crack and it's a good nut —go ahead and put whatever happens down to experience. Wound yourself or him—whatever happens it can't spoil you because economically you're a boy, not a girl."

Rosemary had never done much thinking, save about the illimitability of her mother's perfections, so this final severance of the umbilical cord disturbed her sleep. A false dawn sent the sky pressing through the tall French windows, and getting up she walked out on the terrace, warm to her bare feet. There were secret noises in the air, an insistent bird achieved an ill-natured triumph with regularity in the trees above the tennis court; footfalls followed a round drive in the rear of the hotel, taking their tone in turn from the dust road, the crushed-stone walk, the cement steps, and then reversing the process in going away. Beyond the inky sea and far up that high, black shadow of a hill lived the Divers. She thought of them both together, heard them still singing faintly a song like rising smoke, like a hymn, very remote in time and far away. Their children slept, their gate was shut for the night.

She went inside and dressing in a light gown and espadrilles went out her window again and along the continuous terrace toward the front door, going fast since she found that other private rooms, exuding sleep, gave upon it. She stopped at the sight of a figure seated on the wide white stairway of the formal entrance—then she saw that it was Luis Campion and that he was weeping.

He was weeping hard and quietly and shaking in the same parts as a weeping woman. A scene in a rôle she had played last year swept over her irresistibly and advancing she touched him on the shoulder. He gave a little yelp before he recognized her.

"What is it?" Her eyes were level and kind and not slanted into him with hard curiosity. "Can I help you?"

"Nobody can help me. I knew it. I have only myself to blame. It's always the same."

"What is it—do you want to tell me?"

He looked at her to see.

"No," he decided. "When you're older you'll know what people who love suffer. The agony. It's better to be cold and young than to love. It's happened to me before but never like this—so accidental—just when everything was going well."

His face was repulsive in the quickening light. Not by a flicker of her personality, a movement of the smallest muscle, did she betray her sudden disgust with whatever it was. But Campion's sensitivity realized it and he changed the subject rather suddenly.

"Abe North is around here somewhere."

"Why, he's staying at the Divers'!"

"Yes, but he's up—don't you know what happened?"

A shutter opened suddenly in a room two stories above and an English voice spat distinctly:

"*Will you kaindlay stup tucking!*"

Rosemary and Luis Campion went humbly down the steps and to a bench beside the road to the beach.

"Then you have no idea what's happened? My dear, the most extraordinary thing—" He was warming up now, hanging on to his revelation. "I've never seen a thing come so suddenly—I have always avoided violent people—they upset me so I sometimes have to go to bed for days."

He looked at her triumphantly. She had no idea what he was talking about.

"My dear," he burst forth, leaning toward her with his whole body as he touched her on the upper leg, to show it was no mere irresponsible venture of his hand—he was so sure of himself. "There's going to be a duel."

"Wh-at?"

"A duel with—we don't know what yet."

"Who's going to duel?"

"I'll tell you from the beginning." He drew a long breath and then said, as if it were rather to her discredit but he wouldn't hold it against her. "Of course, you were in the other automobile. Well, in a way you were lucky—I lost at least two years of my life, it came so suddenly."

"What came?" she demanded.

"I don't know what began it. First she began to talk——"

51

"Who?"

"Violet McKisco." He lowered his voice as if there were people under the bench. "But don't mention the Divers because he made threats against anybody who mentioned it."

"Who did?"

"Tommy Barban, so don't you say I so much as mentioned them. None of us ever found out anyhow what it was Violet had to say because he kept interrupting her, and then her husband got into it and now, my dear, we have the duel. This morning—at five o'clock—in an hour." He sighed suddenly thinking of his own griefs. "I almost wish it were I. I might as well be killed now I have nothing to live for." He broke off and rocked to and fro with sorrow.

Again the iron shutter parted above and the same British voice said:

*"Rilly, this must stup immejetely."*

Simultaneously Abe North, looking somewhat distracted, came out of the hotel, perceived them against the sky, white over the sea. Rosemary shook her head warningly before he could speak and they moved another bench further down the road. Rosemary saw that Abe was a little tight.

"What are *you* doing up?" he demanded.

"I just got up." She started to laugh, but remembering the voice above, she restrained herself.

"Plagued by the nightingale,"[10] Abe suggested, and repeated, "probably plagued by the nightingale. Has this sewing-circle member told you what happened?"

Campion said with dignity:

"I only know what I heard with my own ears."

He got up and walked swiftly away; Abe sat down beside Rosemary.

"Why did you treat him so badly?"

"Did I?" he asked surprised. "He's been weeping around here all morning."

"Well, maybe he's sad about something."

"Maybe he is."

"What about a duel? Who's going to duel? I thought there was something strange in that car. Is it true?"

"It certainly is coo-coo but it seems to be true."

52

## X

THE trouble began at the time Earl Brady's car passed the
Divers' car stopped on the road—Abe's account melted
impersonally into the thronged night—Violet McKisco was
telling Mrs. Abrams something she had found out about
the Divers—she had gone upstairs in their house and she had
come upon something there which had made a great impression on her. But Tommy is a watch-dog about the Divers.
As a matter of fact she is inspiring and formidable—but it's a
mutual thing, and the fact of The Divers together is more
important to their friends than many of them realize. Of
course it's done at a certain sacrifice—sometimes they seem
just rather charming figures in a ballet, and worth just the
attention you give a ballet, but it's more than that—you'd
have to know the story. Anyhow Tommy is one of those
men that Dick's passed along to Nicole and when Mrs.
McKisco kept hinting at her story, he called them on it. He
said:

"Mrs. McKisco, please don't talk further about Mrs.
Diver."

"I wasn't talking to you," she objected.

"I think it's better to leave them out."

"Are they so sacred?"

"Leave them out. Talk about something else."

He was sitting on one of the two little seats beside
Campion. Campion told me the story.

"Well, you're pretty high-handed," Violet came back.

You know how conversations are in cars late at night,
some people murmuring and some not caring, giving up
after the party, or bored or asleep. Well, none of them knew
just what happened until the car stopped and Barban cried
in a voice that shook everybody, a voice for cavalry:

"Do you want to step out here—we're only a mile from
the hotel and you can walk it or I'll drag you there. *You've
got to shut up and shut your wife up!*"

"You're a bully," said McKisco. "You know you're

stronger muscularly than I am. But I'm not afraid of you—what they ought to have is the code duello——"

There's where he made his mistake because Tommy, being French, leaned over and clapped him one, and then the chauffeur drove on. That was where you passed them. Then the women began. That was still the state of things when the car got to the hotel.

Tommy telephoned some man in Cannes to act as second and McKisco said he wasn't going to be seconded by Campion, who wasn't crazy for the job anyhow, so he telephoned me not to say anything but to come right down. Violet McKisco collapsed and Mrs. Abrams took her to her room and gave her a bromide whereupon she fell comfortably asleep on the bed. When I got there I tried to argue with Tommy but the latter wouldn't accept anything short of an apology and McKisco rather spunkily wouldn't give it.

When Abe had finished Rosemary asked thoughtfully:

"Do the Divers know it was about them?"

"No—and they're not ever going to know they had anything to do with it. That damn Campion had no business talking to you about it, but since he did—I told the chauffeur I'd get out the old musical saw if he opened his mouth about it. This fight's between two men—what Tommy needs is a good war."

"I hope the Divers don't find out," Rosemary said.

Abe peered at his watch.

"I've got to go up and see McKisco—do you want to come?—he feels sort of friendless—I bet he hasn't slept."

Rosemary had a vision of the desperate vigil that high-strung, badly organized man had probably kept. After a moment balanced between pity and repugnance she agreed, and full of morning energy, bounced upstairs beside Abe.

McKisco was sitting on his bed with his alcoholic combativeness vanished, in spite of the glass of champagne in his hand. He seemed very puny and cross and white. Evidently he had been writing and drinking all night. He stared confusedly at Abe and Rosemary and asked:

"Is it time?"

"No, not for half an hour."

The table was covered with papers which he assembled with some difficulty into a long letter; the writing on the last pages was very large and illegible. In the delicate light of electric lamps fading, he scrawled his name at the bottom, crammed it into an envelope and handed it to Abe. "For my wife."

"You better souse your head in cold water," Abe suggested.

"You think I'd better?" inquired McKisco doubtfully. "I don't want to get too sober."

"Well, you look terrible now."

Obediently McKisco went into the bathroom.

"I'm leaving everything in an awful mess," he called. "I don't know how Violet will get back to America. I don't carry any insurance. I never got around to it."

"Don't talk nonsense, you'll be right here eating breakfast in an hour."

"Sure, I know." He came back with his hair wet and looked at Rosemary as if he saw her for the first time. Suddenly tears stood in his eyes. "I never have finished my novel. That's what makes me so sore. You don't like me," he said to Rosemary, "but that can't be helped. I'm primarily a literary man." He made a vague discouraged sound and shook his head helplessly. "I've made lots of mistakes in my life—many of them. But I've been one of the most prominent—in some ways——"

He gave this up and puffed at a dead cigarette.

"I do like you," said Rosemary, "but I don't think you ought to fight a duel."

"Yeah, I should have tried to beat him up, but it's done now. I've let myself be drawn into something that I had no right to be. I have a very violent temper—" He looked closely at Abe as if he expected the statement to be challenged. Then with an aghast laugh he raised the cold cigarette butt toward his mouth. His breathing quickened.

"The trouble was I suggested the duel—if Violet had only kept her mouth shut I could have fixed it. Of course even now I can just leave, or sit back and laugh at the whole

55

thing—but I don't think Violet would ever respect me again."

"Yes, she would," said Rosemary. "She'd respect you more."

"No—you don't know Violet. She's very hard when she gets an advantage over you. We've been married twelve years, we had a little girl seven years old and she died and after that you know how it is. We both played around on the side a little, nothing serious but drifting apart—she called me a coward out there to-night."

Troubled, Rosemary didn't answer.

"Well, we'll see there's as little damage done as possible," said Abe. He opened the leather case. "These are Barban's duelling pistols—I borrowed them so you could get familiar with them. He carries them in his suitcase." He weighed one of the archaic weapons in his hand. Rosemary gave an exclamation of uneasiness and McKisco looked at the pistols anxiously.

"Well—it isn't as if we were going to stand up and pot each other with forty-fives," he said.

"I don't know," said Abe cruelly; "the idea is you can sight better along a long barrel."

"How about distance?" asked McKisco.

"I've inquired about that. If one or the other parties has to be definitely eliminated they make it eight paces, if they're just good and sore it's twenty paces, and if it's only to vindicate their honor it's forty paces. His second agreed with me to make it forty."

"That's good."

"There's a wonderful duel in a novel of Pushkin's," recollected Abe. "Each man stood on the edge of a precipice, so if he was hit at all he was done for."

This seemed very remote and academic to McKisco, who stared at him and said, "What?"

"Do you want to take a quick dip and freshen up?"

"No—no, I couldn't swim." He sighed. "I don't see what it's all about," he said helplessly. "I don't see why I'm doing it."

It was the first thing he had ever done in his life. Actually he was one of those for whom the sensual world does not exist, and faced with a concrete fact he brought to it a vast surprise.

"We might as well be going," said Abe, seeing him fail a little.

"All right." He drank off a stiff drink of brandy, put the flask in his pocket, and said with almost a savage air: "What'll happen if I kill him—will they throw me in jail?"

"I'll run you over the Italian border."

He glanced at Rosemary—and then said apologetically to Abe:

"Before we start there's one thing I'd like to see you about alone."

"I hope neither of you gets hurt," Rosemary said. "I think it's very foolish and you ought to try to stop it."

## XI

SHE found Campion downstairs in the deserted lobby.

"I saw you go upstairs," he said excitedly. "Is he all right? When is the duel going to be?"

"I don't know." She resented his speaking of it as a circus, with McKisco as the tragic clown.

"Will you go with me?" he demanded, with the air of having seats. "I've hired the hotel car."

"I don't want to go."

"Why not? I imagine it'll take years off my life but I wouldn't miss it for words. We could watch it from quite far away."

"Why don't you get Mr. Dumphry to go with you?"

His monocle fell out, with no whiskers to hide in—he drew himself up.

"I never want to see him again."

"Well, I'm afraid I can't go. Mother wouldn't like it."

As Rosemary entered her room Mrs. Speers stirred sleepily and called to her:

"Where've you been?"

"I just couldn't sleep. You go back to sleep, Mother."

"Come in my room." Hearing her sit up in bed, Rosemary went in and told her what had happened.

[ "Why don't you go and see it?" Mrs. Speers suggested. "You needn't go up close and you might be able to help afterwards."

Rosemary did not like the picture of herself looking on and she demurred, but Mrs. Speer's consciousness was still clogged with sleep and she was reminded of night calls to death and calamity when she was the wife of a doctor. "I like you to go places and do things on your own initiative without me—you did much harder things for Rainy's publicity stunts." ]

Still Rosemary did not see why she should go, but she obeyed the sure, clear voice that had sent her into the stage entrance of the Odéon in Paris when she was twelve and greeted her when she came out again.

She thought she was reprieved when from the steps she saw Abe and McKisco drive away—but after a moment the hotel car came around the corner. Squealing delightedly Luis Campion pulled her in beside him.

"I hid there because they might not let us come. I've got my movie camera, you see."

She laughed helplessly. He was so terrible that he was no longer terrible, only dehumanized.

"I wonder why Mrs. McKisco didn't like the Divers?" she said. "They were very nice to her."

"Oh, it wasn't that. It was something she saw. We never did find exactly what it was because of Barban."

"Then that wasn't what made you so sad."

"Oh, no," he said, his voice breaking, "that was something else that happened when we got back to the hotel. But now I don't care—I wash my hands of it completely."

They followed the other car east along the shore past Juan-les-Pins, where the skeleton of the new Casino was rising. It was past four and under a blue-gray sky the first fishing boats were creaking out into a glaucous sea. Then they turned off the main road and into the back country.

"It's the golf course," cried Campion. "I'm sure that's where it's going to be."

He was right. When Abe's car pulled up ahead of them the east was crayoned red and yellow, promising a sultry day. Ordering the hotel car into a grove of pines Rosemary and Campion kept in the shadow of a wood and skirted the bleached fairway where Abe and McKisco were walking up and down, the latter raising his head at intervals like a rabbit scenting. Presently there were moving figures over by a farther tee and the watchers made out Barban and his French second—the latter carried the box of pistols under his arm.

Somewhat appalled, McKisco slipped behind Abe and took a long swallow of brandy. He walked on choking and would have marched directly up into the other party, but Abe stopped him and went forward to talk to the Frenchman. The sun was over the horizon.

Campion grabbed Rosemary's arm.

"I can't stand it," he squeaked, almost voiceless. "It's too much. This will cost me——"

"Let go," Rosemary said peremptorily. She breathed a frantic prayer in French.

The principals faced each other, Barban with the sleeve rolled up from his arm. His eyes gleamed restlessly in the sun, but his motion was deliberate as he wiped his palm on the seam of his trousers. McKisco, reckless with brandy, pursed his lips in a whistle and pointed his long nose about nonchalantly, until Abe stepped forward with a handkerchief in his hand. The French second stood with his face turned away. Rosemary caught her breath in terrible pity and gritted her teeth with hatred for Barban; then:

"One—two—three!" Abe counted in a strained voice.

They fired at the same moment. McKisco swayed but recovered himself. Both shots had missed.

"Now, that's enough!" cried Abe.

The duellists walked in, and everyone looked at Barban inquiringly.

"I declare myself unsatisfied."

"What? Sure you're satisfied," said Abe impatiently. "You just don't know it."

"Your man refuses another shot?"

"You're damn right, Tommy. You insisted on this and my client went through with it."

Tommy laughed scornfully.

"The distance was ridiculous," he said. "I'm not accustomed to such farces—your man must remember he's not now in America."

"No use cracking at America," said Abe rather sharply. And then, in a more conciliatory tone, "This has gone far enough, Tommy." They parleyed briskly for a moment—then Barban nodded and bowed coldly to his late antagonist.

"No shake hand?" suggested the French doctor.

"They already know each other," said Abe.

He turned to McKisco.

"Come on, let's get out."

As they strode off, McKisco, in exultation, gripped his arm.

"Wait a minute!" Abe said. "Tommy wants his pistol back. He might need it again."

McKisco handed it over.

"To hell with him," he said in a tough voice. "Tell him he can——"

"Shall I tell him you want another shot?"

"Well, I did it," cried McKisco, as they went along. "And I did it pretty well, didn't I? I wasn't yellow."

"You were pretty drunk," said Abe bluntly.

"No, I wasn't."

"All right, then, you weren't."

"Why would it make any difference if I had a drink or so?"

As his confidence mounted he looked resentfully at Abe.

"What difference does that make?" he repeated.

"If you can't see it, there's no use going into it."

"Don't you know everybody was drunk all the time during the war?"

"Well, let's forget it."

But the episode was not quite over. There were urgent footsteps in the heather behind them and the doctor drew up alongside.

"Pardon, Messieurs," he panted. "Voulez-vous régler mes honoraires? Naturellement c'est pour soins médicaux seulement. M. Barban n'a qu'un billet de mille et ne peut pas les régler et l'autre a laissé son porte-monnaie chez lui."

"Trust a Frenchman to think of that," said Abe, and then to the doctor, "Combien?"

"Let me pay this," said McKisco.

"No, I've got it. We were all in about the same danger."

Abe paid the doctor while McKisco suddenly turned into the bushes and was sick there. Then paler than before he strutted on with Abe toward the car through the now rosy morning.

Campion lay gasping on his back in the shrubbery, the only casualty of the duel, while Rosemary suddenly hysterical with laughter kept kicking at him with her espadrille. She did this persistently until she roused him— the only matter of importance to her now was that in a few hours she would see the person whom she still referred to in her mind as "the Divers" on the beach.

## XII

THEY were at Voisins waiting for Nicole, six of them, Rosemary, the Norths, Dick Diver and two young French musicians. They were looking over the other patrons of the restaurant to see if they had repose—Dick said no American men had any repose, except himself, and they were seeking an example to confront him with. Things looked black for them—not a man had come into the restaurant for ten minutes without raising his hand to his face.

"We ought never to have given up waxed mustaches," said Abe. "Nevertheless Dick isn't the *only* man with repose——"

"Oh, yes, I am."

"—but he may be the only sober man with repose."

A well-dressed American had come in with two women who swooped and fluttered unself-consciously around a table. Suddenly, he perceived that he was being watched—whereupon his hand rose spasmodically and arranged a phantom bulge in his necktie. In another unseated party a man endlessly patted his shaven cheek with his palm, and his companion mechanically raised and lowered the stub of a cold cigar. The luckier ones fingered eyeglasses and facial hair, the unequipped stroked blank mouths, or even pulled desperately at the lobes of their ears.

A well-known general came in, and Abe, counting on the man's first year at West Point—that year during which no cadet can resign and from which none ever recovers—made a bet with Dick of five dollars.

His hands hanging naturally at his sides, the general waited to be seated. Once his arms swung suddenly backward like a jumper's and Dick said, "Ah!" supposing he had lost control, but the general recovered and they breathed again—the agony was nearly over, the garçon was pulling out his chair. . . .

With a touch of fury the conqueror shot up his hand and scratched his gray immaculate head.

"You see," said Dick smugly, "I'm the only one."

Rosemary was quite sure of it and Dick, realizing that he never had a better audience, made the group into so bright a unit that Rosemary felt an impatient disregard for all who were not at their table. They had been two days in Paris but actually they were still under the beach umbrella. When, as at the ball of the Corps des Pages the night before, the surroundings seemed formidable to Rosemary, who had yet to attend a Mayfair party in Hollywood, Dick would bring the scene within range by greeting a few people, a sort of selection—the Divers seemed to have a large acquaintance, but it was always as if the person had not seen them for a long, long time, and was utterly bowled over, "Why, where do you *keep* yourselves?"—and then re-create the unity of his own party by destroying the outsiders softly but permanently with an ironic coup de grâce. Presently Rosemary seemed to have known those people herself in some deplorable past, and then got on to them, rejected them, discarded them.

Their own party was overwhelmingly American and sometimes scarcely American at all. It was themselves he gave back to them, blurred by the compromises of how many years.

Into the dark, smoky restaurant, smelling of the rich raw foods on the buffet, slid Nicole's sky-blue suit like a stray segment of the weather outside. Seeing from their eyes how beautiful she was, she thanked them with a smile of radiant appreciation. They were all very nice people for a while, very courteous and all that. Then they grew tired of it and they were funny and bitter, and finally they made a lot of plans. They laughed at things that they would not remember clearly afterward—laughed a lot and the men drank three bottles of wine. The trio of women at the table were representative of the enormous flux of American life. Nicole was the granddaughter of a self-made American capitalist and the granddaughter of a Count of the House of Lippe Weissenfeld. Mary North was the daughter of a journeyman paper-hanger and a descendant of President Tyler.[11] Rosemary was from the middle of the middle class, catapulted by her mother onto the uncharted heights of Hollywood. Their point of resemblance to each other and their difference from so many American women, lay in the fact that they were all happy to exist in a man's world—they preserved their individuality through men and not by opposition to them. They would all three have made alternatively good courtesans or good wives not by the accident of birth but through the greater accident of finding their man or not finding him.

So Rosemary found it a pleasant party, that luncheon, nicer in that there were only seven people, about the limit of a good party. Perhaps, too, the fact that she was new to their world acted as a sort of catalytic agent to precipitate out all their old reservations about one another. After the table broke up, a waiter directed Rosemary back into the dark hinterland of all French restaurants, where she looked up a phone number by a dim orange bulb, and called Franco-American Films. Sure, they had a print of "Daddy's Girl"—it was out for the moment, but they would run it off

*social status*

later in the week for her at 341 rue des Saints Anges—ask for Mr. Crowder.

The semi-booth gave on the vestiaire and as Rosemary hung up the receiver she heard two low voices not five feet from her on the other side of a row of coats.

"—So you love me?"

"Oh, *do* I!"

It was Nicole—Rosemary hesitated in the door of the booth—then she heard Dick say:

"I want you terribly—let's go to the hotel now." Nicole gave a little gasping sigh. For a moment the words conveyed nothing at all to Rosemary—but the tone did. The vast secretiveness of it vibrated to herself.

"I want you."

"I'll be at the hotel at four."[12]

Rosemary stood breathless as the voices moved away. She was at first even astonished—she had seen them in their relation to each other as people without personal exigencies —as something cooler. Now a strong current of emotion flowed through her, profound and unidentified. She did not know whether she was attracted or repelled, but only that she was deeply moved. It made her feel very alone as she went back into the restaurant, but it was touching to look in upon, and the passionate gratitude of Nicole's "Oh, *do* I!" echoed in her mind. The particular mood of the passage she had witnessed lay ahead of her; but however far she was from it her stomach told her it was all right—she had none of the aversion she had felt in the playing of certain love scenes in pictures.

Being far away from it she nevertheless irrevocably participated in it now, and shopping with Nicole she was much more conscious of the assignation than Nicole herself. She looked at Nicole in a new way, estimating her attractions. Certainly she was the most attractive woman Rosemary had ever met—with her hardness, her devotions and loyalties, and a certain elusiveness, which Rosemary, thinking now through her mother's middle-class mind, associated with her attitude about money. Rosemary spent money she had earned—she was here in Europe due to the fact that she had gone in the pool six times that January day with her temperature roving from 99° in the early morning to 103°, when her mother stopped it.

With Nicole's help Rosemary bought two dresses and two hats and four pairs of shoes with her money. Nicole bought from a great list that ran two pages, and bought the things in the windows besides. Everything she liked that she couldn't possibly use herself, she bought as a present for a friend. She bought colored beads, folding beach cushions, artificial flowers, honey, a guest bed, bags, scarfs, love birds, miniatures for a doll's house and three yards of some new cloth the color of prawns.[13] She bought a dozen bathing suits, a rubber alligator, a travelling chess set of gold and ivory, big linen handkerchiefs for Abe, two chamois leather jackets of kingfisher blue and burning bush from Hermès[14]—bought all these things not a bit like a high-class courtesan buying underwear and jewels, which were after all professional equipment and insurance—but with an entirely different point of view. Nicole was the product of much ingenuity and toil. For her sake trains began their run at Chicago and traversed the round belly of the continent to California; chicle factories fumed and link belts grew link by link in factories; men mixed toothpaste in vats and drew mouth-wash out of copper hogsheads; girls canned tomatoes quickly in August or worked rudely at the Five-and-Tens on Christmas Eve; half-breed Indians toiled on Brazilian coffee plantations and dreamers were muscled out of patent rights in new tractors—these were some of the people who gave a tithe to Nicole, and as the whole system swayed and thundered onward it lent a feverish bloom to such processes of hers as wholesale buying, like the flush of a fireman's face holding his post before a spreading blaze. She illustrated very simple principles, containing in herself her own doom, but illustrated them so accurately that there was grace in the procedure, and presently Rosemary would try to imitate it.

It was almost four. Nicole stood in a shop with a love bird on her shoulder, and had one of her infrequent outbursts of speech.

"Well, what if you hadn't gone in that pool that day—I

65

sometimes wonder about such things. Just before the war we were in Berlin—I was thirteen, it was just before Mother died. My sister was going to a court ball and she had three of the royal princes on her dance card, all arranged by a chamberlain and everything. Half an hour before she was going to start she had a side ache and a high fever. The doctor said it was appendicitis and she ought to be operated on. But Mother had her plans made, so Baby went to the ball and danced till two with an ice pack strapped on under her evening dress. She was operated on at seven o'clock next morning."

It was good to be hard, then; all nice people were hard on themselves. But it was four o'clock and Rosemary kept thinking of Dick waiting for Nicole now at the hotel. She must go there, she must not make him wait for her. She kept thinking, "Why don't you go?" and then suddenly, "Or let me go if you don't want to." But Nicole went to one more place to buy corsages for them both and sent one to Mary North. Only then she seemed to remember and with sudden abstraction she signalled for a taxi.

"Good-by," said Nicole. "We had fun, didn't we?"

"Loads of fun," said Rosemary. It was more difficult than she thought and her whole self protested as Nicole drove away.

## XIII

DICK turned the corner of the traverse and continued along the trench walking on the duckboard. He came to a periscope, looked through it a moment, then he got up on the step and peered over the parapet. In front of him beneath a dingy sky was Beaumont-Hamel; to his left the tragic hill of Thiepval. Dick stared at them through his field glasses, his throat straining with sadness.

He went on along the trench, and found the others waiting for him in the next traverse. He was full of excitement and he wanted to communicate it to them, to make them

66

understand about this, though actually Abe North had seen battle service and he had not.

"This land here cost twenty lives a foot that summer," he said to Rosemary. She looked out obediently at the rather bare green plain with its low trees of six years' growth. If Dick had added that they were now being shelled she would have believed him that afternoon. Her love had reached a point where now at last she was beginning to be unhappy, to be desperate. She didn't know what to do—she wanted to talk to her mother.

"There are lots of people dead since and we'll all be dead soon," said Abe consolingly.

Rosemary waited tensely for Dick to continue.

"See that little stream—we could walk to it in two minutes. It took the British a month to walk to it—a whole empire walking very slowly, dying in front and pushing forward behind. And another empire walked very slowly backward a few inches a day, leaving the dead like a million bloody rugs. No Europeans will ever do that again in this generation."

"Why, they've only just quit over in Turkey," said Abe. "And in Morocco——"

"That's different. This western-front business couldn't be done again, not for a long time. The young men think they could do it but they couldn't. They could fight the first Marne[15] again but not this. This took religion and years of plenty and tremendous sureties and the exact relation that existed between the classes. The Russians and Italians weren't any good on this front. You had to have a whole-souled sentimental equipment going back further than you could remember. You had to remember Christmas, and postcards of the Crown Prince and his fiancée, and little cafés in Valence and beer gardens in Unter den Linden and weddings at the mairie, and going to the Derby, and your grandfather's whiskers."

"General Grant invented this kind of battle at Petersburg in sixty-five."

"No, he didn't—he just invented mass butchery. This kind of battle was invented by Lewis Carroll and Jules Verne and whoever wrote *Undine*,[16] and country deacons bowling and marraines in Marseilles and girls seduced in the back lanes of Württemberg and Westphalia. Why, this was a love battle—there was a century of middle-class love spent here. This was the last love battle."

"You want to hand over this battle to D. H. Lawrence," said Abe.

"All my beautiful lovely safe world blew itself up here with a great gust of high explosive love," Dick mourned persistently. "Isn't that true, Rosemary?"

"I don't know," she answered with a grave face. "You know everything."

They dropped behind the others. Suddenly a shower of earth gobs and pebbles came down on them and Abe yelled from the next traverse:

"The war spirit's getting into me again. I have a hundred years of Ohio love behind me and I'm going to bomb out this trench." His head popped up over the embankment. "You're dead—don't you know the rules? That was a grenade."

Rosemary laughed and Dick picked up a retaliatory handful of stones and then put them down.

"I couldn't kid here," he said rather apologetically. "The silver cord is cut and the golden bowl is broken[17] and all that, but an old romatic like me can't do anything about it."

"I'm romantic too."

They came out of the neat restored trench, and faced a memorial to the Newfoundland dead. Reading the inscription Rosemary burst into sudden tears. Like most women she liked to be told how she should feel, and she liked Dick's telling her which things were ludicrous and which things were sad. But most of all she wanted him to know how she loved him, now that the fact was upsetting everything, now that she was walking over the battle-field in a thrilling dream.

After that they got in their car and started back toward Amiens. A thin warm rain was falling on the new scrubby woods and underbrush and they passed great funeral pyres of sorted duds, shells, bombs, grenades, and equipment,

68

helmets, bayonets, gun stocks and rotten leather, abandoned six years in the ground. And suddenly around a bend the white caps of a great sea of graves. Dick asked the chauffeur to stop.

"There's that girl—and she still has her wreath."

They watched as he got out and went over to the girl, who stood uncertainly by the gate with a wreath in her hand. Her taxi waited. She was a red-haired girl from Tennessee whom they had met on the train this morning, come from Knoxville to lay a memorial on her brother's grave. There were tears of vexation on her face.

"The War Department must have given me the wrong number," she whimpered. "It had another name on it. I been lookin' for it since two o'clock, and there's so many graves."

"Then if I were you I'd just lay it on any grave without looking at the name," Dick advised her.

"You reckon that's what I ought to do?"

"I think that's what he'd have wanted you to do."

It was growing dark and the rain was coming down harder. She left the wreath on the first grave inside the gate, and accepted Dick's suggestion that she dismiss her taxi-cab and ride back to Amiens with them.

Rosemary shed tears again when she heard of the mishap —altogether it has been a watery day, but she felt that she had learned something, though exactly what it was she did not know. Later she remembered all the hours of the afternoon as happy—one of those uneventful times that seem at the moment only a link between past and future pleasure but turn out to have been the pleasure itself.

Amiens was an echoing purple town, still sad with the war, as some railroad stations were: the Gare du Nord and Waterloo station in London. In the daytime one is deflated by such towns, with their little trolley cars of twenty years ago crossing the great gray cobble-stoned squares in front of the cathedral, and the very weather seems to have a quality of the past, faded weather like that of old photographs. But after dark all that is most satisfactory in French life swims back into the picture—the sprightly tarts, the men arguing with a hundred Voilàs in the cafés, the couples drifting, head to head, toward the satisfactory inexpensiveness of nowhere. Waiting for the train they sat in a big arcade, tall enough to release the smoke and chatter and music upward and obligingly the orchestra launched into "Yes, We Have No Bananas"—they clapped, because the leader looked so pleased with himself. The Tennessee girl forgot her sorrow and enjoyed herself, even began flirtations of tropical eye-rollings and pawings, with Dick and Abe. They teased her gently.

Then, leaving infinitesimal sections of Württembergers, Prussian Guards, chasseurs alpins, Manchester mill hands and Old Etonians to pursue their eternal dissolution under the warm rain, they took the train for Paris. They ate sandwiches of mortadel sausage and bel paese cheese made up in the station restaurant, and drank Beaujolais. Nicole was abstracted, biting her lip restlessly and reading over the guide-books to the battle-field that Dick had brought along —indeed, he had made a quick study of the whole affair, simplifying it always until it bore a faint resemblance to one of his own parties.

## XIV

WHEN they reached Paris Nicole was too tired to go on to the grand illumination at the Decorative Arts Exposition as they had planned. They left her at the Hôtel Roi George, and as she disappeared between the intersecting planes made by lobby lights of the glass doors, Rosemary's oppression lifted. Nicole was a force—not necessarily well disposed or predictable like her mother—an incalculable force. Rosemary was somewhat afraid of her.

At eleven she sat with Dick and the Norths at a houseboat café just opened on the Seine. The river shimmered with lights from the bridges and cradled many cold moons. On Sundays sometimes when Rosemary and her mother had lived in Paris they had taken the little steamer up to

70

Suresnes and talked about plans for the future. They had little money but Mrs. Speers was so sure of Rosemary's beauty and had implanted in her so much ambition, that she was willing to gamble the money on "advantages"; Rosemary in turn was to repay her mother when she got her start. . . . ⌡

Since reaching Paris Abe North had had a thin vinous fur over him; his eyes were bloodshot from sun and wine. Rosemary realized for the first time that he was always stopping in places to get a drink, and she wondered how Mary North liked it. Mary was quiet, so quiet save for her frequent laughter that Rosemary had learned little about her. She liked the straight dark hair brushed back until it met some sort of natural cascade that took care of it—from time to time it eased with a jaunty slant over the corner of her temple, until it was almost in her eye when she tossed her head and caused it to fall sleek into place once more.

"We'll turn in early to-night, Abe, after this drink." Mary's voice was light but it held a little flicker of anxiety. "You don't want to be poured on the boat."

"It's pretty late now," Dick said. "We'd all better go."

The noble dignity of Abe's face took on a certain stubbornness, and he remarked with determination:

"Oh, no." He paused gravely. "Oh, no, not yet. We'll have another bottle of champagne."

"No more for me," said Dick.

"It's Rosemary I'm thinking of. She's a natural alcoholic —keeps a bottle of gin in the bathroom and all that—her mother told me."

He emptied what was left of the first bottle into Rosemary's glass. She had made herself quite sick the first day in Paris with quarts of lemonade; after that she had taken nothing with them, but now she raised the champagne and drank at it.

"But what's this?" exclaimed Dick. "You told me you didn't drink."

"I didn't say I was never going to."

"What about your mother?"

"I'm just going to drink this one glass." She felt some

71

necessity for it. Dick drank, not too much, but he drank, and perhaps it would bring her closer to him, be a part of the equipment for what she had to do. She drank it quickly, choked and then said, "Besides, yesterday was my birthday —I was eighteen."

"Why didn't you tell us?" they said indignantly.

"I knew you'd make a fuss over it and go to a lot of trouble." She finished the champagne. "So this is the celebration."

"It most certainly is not," Dick assured her. "The dinner to-morrow night is your birthday party and don't forget it. Eighteen—why that's a terribly important age."

"I used to think until you're eighteen nothing matters," said Mary.

"That's right," Abe agreed. "And afterward it's the same way."

"Abe feels that nothing matters till he gets on the boat," said Mary. "This time he really has got everything planned out when he gets to New York." She spoke as though she were tired of saying things that no longer had a meaning for her, as if in reality the course that she and her husband followed, or failed to follow, had become merely an intention.

"He'll be writing music in America and I'll be working at singing in Munich, so when we get together again there'll be nothing we can't do."

"That's wonderful," agreed Rosemary, feeling the champagne.

"Meanwhile, another touch of champagne for Rosemary. Then she'll be more able to rationalize the acts of her lymphatic glands. They only begin to function at eighteen."

Dick laughed indulgently at Abe, whom he loved, and in whom he had long lost hope: "That's medically incorrect and we're going." Catching the faint patronage Abe said lightly:

"Something tells me I'll have a new score on Broadway long before you've finished your scientific treatise."

"I hope so," said Dick evenly. "I hope so. I may even abandon what you call my 'scientific treatise.'"

"Oh, Dick!" Mary's voice was startled, was shocked.

Rosemary had never before seen Dick's face utterly expressionless; she felt that this announcement was something momentous and she was inclined to exclaim with Mary, "Oh, Dick!"

But suddenly Dick laughed again, added to his remark "—abandon it for another one," and got up from the table.

"But Dick, sit down. I want to know——"

"I'll tell you some time. Good night, Abe. Good night, Mary."

"Good night, dear Dick." Mary smiled as if she were going to be perfectly happy sitting there on the almost deserted boat. She was a brave, hopeful woman and she was following her husband somewhere, changing herself to this kind of person or that, without being able to lead him a step out of his path, and sometimes realizing with discouragement how deep in him the guarded secret of her direction lay. And yet an air of luck clung about her, as if she were a sort of token. . . .

## XV

"What is it you are giving up?" demanded Rosemary, facing Dick earnestly in the taxi.

"Nothing of importance."

"Are you a scientist?"

"I'm a doctor of medicine."

"Oh-h!" She smiled delightedly. "My father was a doctor too. Then why don't you—" she stopped.

"There's no mystery. I didn't disgrace myself at the height of my career, and hide away on the Riviera. I'm just not practising. You can't tell, I'll probably practise again some day."

Rosemary put up her face quietly to be kissed. He looked at her for a moment as if he didn't understand. Then holding her in the hollow of his arm he rubbed his cheek against her cheek's softness, and then looked down at her for another long moment.

73

*child, not an adult.*

"Such a lovely child," he said gravely.

She smiled up at him; her hands playing conventionally with the lapels of his coat. "I'm in love with you and Nicole. Actually that's my secret—I can't even talk about you to anybody because I don't want any more people to know how wonderful you are. Honestly—I love you and Nicole—I do."

—So many times he had heard this—even the formula was the same.

Suddenly she came toward him, her youth vanishing as she passed inside the focus of his eyes and he had kissed her breathlessly as if she were any age at all. Then she lay back against his arm and sighed.

"I've decided to give you up," she said.

Dick started—had he said anything to imply that she possessed any part of him?

"But that's very mean," he managed to say lightly, "just when I was getting interested."

"I've loved you so—" As if it had been for years. She was weeping a little now. "I've loved you so-o-o."

Then he should have laughed, but he heard himself saying, "Not only are you beautiful but you are somehow on the grand scale. Everything you do, like pretending to be in love or pretending to be shy gets across."

In the dark cave of the taxi, fragrant with the perfume Rosemary had bought with Nicole, she came close again, clinging to him. He kissed her without enjoying it. He knew that there was passion there, but there was no shadow of it in her eyes or on her mouth; there was a faint spray of champagne on her breath. She clung nearer desperately and once more he kissed her and was chilled by the innocence of her kiss, by the glance that at the moment of contact looked beyond him out into the darkness of the night, the darkness of the world. She did not know yet that splendor is something in the heart; at the moment when she realized that and melted into the passion of the universe he could take her without question or regret.

Her room in the hotel was diagonally across from theirs

74

and nearer the elevator. When they reached the door she said suddenly:

"I know you don't love me—I don't expect it. But you said I should have told you about my birthday. Well, I did, and now for my birthday present I want you to come into my room a minute while I tell you something. Just one minute."

They went in and he closed the door, and Rosemary stood close to him, not touching him. The night had drawn the color from her face—she was pale as pale now, she was a white carnation left after a dance.

"When you smile—" He had recovered his _paternal attitude_, perhaps because of Nicole's silent proximity, "I always think I'll see a gap where you've lost some baby teeth."

But he was too late—she came close up against him with a forlorn whisper.

"Take me."

"Take you where?"

Astonishment froze him rigid.

"Go on," she whispered. "Oh, please go on, whatever they do. I don't care if I don't like it—I never expected to— I've always hated to think about it but now I don't. I want you to."

She was astonished at herself—she had never imagined she could talk like that. She was calling on things she had read, seen, dreamed through a decade of convent hours. Suddenly she knew too that it was one of her greatest rôles and she flung herself into it more passionately.

"This is not as it should be," Dick deliberated. "Isn't it just the champagne? Let's more or less forget it."

"Oh, no, _now_. I want you to do it now, take me, show me, I'm absolutely yours and I want to be."

"For one thing, have you thought how much it would hurt Nicole?"

"She won't know—this won't have anything to do with her."

He continued kindly.

75

"Then there's the fact that I love Nicole."

"But you can love more than just one person, can't you? Like I love Mother and I love you—more. I love you more now."

"—the fourth place you're not in love with me but you might be afterwards, and that would begin your life with a terrible mess."

"No, I promise I'll never see you again. I'll get Mother and go to America right away."

He dismissed this. He was remembering too vividly the youth and freshness of her lips. He took another tone.

"You're just in that mood."

"Oh, please, I don't care even if I had a baby. I could go into Mexico like a girl at the studio. Oh, this is so different from anything I ever thought—I used to hate it when they kissed me seriously." He saw she was still under the impression that it must happen. "Some of them had great big teeth, but you're all different and beautiful. I want you to do it."

"I believe you think people just kiss some way and you want me to kiss you."

"Oh, don't tease me—I'm not a baby. I know you're not in love with me." She was suddenly humble and quiet. "I didn't expect that much. I know I must seem just nothing to you."

"Nonsense. But you seem young to me." His thoughts added, "—there'd be so much to teach you."

Rosemary waited, breathing eagerly till Dick said: "And lastly things aren't arranged so that this could be as you want."

Her face drooped with dismay and disappointment and Dick said automatically, "We'll have to simply—" He stopped himself, followed her to the bed, sat down beside her while she wept. He was suddenly confused, not about the ethics of the matter, for the impossibility of it was sheerly indicated from all angles, but simply confused, and for a moment his usual grace, the tensile strength of his balance, was absent.

"I knew you wouldn't," she sobbed. "It was just a forlorn hope."

He stood up.

"Good night, child. This is a damn shame. Let's drop it out of the picture." He gave her two lines of hospital patter to go to sleep on. "So many people are going to love you and it might be nice to meet your first love all intact, emotionally too. That's an old-fashioned idea, isn't it?" She looked up at him as he took a step toward the door; she looked at him without the slightest idea as to what was in his head, she saw him take another step in slow motion, turn and look at her again, and she wanted for a moment to hold him and devour him, wanted his mouth, his ears, his coat collar, wanted to surround him and engulf him; she saw his hand fall on the doorknob. Then she gave up and sank back on the bed. When the door closed she got up and went to the mirror, where she began brushing her hair, sniffling a little. One hundred and fifty strokes Rosemary gave it, as usual, then a hundred and fifty more. She brushed it until her arm ached, then she changed arms and went on brushing. . . .

*D. D. tries to make her feel better by reassuring her* [handwritten marginalia]

## XVI

SHE woke up cooled and shamed. The sight of her beauty in the mirror did not reassure her but only awakened the ache of yesterday and a letter, forwarded by her mother, from the boy who had taken her to the Yale prom last fall, which announced his presence in Paris, was no help—all that seemed far away. She emerged from her room for the ordeal of meeting the Divers weighted with a double trouble. But it was hidden by a sheath as impermeable as Nicole's when they met and went together to a series of fittings. It was consoling, though, when Nicole remarked, apropos of a distraught saleswoman: "Most people think everybody feels about them much more violently than they actually do—they think other people's opinions of them

77

swing through great arcs of approval or disapproval."
Yesterday in her expansiveness Rosemary would have
resented that remark—to-day in her desire to minimize
what had happened she welcomed it eagerly. She admired
Nicole for her beauty and her wisdom, and also for the first
time in her life she was jealous. Just before leaving Gausse's
Hôtel her mother had said in that casual tone, which
Rosemary knew concealed her most significant opinions,
that Nicole was a great beauty, with the frank implication
that Rosemary was not. This did not bother Rosemary, who
had only recently been allowed to learn that she was even
personable; so that her prettiness never seemed exactly her
own but rather an acquirement, like her French. Nevertheless, in the taxi she looked at Nicole, matching herself against
her. There were all the potentialities for romantic love in
that lovely body and in the delicate mouth, sometimes
tight, sometimes expectantly half open to the world. Nicole
had been a beauty as a young girl and she would be a
beauty later when her skin stretched tight over her high
cheek-bones—the essential structure was there. She had
been white-Saxon-blonde but she was more beautiful now
that her hair had darkened than when it had been like a
cloud and more beautiful than she.

"We lived there," Rosemary suddenly pointed to a
building in the rue des Saints-Pères.

"That's strange. Because when I was twelve Mother and
Baby and I once spent a winter there," and she pointed to a
hotel directly across the street. The two dingy fronts stared
at them, gray echoes of girlhood.

"We'd just built our Lake Forest house and we were
economizing," Nicole continued. "At least Baby and I and
the governess economized and Mother travelled."

"We were economizing too," said Rosemary, realizing
that the word meant different things to them.

"Mother always spoke of it very carefully as a small
hotel—" Nicole gave her quick magnetic little laugh, "—I
mean instead of saying a 'cheap' hotel. If any swanky
friends asked us our address we'd never say, 'We're in a
dingy little hole over in the apache quarter where we're

glad of running water,'—we'd say 'We're in a small hotel.' As if all the big ones were too noisy and vulgar for us. Of course the friends always saw through us and told everyone about it, but Mother always said it showed we knew our way around Europe. She did, of course: she was born a German citizen. But her mother was American, and she was brought up in Chicago, and she was more American than European."

They were meeting the others in two minutes, and Rosemary reconstructed herself once more as they got out of the taxi in the rue Guynemer, across from the Luxembourg Gardens. They were lunching in the Norths' already dismantled apartment high above the green mass of leaves. The day seemed different to Rosemary from the day before. When she saw him face to face their eyes met and brushed like birds' wings. After that everything was all right, everything was wonderful, she knew that he was beginning to fall in love with her. She felt wildly happy, felt the warm sap of emotion being pumped through her body. A cool, clear confidence deepened and sang in her. She scarcely looked at Dick but she knew everything was all right.

After luncheon the Divers and the Norths and Rosemary went to the Franco-American Films, to be joined by Collis Clay, her young man from New Haven, to whom she had telephoned. He was a Georgian, with the peculiarly regular, even stencilled ideas of Southerners who are educated in the North. Last winter she had thought him attractive—once they held hands in an automobile going from New Haven to New York; now he no longer existed for her.

In the projection room she sat between Collis Clay and Dick while the mechanic mounted the reels of "Daddy's Girl" and a French executive fluttered about her trying to talk American slang. "Yes, boy," he said when there was trouble with the projector, "I have not any benenas." Then the lights went out, there was the sudden click and a flickering noise and she was alone with Dick at last. They looked at each other in the half darkness.

"Dear Rosemary," he murmured. Their shoulders touched. Nicole stirred restlessly at the end of the row and

Abe coughed convulsively and blew his nose; then they all settled down and the picture ran.

There she was—the school girl of a year ago, hair down her back and rippling out stiffly like the solid hair of a Tanagra figure; there she was—*so* young and innocent—the product of her mother's loving care; there she was— embodying all the immaturity of the race, cutting a new cardboard paper doll to pass before its empty harlot's mind. She remembered how she had felt in that dress, especially fresh and new under the fresh young silk.

Daddy's girl. Was it a 'itty-bitty bravekins and did it suffer? Ooo-ooo-tweet, de tweetest thing, wasn't she dest too tweet? Before her tiny fist the forces of lust and corruption rolled away; nay, the very march of destiny stopped; inevitably became evitable, syllogism, dialectic, all rationality fell away. Women would forget the dirty dishes at home and weep, even within the picture one woman wept so long that she almost stole the film away from Rosemary. She wept all over a set that cost a fortune, in a Duncan Phyfe dining-room, in an aviation port, and during a yacht-race that was only used in two flashes, in a subway and finally in a bathroom. But Rosemary triumphed. Her fineness of character, her courage and steadfastness intruded upon by the vulgarity of the world, and Rosemary showing what it took with a face that had not yet become mask-like—yet it was actually so moving that the emotions of the whole row of people went out to her at intervals during the picture. There was a break once and the light went on and after the chatter of applause Dick said to her sincerely: "I'm simply astounded. You're going to be one of the best actresses on the stage."

Then back to "Daddy's Girl": happier days now, and a lovely shot of Rosemary and her parent united at the last in a father complex so apparent that Dick winced for all psychologists at the vicious sentimentality. The screen vanished, the lights went on, the moment had come.

"I've arranged one other thing," announced Rosemary to the company at large, "I've arranged a test for Dick."

"A what?"

"A screen test, they'll take one now."

There was an awful silence—then an irrepressible chortle from the Norths. Rosemary watched Dick comprehend what she meant, his face moving first in an Irish way; simultaneously she realized that she had made some mistake in the playing of her trump and still she did not suspect that the card was at fault.

"I don't want a test," said Dick firmly; then, seeing the situation as a whole, he continued lightly, "Rosemary, I'm disappointed. The pictures make a fine career for a woman —but my God, they can't photograph me. I'm an old scientist all wrapped up in his private life."

Nicole and Mary urged him ironically to seize the opportunity; they teased him, both faintly annoyed at not having been asked for a sitting. But Dick closed the subject with a somewhat tart discussion of actors: "The strongest guard is placed at the gateway to nothing," he said. "Maybe because the condition of emptiness is too shameful to be divulged."

In the taxi with Dick and Collis Clay—they were dropping Collis, and Dick was taking Rosemary to a tea from which Nicole and the Norths had resigned in order to do the things Abe had left undone till the last—in the taxi Rosemary reproached him.

"I thought if the test turned out to be good I could take it to California with me. And then maybe if they liked it you'd come out and be my leading man in a picture."

He was overwhelmed. "It was a darn sweet thought, but I'd rather look at *you*. You were about the nicest sight I ever looked at."

"That's a great picture," said Collis. "I've seen it four times. I know one boy at New Haven who's seen it a dozen times—he went all the way to Hartford to see it one time. And when I brought Rosemary up to New Haven he was so shy he wouldn't meet her. Can you beat that? This little girl knocks them cold."

Dick and Rosemary looked at each other, wanting to be alone, but Collis failed to understand.

"I'll drop you where you're going," he suggested. "I'm staying at the Lutétia."

81

"We'll drop you," said Dick.

"It'll be easier for me to drop you. No trouble at all."

"I think it will be better if we drop you."

"But—" began Collis; he grasped the situation at last and began discussing with Rosemary when he would see her again.

Finally, he was gone, with the shadowy unimportance but the offensive bulk of the third party. The car stopped unexpectedly, unsatisfactorily, at the address Dick had given. He drew a long breath.

"Shall we go in?"

"I don't care," Rosemary said. "I'll do anything you want."

He considered.

"I almost have to go in—she wants to buy some pictures from a friend of mine who needs the money."

Rosemary smoothed the brief expressive disarray of her hair.

'We'll stay just five minutes," he decided. "You're not going to like these people."

She assumed that they were dull and stereotyped people, or gross and drunken people, or tiresome, insistent people, or any of the sorts of people that the Divers avoided. She was entirely unprepared for the impression that the scene made on her.

## XVII

IT was a house hewn from the frame of Cardinal de Retz's[18] palace in the rue Monsieur, but once inside the door there was nothing of the past, nor of any present that Rosemary knew. The outer shell, the masonry, seemed rather to enclose the future so that it was an electric-like shock, a definite nervous experience, perverted as a breakfast of oatmeal and hashish, to cross that threshold, if it could be so called, into the long hall of blue steel, silver-gilt, and the myriad facets of many oddly bevelled mirrors. The effect was unlike that of any part of the Decorative Arts Exhibition—for there were people *in* it, not in front of it. Rosemary had the detached false-and-exalted feeling of being on a set and she guessed that every one else present had that feeling too.

There were about thirty people, mostly women, and all fashioned by Louisa M. Alcott or Madame de Ségur;[19] and they functioned on this set as cautiously, as precisely, as does a human hand picking up jagged broken glass. Neither individually nor as a crowd could they be said to dominate the environment, as one comes to dominate a work of art he may possess, no matter how esoteric. No one knew what this room meant because it was evolving into something else, becoming everything a room was not; to exist in it was as difficult as walking on a highly polished moving stairway, and no one could succeed at all save with the aforementioned qualities of a hand moving among broken glass—which qualities limited and defined the majority of those present.

These were of two sorts. There were the Americans and English who had been dissipating all spring and summer, so that now everything they did had a purely nervous inspiration. They were very quiet and lethargic at certain hours and then they exploded into sudden quarrels and breakdowns and seductions. The other class, who might be called the exploiters, was formed by the sponges, who were sober, serious people by comparison, with a purpose in life and no time for fooling. These kept their balance best in that environment, and what tone there was, beyond the apartment's novel organization of light values, came from them.

The Frankenstein took down Dick and Rosemary at a gulp—it separated them immediately and Rosemary suddenly discovered herself to be an insincere little person, living all in the upper registers of her throat and wishing the director would come. There was however such a wild beating of wings in the room that she did not feel her position was more incongruous than any one else's. In addition, her training told and after a series of semi-military turns, shifts, and marches she found herself presumably talking to a neat, slick girl with a lovely boy's face, but actually absorbed by a

83

conversation taking place on a sort of gun-metal ladder diagonally opposite her and four feet away.

There was a trio of young women sitting on the bench. They were all tall and slender with small heads groomed like manikins' heads, and as they talked the heads waved gracefully about above their dark tailored suits, rather like long-stemmed flowers and rather like cobras' hoods.

"Oh, they give a good show," said one of them, in a deep rich voice. "Practically the best show in Paris—I'd be the last one to deny that. But after all—" She sighed. "Those phrases he uses over and over—'Oldest inhabitant gnawed by rodents.' You laugh once."

"I prefer people whose lives have more corrugated surfaces," said the second, "and I don't like her."

"I've never really been able to get very excited about them, or their entourage either. Why, for example, the entirely liquid Mr. North?"

"He's out," said the first girl. "But you must admit that the party in question can be one of the most charming human beings you have ever met."

It was the first hint Rosemary had had that they were talking about the Divers, and her body grew tense with indignation. But the girl talking to her, in the starched blue shirt with the bright blue eyes and the red cheeks and the very gray suit, a poster of a girl, had begun to play up. Desperately she kept sweeping things from between them, afraid that Rosemary couldn't see her, sweeping them away until presently there was not so much as a veil of brittle humor hiding the girl, and with distaste Rosemary saw her plain.

"Couldn't you have lunch, or maybe dinner, or lunch the day after?" begged the girl. Rosemary looked about for Dick, finding him with the hostess, to whom he had been talking since they came in. Their eyes met and he nodded slightly, and simultaneously the three cobra women noticed her; their long necks darted toward her and they fixed finely critical glances upon her. She looked back at them defiantly, acknowledging that she had heard what they said. Then she threw off her exigent vis-à-vis with a polite but clipped

parting that she had just learned from Dick, and went over
to join him. The hostess—she was another tall rich American
girl, promenading insouciantly upon the national prosperity
—was asking Dick innumerable questions about Gausse's
Hôtel, whither she evidently wanted to come, and battering
persistently against his reluctance. Rosemary's presence
reminded her that she had been recalcitrant as a hostess and
glancing about she said: "Have you met any one amusing,
have you met Mr.—" Her eyes groped for a male who might
interest Rosemary, but Dick said they must go. They left
immediately, moving over the brief threshold of the future to
the sudden past of the stone façade without.

"Wasn't it terrible?" he said.

"Terrible," she echoed obediently.

"Rosemary?"

She murmured, "What?" in an awed voice.

"I feel terribly about this."

She was shaken with audibly painful sobs. "Have you got
a handkerchief?" she faltered. But there was little time to
cry, and lovers now they fell ravenously on the quick seconds
while outside the taxi windows the green and cream twilight
faded, and the fire-red, gas-blue, ghost-green signs began to
shine smokily through the tranquil rain. It was nearly six,
the streets were in movement, the bistros gleamed, the Place
de la Concorde moved by in pink majesty as the cab turned
north.

They looked at each other at last, murmuring names that
were a spell. Softly the two names lingered on the air, died
away more slowly than other words, other names, slower
than music in the mind.

"I don't know what came over me last night," Rosemary
said. "That glass of champagne? I've never done anything
like that before."

"You simply said you loved me."

"I do love you—I can't change that." It was time for
Rosemary to cry, so she cried a little in her handkerchief.

"I'm afraid I'm in love with you," said Dick, "and that's
not the best thing that could happen."

Again the names—then they lurched together as if the

85

taxi had swung them. Her breasts crushed flat against him, her mouth was all new and warm, owned in common. They stopped thinking with an almost painful relief, stopped seeing; they only breathed and sought each other. They were both in the gray gentle world of a mild hangover of fatigue when the nerves relax in bunches like piano strings, and crackle suddenly like wicker chairs. Nerves so raw and tender must surely join other nerves, lips to lips, breast to breast. . . .⌉

They were still in the happier stage of love. They were full of brave illusions about each other, tremendous illusions, so that the communion of self with self seemed to be on a plane where no other human relations mattered. They both seemed to have arrived there with an extraordinary innocence as though a series of pure accidents had driven them together, so many accidents that at last they were forced to conclude that they were for each other. They had arrived with clean hands, or so it seemed, after no traffic with the merely curious and clandestine.

But for Dick that portion of the road was short; the turning came before they reached the hotel.

"There's nothing to do about it," he said, with a feeling of panic. "I'm in love with you but it doesn't change what I said last night."

"That doesn't matter now. I just wanted to make you love me—if you love me everything's all right."

"Unfortunately I do. But Nicole mustn't know—she mustn't suspect even faintly. Nicole and I have got to go on together. In a way that's more important than just wanting to go on."

"Kiss me once more."

He kissed her, but momentarily he had left her.

"Nicole mustn't suffer—she loves me and I love her—you understand that."

She did understand—it was the sort of thing she understood well, not hurting people. She knew the Divers loved each other because it had been her primary assumption. She had thought however that it was a rather cooled relation, and actually rather like the love of herself and her mother.

86

When people have so much for outsiders didn't it indicate a lack of inner intensity?

"And I mean love," he said, guessing her thoughts. "Active love—it's more complicated than I can tell you. It was responsible for that crazy duel."

"How did you know about the duel? I thought we were to keep it from you."

"Do you think Abe can keep a secret?" He spoke with incisive irony. "Tell a secret over the radio, publish it in a tabloid, but never tell it to a man who drinks more than three or four a day."

She laughed in agreement, staying close to him.

"So you understand my relations with Nicole are compli- *D.D.*
cated. She's not very strong—she looks strong but she isn't. *wants*
And this makes rather a mess." *to protect his wife*

"Oh, say that later! But kiss me now—love me now. I'll love you and never let Nicole see."

"You darling."

They reached the hotel and Rosemary walked a little behind him, to admire him, to adore him. His step was alert as if he had just come from some great doings and was hurrying on toward others. Organizer of private gaiety, curator of a richly incrusted happiness. His hat was a perfect hat and he carried a heavy stick and yellow gloves. She thought what a good time they would all have being with him to-night.

They walked upstairs—five flights. At the first landing they stopped and kissed; she was careful on the next landing, on the third more careful still. On the next—there were two more—she stopped half way and kissed him fleetingly good-by. At his urgency she walked down with him to the one below for a minute—and then up and up. Finally it was good-by with their hands stretching to touch along the diagonal of the banister and then the fingers slipping apart. Dick went back downstairs to make some arrangements for the evening—Rosemary ran to her room and wrote a letter to her mother; she was conscience-stricken because she did not miss her mother at all. *Starting to grow up.*

## XVIII

ALTHOUGH the Divers were honestly apathetic to organized fashion, they were nevertheless too acute to abandon its contemporaneous rhythm and beat—Dick's parties were all concerned with excitement, and a chance breath of fresh night air was the more precious for being experienced in the intervals of the excitement.

The party that night moved with the speed of a slapstick comedy. They were twelve, they were sixteen, they were quartets in separate motors bound on a quick odyssey over Paris. Everything had been foreseen. People joined them as if by magic, accompanied them as specialists, almost guides, through a phase of the evening, dropped out and were succeeded by other people, so that it appeared as if the freshness of each one had been husbanded for them all day. Rosemary appreciated how different it was from any party in Hollywood, no matter how splendid in scale. There was, among many diversions, the car of the Shah of Persia. Where Dick had commandeered this vehicle, what bribery was employed, these were facts of irrelevance. Rosemary accepted it as merely a new facet of the fabulous, which for two years had filled her life. The car had been built on a special chassis in America. Its wheels were of silver, so was the radiator. The inside of the body was inlaid with innumerable brilliants which would be replaced with true gems by the court jeweller when the car arrived in Teheran the following week. There was only one real seat in back, because the Shah must ride alone, so they took turns riding in it and sitting on the marten fur that covered the floor.

But always there was Dick. Rosemary assured the image of her mother, ever carried with her, that never, never had she known any one so nice, so thoroughly nice as Dick was that night. She compared him with the two Englishmen, whom Abe addressed conscientiously as "Major Hengest and Mr. Horsa," and with the heir to a Scandinavian throne and the novelist just back from Russia, and with Abe, who was desperate and witty, and with Collis Clay, who joined them somewhere and stayed along—and felt there was no comparison. The enthusiasm, the selflessness behind the whole performance ravished her, the technic of moving many varied types, each as immobile, as dependent on supplies of attention as an infantry battalion is dependent on rations, appeared so effortless that he still had pieces of his own most personal self for everyone.

—Afterward she remembered the times when she had felt the happiest. The first time was when she and Dick danced together and she felt her beauty sparkling bright against his tall, strong form as they floated, hovering like people in an amusing dream—he turned her here and there with such a delicacy of suggestion that she was like a bright bouquet, a piece of precious cloth being displayed before fifty eyes. There was a moment when they were not dancing at all, simply clinging together. Some time in the early morning they were alone, and her damp powdery young body came up close to him in a crush of tired cloth, and stayed there, crushed against a background of other people's hats and wraps. . . .

The time she laughed most was later, when six of them, the best of them, noblest relics of the evening, stood in the dusky front lobby of the Ritz telling the night concierge that General Pershing[20] was outside and wanted caviare and champagne. "He brooks no delay. Every man, every gun is at his service." Frantic waiters emerged from nowhere, a table was set in the lobby, and Abe came in representing General Pershing while they stood up and mumbled remembered fragments of war songs at him. In the waiters' injured reaction to this anti-climax they found themselves neglected, so they built a waiter trap—a huge and fantastic device constructed of all the furniture in the lobby and functioning like one of the bizarre machines of a Goldberg cartoon.[21] Abe shook his head doubtfully at it.

"Perhaps it would be better to steal a musical saw and——"

"That's enough," Mary interrupted. "When Abe begins bringing up that it's time to go home." Anxiously she confided to Rosemary:

89

"I've got to get Abe home. His boat train leaves at eleven. It's so important—I feel the whole future depends on his catching it, but whenever I argue with him he does the exact opposite."

"I'll try and persuade him," offered Rosemary.

"Would you?" Mary said doubtfully. "Maybe you could."

Then Dick came up to Rosemary:

"Nicole and I are going home and we thought you'd want to go with us."

Her face was pale with fatigue in the false dawn. Two wan dark spots in her cheek marked where the color was by day.

"I can't," she said. "I promised Mary North to stay along with them—or Abe'll never go to bed. Maybe you could do something."

"Don't you know you can't do anything about people?" he advised her. "If Abe was my room-mate in college, tight for the first time, it'd be different. Now there's nothing to do."

"Well, I've got to stay. He says he'll go to bed if we only come to the Halles with him," she said, almost defiantly.

He kissed the inside of her elbow quickly.

"Don't let Rosemary go home alone," Nicole called to Mary as they left. "We feel responsible to her mother."

—Later Rosemary and the Norths and a manufacturer of dolls' voices from Newark and ubiquitous Collis and a big splendidly dressed oil Indian named George T. Horse-protection were riding along on top of thousands of carrots in a market wagon. The earth in the carrot beards was fragrant and sweet in the darkness, and Rosemary was so high up in the load that she could hardly see the others in the long shadow between infrequent street lamps. Their voices came from far off, as if they were having experiences different from hers, different and far away, for she was with Dick in her heart, sorry she had come with the Norths, wishing she was at the hotel and him asleep across the hall, or that he was here beside her with the warm darkness streaming down.

"Don't come up," she called to Collis, "the carrots will all roll." She threw one at Abe who was sitting beside the driver, stiffly like an old man. . . .

Later she was homeward bound at last in broad daylight, with the pigeons already breaking over Saint-Sulpice. All of them began to laugh spontaneously because they knew it was still last night while the people in the streets had the delusion that it was bright hot morning.

"At last I've been on a wild party," thought Rosemary, "but it's no fun when Dick isn't there."

She felt a little betrayed and sad, but presently a moving object came into sight. It was a huge horse-chestnut tree in full bloom bound for the Champs-Élysées, strapped now into a long truck and simply shaking with laughter—like a lovely person in an undignified position yet confident none the less of being lovely. Looking at it with fascination Rosemary identified herself with it, and laughed cheerfully with it, and everything all at once seemed gorgeous.

## XIX

ABE left from the Gare Saint-Lazare at eleven—he stood alone under the fouled glass dome, relic of the seventies, era of the Crystal Palace; his hands, of that vague gray color that only twenty-four hours can produce, were in his coat pockets to conceal the trembling fingers. With his hat removed it was plain that only the top layer of his hair was brushed back—the lower levels were pointed resolutely sidewise. He was scarcely recognizable as the man who had swum upon Gausse's beach a fortnight ago.

He was early; he looked from left to right with his eyes only; it would have taken nervous forces out of his control to use any other part of his body. New-looking baggage went past him; presently prospective passengers, with dark little bodies, were calling: "Jew-uls-*Hoo-oo!*" in dark piercing voices.

At the minute when he wondered whether or not he had

time for a drink at the buffet, and began clutching at the soggy wad of thousand-franc notes in his pocket, one end of his pendulous glance came to rest upon the apparition of Nicole at the stairhead. He watched her—she was self-revelatory in her little expressions as people seem to some-one waiting for them, who as yet is himself unobserved. She was frowning, thinking of her children, less gloating over them than merely animally counting them—a cat checking her cubs with a paw.

When she saw Abe, the mood passed out of her face; the glow of the morning skylight was sad, and Abe made a gloomy figure with dark circles that showed through the crimson tan under his eyes. They sat down on a bench.

"I came because you asked me," said Nicole defensively. Abe seemed to have forgotten why he asked her and Nicole was quite content to look at the travellers passing by.

"That's going to be the belle of your boat—that one with all the men to say good-by—you see why she bought that dress?" Nicole talked faster and faster. "You see why nobody else would buy it except the belle of the world cruise? See? No? Wake up! That's a story dress—that extra material tells a story and somebody on world cruise would be lonesome enough to want to hear it."

She bit close her last words; she had talked too much for her; and Abe found it difficult to gather from her serious set face that she had spoken at all. With an effort he drew himself up to a posture that looked as if he were standing up while he was sitting down.

"The afternoon you took me to that funny ball—you know, St. Genevieve's—" he began.

"I remember. It was fun, wasn't it?"

"No fun for me. I haven't had fun seeing you this time. I'm tired of you both, but it doesn't show because you're even more tired of me—you know what I mean. If I had any enthusiasm, I'd go on to new people."

There was a rough nap on Nicole's velvet gloves as she slapped him back:

"Seems rather foolish to be unpleasant, Abe. Anyhow

you don't mean that. I can't see why you've given up about everything."

Abe considered, trying hard not to cough or blow his nose.

"I suppose I got bored; and then it was such a long way to go back in order to get anywhere."

Often a man can play the helpless child in front of a woman, but he can almost never bring it off when he feels most like a helpless child.

"No excuse for it," Nicole said crisply.

Abe was feeling worse every minute—he could think of nothing but disagreeable and sheerly nervous remarks. Nicole thought that the correct attitude for her was to sit staring straight ahead, hands in her lap. For a while there was no communication between them—each was racing away from the other, breathing only insofar as there was blue space ahead, a sky not seen by the other. Unlike lovers they possessed no past; unlike man and wife, they possessed no future; yet up to this morning Nicole had liked Abe better than any one except Dick—and he had been heavy, belly-frightened, with love for her for years.

"Tired of women's worlds," he spoke up suddenly.

"Then why don't you make a world of your own?"

"Tired of friends. The thing is to have sycophants."

Nicole tried to force the minute hand around on the station clock, but, "You agree?" he demanded.

"I am a woman and my business is to hold things together."

"My business is to tear them apart."

"When you get drunk you don't tear anything apart except yourself," she said, cold now, and frightened and unconfident. The station was filling but no one she knew came. After a moment her eyes fell gratefully on a tall girl with straw hair like a helmet, who was dropping letters in the mail slot.

"A girl I have to speak to, Abe. Abe, wake up! You fool!"

Patiently Abe followed her with his eyes. The woman turned in a startled way to greet Nicole, and Abe recognized

93

her as some one he had seen around Paris. He took advantage of Nicole's absence to cough hard and retchingly into his handkerchief, and to blow his nose loud. The morning was warmer and his underwear was soaked with sweat. His fingers trembled so violently that it took four matches to light a cigarette; it seemed absolutely necessary to make his way into the buffet for a drink, but immediately Nicole returned.

"That was a mistake," she said with frosty humor. "After begging me to come and see her, she gave me a good snubbing. She looked at me as if I were rotted." Excited, she did a little laugh, as with two fingers high in the scales. "Let people come to you."

Abe recovered from a cigarette cough and remarked:

"Trouble is when you're sober you don't want to see anybody, and when you're tight nobody wants to see you."

"Who, me?" Nicole laughed again; for some reason the late encounter had cheered her.

"No—me."

"Speak for yourself. I like people, a lot of people—I like——"

Rosemary and Mary North came in sight, walking slowly and searching for Abe, and Nicole burst forth grossly with "Hey! Hi! Hey!" and laughed and waved the package of handkerchiefs she had bought for Abe.

They stood in an uncomfortable little group weighted down by Abe's gigantic presence: he lay athwart them like the wreck of a galleon, dominating with his presence his own weakness and self-indulgence, his narrowness and bitterness. All of them were conscious of the solemn dignity that flowed from him, of his achievement, fragmentary, suggestive and surpassed. But they were frightened at his survivant will, once a will to live, now become a will to die.

Dick Diver came and brought with him a fine glowing surface on which the three women sprang like monkeys with cries of relief, perching on his shoulders, on the beautiful crown of his hat or the gold head of his cane. Now, for a moment, they could disregard the spectacle of Abe's gigantic obscenity. Dick saw the situation quickly and grasped it

94

quietly. He pulled them out of themselves into the station, making plain its wonders. Nearby, some Americans were saying good-by in voices that mimicked the cadence of water running into a large old bathtub. Standing in the station, with Paris in back of them, it seemed as if they were vicariously leaning a little over the ocean, already undergoing a sea-change, a shifting about of atoms to form the essential molecule of a new people.

So the well-to-do Americans poured through the station onto the platforms with frank new faces, intelligent, considerate, thoughtless, thought-for. An occasional English face among them seemed sharp and emergent. When there were enough Americans on the platform the first impression of their immaculacy and their money began to fade into a vague racial dusk that hindered and blinded both them and their observers.

Nicole seized Dick's arm crying, "Look!" Dick turned in time to see what took place in half a minute. At a Pullman entrance two cars off, a vivid scene detached itself from the tenor of many farewells. The young woman with the helmet-like hair to whom Nicole had spoken made an odd dodging little run away from the man to whom she was talking and plunged a frantic hand into her purse; then the sound of two revolver shots cracked the narrow air of the platform. Simultaneously the engine whistled sharply and the train began to move, momentarily dwarfing the shots in significance. Abe waved again from his window, oblivious to what had happened. But before the crowd closed in, the others had seen the shots take effect, seen the target sit down upon the platform.

Only after a hundred years did the train stop; Nicole, Mary, and Rosemary waited on the outskirts while Dick fought his way through. It was five minutes before he found them again—by this time the crowd had split into two sections, following, respectively, the man on a stretcher and the girl walking pale and firm between distraught gendarmes.

"It was Maria Wallis," Dick said hurriedly. "The man she shot was an Englishman—they had an awful time finding out who, because she shot him through his identification card." They were walking quickly from the train, swayed along with the crowd. "I found out what poste de police they're taking her to so I'll go there——"

"But her sister lives in Paris," Nicole objected. "Why not phone her? Seems very peculiar nobody thought of that. She's married to a Frenchman, and he can do more than we can."

Dick hesitated, shook his head and started off.

"Wait!" Nicole cried after him. "That's foolish—how can you do any good—with your French?"

"At least I'll see they don't do anything outrageous to her."

"They're certainly going to hold on to her," Nicole assured him briskly. "She *did* shoot the man. The best thing is to phone right away to Laura—she can do more than we can."

Dick was unconvinced—also he was showing off for Rosemary.

"You wait," said Nicole firmly, and hurried off to a telephone booth.

"When Nicole takes things into her hands," he said with affectionate irony, "there is nothing more to be done."

He saw Rosemary for the first time that morning. They exchanged glances, trying to recognize the emotions of the day before. For a moment each seemed unreal to the other —then the slow warm hum of love began again.

"You like to help everybody, don't you?" Rosemary said.

"I only pretend to."

"Mother likes to help everybody—of course she can't help as many people as you do." She sighed. "Sometimes I think I'm the most selfish person in the world."

For the first time the mention of her mother annoyed rather than amused Dick. He wanted to sweep away her mother, remove the whole affair from the nursery footing upon which Rosemary persistently established it. But he realized that this impulse was a loss of control—what would become of Rosemary's urge toward him if, for even a moment, he relaxed. He saw, not without panic, that the affair was sliding to rest; it could not stand still, it must go on or go back; for the first time it occurred to him that Rosemary had her hand on the lever more authoritatively than he.

Before he had thought out a course of procedure, Nicole returned.

"I found Laura. It was the first news she had and her voice kept fading away and then getting loud again—as if she was fainting and then pulling herself together. She said she knew something was going to happen this morning."

"Maria ought to be with Diaghileff," said Dick in a gentle tone, in order to bring them back to quietude. "She has a nice sense of decor—not to say rhythm. Will any of us ever see a train pulling out without hearing a few shots?"

They bumped down the wide steel steps. "I'm sorry for the poor man," Nicole said. "Course that's why she talked so strange to me—she was getting ready to open fire."

She laughed, Rosemary laughed too, but they were both horrified, and both of them deeply wanted Dick to make a moral comment on the matter and not leave it to them. This wish was not entirely conscious, especially on the part of Rosemary, who was accustomed to having shell fragments of such events shriek past her head. But a totality of shock had piled up in her too. For the moment, Dick was too shaken by the impetus of his newly recognized emotion to resolve things into the pattern of the holiday, so the women, missing something, lapsed into a vague unhappiness.

Then, as if nothing had happened, the lives of the Divers and their friends flowed out into the street.

However, everything had happened—Abe's departure and Mary's impending departure for Salzburg this after-noon had ended the time in Paris. Or perhaps the shots, the concussions that had finished God knew what dark matter, had terminated it. The shots had entered into all their lives: *affects everyone* echoes of violence followed them out onto the pavement where two porters held a post-mortem beside them as they waited for a taxi.

"Tu as vu le revolver? Il était très petite, vraie perle—un jouet."

"Mais, assez puissant!" said the other porter sagely. "Tu as vu sa chemise? Assez de sang pour se croire à la guerre."

# XX

In the square, as they came out, a suspended mass of gasoline exhaust cooked slowly in the July sun. It was a terrible thing—unlike pure heat it held no promise of rural escape but suggested only roads choked with the same foul asthma. During their luncheon, outdoors, across from the Luxembourg Gardens, Rosemary had cramps and felt fretful and full of impatient lassitude—it was the foretaste of this that had inspired her self-accusation of selfishness in the station.

Dick had no suspicion of the sharpness of the change; he was profoundly unhappy and the subsequent increase of egotism tended momentarily to blind him to what was going on round about him, and deprive him of the long ground-swell of imagination that he counted on for his judgments.

After Mary North left them, accompanied by the Italian singing teacher who had joined them for coffee and was taking her to her train, Rosemary, too, stood up, bound for an engagement at her studio: "meet some officials."

"And oh—" she proposed "—if Collis Clay, that Southern boy—if he comes while you are still sitting here, just tell him I couldn't wait; tell him to call me to-morrow."

Too insouciant, in reaction from the late disturbance, she had assumed the privileges of a child—the result being to remind the Divers of their exclusive love for their own children; Rosemary was sharply rebuked in a short passage between the women: "You'd better leave the message with a waiter," Nicole's voice was stern and unmodulated, "we're leaving immediately."

Rosemary got it, took it without resentment.

"I'll let it go then. Good-by, you darlings."

Dick asked for the check; the Divers relaxed, chewing tentatively on toothpicks.

"Well—" they said together.

He saw a flash of unhappiness on her mouth, so brief that only he would have noticed, and he could pretend not to have seen. What did Nicole think? Rosemary was one of a dozen people he had "worked over" in the past years: these had included a French circus clown, Abe and Mary North, a pair of dancers, a writer, a painter, a comedienne from the Grand Guignol, a half-crazy pederast from the Russian Ballet, a promising tenor they had staked to a year in Milan. Nicole well knew how seriously these people interpreted his interest and enthusiasm; but she realized also that, except while their children were being born, Dick had not spent a night apart from her since their marriage. On the other hand, there was a pleasingness about him that simply had to be used—those who possessed that pleasingness had to keep their hands in, and go along attaching people that they had no use to make of.

Now Dick hardened himself and let minutes pass without making any gesture of confidence, any representation of constantly renewed surprise that they were one together.

Collis Clay out of the South edged a passage between the closely packed tables and greeted the Divers cavalierly. Such salutations always astonished Dick—acquaintances saying "Hi!" to them, or speaking only to one of them. He felt so intensely about people that in moments of apathy he preferred to remain concealed; that one could parade a casualness into his presence was a challenge to the key on which he lived.

Collis, unaware that he was without a wedding garment, heralded his arrival with: "I reckon I'm late—the beyed has flown." Dick had to wrench something out of himself before he could forgive him for not having first complimented Nicole.

She left almost immediately and he sat with Collis, finishing the last of his wine. He rather liked Collis—he was "post-war"; less difficult than most of the Southerners he had known at New Haven a decade previously. Dick listened with amusement to the conversation that accompanied the slow, profound stuffing of a pipe. In the early afternoon children and nurses were trekking into the Luxembourg Gardens; it was the first time in months that Dick had let this part of the day out of his hands.

Suddenly his blood ran cold as he realized the content of Collis's confidential monologue.

"—she's not so cold as you'd probably think. I admit I thought she was cold for a long time. But she got into a jam with a friend of mine going from New York to Chicago at Easter—a boy named Hillis she thought was pretty nutsey at New Haven—she had a compartment with a cousin of mine but she and Hillis wanted to be alone, so in the afternoon my cousin came and played cards in our compartment. Well, after about two hours we went back and there was Rosemary and Bill Hillis standing in the vestibule arguing with the conductor—Rosemary white as a sheet. Seems they locked the door and pulled down the blinds and I guess there was some heavy stuff going on when the conductor came for the tickets and knocked on the door. They thought it was us kidding them and wouldn't let him in at first, and when they did, he was plenty sore. He asked Hillis if that was his compartment and whether he and Rosemary were married that they locked the door, and Hillis lost his temper trying to explain there was nothing wrong. He said the conductor had insulted Rosemary and he wanted him to fight, but that conductor could have made trouble—and believe me I had an awful time smoothing it over."

With every detail imagined, with even envy for the pair's community of misfortune in the vestibule, Dick felt a change taking place within him. Only the image of a third person, even a vanished one, entering into his relation with Rosemary was needed to throw him off his balance and send through him waves of pain, misery, desire, desperation. The vividly pictured hand on Rosemary's cheek, the quicker breath, the white excitement of the event viewed from outside, the inviolable secret warmth within.

—Do you mind if I pull down the curtain?

—Please do. It's too light in here.

Collis Clay was now speaking about fraternity politics at New Haven, in the same tone, with the same emphasis. Dick had gathered that he was in love with Rosemary in some curious way Dick could not have understood. The affair with Hillis seemed to have made no emotional impression on Collis save to give him the joyful conviction that Rosemary was "human."

"Bones got a wonderful crowd," he said. "We all did, as a matter of fact. New Haven's so big now the sad thing is the men we have to leave out."

—Do you mind if I pull down the curtain?

—Please do. It's too light in here.

. . . Dick went over Paris to his bank—writing a check, he looked along the row of men at the desks deciding to which one he would present it for an O. K. As he wrote he engrossed himself in the material act, examining meticulously the pen, writing laboriously upon the high glass-topped desk. Once he raised glazed eyes to look toward the mail department, then glazed his spirit again by concentration upon the objects he dealt with.

Still he failed to decide to whom the check should be presented, which man in the line would guess least of the unhappy predicament in which he found himself and, also, which one would be least likely to talk. There was Perrin, the suave New Yorker, who had asked him to luncheons at the American Club, there was Casasus, the Spaniard, with whom he usually discussed a mutual friend in spite of the fact that the friend had passed out of his life a dozen years before; there was Muchhause, who always asked him whether he wanted to draw upon his wife's money or his own.

As he entered the amount on the stub, and drew two lines under it, he decided to go to Pierce, who was young and for whom he would have to put on only a small show. It was often easier to give a show than to watch one.

He went to the mail desk first—as the woman who served him pushed up with her bosom a piece of paper that had nearly escaped the desk, he thought how differently women use their bodies from men. He took his letters aside to open: There was a bill for seventeen <u>psychiatric books</u> from a German concern, a bill from Brentano's, a letter from Buffalo from his father, in a handwriting that year by year became more indecipherable; there was a card from Tommy Barban postmarked Fez and bearing a facetious communication; there were letters from doctors in Zurich, both in German; a disputed bill from a plasterer in Cannes; a bill from a furniture maker; a letter from the publisher of a medical journal in Baltimore, miscellaneous announcements and an invitation to a showing of pictures by an incipient artist; also there were three letters for Nicole, and a letter for Rosemary sent in his care.

—Do you mind if I pull down the curtain?

He went toward Pierce but he was engaged with a woman, and Dick saw with his heels that he would have to present his check to Casasus at the next desk, who was free.

"How are you, Diver?" Casasus was genial. He stood up, his mustache spreading with his smile. "We were talking about Featherstone the other day and I thought of you—he's out in California now."

Dick widened his eyes and bent forward a little.

"In Ca*lifornia*?"

"That's what I heard."

Dick held the check poised; to focus the attention of Casasus upon it he looked toward Pierce's desk, holding the latter for a moment in a friendly eye-play conditioned by an old joke of three years before when Pierce had been involved with a Lithuanian countess. Pierce played up with a grin until Casasus had authorized the check and had no further recourse to detain Dick, whom he liked, than to stand up holding his pince-nez and repeat, "Yes, he's in California."

Meanwhile Dick had seen that Perrin, at the head of the line of desks, was in conversation with the heavyweight champion of the world; from a sidesweep of Perrin's eye Dick saw that he was considering calling him over and introducing him, but that he finally decided against it.

Cutting across the social mood of Casasus with the intensity he had accumulated at the glass desk—which is to say he looked hard at the check, studying it, and then fixed his eyes on grave problems beyond the first marble pillar to the right of the banker's head and made a business of shifting the cane, hat, and letters he carried—he said good-by and went out. He had long ago purchased the doorman; his taxi sprang to the curb.

"I want to go to the Films Par Excellence Studio—it's on a little street in Passy. Go to the Muette. I'll direct you from there."

He was rendered so uncertain by the events of the last forty-eight hours that he was not even sure of what he wanted to do; he paid off the taxi at the Muette and walked in the direction of the studio, crossing to the opposite side of the street before he came to the building. Dignified in his fine clothes, with their fine accessories, he was yet swayed and driven as an animal. Dignity could come only with an overthrowing of his past, of the effort of the last six years. He went briskly around the block with the fatuousness of one of Tarkington's[22] adolescents hurrying at the blind places lest he miss Rosemary's coming out of the studio. It was a melancholy neighborhood. Next door to the place he saw a sign: "1000 chemises." The shirts filled the window, piled, cravated, stuffed, or draped with shoddy grace on the show-case floor: "1000 chemises"—count them! On either side he read: "Papeterie," "Pâtisserie," "Solde," "Réclame"—and Constance Talmadge in "Déjeuner de Soleil," and farther away there were more sombre announcements: "Vêtements Ecclésiastiques," "Déclaration de Décès" and "Pompes Funèbres." Life and death.

He knew that what he was now doing marked a turning point in his life—it was out of line with everything that had preceded it—even out of line with what effect he might hope to produce upon Rosemary. Rosemary saw him always as a model of correctness—his presence walking around this block was an intrusion. But Dick's necessity of behaving as he did was a projection of some submerged reality: he was compelled to walk there, or stand there, his shirt-sleeve fitting his wrist and his coat sleeve encasing his shirt-sleeve like a sleeve valve, his collar molded plastically to his neck,

his red hair cut exactly, his hand holding his small brief-
case like a dandy—just as another man once found it necessary to stand in front of a church in Ferrara,[23] in sackcloth and
ashes. Dick was paying some tribute to things unforgotten,
unshriven, unexpurgated.

## XXI

AFTER three-quarters of an hour of standing around, he
became suddenly involved in a human contact. It was just
the sort of thing that was likely to happen to him when he
was in the mood of not wanting to see any one. So rigidly
did he sometimes guard his exposed self-consciousness that
frequently he defeated his own purposes; as an actor who
underplays a part sets up a craning forward, a stimulated
emotional attention in an audience, and seems to create in
others an ability to bridge the gap he has left open. Similarly
we are seldom sorry for those who need and crave our pity—
we reserve this for those who, by other means, make us
exercise the abstract function of pity.

So Dick might, himself, have analyzed the incident that
ensued. As he paced the rue des Saints Anges he was
spoken to by a thin-faced American, perhaps thirty, with an
air of being scarred and a slight but sinister smile. As Dick
gave him the light he requested, he placed him as one of a
type of which he had been conscious since early youth—a
type that loafed about tobacco stores with one elbow on the
counter and watched, through heaven knew what small
chink of the mind, the people who came in and out. Intimate
to garages, where he had vague business conducted in
undertones, to barber shops, to the lobbies of theatres—in
such places, at any rate, Dick placed him. Sometimes the
face bobbed up in one of Tad's[24] more savage cartoons—in
boyhood Dick had often thrown an uneasy glance at the dim
borderland of crime on which he stood.

"How do you like Paris, Buddy?"

Not waiting for an answer the man tried to fit in his

footsteps with Dick's: "Where you from?" he asked encouragingly.

"From Buffalo."

"I'm from San Antone—but I been over here since the war."

"You in the army?"

"*I'll* say I was. Eighty-fourth Division—ever heard of that outfit?"

The man walked a little ahead of him and fixed him with eyes that were practically menacing.

"Staying in Paris awhile, Buddy? Or just passing through?"

"Passing through."

"What hotel you staying at?"

Dick had begun laughing to himself—the party had the intention of rifling his room that night. His thoughts were read apparently without self-consciousness.

"With a build like yours you oughtn't to be afraid of me, Buddy. There's a lot of bums around just laying for American tourists, but you needn't be afraid of me."

Becoming bored, Dick stopped walking: "I just wonder why you've got so much time to waste."

"I'm in business here in Paris."

"In what line?"

"Selling papers."

The contrast between the formidable manner and the mild profession was absurd—but the man amended it with:

"Don't worry; I made plenty money last year—ten or twenty francs for a Sunny Times that cost six."

He produced a newspaper clipping from a rusty wallet and passed it over to one who had become a fellow stroller— the cartoon showed a stream of Americans pouring from the gangplank of a liner freighted with gold.

"Two hundred thousand—spending ten million a summer."

"What you doing out here in Passy?"

His companion looked around cautiously. "Movies," he said darkly. "They got an American studio over there. And they need guys can speak English. I'm waiting for a break."

Dick shook him off quickly and firmly.

It had become apparent that Rosemary either had escaped on one of his early circuits of the block or else had left before he came into the neighborhood; he went into the bistro on the corner, bought a lead disk and, squeezed in an alcove between the kitchen and the foul toilet, he called the Roi George. He recognized Cheyne-Stokes tendencies[25] in his respiration—but like everything the symptom served only to turn him in toward his emotion. He gave the number of the hotel; then stood holding the phone and staring into the café; after a long while a strange little voice said hello.

"This is Dick—I had to call you."

A pause from her—then bravely, and in key with his emotion: "I'm glad you did."

"I came to meet you at your studio—I'm out in Passy across the way from it. I thought maybe we'd ride around through the Bois."

"Oh, I only stayed there a minute! I'm so sorry." A silence.

"Rosemary."

"Yes, Dick."

"Look, I'm in an extraordinary condition about you. When a child can disturb a middle-aged gent—things get difficult."

"You're not middle-aged, Dick—you're the youngest person in the world."

"Rosemary?" Silence while he stared at a shelf that held the humbler poisons of France—bottles of Otard, Rhum St. James, Marie Brizard, Punch Orangeade, Fernet Branca, Cherry Rocher, and Armagnac.

"Are you alone?"

—*Do you mind if I pull down the curtain?*

"Who do you think I'd be with?"

"That's the state I'm in. I'd like to be with you now."

Silence, then a sigh and an answer. "I wish you were with me now."

There was the hotel room where she lay behind a telephone number, and little gusts of music wailed around her—

"And two—for tea.
And me for you,
And you for me
Alow-own."

There was the remembered dust of powder over her tan—when he kissed her face it was damp around the corners of her hair; there was the flash of a white face under his own, the arc of a shoulder.

"It's impossible," he said to himself. In a minute he was out in the street marching along toward the Muette, or away from it, his small brief-case still in his hand, his gold-headed stick held at a sword-like angle.

Rosemary returned to her desk and finished a letter to her mother.

"—I only saw him for a little while but I thought he was wonderful looking. I fell in love with him (Of course I Do Love Dick Best but you know what I mean). He really is going to direct the picture and is leaving immediately for Hollywood, and I think we ought to leave, too. Collis Clay has been here. I like him all right but have not seen much of him because of the Divers, who really are divine, about the Nicest People I ever Knew. I am feeling not very well to-day and am taking the Medicine, though see No need for it. I'm not even Going to Try to tell you All that's Happened until I see *You!!!* So when you get this letter *wire, wire, wire!* Are you coming north or shall I come south with the Divers?"

At six Dick called Nicole.

"Have you any special plans?" he asked. "Would you like to do something quiet—dinner at the hotel and then a play?"

"Would you? I'll do whatever you want. I phoned Rosemary a while ago and she's having dinner in her room. I think this upset all of us, don't you?"

"It didn't upset me," he objected. "Darling, unless you're physically tired let's do something. Otherwise we'll get south and spend a week wondering why we didn't see Boucher. It's better than brooding——"

This was a blunder and Nicole took him up sharply.

"Brooding about what?"

"About Maria Wallis."

She agreed to go to a play. It was a tradition between them that they should never be too tired for anything, and they found it made the days better on the whole and put the evenings more in order. When, inevitably, their spirits flagged they shifted the blame to the weariness and fatigue of others. Before they went out, as fine-looking a couple as could be found in Paris, they knocked softly at Rosemary's door. There was no answer; judging that she was asleep they walked into a warm strident Paris night, snatching a vermouth and bitters in the shadow by Fouquet's bar.

## XXII

NICOLE awoke late, murmuring something back into her dream before she parted her long lashes tangled with sleep. Dick's bed was empty—only after a minute did she realize that she had awakened by a knock at their salon door.

"Entrez!" she called, but there was no answer, and after a moment she slipped on a dressing-gown and went to open it. A sergent de ville confronted her courteously and stepped inside the door.

"Mr. Afghan North—he is here?"

"What? No—he's gone to America."

"When did he leave, Madame?"

"Yesterday morning."

He shook his head and waved his forefinger at her in a quicker rhythm.

"He was in Paris last night. He is registered here but his room is not occupied. They told me I had better ask at this room."

"Sounds very peculiar to me—we saw him off yesterday morning on the boat train."

"Be that as it may, he has been seen here this morning. Even his carte d'identité has been seen. And there you are."

"We know nothing about it," she proclaimed in amazement.

He considered. He was an ill-smelling, handsome man.

"You were not with him at all last night?"

"But no."

"We have arrested a Negro. We are convinced we have at last arrested the correct Negro."

"I assure you that I haven't an idea what you're talking about. If it's the Mr. Abraham North, the one we know, well, if he was in Paris last night we weren't aware of it."

The man nodded, sucked his upper lip, convinced but disappointed.

"What happened?" Nicole demanded.

He showed his palms, puffing out his closed mouth. He had begun to find her attractive and his eyes flickered at her.

"What do you wish, Madame? A summer affair. Mr. Afghan North was robbed and he made a complaint. We have arrested the miscreant. Mr. Afghan should come to identify him and make the proper charges."

Nicole pulled her dressing-gown closer around her and dismissed him briskly. Mystified she took a bath and dressed. By this time it was after ten and she called Rosemary but got no answer—then she phoned the hotel office and found that Abe had indeed registered, at six-thirty this morning. His room, however, was still unoccupied. Hoping for a word from Dick she waited in the parlor of the suite; just as she had given up and decided to go out, the office called and announced:

"Meestaire Crawshow, un nègre."

"On what business?" she demanded.

"He says he knows you and the doctaire. He says there is a Meestaire Freeman into prison that is a friend of all the world. He says there is injustice and he wishes to see Meestaire North before he himself is arrested."

"We know nothing about it." Nicole disclaimed the whole business with a vehement clap of the receiver. Abe's bizarre reappearance made it plain to her how fatigued she was with his dissipation. Dismissing him from her mind she went out, ran into Rosemary at the dressmaker's, and shopped with her for artificial flowers and all-colored strings of colored beads on the rue de Rivoli. She helped Rosemary choose a diamond for her mother, and some scarfs and novel cigarette cases to take home to business associates in California. For her son she bought Greek and Roman soldiers, a whole army of them, costing over a thousand francs. Once again they spent their money in different ways, and again Rosemary admired Nicole's method of spending. Nicole was sure that the money she spent was hers—Rosemary still thought her money was miraculously lent to her and she must consequently be very careful of it.

It was fun spending money in the sunlight of the foreign city, with healthy bodies under them that sent streams of color up to their faces; with arms and hands, legs and ankles that they stretched out confidently, reaching or stepping with the confidence of women lovely to men.

When they got back to the hotel and found Dick, all bright and new in the morning, both of them had a moment of complete childish joy.

He had just received a garbled telephone call from Abe who so it appeared, had spent the forenoon in hiding.

"It was one of the most extraordinary telephone conversations I've ever held."

Dick had talked not only to Abe but to a dozen others. On the phone these supernumeraries had been typically introduced as: "—man wants to talk to you is in the Teput Dome,²⁶ well he says he was in it—what is it?

"Hey, somebody, shut-up—anyhow, he was in some shandel-scandal and he kaa *possi*bly go home. My own *per*sonal is that—my personal is he's had a—" Gulps sounded and thereafter what the party had, rested with the unknown.

The phone yielded up a supplementary offer:

"I thought it would appeal to you anyhow as a psychologist." The vague personality who corresponded to this statement was eventually hung on to the phone; in the sequence he failed to appeal to Dick, as a psychologist, or indeed as anything else. Abe's conversation flowed on as follows:

"Hello."

"Well?"

"Well, hello."

"Who are you?"

"Well." There were interpolated snorts of laughter.

"Well, I'll put somebody else on the line."

Sometimes Dick could hear Abe's voice, accompanied by scufflings, droppings of the receiver, far-away fragments such as, "No, I don't, Mr. North. . . ." Then a pert decided voice had said: "If you are a friend of Mr. North you will come down and take him away."

Abe cut in, solemn and ponderous, beating it all down with an overtone of earth-bound determination.

"Dick, I've launched a race riot in Montmartre. I'm going over and get Freeman out of jail. If a Negro from Copenhagen that makes shoe polish—hello, can you hear me—well, look, if anybody comes there—" Once again the receiver was a chorus of innumerable melodies.

"Why you back in Paris?" Dick demanded.

"I got as far as Évreux, and I decided to take a plane back so I could compare it with St. Sulpice. I mean I don't intend to bring St. Sulpice back to Paris. I don't even mean Baroque! I meant St. Germain. For God's sake, wait a minute and I'll put the chasseur on the wire."

"For God's sake, don't."

"Listen—did Mary get off all right?"

"Yes."

"Dick, I want you to talk with a man I met here this morning, the son of a naval officer that's been to every doctor in Europe. Let me tell you about him——"

Dick had rung off at this point—perhaps that was a piece of ingratitude for he needed grist for the grinding activity of his mind.

"Abe used to be so nice," Nicole told Rosemary. "So nice. Long ago—when Dick and I were first married. If you had known him then. He'd come to stay with us for weeks and weeks and we scarcely knew he was in the house. Sometimes he'd play—sometimes he'd be in the library with a muted piano, making love to it by the hour—Dick, do you remember that maid? She thought he was a ghost and sometimes Abe used to meet her in the hall and moo at her, and it cost us a whole tea service once—but we didn't care."

So much fun—so long ago. Rosemary envied them their fun, imagining a life of leisure unlike her own. She knew little of leisure but she had the respect for it of those who have never had it. She thought of it as a resting, without realizing that the Divers were as far from relaxing as she was herself.

"What did this to him?" she asked. "Why does he have to drink?"

Nicole shook her head right and left, disclaiming responsibility for the matter: "So many smart men go to pieces nowadays."

"And when haven't they?" Dick asked. "Smart men play close to the line because they have to—some of them can't stand it, so they quit."

"It must lie deeper than that." Nicole clung to her conservatism; also she was irritated that Dick should contradict her before Rosemary. "Artists like—well, like Fernand don't seem to have to wallow in alcohol. Why is it just Americans who dissipate?"

There were so many answers to this question that Dick decided to leave it in the air, to buzz victoriously in Nicole's ears. He had become intensely critical of her. Though he thought she was the most attractive human creature he had ever seen, though he got from her everything he needed, he scented battle from afar, and subconsciously he had been hardening and arming himself, hour by hour. He was not given to self-indulgence and he felt comparatively graceless at this moment of indulging himself, blinding his eyes with the hope that Nicole guessed at only an emotional excitement about Rosemary. He was not sure—last night at the theatre she had referred pointedly to Rosemary as a child.

The trio lunched downstairs in an atmosphere of carpets and padded waiters, who did not march at the stomping quick-step of those men who brought good food to the tables whereon they had recently dined. Here there were families of Americans staring around at families of Americans, and trying to make conversation with one another.

There was a party at the next table that they could not account for. It consisted of an expansive, somewhat secretarial, would-you-mind-repeating young man, and a score of women. The women were neither young nor old nor of any particular social class; yet the party gave the impression of a unit, held more closely together for example than a group of wives stalling through a professional congress of their husbands. Certainly it was more of a unit than any conceivable tourist party.

An instinct made Dick suck back the grave derision that formed on his tongue; he asked the waiter to find out who they were.

"Those are the gold-star muzzers," explained the waiter.

Aloud and in low voices they exclaimed. Rosemary's eyes filled with tears.

"Probably the young ones are the wives," said Nicole.

Over his wine Dick looked at them again; in their happy faces, the dignity that surrounded and pervaded the party, he perceived all the maturity of an older America. For a while the sobered women who had come to mourn for their dead, for something they could not repair, made the room beautiful. Momentarily, he sat again on his father's knee, riding with Mosby[27] while the old loyalties and devotions fought on around him. Almost with an effort he turned back to his two women at the table and faced the whole new world in which he believed.

—Do you mind if I pull down the curtain?

# XXIII

ABE NORTH was still in the Ritz bar, where he had been since nine in the morning. When he arrived seeking sanctuary the windows were open and great beams were busy at pulling up the dust from smoky carpets and cushions. Chasseurs tore through the corridors, liberated and disembodied, moving for the moment in pure space. The sitdown bar for women, across from the bar proper, seemed very small—it was hard to imagine what throngs it could accommodate in the afternoon.

The famous Paul, the concessionnaire, had not arrived, but Claude, who was checking stock, broke off his work with no improper surprise to make Abe a pick-me-up. Abe sat on a bench against a wall. After two drinks he began to feel better—so much better that he mounted to the barber's shop and was shaved. When he returned to the bar Paul had arrived—in his custom-built motor, from which he had disembarked correctly at the Boulevard des Capucines. Paul liked Abe and came over to talk.

"I was supposed to ship home this morning," Abe said. "I mean yesterday morning, or whatever this is."

"Why din you?" asked Paul.

Abe considered, and happened finally to a reason: "I was reading a serial in Liberty and the next installment was due here in Paris—so if I'd sailed I'd have missed it—then I never would have read it."

"It must be a very good story."

"It's a terr-r-rible story."

Paul arose chuckling and paused, leaning on the back of a chair:

"If you really want to get off, Mr. North, there are friends of yours going to-morrow on the France—Mister what is this name—and Slim Pearson. Mister—I'll think of it—tall with a new beard."

"Yardly," Abe supplied.

"Mr. Yardly. They're both going on the France."

He was on his way to his duties but Abe tried to detain him: "If I didn't have to go by way of Cherbourg. The baggage went that way."

"Get your baggage in New York," said Paul, receding.

The logic of the suggestion fitted gradually into Abe's pitch—he grew rather enthusiastic about being cared for, or rather about prolonging his state of irresponsibility.

Other clients had meanwhile drifted in to the bar: first came a huge Dane whom Abe had somewhere encountered. The Dane took a seat across the room, and Abe guessed he would be there all the day, drinking, lunching, talking or reading newspapers. He felt a desire to out-stay him. At eleven the college boys began to step in, stepping gingerly lest they tear one another bag from bag. It was about then he had the chasseur telephone to the Divers; by the time he was in touch with them he was in touch also with other friends—and his hunch was to put them all on different phones at once—the result was somewhat general. From time to time his mind reverted to the fact that he ought to go over and get Freeman out of jail, but he shook off all facts as parts of the nightmare.

By one o'clock the bar was jammed; amidst the consequent mixture of voices the staff of waiters functioned, pinning down their clients to the facts of drink and money.

"That makes two stingers ... and one more ... two martinis and one ... nothing for you, Mr. Quarterly ... that makes three rounds. That makes seventy-five francs, Mr. Quarterly. Mr. Schaeffer said he had this—you had the last ... I can only do what you say ... thanks veramuch."

In the confusion Abe had lost his seat; now he stood gently swaying and talking to some of the people with whom he had involved himself. A terrier ran a leash around his legs but Abe managed to extricate himself without upsetting and became the recipient of profuse apologies. Presently he was invited to lunch, but declined. It was almost Briglith, he explained, and there was something he had to do at Briglith. A little later, with the exquisite manners of the alcoholic that are like the manners of a prisoner or a family servant, he said good-by to an acquaintance, and turning around discovered that the bar's great moment was over as precipitately as it had begun.

Across from him the Dane and his companions had ordered luncheon. Abe did likewise but scarcely touched it. Afterwards, he just sat, happy to live in the past. The drink made past happy things contemporary with the present, as if they were still going on, contemporary even with the future as if they were about to happen again.

At four the chasseur approached him:

"You wish to see a colored fellow of the name Jules Peterson?"

"God! How did he find me?"

"I didn't tell him you were present."

"Who did?" Abe fell over his glasses but recovered himself.

"Says he's already been around to all the American bars and hotels."

"Tell him I'm not here—" As the chasseur turned away Abe asked: "Can he come in here?"

"I'll find out."

Receiving the question Paul glanced over his shoulder; he shook his head, then seeing Abe he came over.

"I'm sorry; I can't allow it."

Abe got himself up with an effort and went out to the rue Cambon.

## XXIV

WITH his miniature leather brief-case in his hand Richard Diver walked from the seventh arrondissement—where he left a note for Maria Wallis signed "Dicole," the word with which he and Nicole had signed communications in the first days of love—to his shirt-makers where the clerks made a fuss over him out of proportion to the money he spent. Ashamed at promising so much to these poor Englishmen, with his fine manners, his air of having the key to security, ashamed of making a tailor shift an inch of silk on his arm. Afterward he went to the bar of the Crillon and drank a small coffee and two fingers of gin.

As he entered the hotel the halls had seemed unnaturally bright; when he left he realized that it was because it had already turned dark outside. It was a windy four-o'clock night with the leaves on the Champs-Élysées singing and failing, thin and wild. Dick turned down the rue de Rivoli, walking two squares under the arcades to his bank where there was mail. Then he took a taxi and started up the Champs-Élysées through the first patter of rain, sitting alone with his love.

Back at two o'clock in the Roi George corridor the beauty of Nicole had been to the beauty of Rosemary as the beauty of Leonardo's girl was to that of the girl of an illustrator. Dick moved on through the rain, demoniac and frightened, the passions of many men inside him and nothing simple that he could see.

Rosemary opened her door full of emotions no one else knew of. She was now what is sometimes called a "little wild thing"—by twenty-four full hours she was not yet unified and she was absorbed in playing around with chaos; as if her destiny were a picture puzzle—counting benefits, counting hopes, telling off Dick, Nicole, her mother, the director she met yesterday, like stops on a string of beads.

When Dick knocked she had just dressed and been watching the rain, thinking of some poem, and of full gutters in Beverly Hills. When she opened the door she saw him as something fixed and Godlike as he had always been, as older people are to younger, rigid and unmalleable. Dick saw her with an inevitable sense of disappointment. It took him a moment to respond to the unguarded sweetness of her smile, her body calculated to a millimeter to suggest a bud yet guarantee a flower. He was conscious of the print of her wet foot on a rug through the bathroom door.

"Miss Television,"[28] he said with a lightness he did not feel. He put his gloves, his brief-case on the dressing table, his stick against the wall. His chin dominated the lines of pain around his mouth, forcing them up into his forehead and the corner of his eyes, like fear that cannot be shown in public.

"Come and sit on my lap close to me," he said softly, "and let me see about your lovely mouth."

She came over and sat there and while the dripping slowed down outside—drip—dri-i-ip, she laid her lips to the beautiful cold image she had created.

Presently she kissed him several times in the mouth, her face getting big as it came up to him; he had never seen anything so dazzling as the quality of her skin, and since sometimes beauty gives back the images of one's best thoughts he thought of his responsibility about Nicole, and of the possibility of her being two doors down across the corridor.

"The rain's over," he said. "Do you see the sun on the slate?"

Rosemary stood up and leaned down and said her most sincere thing to him:

"Oh, we're such *actors*—you and I."

She went to her dresser and the moment that she laid her comb flat against her hair there was a slow persistent knocking at the door.

They were shocked motionless; the knock was repeated insistently, and in the sudden realization that the door was not locked Rosemary finished her hair with one stroke, nodded at Dick who had quickly jerked the wrinkles out of the bed where they had been sitting, and started for the door. Dick said in quite a natural voice, not too loud:

"—so if you don't feel up to going out, I'll tell Nicole and we'll have a very quiet last evening."

The precautions were needless for the situation of the parties outside the door was so harassed as to preclude any but the most fleeting judgments on matters not pertinent to themselves. Standing there was Abe, aged by several months in the last twenty-four hours, and a very frightened, concerned colored man whom Abe introduced as Mr. Peterson of Stockholm.

"He's in a terrible situation and it's my fault," said Abe. "We need some good advice."

"Come in our rooms," said Dick.

Abe insisted that Rosemary come too and they crossed the hall to the Divers' suite. Jules Peterson, a small, respectable Negro, on the suave model that heels the Republican party in the border states, followed.

It appeared that the latter had been a legal witness to the early morning dispute in Montparnasse; he had accompanied Abe to the police station and supported his assertion that a thousand-franc note had been seized out of his hand by a Negro, whose identification was one of the points of the case. Abe and Jules Peterson, accompanied by an agent of police, returned to the bistro and too hastily identified as the criminal a Negro, who, so it was established after an hour, had only entered the place after Abe left. The police had further complicated the situation by arresting the prominent Negro restaurateur, Freeman, who had only drifted through the alcoholic fog at a very early stage and then vanished. The true culprit, whose case, as reported by his friends, was that he had merely commandeered a fifty-franc note to pay for drinks that Abe had ordered, had only recently and in a somewhat sinister rôle, reappeared upon the scene.

In brief, Abe had succeeded in the space of an hour in entangling himself with the personal lives, consciences, and emotions of one Afro-European and three Afro-Americans inhabiting the Latin Quarter. The disentanglement was not even faintly in sight and the day had passed in an atmosphere of unfamiliar Negro faces bobbing up in unexpected places and around unexpected corners, and insistent Negro voices on the phone.

In person, Abe had succeeded in evading all of them, save Jules Peterson. Peterson was rather in the position of the friendly Indian who had helped a white. The Negroes who suffered from the betrayal were not so much after Abe as after Peterson, and Peterson was very much after what protection he might get from Abe.

Up in Stockholm Peterson had failed as a small manufacturer of shoe polish and now possessed only his formula and sufficient trade tools to fill a small box; however, his new protector had promised in the early hours to set him up in business in Versailles. Abe's former chauffeur was a shoemaker there and Abe had handed Peterson two hundred francs on account.

Rosemary listened with distaste to this rigmarole; to appreciate its grotesquerie required a more robust sense of humor than hers. The little man with his portable manufactory, his insincere eyes that, from time to time, rolled white semicircles of panic into view; the figure of Abe, his face as blurred as the gaunt fine lines of it would permit—all this was as remote from her as sickness.

"I ask only a chance in life," said Peterson with the sort of precise yet distorted intonation peculiar to colonial countries. "My methods are simple, my formula is so good that I was drove away from Stockholm, ruined, because I did not care to dispose of it."

Dick regarded him politely—interest formed, dissolved, he turned to Abe:

"You go to some hotel and go to bed. After you're all straight Mr. Peterson will come and see you."

"But don't you appreciate the mess that Peterson's in?" Abe protested.

"I shall wait in the hall," said Mr. Peterson with delicacy. "It is perhaps hard to discuss my problems in front of me."

He withdrew after a short travesty of a French bow; Abe pulled himself to his feet with the deliberation of a locomotive.

"I don't seem highly popular to-day."

"Popular but not probable," Dick advised him. "My advice is to leave this hotel—by way of the bar, if you want. Go to the Chambord, or if you'll need a lot of service, go over to the Majestic."

"Could I annoy you for a drink?"

"There's not a thing up here," Dick lied.

Resignedly Abe shook hands with Rosemary; he composed his face slowly, holding her hand a long time and forming sentences that did not emerge.

"You are the most—one of the most——"

She was sorry, and rather revolted at his dirty hands, but she laughed in a well-bred way, as though it were nothing unusual to her to watch man walking in a slow dream.

Often people display a curious respect for a man drunk, rather like the respect of simple races for the insane. Respect rather than fear. There is something awe-inspiring in one who has lost all inhibitions, who will do anything. Of course we make him pay afterward for his moment of superiority, his moment of impressiveness. Abe turned to Dick with a last appeal.

"If I go to a hotel and get all steamed and curry-combed, and sleep awhile, and fight off these Senegalese—could I come and spend the evening by the fireside?"

Dick nodded at him, less in agreement than in mockery and said: "You have a high opinion of your current capacities."

"I bet if Nicole was here she'd let me come back."

"All right." Dick went to a trunk tray and brought a box to the central table; inside were innumerable cardboard letters.

"You can come if you want to play anagrams."

Abe eyed the contents of the box with physical revulsion, as though he had been asked to eat them like oats.

"What are anagrams? Haven't I had enough strange——"

"It's a quiet game. You spell words with them—any word except alcohol."

"I bet you can spell alcohol," Abe plunged his hand among the counters. "Can I come back if I can spell alcohol?"

"You can come back if you want to play anagrams."

Abe shook his head resignedly.

"If you're in that frame of mind there's no use—I'd just be in the way." He waved his finger reproachfully at Dick. "But remember what George the Third said, that if Grant[29] was drunk he wished he would bite the other generals."

With a last desperate glance at Rosemary from the golden corners of his eyes, he went out. To his relief Peterson was no longer in the corridor. Feeling lost and homeless he went back to ask Paul the name of that boat.

# XXV

WHEN he had tottered out, Dick and Rosemary embraced fleetingly. There was a dust of Paris over both of them through which they scented each other: the rubber guard on Dick's fountain pen, the faintest odor of warmth from Rosemary's neck and shoulders. For another half-minute Dick clung to the situation; Rosemary was first to return to reality.

"I must go, youngster," she said.

They blinked at each other across a widening space, and Rosemary made an exit that she had learned young, and on which no director had ever tried to improve.

She opened the door of her room and went directly to her desk where she had suddenly remembered leaving her wristwatch. It was there; slipping it on she glanced down at the daily letter to her mother, finishing the last sentence in her mind. Then, rather gradually, she realized without turning about that she was not alone in the room.

In an inhabited room there are refracting objects only half noticed: varnished wood, more or less polished brass, silver and ivory, and beyond these a thousand conveyers of light and shadow so mild that one scarcely thinks of them as that, the tops of picture-frames, the edges of pencils or ash-trays, of crystal or china ornaments; the totality of this refraction— appealing to equally subtle reflexes of the vision as well as to those associational fragments in the subconscious that we seem to hang on to, as a glass-fitter keeps the irregularly shaped pieces that may do some time—this fact might account for what Rosemary afterward mystically described as "realizing" that there was some one in the room, before she could determine it. But when she did realize it she turned swift in a sort of ballet step and saw that a dead Negro was stretched upon her bed.

_murder_

As she cried "aaouu!" and her still unfastened wristwatch banged against the desk she had the preposterous idea that it was Abe North. Then she dashed for the door and across the hall.

Dick was straightening up; he had examined the gloves worn that day and thrown them into a pile of soiled gloves in a corner of a trunk. He had hung up coat and vest and spread his shirt on another hanger—a trick of his own. "You'll wear a shirt that's a little dirty where you won't wear a mussed shirt." Nicole had come in and was dumping one of Abe's extraordinary ash-trays into the waste-basket when Rosemary tore into the room.

"*Dick! Dick!* Come and see!"

Dick jogged across the hall into her room. He knelt to Peterson's heart, and felt the pulse—the body was warm, the face, harassed and indirect in life, was gross and bitter in death; the box of materials was held under one arm but the shoe that dangled over the bedside was bare of polish and its sole was worn through. By French law Dick had no right to touch the body but he moved the arm a little to see something—there was a stain on the green coverlet, there would be faint blood on the blanket beneath.

Dick closed the door and stood thinking; he heard cautious steps in the corridor and then Nicole calling him by name. Opening the door he whispered: "Bring the couverture and top blanket from one of our beds—don't let any one see you." Then, noticing the strained look on her face, he added quickly, "Look here, you mustn't get upset over this—it's only some nigger scrap."

"I want it to be over."

The body, as Dick lifted it, was light and ill-nourished. He held it so that further hemorrhages from the wound would flow into the man's clothes. Laying it beside the bed he stripped off the coverlet and top blanket and then opening the door an inch, listened—there was a clank of dishes down the hall followed by a loud patronizing "Merci, Madame," but the waiter went in the other direction, toward the service stairway. Quickly Dick and Nicole exchanged bundles across the corridor; after spreading this covering on Rosemary's bed, Dick stood sweating in the warm twilight, considering. Certain points had become apparent to him in the moment following his examination of the body; first, that Abe's first hostile Indian had tracked the friendly Indian and discovered him in the corridor, and when the latter had taken desperate refuge in Rosemary's room, had hunted down and slain him; second, that if the situation were allowed to develop naturally, no power on earth could keep the smear off Rosemary—the paint was scarcely dry on the Arbuckle case.[30] Her contract was contingent upon an obligation to continue rigidly and unexceptionally as "Daddy's Girl."

*D.D.*
*protecting*
*R's*
*career*

Automatically Dick made the old motion of turning up his sleeves though he wore a sleeveless undershirt, and bent over the body. Getting a purchase on the shoulders of the coat he kicked open the door with his heel, and dragged the body quickly into a plausible position in the corridor. He came back into Rosemary's room and smoothed back the grain of the plush floor rug. Then he went to the phone in his suite and called the manager-owner of the hotel.

"McBeth?[31]—it's Doctor Diver speaking—something very important. Are we on a more or less private line?"

It was good that he had made the extra effort which had firmly entrenched him with Mr. McBeth. Here was one use for all the pleasingness that Dick had expended over a large area he would never retrace. . . .

"Going out of the suite we came on a dead Negro . . . in the hall . . . no, no, he's a civilian. Wait a minute now—I knew you didn't want any guests to blunder on the body so I'm phoning you. Of course I must ask you to keep my name out of it. I don't want any French red tape just because I discovered the man."

What exquisite consideration for the hotel! Only because Mr. McBeth, with his own eyes, had seen these traits in Doctor Diver two nights before, could he credit the story without question.

In a minute Mr. McBeth arrived and in another minute he was joined by a gendarme. In the interval he found time to whisper to Dick, "You can be sure the name of any guest will be protected. I'm only too grateful to you for your pains."

Mr. McBeth took an immediate step that may only be imagined, but that influenced the gendarme so as to make him pull his mustaches in a frenzy of uneasiness and greed. He made perfunctory notes and sent a telephone call to his post. Meanwhile with a celerity that Jules Peterson, as a business man, would have quite understood, the remains were carried into another apartment of one of the most fashionable hotels in the world.

Dick went back to his salon.

"What *hap*pened?" cried Rosemary. "Do all the Americans in Paris just shoot at each other all the time?"

"This seems to be the open season," he answered. "Where's Nicole?"

"I think she's in the bathroom."

She adored him for saving her—disasters that could have attended upon the event had passed in prophecy through her mind; and she had listened in wild worship to his strong, sure, polite voice making it all right. But before she reached him in a sway of soul and body his attention focussed on something else: he went into the bedroom and toward the bathroom. And now Rosemary, too, could hear, louder and louder, a verbal inhumanity that penetrated the keyholes *secrets* and the cracks in the doors, swept into the suite and in the shape of horror took form again.

With the idea that Nicole had fallen in the bathroom and hurt herself, Rosemary followed Dick. That was not *D.D. doesn't want R. to know* the condition of affairs at which she stared before Dick shouldered her back and brusquely blocked her view.

Nicole knelt beside the tub swaying sidewise and sidewise. "It's you!" she cried, "—it's you come to intrude on the only privacy I have in the world—with your spread with red blood on it. I'll wear it for you—I'm not ashamed, though it was such a pity. On All Fools Day we had a party on the Zürichsee, and all the fools were there, and I wanted to come dressed in a spread but they wouldn't let me——"

"Control yourself!" *Nicole's breakdown*

"—so I sat in the bathroom and they brought me a *cape & mask?* domino and said wear that. I did. What else could I do?"

"Control yourself, Nicole!"

"I never expected you to love me—it was too late—only don't come in the bathroom, the only place I can go for

125

*Jealousy*

privacy, dragging spreads with red blood on them and asking me to fix them."

"Control yourself. Get up——"

Rosemary, back in the salon, heard the bathroom door bang, and stood trembling: now she knew what Violet McKisco had seen in the bathroom at Villa Diana. She answered the ringing phone and almost cried with relief when she found it was Collis Clay, who had traced her to the Divers' apartment. She asked him to come up while she got her hat, because she was afraid to go into her room alone.

Jealousy → Dick in room w/ Rosemary

**BOOK II**

objective is
Dick

- Dick being 'bought' by Warren family
  in marriage to Nicole.

- façades

- Warren family = ducal
                  'ducke

# I

In the spring of 1917, when Doctor Richard Diver first arrived in Zurich, he was twenty-six years old, a fine age for a man, indeed the very acme of bachelorhood. Even in war-time days, it was a fine age for Dick, who was already too valuable, too much of a capital investment to be shot off in a gun. Years later it seemed to him that even in this sanctuary he did not escape lightly, but about that he never fully made up his mind—in 1917 he laughed at the idea, saying apologetically that the war didn't touch him at all. Instructions from his local board were that he was to complete his studies in Zurich and take a degree as he had planned.

Switzerland was an island, washed on one side by the waves of thunder around Gorizia and on another by the cataracts along the Somme and the Aisne. For once there seemed more intriguing strangers than sick ones in the cantons, but that had to be guessed at—the men who whispered in the little cafés of Berne and Geneva were as likely to be diamond salesmen or commercial travellers. However, no one had missed the long trains of blinded or one-legged men, or dying trunks, that crossed each other between the bright lakes of Constance and Neuchâtel. In the bier-halls and shop-windows were bright posters presenting the Swiss defending their frontiers in 1914—with inspiring ferocity young men and old men glared down from the mountains at phantom French and Germans; the purpose was to assure the Swiss heart that it had shared the contagious glory of those days. As the massacre continued the posters withered away, and no country was more surprised than its sister republic when the United States bungled its way into the war.

Doctor Diver had seen around the edges of the war by that time: he was an Oxford Rhodes Scholar from Connecticut in 1914. He returned home for a final year at

Johns Hopkins, and took his degree. In 1916 he managed to get to Vienna under the impression that, if he did not make haste, the great Freud would eventually succumb to an aeroplane bomb. Even then Vienna was old with death but Dick managed to get enough coal and oil to sit in his room in the Damenstiftgasse and write the pamphlets that he later destroyed, but that, rewritten, were the backbone of the book he published in Zurich in 1920.

Most of us have a favorite, a heroic period, in our lives and that was Dick Diver's. For one thing he had no idea that he was charming, that the affection he gave and inspired was anything unusual among healthy people. In his last year at New Haven some one referred to him as "lucky Dick"—the name lingered in his head.

"Lucky Dick, you big stiff," he would whisper to himself, walking around the last sticks of flame in his room. "You hit it, my boy. Nobody knew it was there before you came along."

At the beginning of 1917, when it was becoming difficult to find coal, Dick burned for fuel almost a hundred textbooks that he had accumulated; but only, as he laid each one on the fire, with an assurance chuckling inside him that he was himself a digest of what was within the book, that he could brief it five years from now, if it deserved to be briefed. This went on at any odd hour, if necessary, with a floor rug over his shoulders, with the fine quiet of the scholar which is nearest of all things to heavenly peace—but which, as will presently be told, had to end.

For its temporary continuance he thanked his body that had done the flying rings at New Haven, and now swam in the winter Danube. With Elkins, second secretary at the Embassy, he shared an apartment, and there were two nice girl visitors—which was that and not too much of it, nor too much of the Embassy either. His contact with Ed Elkins aroused in him a first faint doubt as to the quality of his mental processes; he could not feel that they were profoundly different from the thinking of Elkins—Elkins, who would name you all the quarterbacks at New Haven for thirty years.

130

"—And Lucky Dick can't be one of these clever men; he must be less intact, even faintly destroyed. If life won't do it for him it's not a substitute to get a disease, or a broken heart, or an inferiority complex, though it'd be nice to build out some broken side till it was better than the original structure."

He mocked at his reasoning, calling it specious and "American"—his criterion of uncerebral phrase-making was that it was American. He knew, though, that the price of his intactness was incompleteness.

"The best I can wish you, my child," so said the Fairy Blackstick[32] in Thackeray's *The Rose and the Ring*, "is a little misfortune."

In some moods he griped at his own reasoning: Could I help it that Pete Livingstone sat in the locker-room Tap Day when everybody looked all over hell for him? And I got an election when otherwise I wouldn't have got Elihu, knowing so few men. He was good and right and I ought to have sat in the locker-room instead. Maybe I would, if I'd thought I had a chance at an election. But Mercer kept coming to my room all those weeks. I guess I knew I had a chance all right, all right. But it would have served me right if I'd swallowed my pin in the shower and set up a conflict.

After the lectures at the university he used to argue this point with a young Rumanian intellectual who reassured him: "There's no evidence that Goethe ever had a 'conflict' in the modern sense, or a man like Jung, for instance. You're not a romantic philosopher—you're a scientist. Memory, force, character—especially good sense. That's going to be your trouble—judgment about yourself. Once I knew a man who worked two years on the brain of an armadillo, with the idea that he would sooner or later know more about the brain of an armadillo than any one. I kept arguing with him that he was not really pushing out the extension of the human range—it was too arbitrary. And sure enough, when he sent his work to the medical journal they refused it—they had just accepted a thesis by another man on the same subject."

Dick got up to Zurich on less Achilles' heels than would be required to equip a centipede, but with plenty—the illusions of eternal strength and health, and of the essential goodness of people; illusions of a nation, the lies of generations of frontier mothers who had to croon falsely that there were no wolves outside the cabin door. After he took his degree, he received his orders to join a neurological unit forming in Bar-sur-Aube.

*idealist*

In France, to his disgust, the work was executive rather than practical. In compensation he found time to complete the short textbook and assemble the material for his next venture. He returned to Zurich in the spring of 1919 discharged.

The foregoing has the ring of a biography, without the satisfaction of knowing that the hero, like Grant, lolling in his general store in Galena, is ready to be called to an intricate destiny. Moreover it is confusing to come across a youthful photograph of some one known in a rounded maturity and gaze with a shock upon a fiery, wiry, eagle-eyed stranger. Best to be reassuring—Dick Diver's moment now began.

*Ulysses S. Grant*

## II

It was a damp April day, with long diagonal clouds over the Albishorn and water inert in the low places. Zurich is not unlike an American city. Missing something ever since his arrival two days before, Dick perceived that it was the sense he had had in finite French lanes that there was nothing more. In Zurich there was a lot besides Zurich—the roofs upled the eyes to tinkling cow pastures, which in turn modified hilltops further up—so life was a perpendicular starting off to a postcard heaven. The Alpine lands, home of the toy and the funicular, the merry-go-round and the thin chime, were not a being *here*, as in France, with French vines growing over one's feet on the ground.

In Salzburg once Dick had felt the superimposed quality

of a bought and borrowed century of music; once in the laboratories of the University in Zurich, delicately poking at the cervical of a brain, he had felt like a toy-maker rather than like the tornado who had hurried through the old red buildings of Hopkins, two years before, unstayed by the irony of the gigantic Christ in the entrance hall.

Yet he had decided to remain another two years in Zurich, for he did not underestimate the value of toy-making, of infinite precision, of infinite patience.

To-day he went out to see Franz Gregorovious at Dohmler's clinic on the Zürichsee. Franz, resident pathologist at the clinic, a Vaudois by birth, a few years older than Dick, met him at the tram stop. He had a dark and magnificent aspect of Cagliostro about him, contrasted with holy eyes; he was the third of the Gregoroviouses—his grandfather had instructed Kraepelin[33] when psychiatry was just emerging from the darkness of all time. In personality he was proud, fiery, and sheep-like—he fancied himself as a hypnotist. If the original genius of the family had grown a little tired, Franz would without doubt become a fine clinician.

On the way to the clinic he said: "Tell me of your experiences in the war. Are you changed like the rest? You have the same stupid and unaging American face, except I know you're not stupid, Dick."

"I didn't see any of the war—you must have gathered that from my letters Franz."

"That doesn't matter—we have some shell-shocks who merely heard an air raid from a distance. We have a few who merely read newspapers."

"It sounds like nonsense to me."

"Maybe it is, Dick. But, we're a rich person's clinic—we don't use the word nonsense. Frankly, did you come down to see me or to see that girl?" *Nicole?*

They looked sideways at each other; Franz smiled enigmatically.

"Naturally I saw all the first letters," he said in his official basso. "When the change began, delicacy prevented me from opening any more. Really it had become your case."

"Then she's well?" Dick demanded.

133

"Perfectly well, I have charge of her, in fact I have charge of the majority of the English and American patients. They call me Doctor Gregory."

"Let me explain about that girl," Dick said. "I only saw her one time, that's a fact. When I came out to say good-by to you just before I went over to France. It was the first time I put on my uniform and I felt very bogus in it—went around saluting privates and all that."

"Why didn't you wear it to-day?"

"Hey! I've been discharged three weeks. Here's the way I happened to see that girl. When I left you I walked down toward that building of yours on the lake to get my bicycle."

"Toward the Cedars?"

"—a wonderful night, you know—moon over that mountain——"

"The Krenzegg."

"—I caught up with a nurse and a young girl. I didn't think the girl was a patient; I asked the nurse about tram times and we walked along. The girl was about the prettiest thing I ever saw."

"She still is."

"She'd never seen an American uniform and we talked, and I didn't think anything about it." He broke off, recognizing a familiar perspective, and then resumed: "—except, Franz, I'm not as hard-boiled as you are yet; when I see a beautiful shell like that I can't help feeling a regret about what's inside it. That was absolutely all—till the letters began to come."

"It was the best thing that could have happened to her," said Franz dramatically, "a transference[34] of the most fortuitous kind. That's why I came down to meet you on a very busy day. I want you to come into my office and talk a long time before you see her. In fact, I sent her into Zurich to do errands." His voice was tense with enthusiasm. "In fact, I sent her without a nurse, with a less stable patient. I'm intensely proud of this case, which I handled, with your accidental assistance."

The car had followed the shore of the Zürichsee into a fertile region of pasture farms and low hills, steepled with châlets. The sun swam out into a blue sea of sky and suddenly it was a Swiss valley at its best—pleasant sounds and murmurs and a good fresh smell of health and cheer.

Professor Dohmler's plant consisted of three old buildings and a pair of new ones, between a slight eminence and the shore of the lake. At its founding, ten years before, it had been the first modern clinic for mental illness; at a casual glance no layman would recognize it as a refuge for the broken, the incomplete, the menacing, of this world, though two buildings were surrounded with vine-softened walls of a deceptive height. Some men raked straw in the sunshine; here and there, as they rode into the grounds, the car passed the white flag of a nurse waving beside a patient on a path.

*mental Clinic*

After conducting Dick to his office, Franz excused himself for half an hour. Left alone Dick wandered about the room and tried to reconstruct Franz from the litter of his desk, from his books and the books of and by his father and grandfather; from the Swiss piety of a huge claret-colored photo of the former on the wall. There was smoke in the room; pushing open a French window, Dick let in a cone of sunshine. Suddenly his thoughts swung to the patient, the girl.

He had received about fifty letters from her written over a period of eight months. The first one was apologetic, explaining that she had heard from America how girls wrote to soldiers whom they did not know. She had obtained the name and address from Doctor Gregory and she hoped he would not mind if she sometimes sent word to wish him well, etc., etc.

So far it was easy to recognize the tone—from *Daddy-Long-Legs* and *Molly-Make-Believe*,[35] sprightly and sentimental epistolary collections enjoying a vogue in the States. But there the resemblance ended.

The letters were divided into two classes, of which the first class, up to about the time of the Armistice, was of marked pathological turn, and of which the second class, running from thence up to the present, was entirely normal, and displayed a richly maturing nature. For these latter letters Dick had come to wait eagerly in the last dull months at Bar-sur-Aube—yet even from the first letters he had pieced together more than Franz would have guessed of the story.

MON CAPITAINE:

I thought when I saw you in your uniform you were so handsome. Then I thought Je m'en fiche French too and German. You thought I was pretty too but I've had that before and a long time I've stood it. If you come here again with that attitude base and criminal and not even faintly what I had been taught to associate with the role of gentleman then heaven help you. However, you seem quieter than the others, all soft like a big cat. I

(2)

have only gotten to like boys who are rather sissies. Are you a sissy? There were some somewhere.

Excuse all this, it is the third letter I have written you and will send immediately or will never send. I've thought a lot about moonlight too, and there are many witnesses I could find if I could only be out of here.

(3)

They said you were a doctor, but so long as you are a cat it is different. My head aches so, so excuse this walking there like an ordinary with a white cat will explain, I think. I can speak three languages, four with English, and am sure I could be useful interpreting if you arrange such thing in France I'm sure I could control everything with the belts all bound around everybody like it was Wednesday. It is now Saturday and you are far away, per-

(4)

haps killed.

Come back to me some day, for I will be here always on this green hill. Unless they will let me write my father, whom I loved dearly.

Excuse this. I am not myself today. I will write when I feel better.

Cherio

NICOLE WARREN.

Excuse all this.

**CAPTAIN DIVER:**

I know introspection is not good for a highly nervous state like mine, but I would like you to know where I stand. Last year or whenever it was in Chicago when I got so I couldn't speak to servants or walk in the street I kept waiting for some one to tell me. It was the duty of some one who understood. The blind must be led. Only no one would tell me everything—they would just tell me half and I was already too muddled to put two and two together. [One man was nice—he was a French officer and he understood. He gave me a flower and said it was "plus petite

(2)   *"deflowering"*

et moins entendue." We were friends. Then he took it away.] I grew sicker and there was no one to explain to me. They had a song about Joan of Arc that they used to sing at me but that was just mean—it would just make me cry, for there was nothing the matter with my head then. They kept making reference to sports, too, but I didn't care by that time. <u>So there was that day I went walking on Michigan Boulevard on and on for miles and finally</u>

(3)

<u>they followed me in an automobile, but I wouldn't get in. Finally they pulled me in and there were nurses.</u> After that time I began to realize it all, because I could feel what was happening in others. So you see how I stand. And what good can it be for me to stay here with the doctors harping constantly on the things I was here to get over. So today I have written my father to come and take

(4)

me away. I am glad you are so interested in examining people and sending them back. It must be so much fun.

And again, from another letter:

You might pass up your next examination and write me a letter. They just sent me some phonograph records in case I should forget my lesson and I broke them all so the nurse won't speak to me. They were in English, so that the nurses would not understand. One doctor in Chicago said I was bluffing, but what he really meant was that I was a twin six and he had never seen one before. But I was very busy being mad then, so I didn't care what he said, when I am very busy being mad I don't usually care what they say, not if I were a million girls.

You told me that night you'd teach me to play. Well, I think

*Nicole's father*

love is all there is or should be. Anyhow I am glad your interest in examinations keeps you busy.

Tout à vous,

NICOLE WARREN.

There were other letters among whose helpless cæsuras lurked darker rhythms:

DEAR CAPTAIN DIVER:

I write to you because there is no one else to whom I can turn and it seems to me if this farcicle situation is apparent to one as sick as me it should be apparent to you. The mental trouble is all over and besides that I am completely broken and humiliated, if that was what they wanted. My family have shamefully neglected me, there's no use asking them for help or pity. I have had enough and it is simply ruining my health and wasting my time

pretending that what is the matter with my head is curable.

Here I am in what appears to be a semi-insane-asylum, all because nobody saw fit to tell me the truth about anything. If I had only known what was going on like I know now I could have stood it I guess for I am pretty strong, but those who should have, did not see fit to enlighten me. And now, when I know and

have paid such a price for knowing, they sit there with their dogs lives and say I should believe what I did believe. Especially one does but I know now.

I am lonesome all the time far away from friends and family across the Atlantic I roam all over the place in a half daze. If you could get me a position as interpreter (I know French and

German like a native, fair Italian and a little Spanish) or in the Red Cross Ambulance or as a train nurse, though I would have to train you would prove a great blessing.

And again:

Since you will not accept my explanation of what is the matter you could at least explain to me what you think, because you have a kind cat's face, and not that funny look that seems to be so fashionable here. Dr. Gregory gave me a snapshot of you, not as handsome as you are in your uniform, but younger looking.

MON CAPITAINE:

It was fine to have your postcard. I am so glad you take such interest in disqualifying nurses—oh, I understood your note very well indeed. Only I thought from the moment I met you that you were different.

DEAR CAPITAINE:

I think one thing today and another tomorrow. That is really all that's the matter with me, except a crazy defiance and a lack of proportion. I would gladly welcome any alienist you might suggest. Here they lie in their bath tubs and sing Play in Your Own Backyard as if I had my backyard to play in or any hope

(2)

which I can find by looking either backward or forward. They tried it again in the candy store again and I almost hit the man with the weight, but they held me.

I am not going to write you any more. I am too unstable.

And then a month with no letters. And then suddenly the change.

—I am slowly coming back to life. . . .
—Today the flowers and the clouds. . . .
—The war is over and I scarcely knew there was a war. . . .
—How kind you have been! You must be very wise behind your face like a white cat, except you don't look like that in the picture Dr. Gregory gave me. . . .
—Today I went to Zurich, how strange a feeling to see a city again.
—Today we went to Berne, it was so nice with the clocks.
—Today we climbed high enough to find asphodel and edelweiss. . . .

After that the letters were fewer, but he answered them all. There was one:

I wish someone were in love with me like boys were ages ago before I was sick. I suppose it will be years, though, before I could think of anything like that.

139

But when Dick's answer was delayed for any reason, there was a fluttering burst of worry—like a worry of a lover: "Perhaps I have bored you," and "Afraid I have presumed," and "I keep thinking at night you have been sick."

In actuality Dick was sick with the flu. When he recovered, all except the formal part of his correspondence was sacrificed to the consequent fatigue, and shortly afterward the memory of her became overlaid by the vivid presence of a Wisconsin telephone girl at headquarters in Bar-sur-Aube. She was red-lipped like a poster, and known obscenely in the messes as "The Switchboard."

Franz came back into his office feeling self-important. Dick thought he would probably be a fine clinician, for the sonorous or staccato cadences by which he disciplined nurse or patient came not from his nervous system but from a tremendous and harmless vanity. His true emotions were more ordered and kept to himself.

"Now about the girl, Dick," he said. "Of course, I want to find out about you and tell you about myself, but first about the girl, because I have been waiting to tell you about it so long."

He searched for and found a sheaf of papers in a filing cabinet but after shuffling through them he found they were in his way and put them on his desk. Instead he told Dick the story.

### III

ABOUT a year and a half before, Doctor Dohmler had some vague correspondence with an American gentleman living in Lausanne, a Mr. Devereux Warren,[36] of the Warren family of Chicago. A meeting was arranged and one day Mr. Warren arrived at the clinic with his daughter Nicole, a girl of sixteen. She was obviously not well and the nurse who was with her took her to walk about the grounds while Mr. Warren had his consultation.

Warren was a strikingly handsome man looking less than

forty. He was a fine American type in every way, tall, broad, well-made—"un homme très chic," as Doctor Dohmler described him to Franz. His large gray eyes were sun-veined from rowing on Lake Geneva, and he had that special air about him of having known the best of this world. The conversation was in German, for it developed that he had been educated at Göttingen. He was nervous and obviously very moved by his errand.

"Doctor Dohmler, my daughter isn't right in the head. I've had lots of specialists and nurses for her and she's taken a couple of rest cures but the thing has grown too big for me and I've been strongly recommended to come to you."

"Very well," said Doctor Dohmler. "Suppose you start at the beginning and tell me everything."

"There isn't any beginning, at least there isn't any insanity in the family that I know of, on either side. Nicole's mother died when she was eleven and I've sort of been father and mother both to her, with the help of governesses—father and mother both to her."

He was very moved as he said this. Doctor Dohmler saw that there were tears in the corners of his eyes and noticed for the first time that there was whiskey on his breath.

"As a child she was a darling thing—everybody was crazy about her, everybody that came in contact with her. She was smart as a whip and happy as the day is long. She liked to read or draw or dance or play the piano—anything. I used to hear my wife say she was the only one of our children who never cried at night. I've got an older girl, too, and there was a boy that died, but Nicole was—Nicole was—Nicole——"

He broke off and Doctor Dohmler helped him.

"She was a perfectly normal, bright, happy child."

"Perfectly."

Doctor Dohmler waited. Mr. Warren shook his head, blew a long sigh, glanced quickly at Doctor Dohmler and then at the floor again.

"About eight months ago, or maybe it was six months ago or maybe ten—I try to figure but I can't remember exactly where we were when she began to do funny things—crazy things. Her sister was the first one to say anything to me about it—because Nicole was always the same to me," he added rather hastily, as if some one had accused him of being to blame, "—the same loving little girl. The first thing was about a valet."

"Oh, yes," said Doctor Dohmler, nodding his venerable head, as if, like Sherlock Holmes, he had expected a valet and only a valet to be introduced at this point.

"I had a valet—been with me for years—Swiss, by the way." He looked up for Doctor Dohmler's patriotic approval. "And she got some crazy idea about him. She thought he was making up to her—of course, at the time I believed her and I let him go, but I know now it was all nonsense."

"What did she claim he had done?"

"That was the first thing—the doctors couldn't pin her down. She just looked at them as if they ought to know what he'd done. But she certainly meant he'd made some kind of indecent advances to her—she didn't leave us in any doubt of that."

"I see."

"Of course, I've read about women getting lonesome and thinking there's a man under the bed and all that, but why should Nicole get such an idea? She could have all the young men she wanted. We were in Lake Forest—that's a summer place near Chicago where we have a place—and she was out all day playing golf or tennis with boys. And some of them pretty gone on her at that.

All the time Warren was talking to the dried old package of Doctor Dohmler, one section of the latter's mind kept thinking intermittently of Chicago. Once in his youth he could have gone to Chicago as fellow and docent at the university, and perhaps become rich there and owned his own clinic instead of being only a minor shareholder in a clinic. But when he had thought of what he considered his own thin knowledge spread over that whole area, over all those wheat fields, those endless prairies, he had decided against it. But he had read about Chicago in those days, about the great feudal families of Armour, Palmer, Field,

Crane, Warren, Swift, and McCormick and many others, and since that time not a few patients had come to him from that stratum of Chicago and New York.

"She got worse," continued Warren. "She had a fit or something—the things she said got crazier and crazier. Her sister wrote some of them down—" He handed a much-folded piece of paper to the doctor. "Almost always about men going to attack her, men she knew or men on the street—anybody——" *Schizo-phrenic*

He told of their alarm and distress, of the horrors families go through under such circumstances, of the ineffectual efforts they had made in America, finally of the faith in a change of scene that had made him run the submarine blockade and bring his daughter to Switzerland.

"—on a United States cruiser," he specified with a touch of hauteur. "It was possible for me to arrange that, by a stroke of luck. And, may I add," he smiled apologetically, "that as they say: money is no object."

"Certainly not," agreed Dohmler dryly.

He was wondering why and about what the man was lying to him. Or, if he was wrong about that, what was the falsity that pervaded the whole room, the handsome figure in tweeds sprawling in his chair with a sportsman's ease? That was a tragedy out there, in the February day, the young bird with wings crushed somehow, and inside here it was all too thin, thin and wrong.

"I would like—to talk to her—a few minutes now," said Doctor Dohmler, going into English as if it would bring him closer to Warren.

Afterward when Warren had left his daughter and returned to Lausanne, and several days had passed, the doctor and Franz entered upon Nicole's card:

Diagnostic: Schizophrénie. Phase aiguë en décroissance. La peur des hommes est un symptôme de la maladie, et n'est point constitutionnelle. . . . Le pronostic doit rester réservé.*

*Diagnosis: Divided Personality, Acute and down-hill phase of the illness. The fear of men is a symptom of the illness and is not at all constitutional. . . . The prognosis must be reserved.

143

And then they waited with increasing interest as the days passed for Mr. Warren's promised second visit.

It was slow in coming. After a fortnight Doctor Dohmler wrote. Confronted with further silence he committed what was for those days "une folie," and telephoned to the Grand Hotel at Vevey. He learned from Mr. Warren's valet that he was at the moment packing to sail for America. But reminded that the forty francs Swiss for the call would show up on the clinic books, the blood of the Tuileries Guard rose to Doctor Dohmler's aid and Mr. Warren was got to the phone.

"It is—absolutely necessary—that you come. Your daughter's health—all depends. I can take no responsibility."

"But look here, Doctor, that's just what you're for. I have a hurry call to go home!"

Doctor Dohmler had never yet spoken to any one so far away but he dispatched his ultimatum so firmly into the phone that the agonized American at the other end yielded. Half an hour after this second arrival on the Zürichsee, Warren had broken down, his fine shoulders shaking with awful sobs inside his easy-fitting coat, his eyes redder than the very sun on Lake Geneva, and they had the awful story.

"It just happened," he said hoarsely. "I don't know—I don't know.

"After her mother died when she was little she used to come into my bed every morning, sometimes she'd sleep in my bed. I was sorry for the little thing. Oh, after that, whenever we went places in an automobile or a train we used to hold hands. She used to sing to me. We used to say, 'Now let's not pay any attention to anybody else this afternoon— let's just have each other—for this morning you're mine.' " A broken sarcasm came into his voice. "People used to say what a wonderful father and daughter we were—they used to wipe their eyes. We were just like lovers—and then all at once we were lovers—and ten minutes after it happened I could have shot myself—except I guess I'm such a God-damned degenerate I didn't have the nerve to do it."

"Then what?" said Doctor Dohmler, thinking again of

*incest*

*incest*

7

144

Chicago and of a mild pale gentleman with a pince-nez who had looked him over in Zurich thirty years before. "Did this thing go on?"

"Oh, no! She almost—she seemed to freeze up right away. She'd just say, 'Never mind, never mind, Daddy. It doesn't matter. Never mind.'"

"There were no consequences?"

"No." He gave one short conclusive sob and blew his nose several times. "Except now there's plenty of consequences."

As the story concluded Dohmler sat back in the focal armchair of the middle class and said to himself sharply, "Peasant!"—it was one of the few absolute worldly judgments that he had permitted himself for twenty years. Then he said:

"I would like for you to go to a hotel in Zurich and spend the night and come see me in the morning."

"And then what?"

Doctor Dohmler spread his hands wide enough to carry a young pig.

"Chicago," he suggested. *Sends away Nicole's father.*

## IV

"THEN we knew where we stood," said Franz. "Dohmler told Warren we would take the case if he would agree to keep away from his daughter indefinitely, with an absolute minimum of five years. After Warren's first collapse, he seemed chiefly concerned as to whether the story would ever leak back to America.

"We mapped out a routine for her and waited. The prognosis was bad—as you know, the percentage of cures, even so-called social cures, is very low at that age.

"These first letters looked bad," agreed Dick.

"Very bad—very typical. I hesitated about letting the first one get out of the clinic. Then I thought it will be good for Dick to know we're carrying on here. It was generous of you to answer them."

Dick sighed. "She was such a pretty thing—she enclosed a lot of snapshots of herself. And for a month there I didn't have anything to do. All I said in my letters was 'Be a good girl and mind the doctors.' "

"That was enough—it gave her somebody to think of outside. For a while she didn't have anybody—only one sister that she doesn't seem very close to. Besides, reading her letters helped us here—they were a measure of her condition."

"I'm glad."

"You see now what happened? She felt complicity—that's neither here nor there, except as we want to revalue her ultimate stability and strength of character. First came this shock. Then she went off to a boarding-school and heard the girls talking—so from sheer self-protection she developed the idea that she had had no complicity—and from there it was easy to slide into a phantom world where all men, the more you liked them and trusted them, the more evil——"

"Did she ever go into the—horror directly?"

"No, and as a matter of fact when she began to seem normal, about October, we were in a predicament. If she had been thirty years old we would have let her make her own adjustment, but she was so young we were afraid she might harden with it all twisted inside her. So Doctor Dohmler said to her frankly, 'Your duty now is to yourself. This doesn't by any account mean the end of anything for you—your life is just at its beginning,' and so forth and so forth. She really has an excellent mind, so he gave her a little Freud to read, not too much, and she was very interested. In fact, we've made rather a pet of her around here. But she is reticent," he added; he hesitated: "We have wondered if in her recent letters to you which she mailed herself from Zurich, she has said anything that would be illuminating about her state of mind and her plans for the future."

Dick considered.

"Yes and no—I'll bring the letters out here if you want. She seems hopeful and normally hungry for life—even rather romantic. Sometimes she speaks of 'the past' as people speak who have been in prison. But you never know whether they refer to the crime or the imprisonment or the whole experience. After all I'm only a sort of stuffed figure in her life."

"Of course, I understand your position exactly, and I express our gratitude once again. That was why I wanted to see you before you see her."

Dick laughed.

"You think she's going to make a flying leap at my person?"

"No, not that. But I want to ask you to go very gently. You are attractive to women, Dick."

"Then God help me! Well, I'll be gentle and repulsive— I'll chew garlic whenever I'm going to see her and wear a stubble beard. I'll drive her to cover."

"Not garlic!" said Franz, taking him seriously. "You don't want to compromise your career. But you're partly joking."

"—and I can limp a little. And there's no real bathtub where I'm living, anyhow."

"You're entirely joking," Franz relaxed—or rather assumed the posture of one relaxed. "Now tell me about yourself and your plans?"

"I've only got one, Franz, and that's to be a good psychologist—maybe to be the greatest one that ever lived."

Franz laughed pleasantly, but he saw that this time Dick wasn't joking.

"That's very good—and very American," he said. "It's more difficult for us." He got up and went to the French window. "I stand here and I see Zurich—there is the steeple of the Gross-Münster. In its vault my grandfather is buried. Across the bridge from it lies my ancestor Lavater, who would not be buried in any church. Nearby is the statue of another ancestor, Heinrich Pestalozzi, and one of Doctor Alfred Escher. And over everything there is always Zwingli —I am continually confronted with a pantheon of heroes."[37]

"Yes, I see." Dick got up. "I was only talking big. Everything's just starting over. Most of the Americans in France are frantic to get home, but not me—I draw military pay all the rest of the year if I only attend lectures at the university.

How's that for a government on the grand scale that knows its future great men? Then I'm going home for a month and see my father. Then I'm coming back—I've been offered a job."

"Where?"

"Your rivals—Gisler's clinic on Interlaken."

"Don't touch it," Franz advised him. "They've had a dozen young men there in a year. Gisler's a manic-depressive himself, his wife and her lover run the clinic—of course, you understand that's confidential."

"How about your old scheme for America?" asked Dick lightly. "We were going to New York and start an up-to-date establishment for billionaires."

"That was students' talk."

Dick dined with Franz and his bride and a small dog with a smell of burning rubber, in their cottage on the edge of the grounds. He felt vaguely oppressed, not by the atmosphere of modest retrenchment, nor by Frau Gregorovious, who might have been prophesied, but by the sudden contracting of horizons to which Franz seemed so reconciled. For him the boundaries of asceticism were differently marked—he could see it as a means to an end, even as a carrying on with a glory it would itself supply, but it was hard to think of deliberately cutting life down to the scale of an inherited suit. The domestic gestures of Franz and his wife as they turned in a cramped space lacked grace and adventure. The post-war months in France, and the lavish liquidations taking place under the ægis of American splendor, had affected Dick's outlook. Also, men and women had made much of him, and perhaps what had brought him back to the centre of the great Swiss watch was an intuition that this was not too good for a serious man.

He made Kaethe Gregorovious feel charming, meanwhile becoming increasingly restless at the all-pervading cauliflower—simultaneously hating himself too for this incipience of he knew not what superficiality.

"God, am I like the rest after all?"—so he used to think starting awake at night—"Am I like the rest?"

This was poor material for a socialist but good material

for those who do much of the world's rarest work. The truth was that for some months he had been going through that partitioning of the things of youth wherein it is decided whether or not to die for what one no longer believes. In the dead white hours in Zurich staring into a stranger's pantry across the upshine of a street-lamp, he used to think that he wanted to be good, he wanted to be kind, he wanted to be brave and wise, but it was all pretty difficult. He wanted to be loved, too, if he could fit it in.

= p.
325

# V

THE veranda of the central building was illuminated from open French windows, save where the black shadows of stripling walls and the fantastic shadows of iron chairs slithered down into a gladiola bed. From the figures that shuffled between the rooms Miss Warren emerged first in glimpses and then sharply when she saw him; as she crossed the threshold her face caught the room's last light and brought it outside with her. She walked to a rhythm—all that week there had been singing in her ears, summer songs of ardent skies and wild shade, and with his arrival the singing had become so loud she could have joined in with it.

"How do you do, captain," she said, unfastening her eyes from his with difficulty, as though they had become entangled. "Shall we sit out here?" She stood still, her glance moving about for a moment. "It's summer practically."

A woman had followed her out, a dumpy woman in a shawl, and Nicole presented Dick: "Señora——"

Franz excused himself and Dick grouped three chairs together.

"The lovely night," the Señora said.

"Muy bella," agreed Nicole; then to Dick, "Are you here for a long time?"

"I'm in Zurich for a long time, if that's what you mean."

"This is really the first night of real spring," the Señora suggested.

149

"To stay?"

"At least till July."

"I'm leaving in June."

"June is a lovely month here," the Señora commented. "You should stay for June and then leave in July when it gets really too hot."

"You're going where?" Dick asked Nicole.

"Somewhere with my sister—somewhere exciting, I hope, because I've lost so much time. But perhaps they'll think I ought to go to a quiet place at first—perhaps Como. Why don't you come to Como?"

"Ah, Como—" began the Señora.

Within the building a trio broke into Suppé's "Light Cavalry." Nicole took advantage of this to stand up and the impression of her youth and beauty grew on Dick until it welled up inside him in a compact paroxysm of emotion. She smiled, a moving childish smile that was like all the lost youth in the world.

"The music's too loud to talk against—suppose we walk around. Buenas noches, Señora."

"G't night—g't night."[38]

They went down two steps to the path—where in a moment a shadow cut across it. She took his arm.

"I have some phonograph records my sister sent me from America," she said. "Next time you come here I'll play them for you—I know a place to put the phonograph where no one can hear."

"That'll be nice."

"Do you know 'Hindustan'?" she asked wistfully. "I'd never heard it before, but I like it. And I've got 'Why Do They Call Them Babies?' and 'I'm Glad I Can Make You Cry.' I suppose you've danced to all those tunes in Paris?"

"I haven't been to Paris."

Her cream-colored dress, alternately blue or gray as they walked, and her very blonde hair, dazzled Dick—whenever he turned toward her she was smiling a little, her face lighting up like an angel's when they came into the range of a roadside arc. She thanked him for everything, rather as if he had taken her to some party, and as Dick became less

150

and less certain of his relation to her, her confidence increased—there was that excitement about her that seemed to reflect all the excitement of the world.

"I'm not under any restraint at all," she said. "I'll play you two good tunes called 'Wait Till the Cows Come Home' and 'Good-by, Alexander.' "

He was late the next time, a week later, and Nicole was waiting for him at a point in the path which he would pass walking from Franz's house. Her hair drawn back of her ears brushed her shoulders in such a way that the face seemed to have just emerged from it, as if this were the exact moment when she was coming from a wood into clear moonlight. The unknown yielded her up; Dick wished she had no background, that she was just a girl lost with no address save the night from which she had come. They went to the cache where she had left the phonograph, turned a corner by the workshop, climbed a rock, and sat down behind a low wall, facing miles and miles of rolling night.

They were in America now, even Franz with his conception of Dick as an irresistible Lothario would never have guessed that they had gone so far away. They were so sorry, dear; they went down to meet each other in a taxi, honey; they had preferences in smiles and had met in Hindustan, and shortly afterward they must have quarrelled, for nobody knew and nobody seemed to care—yet finally one of them had gone and left the other crying, only to feel blue, to feel sad.

The thin tunes, holding lost times and future hopes in liaison, twisted upon the Swiss night. In the lulls of the phonograph a cricket held the scene together with a single note. By and by Nicole stopped playing the machine and sang to him:

"Lay a silver dollar
On the ground
And watch it roll
Because it's round—"

On the pure parting of her lips no breath hovered. Dick stood up suddenly.

"What's the matter, you don't like it?"

"Of course I do."

"Our cook at home taught it to me:

> 'A woman never knows
> What a good man she's got
> Till after she turns him down. . . .'

"You like it?"

She smiled at him, making sure that the smile gathered up everything inside her and directed it toward him, making him a profound promise of herself for so little, for the beat of a response, the assurance of a complementary vibration in him. Minute by minute the sweetness drained down into her out of the willow trees, out of the dark world.

She stood up too, and stumbling over the phonograph, was momentarily against him, leaning into the hollow of his rounded shoulder.

"I've got one more record," she said. "Have you heard 'So Long, Letty'? I suppose you have."

"Honestly, you don't understand—I haven't heard a thing."

Nor known, nor smelt, nor tasted, he might have added; only hot-cheeked girls in hot secret rooms. The young maidens he had known at New Haven in 1914 kissed men, saying "There!," hands at the man's chest to push him away. Now there was this scarcely saved waif of disaster *Nicole* bringing him the essence of a continent. . . .

# VI

IT was May when he next found her. The luncheon in Zurich was a council of caution; obviously the logic of his life tended away from the girl; yet when a stranger stared at her from a nearby table, eyes burning disturbingly like an uncharted light, he turned to the man with an urbane version of intimidation and broke the regard.

"He was just a peeper," he explained cheerfully. "He was

just looking at your clothes. Why do you have so many different clothes?"

"Sister says we're very rich," she offered humbly. "Since Grandmother is dead."

"I forgive you."

He was enough older than Nicole to take pleasure in her youthful vanities and delights, the way she paused fractionally in front of the hall mirror on leaving the restaurant, so that the incorruptible quicksilver could give her back to herself. He delighted in her stretching out her hands to new octaves now that she found herself beautiful and rich. He tried honestly to divorce her from any obsession that he had stitched her together—glad to see her build up happiness and confidence apart from him; the difficulty was that, eventually, Nicole brought everything to his feet, gifts of sacrificial ambrosia, of worshipping myrtle.

The first week of summer found Dick re-established in Zurich. He had arranged his pamphlets and what work he had done in the service into a pattern from which he intended to make his revise of *A Psychology for Psychiatrists*. He thought he had a publisher; he had established contact with a poor student who would iron out his errors in German. Franz considered it a rash business, but Dick pointed out the disarming modesty of the theme.

"This is stuff I'll never know so well again," he insisted. "I have a hunch it's a thing that only fails to be basic because it's never had material recognition. The weakness of this profession is its attraction for the man a little crippled and broken. Within the walls of the profession he compensates by tending toward the clinical, the 'practical'—he has won his battle without a struggle.

"On the contrary, you are a good man, Franz, because fate selected you for your profession before you were born. You better thank God you had no 'bent'—I got to be a psychiatrist because there was a girl at St. Hilda's in Oxford that went to the same lectures. Maybe I'm getting trite but I don't want to let my current ideas slide away with a few dozen glasses of beer."

"All right," Franz answered. "You are an American.

You can do this without professional harm. I do not like these generalities. Soon you will be writing little books called 'Deep Thoughts for the Layman,' so simplified that they are positively guaranteed not to cause thinking. If my father were alive he would look at you and grunt, Dick. He would take his napkin and fold it so, and hold his napkin ring, this very one"—he held it up, a boar's head was carved in the brown wood—"and he would say, 'Well my impression is—' then he would look at you and think suddenly, 'What is the use?' then he would stop and grunt again; then we would be at the end of dinner."

"I am alone to-day," said Dick testily. "But I may not be alone to-morrow. After that I'll fold up my napkin like your father and grunt."

Franz waited a moment.

"How about our patient?" he asked.

"I don't know."

"Well, you should know about her by now."

"I like her. She's attractive. What do you want me to do—take her up in the edelweiss?"

"No, I thought since you go in for scientific books you might have an idea."

"—devote my life to her?"

Franz called his wife in the kitchen: "Du lieber Gott! Bitte, bringe Dick noch ein Glas Bier."

"I don't want any more if I've got to see Dohmler."

"We think it's best to have a program. Four weeks have passed away—apparently the girl is in love with you. That's not our business if we were in the world, but here in the clinic we have a stake in the matter."

"I'll do whatever Doctor Dohmler says," Dick agreed.

But he had little faith that Dohmler would throw much light on the matter; he himself was the incalculable element involved. By no conscious volition of his own, the thing had drifted into his hands. It reminded him of a scene in his childhood when everyone in the house was looking for the lost key to the silver closet, Dick knowing he had hid it under the handkerchiefs in his mother's top drawer; at that time he had experienced a philosophical detachment, and this was repeated now when he and Franz went together to Professor Dohmler's office.

The professor, his face beautiful under straight whiskers, like a vine-overgrown veranda of some fine old house, disarmed him. Dick knew some individuals with more talent, but no person of a class qualitatively superior to Dohmler.

—Six months later he thought the same way when he saw Dohmler dead, the light out on the veranda, the vines of his whiskers tickling his stiff white collar, the many battles that had swayed before the chink-like eyes stilled forever under the frail delicate lids——

". . . Good morning, sir." He stood formally, thrown back to the army.

Professor Dohmler interlaced his tranquil fingers. Franz spoke in terms half of liaison officer, half of secretary, till his senior cut through him in mid-sentence.

"We have gone a certain way," he said mildly. "It's you, Doctor Diver, who can best help us now."

Routed out, Dick confessed: "I'm not so straight on it myself."

"I have nothing to do with your personal reactions," said Dohmler. "But I have much to do with the fact that this so-called 'transference,'" he darted a short ironic look at Franz which the latter returned in kind, "must be terminated. Miss Nicole does well indeed, but she is in no condition to survive what she might interpret as a tragedy."

Again Franz began to speak, but Doctor Dohmler motioned him silent.

"I realize that your position has been difficult."

"Yes, it has."

Now the professor sat back and laughed, saying on the last syllable of his laughter, with his sharp little gray eyes shining through: "Perhaps you have got sentimentally involved yourself."

Aware that he was being drawn on, Dick, too, laughed.

"She's a pretty girl—anybody responds to that to a certain extent. I have no intention——"

Again Franz tried to speak—again Dohmler stopped him with a question directed pointedly at Dick. "Have you thought of going away?"

"I can't go away."

Doctor Dohmler turned to Franz: "Then we can send Miss Warren away."

"As you think best, Professor Dohmler," Dick conceded. "It's certainly a situation."

Professor Dohmler raised himself like a legless man mounting a pair of crutches.

"But it is a professional situation," he cried quietly.

He sighed himself back into his chair, waiting for the reverberating thunder to die out about the room. Dick saw that Dohmler had reached his climax, and he was not sure that he himself had survived it. When the thunder had diminished Franz managed to get his word in.

"Doctor Diver is a man of fine character," he said. "I feel he only has to appreciate the situation in order to deal correctly with it. In my opinion Dick can co-operate right here, without any one going away."

"How do you feel about that?" Professor Dohmler asked Dick.

Dick felt churlish in the face of the situation; at the same time he realized in the silence after Dohmler's pronouncement that the state of inanimation could not be indefinitely prolonged; suddenly he spilled everything.

"I'm half in love with her—the question of marrying her has passed through my mind."

"Tch! Tch!" uttered Franz.

"Wait." Dohmler warned him. Franz refused to wait: "What! And devote half your life to being doctor and nurse and all—never! I know what these cases are. One time in twenty it's finished in the first push—better never see her again!"

"What do you think?" Dohmler asked Dick.

"Of course Franz is right."

# VII

I⟨T⟩ was late afternoon when they wound up the discussion as to what Dick should do, he must be most kind and yet eliminate himself. When the doctors stood up at last, Dick's eyes fell outside the window to where a light rain was falling—Nicole was waiting, expectant, somewhere in that rain. When, presently, he went out buttoning his oil-skin at the throat, pulling down the brim of his hat, he came upon her immediately under the roof of the main entrance.

"I know a new place we can go," she said. "When I was ill I didn't mind sitting inside with the others in the evening —what they said seemed like everything else. Naturally now I see them as ill and it's—it's——"

"You'll be leaving soon."

"Oh, soon. My sister, Beth, but she's always been called Baby, she's coming in a few weeks to take me somewhere; after that I'll be back here for a last month."

"The older sister?"

"Oh, quite a bit older. She's twenty-four—she's very English. She lives in London with my father's sister. She was engaged to an Englishman but he was killed—I never saw him."

Her face, ivory gold against the blurred sunset that strove through the rain, had a promise Dick had never seen before: the high cheek-bones, the faintly wan quality, cool rather than feverish, was reminiscent of the frame of a promising colt—a creature whose life did not promise to be only a projection of youth upon a grayer screen, but instead, a true growing; the face would be handsome in middle life; it would be handsome in old age: the essential structure and the economy were there.

"What are you looking at?"

"I was just thinking that you're going to be rather happy."

Nicole was frightened: "Am I? All right—things couldn't be worse than they have been."

In the covered woodshed to which she had led him, she sat cross-legged upon her golf shoes, her burberry wound about her and her cheeks stung alive by the damp air. Gravely she returned his gaze, taking in his somewhat proud carriage that never quite yielded to the wooden post against which he leaned; she looked into his face that always tried to discipline itself into molds of attentive seriousness, after excursions into joys and mockeries of its own. That part of him which seemed to fit his reddish Irish coloring she knew least; she was afraid of it, yet more anxious to explore —this was his more masculine side: the other part, the trained part, the consideration in the polite eyes, she expropriated without question, as most women did.

"At least this institution has been good for languages," said Nicole. "I've spoken French with two doctors, and German with the nurses, and Italian, or something like it, with a couple of scrub-women and one of the patients, and I've picked up a lot of Spanish from another."

"That's fine."

He tried to arrange an attitude but no logic seemed forthcoming."

"—Music too. Hope you didn't think I was only interested in ragtime. I practise every day—the last few months I've been taking a course in Zurich on the history of music. In fact it was all that kept me going at times—music and the drawing." She leaned suddenly and twisted a loose strip from the sole of her shoe, and then looked up. "I'd like to draw you just the way you are now."

It made him sad when she brought out her accomplishments for his approval.

"I envy you. At present I don't seem to be interested in anything except my work."

"Oh, I think that's fine for a man," she said quickly. "But for a girl I think she ought to have lots of minor accomplishments and pass them on to her children."

"I suppose so," said Dick with deliberated indifference.

Nicole sat quiet. Dick wished she would speak so that he could play the easy rôle of wet blanket, but now she sat quiet.

"You're all well," he said. "Try to forget the past; don't overdo things for a year or so. Go back to America and be a débutante and fall in love—and be happy."

"I couldn't fall in love." Her injured shoe scraped a cocoon of must from the log on which she sat.

"Sure you can," Dick insisted. "Not for a year maybe, but sooner or later." Then he added brutally: "You can have a perfectly normal life with a houseful of beautiful descendants. The very fact that you could make a complete comeback at your age proves that the precipitating factors were pretty near everything. Young woman, you'll be pulling your weight long after your friends are carried off screaming."

—But there was a look of pain in her eyes as she took the rough dose, the harsh reminder.

"I know I wouldn't be fit to marry any one for a long time," she said humbly.

Dick was too upset to say any more. He looked out into the grain field trying to recover his hard brassy attitude.

"You'll be all right—everybody here believes in you. Why, Doctor Gregory is so proud of you that he'll prob-ably——"

"I hate Doctor Gregory."

"Well, you shouldn't."

Nicole's world had fallen to pieces, but it was only a flimsy and scarcely created world; beneath it her emotions and instincts fought on. Was it an hour ago she had waited by the entrance, wearing her hope like a corsage at her belt?

... Dress stay crisp for him, button stay put, bloom narcissus—air stay still and sweet.

"It will be nice to have fun again," she fumbled on. For a moment she entertained a desperate idea of telling him how rich she was, what big houses she lived in, that really she was a valuable property—for a moment she made herself into her grandfather, Sid Warren, the horse-trader. But she survived the temptation to confuse all values and shut these matters into their Victorian side-chambers—even though there was no home left to her, save emptiness and pain.

"I have to go back to the clinic. It's not raining now."

Dick walked beside her, feeling her unhappiness, and wanting to drink the rain that touched her cheek.

"I have some new records," she said. "I can hardly wait to play them. Do you know——"

After supper that evening, Dick thought, he would finish the break; also he wanted to kick Franz's bottom for having partially introduced him to such a sordid business. He waited in the hall. His eyes followed a beret, not wet with waiting like Nicole's beret, but covering a skull recently operated on. Beneath it human eyes peered, found him and came over:

"Bonjour, Docteur."

"Bonjour, Monsieur."

"Il fait beau temps."

"Oui, merveilleux."

"Vous êtes ici maintenant?"

"Non, pour la journée seulement."

"Ah, bon. Alors—au revoir, Monsieur."

Glad at having survived another contact, the wretch in the beret moved away. Dick waited. Presently a nurse came downstairs and delivered him a message.

"Miss Warren asks to be excused, Doctor. She wants to lie down. She wants to have dinner upstairs to-night."

The nurse hung on his response, half expecting him to imply that Miss Warren's attitude was pathological.

"Oh, I see. Well—" He rearranged the flow of his own saliva, the pulse of his heart. "I hope she feels better. Thanks."

He was puzzled and discontent. At any rate it freed him.

Leaving a note for Franz begging off from supper, he walked through the countryside to the tram station. As he reached the platform, with spring twilight gilding the rails and the glass in the slot machines, he began to feel that the station, the hospital, was hovering between being centripetal and centrifugal. He felt frightened. He was glad when the substantial cobble-stones of Zurich clicked once more under his shoes.

He expected to hear from Nicole next day but there was no word. Wondering if she was ill, he called the clinic and talked to Franz.

"She came downstairs to luncheon yesterday and to-day," said Franz. "She seemed a little abstracted and in the clouds. How did it go off?"

Dick tried to plunge over the Alpine crevasse between the sexes.

"We didn't get to it—at least I didn't think we did. I tried to be distant, but I didn't think enough happened to change her attitude if it ever went deep."

Perhaps his vanity had been hurt that there was no coup de grâce to administer.

"From some things she said to her nurse I'm inclined to think she understood."

"All right."

"It was the best thing that could have happened. She doesn't seem over-agitated—only a little in the clouds."

"All right, then."

"Dick, come soon and see me."

# VIII

DURING the next weeks Dick experienced a vast dissatisfaction. The pathological origin and mechanistic defeat of the affair left a flat and metallic taste. Nicole's emotions had been used unfairly—what if they turned out to have been his own? Necessarily he must absent himself from felicity a while[39]—in dreams he saw her walking on the clinic path swinging her wide straw hat. . . .

One time he saw her in person; as he walked past the Palace Hotel, a magnificent Rolls curved into the half-moon entrance. Small within its gigantic proportions, and buoyed up by the power of a hundred superfluous horses, sat Nicole and a young woman who he assumed was her sister. Nicole saw him and momentarily her lips parted in an expression of fright. Dick shifted his hat and passed, yet for a moment the air around him was loud with the circlings of all the goblins on the Gross-Münster. He tried to write the matter out of his mind in a memorandum that went into detail as to the solemn régime before her; the possibilities of another "push" of the malady under the stresses which the world would inevitably supply—in all a memorandum that would have been convincing to any one save to him who had written it.

The total value of this effort was to make him realize once more how far his emotions were involved; thenceforth he resolutely provided antidotes. One was the telephone girl from Bar-sur-Aube, now touring Europe from Nice to Coblenz, in a desperate roundup of the men she had known in her never-to-be-equalled holiday; another was the making of arrangements to get home on a government transport in August; a third was a consequent intensification of work on his proofs for the book that this autumn was to be presented to the German-speaking world of psychiatry.

Dick had outgrown the book; he wanted now to do more spade work; if he got an exchange fellowship he could count on plenty of routine.

Meanwhile he had projected a new work: *An Attempt at a Uniform and Pragmatic Classification of the Neuroses and Psychoses, Based on an Examination of Fifteen Hundred Pre-Kraepelin and Post-Kraepelin Cases as they would be Diagnosed in the Terminology of the Different Contemporary Schools*—and another sonorous paragraph—*Together with a Chronology of Such Subdivisions of Opinion as Have Arisen Independently.*

This title would look monumental in German.*

Going into Montreux Dick pedalled slowly, gaping at the Jugenhorn whenever possible, and blinded by glimpses of the lake through the alleys of the shore hotels. He was

*Ein Versuch die Neurosen und Psychosen gleichmässig und pragmatisch zu klassifizieren auf Grund der Untersuchung von fünfzehn hundert pre-Kraepelin und post-Kraepelin Fällen wie sie diagnostiziert sein würden in der Terminologie von den verschiedenen Schulen der Gegenwart—and another sonorous paragraph— Zusammen mit einer Chronologie solcher Sub-divisionen der Meinung welche unabhängig entstanden sind.

conscious of the groups of English, emergent after four years and walking with detective-story suspicion in their eyes, as though they were about to be assaulted in this questionable country by German train-bands. There were building and awakening everywhere on this mound of débris formed by a mountain torrent. At Berne and at Lausanne on the way south, Dick had been eagerly asked if there would be Americans this year. "By August, if not in June?"

He wore leather shorts, an army shirt, mountain shoes. In his knapsack were a cotton suit and a change of underwear. At the Glion funicular he checked his bicycle and took a small beer on the terrace of the station buffet, meanwhile watching the little bug crawl down the eighty-degree slope of the hill. His ear was full of dried blood from la Tour de Peilz, where he had sprinted under the impression that he was a spoiled athlete. He asked for alcohol and cleared up the exterior while the funicular slid down into port. He saw his bicycle embarked, slung his knapsack into the lower compartment of the car, and followed it in.

Mountain-climbing cars are built on a slant similar to the angle of a hat-brim of a man who doesn't want to be recognized. As water gushed from the chamber under the car, Dick was impressed with the ingenuity of the whole idea—a complementary car was now taking on mountain water at the top and would pull the lightened car up by gravity, as soon as the brakes were released. It must have been a great inspiration. In the seat across, a couple of British were discussing the cable itself.

"The ones made in England always last five or six years. Two years ago the Germans underbid us, and how long do you think their cable lasted?"

"How long?"

"A year and ten months. Then the Swiss sold it to the Italians. They don't have rigid inspections of cables."

"I can see it would be a terrible thing for Switzerland if a cable broke."

The conductor shut a door; he telephoned his confrère among the undulati, and with a jerk the car was pulled upward, heading for a pinpoint on an emerald hill above. After it cleared the low roofs, the skies of Vaud, Valais, Savoy, and Geneva spread around the passengers in cyclorama. On the centre of the lake, cooled by the piercing current of the Rhône, lay the true centre of the Western World. Upon it floated swans like boats and boats like swans, both lost in the nothingness of the heartless beauty. It was a bright day, with sun glittering on the grass beach below and the white courts of the Kursaal. The figures on the courts threw no shadows.

When Chillon and the island palace of Salagnon came into view Dick turned his eyes inward. The funicular was above the highest houses of the shore; on both sides a tangle of foliage and flowers culminated at intervals in masses of color. It was a rail-side garden, and in the car was a sign: Défense de cueillir les fleurs.

Though one must not pick flowers on the way up, the blossoms trailed in as they passed—Dorothy Perkins roses dragged patiently through each compartment slowly waggling with the motion of the funicular, letting go at the last to swing back to their rosy cluster. Again and again these branches went through the car.

In the compartment above and in front of Dick's, a group of English were standing up and exclaiming upon the back-drop of sky, when suddenly there was a confusion among them—they parted to give passage to a couple of young people who made apologies and scrambled over into the rear compartment of the funicular—Dick's compartment. The young man was a Latin with the eyes of a stuffed deer; the girl was Nicole.

The two climbers gasped momentarily from their efforts; as they settled into seats, laughing and crowding the English to the corners, Nicole said, "Hel*lo*." She was lovely to look at; immediately Dick saw that something was different; in a second he realized it was her fine-spun hair, bobbed like Irene Castle's and fluffed into curls. She wore a sweater of powder blue and a white tennis skirt—she was the first morning in May and every taint of the clinic was departed.

"Plunk!" she gasped. "Whoo-oo that guard. They'll

arrest us at the next stop. Doctor Diver, the Conte di Marmora."

"Gee-imminy!" She felt her new hair, panting. "Sister bought first-class tickets—it's a matter of principle with her." She and Marmora exchanged glances and shouted: "Then we found that first-class is the hearse part behind the chauffeur—shut in with curtains for a rainy day, so you can't see anything. But Sister's very dignified—" Again Nicole and Marmora laughed with young intimacy.

"Where you bound?" asked Dick.

"Caux. You, too?" Nicole looked at his costume. "That your bicycle they got up in front?"

"Yes. I'm going to coast down Monday."

"With me on your handle-bars? I mean, really—will you? I can't think of more fun."

"But I will carry you down in my arms," Marmora protested intensely. "I will roller-skate you—or I will throw you and you will fall slowly like a feather."

The delight in Nicole's face—to be a feather again instead of a plummet, to float and not to drag. She was a carnival to watch—at times primly coy, posing, grimacing and gesturing—sometimes the shadow fell and the dignity of old suffering flowed down into her finger tips. Dick wished himself away from her, fearing that he was a reminder of a world well left behind. He resolved to go to the other hotel.

When the funicular came to rest those new to it stirred in suspension between the blues of two heavens. It was merely for a mysterious exchange between the conductor of the car going up and the conductor of the car coming down. Then up and up over a forest path and a gorge—then again up a hill that became solid with narcissus, from passengers to sky. The people in Montreux playing tennis in the lakeside courts were pinpoints now. Something new was in the air; freshness—freshness embodying itself in music as the car slid into Glion and they heard the orchestra in the hotel garden.

When they changed to the mountain train the music was drowned by the rushing water released from the hydraulic

165

chamber. Almost overhead was Caux, where the thousand windows of a hotel burned in the late sun.

But the approach was different—a leather-lunged engine pushed the passengers round and round in a corkscrew, mounting, rising; they chugged through low-level clouds and for a moment Dick lost Nicole's face in the spray of the slanting donkey-engine; they skirted a lost streak of wind with the hotel growing in size at each spiral, until with a vast surprise they were there, on top of the sunshine.

In the confusion of arrival, as Dick slung his knapsack and started forward on the platform to get his bicycle, Nicole was beside him.

"Aren't you at our hotel?" she asked.

"I'm economizing."

"Will you come down and have dinner?" Some confusion with baggage ensued. "This is my sister—Doctor Diver from Zurich."

Dick bowed to a young woman of twenty-five, tall and confident. She was both formidable and vulnerable, he decided, remembering other women with flower-like mouths grooved for bits.

"I'll drop in after dinner," Dick promised. "First I must get acclimated."

He wheeled off his bicycle, feeling Nicole's eyes following him, feeling her helpless first love, feeling it twist around inside him. He went three hundred yards up the slope to the other hotel, he engaged a room and found himself washing without a memory of the intervening ten minutes, only a sort of drunken flush pierced with voices, unimportant voices that did not know how much he was loved.

## IX

THEY were waiting for him and incomplete without him. He was still the incalculable element; Miss Warren and the young Italian wore their anticipation as obviously as Nicole. The salon of the hotel, a room of fabled acoustics, was stripped for dancing but there was a small gallery of Englishwomen of a certain age, with neckbands, dyed hair and faces powdered pinkish gray; and of American women of a certain age, with snowy-white transformations, black dresses and lips of cherry red. Miss Warren and Marmora were at a corner table—Nicole was diagonally across from them forty yards away, and as Dick arrived he heard her voice:

"*Can you hear me? I'm speaking naturally.*"

"Perfectly."

"*Hello, Doctor Diver.*"

"What's this?"

"*You realize the people in the centre of the floor can't hear what I say, but you can?*"

"A waiter told us about it," said Miss Warren. "Corner to corner—it's like wireless."

It was exciting up on the mountain, like a ship at sea. Presently Marmora's parents joined them. They treated the Warrens with respect—Dick gathered that their fortunes had something to do with a bank in Milan that had something to do with the Warren fortunes. But Baby Warren wanted to talk to Dick, wanted to talk to him with the impetus that sent her out vagrantly toward all new men, as though she were on an inelastic tether and considered that she might as well get to the end of it as soon as possible. She crossed and recrossed her knees frequently in the manner of tall restless virgins.

"—Nicole told me that you took part care of her, and had a lot to do with her getting well. What I can't understand is what *we're* supposed to do—they were so indefinite at the sanitarium; they only told me she ought to be natural and gay. I knew the Marmoras were up here so I asked Tino to meet us at the funicular. And you see what happens—the very first thing Nicole has him crawling over the sides of the car as if they were both insane——"

"That was absolutely normal," Dick laughed. "I'd call it a good sign. They were showing off for each other."

"But how can *I* tell? Before I knew it, almost in front of

my eyes, she had her hair cut off, in Zurich, because of a picture in Vanity Fair."

"That's all right. She's a schizoid—a permanent eccentric. You can't change that."

"What is it?"

"Just what I said—an eccentric."

"Well, how can any one tell what's eccentric and what's crazy?"

"Nothing is going to be crazy—Nicole is all fresh and happy, you needn't be afraid."

Baby shifted her knees about—she was a compendium of all the discontented women who had loved Byron a hundred years before, yet, in spite of the tragic affair with the guards' officer there was something wooden and onanistic about her.

"I don't mind the responsibility," she declared, "but I'm in the air. We've never had anything like this in the family before—we know Nicole had some shock and my opinion is it was about a boy, but we don't really know. Father says he would have shot him if he could have found out."

The orchestra was playing "Poor Butterfly"; young Marmora was dancing with his mother. It was a tune new enough to them all. Listening, and watching Nicole's shoulders as she chattered to the elder Marmora, whose hair was dashed with white like a piano keyboard, Dick thought of the shoulders of a violin, and then he thought of the dishonor, the secret. Oh, butterfly—the moments pass into hours——

"Actually *I* have a plan," Baby continued with apologetic hardness. "It may seem absolutely impractical to you but they say Nicole will need to be looked after for a few years. I don't know whether you know Chicago or not——"

"I don't."

"Well, there's a North Side and a South Side and they're very much separated. The North Side is chic and all that, and we've always lived over there, at least for many years, but lots of old families, old Chicago families, if you know what I mean, still live on the South Side. The University is there. I mean it's stuffy to some people, but anyhow it's different from the North Side. I don't know whether you understand."

He nodded. With some concentration he had been able to follow her.

"Now of course we have lots of connections there—Father controls certain chairs and fellowships and so forth at the University, and I thought if we took Nicole home and threw her with that crowd—you see she's quite musical and speaks all these languages—what could be better in her condition than if she fell in love with some good doctor——"

A burst of hilarity surged up in Dick, the Warrens were going to buy Nicole a doctor— You got a nice doctor you can let us use? There was no use worrying about Nicole when they were in the position of being able to buy her a nice young doctor, the paint scarcely dry on him.

"But how about the doctor?" he said automatically.

"There must be many who'd jump at the chance."

The dancers were back, but Baby whispered quickly:

"This is the sort of thing I mean. Now where is Nicole—she's gone off somewhere. Is she upstairs in her room? What am *I* supposed to do? I never know whether it's something innocent or whether I ought to go find her."

"Perhaps she just wants to be by herself—people living alone get used to loneliness." Seeing that Miss Warren was not listening he stopped. "I'll take a look around."

For a moment all the outdoors shut in with mist was like spring with the curtains drawn. Life was gathered near the hotel. Dick passed some cellar windows where bus boys sat on bunks and played cards over a litre of Spanish wine. As he approached the promenade, the stars began to come through the white crests of the high Alps. On the horseshoe walk overlooking the lake Nicole was the figure motionless between two lamp stands, and he approached silently across the grass. She turned to him with an expression of: "Here *you* are," and for a moment he was sorry he had come.

"Your sister wondered."

"Oh!" She was accustomed to being watched. With an effort she explained herself: "Sometimes I get a little—it

169

gets a little too much. I've lived so quietly. To-night that music was too much. It made me want to cry——"

"I understand."

"This has been an awfully exciting day."

"I know."

"I don't want to do anything anti-social—I've caused everybody enough trouble. But to-night I wanted to get away."

It occurred to Dick suddenly, as it might occur to a dying man that he had forgotten to tell where his will was, that Nicole had been "re-educated" by Dohmler and the ghostly generations behind him; it occurred to him also that there would be so much she would have to be told. But having recorded this wisdom within himself, he yielded to the insistent face-value of the situation and said:

"You're a nice person—just keep using your own judgment about yourself."

"You like me?"

"Of course."

"Would you—" They were strolling along toward the dim end of the horseshoe, two hundred yards ahead. "If I hadn't been sick would you—I mean, would I have been the sort of girl you might have—oh, slush, you know what I mean."

He was in for it now, possessed by a vast irrationality. She was so near that he felt his breathing change but again his training came to his aid in a boy's laugh and a trite remark.

"You're teasing yourself, my dear. Once I knew a man who fell in love with his nurse——" The anecdote rambled on, punctuated by their footsteps. Suddenly Nicole interrupted in succinct Chicagoese: "Bull!"

"That's a very vulgar expression."

"What about it?" she flared up. "You don't think I've got any common sense—before I was sick I didn't have any, but I have now. And if I don't know you're the most attractive man I ever met you must think I'm still crazy. It's my hard luck, all right—but don't pretend I don't *know*—I know everything about you and me."

Dick was at an additional disadvantage. He remembered

the statement of the elder Miss Warren as to the young doctors that could be purchased in the intellectual stock-yards of the South Side of Chicago, and he hardened for a moment. "You're a fetching kid, but I couldn't fall in love."

"You won't give me a chance." young

"*What!*"

The impertinence, the right to invade implied, astounded him. Short of anarchy he could not think of any chance that Nicole Warren deserved.

"Give me a chance now."

The voice fell low, sank into her breast and stretched the tight bodice over her heart as she came up close. He felt the young lips, her body sighing in relief against the arm growing stronger to hold her. There were now no more plans than if Dick had arbitrarily made some indissoluble mixture, with atoms joined and inseparable; you could throw it all out but never again could they fit back into atomic scale. As he held her and tasted her, and as she curved in further and further toward him, with her own lips, new to herself, drowned and engulfed in love, yet solaced and triumphant, he was thankful to have an existence at all, if only as a reflection in her wet eyes.

"My God," he gasped, "you're fun to kiss."

That was talk, but Nicole had a better hold on him now and she held it; she turned coquette and walked away, leaving him as suspended as in the funicular of the afternoon. She felt: There, that'll show him, how conceited; how he could do with me; oh, wasn't it wonderful! I've got him, he's mine. Now in the sequence came flight, but it was all so sweet and new that she dawdled, wanting to draw all of it in.

She shivered suddenly. Two thousand feet below she saw the necklace and bracelet of lights that were Montreux and Vevey, beyond them a dim pendant of Lausanne. From down there somewhere ascended a faint sound of dance music. Nicole was up in her head now, cool as cool, trying to collate the sentimentalities of her childhood, as deliberate as a man getting drunk after battle. But she was still afraid of Dick, who stood near her, leaning, characteristically, against the iron fence that rimmed the horseshoe; and this prompted her to say: "I can remember how I stood waiting for you in the garden—holding all my self in my arms like a basket of flowers. It was that to me anyhow—I thought I was sweet—waiting to hand that basket to you."

He breathed over her shoulder and turned her insistently about; she kissed him several times, her face getting big every time she came close, her hands holding him by the shoulders.

"It's raining hard."

Suddenly there was a booming from the wine slopes across the lake; cannons were shooting at hail-bearing clouds in order to break them. The lights of the promenade went off, went on again. Then the storm came swiftly, first falling from the heavens, then doubly falling in torrents from the mountains and washing loud down the roads and stone ditches; with it came a dark, frightening sky and savage filaments of lightning and world-splitting thunder, while ragged, destroying clouds fled along past the hotel. Mountains and lake disappeared—the hotel crouched amid tumult, chaos and darkness.

By this time Dick and Nicole had reached the vestibule, where Baby Warren and the three Marmoras were anxiously awaiting them. It was exciting coming out of the wet fog—with the doors banging, to stand and laugh and quiver with emotion, wind in their ears and rain on their clothes. Now in the ballroom the orchestra was playing a Strauss waltz, high and confusing.

. . . For Doctor Diver to marry a mental patient? How did it happen? Where did it begin?

"Won't you come back after you've changed?" Baby Warren asked after a close scrutiny.

"I haven't got any change, except some shorts."

As he trudged up to his hotel in a borrowed raincoat he kept laughing derisively in his throat.

"*Big* chance—oh, yes. My God!—they decided to buy a doctor? Well, they better stick to whoever they've got in Chicago." Revolted by his harshness he made amends to Nicole, remembering that nothing had ever felt so young as her lips, remembering rain like tears shed for him that lay upon her softly shining porcelain cheeks. . . . The silence of the storm ceasing woke him about three o'clock and he went to the window. Her beauty climbed the rolling slope, it came into the room, rustling ghost-like through the curtains. . . .

. . . He climbed two thousand meters to Rochers de Naye the following morning, amused by the fact that his conductor of the day before was using his day off to climb also.

Then Dick descended all the way to Montreux for a swim, got back to his hotel in time for dinner. Two notes awaited him.

"I'm not ashamed about last night—it was the nicest thing that ever happened to me and even if I never saw you again, Mon Capitaine, I would be glad it happened."

That was disarming enough—the heavy shade of Dohmler retreated as Dick opened the second envelope:

"DEAR DOCTOR DIVER: I phoned but you were out. I wonder if I may ask you a great big favor. Unforeseen circumstances call me back to Paris, and I find I can make better time by way of Lausanne. Can you let Nicole ride as far as Zurich with you, since you are going back Monday? and drop her at the sanitarium? Is this too much to ask?

Sincerely,
BETH EVAN WARREN."

Dick was furious—Miss Warren had known he had a bicycle with him; yet she had so phrased her note that it was impossible to refuse. Throw us together! Sweet propinquity and the Warren money!

He was wrong; Baby Warren had no such intentions. She had looked Dick over with worldly eyes, she had measured him with the warped rule of an Anglophile and found him wanting—in spite of the fact that she found him toothsome. But for her he was too "intellectual" and she pigeonholed him with a shabby-snobby crowd she had once known in London—he put himself out too much to be really of the correct stuff. She could not see how he could be made into her idea of an aristocrat.

In addition to that he was stubborn—she had seen him

173

leave her conversation and get down behind his eyes in that odd way that people did, half a dozen times. She had not liked Nicole's free and easy manner as a child and now she was sensibly habituated to thinking of her as a "gone coon"; and anyhow Doctor Diver was not the sort of medical man she could envisage in the family.

She only wanted to use him innocently as a convenience.

But her request had the effect that Dick assumed she desired. A ride in a train can be a terrible, heavy-hearted or comic thing; it can be a trial flight; it can be a prefiguration of another journey just as a given day with a friend can be long, from the taste of hurry in the morning up to the realization of both being hungry and taking food together. Then comes the afternoon with the journey fading and dying, but quickening again at the end. Dick was sad to see Nicole's meagre joy; yet it was a relief for her, going back to the only home she knew. They made no love that day, but when he left her outside the sad door on the Zürichsee and she turned and looked at him he knew her problem was one they had together for good now.

## X

IN Zurich in September Doctor Diver had tea with Baby Warren.

"I think it's ill advised," she said, "I'm not sure I truly understand your motives."

"Don't let's be unpleasant."

"After all I'm Nicole's sister."

"That doesn't give you the right to be unpleasant." It irritated Dick that he knew so much that he could not tell her. "Nicole's rich, but that doesn't make me an adventurer."

"That's just it," complained Baby stubbornly. "Nicole's rich."

"Just how much money has she got?" he asked.

She started; and with a silent laugh he continued, "You

174

see how silly this is? I'd rather talk to some man in your family——"

"Everything's been left to me," she persisted. "It isn't we think you're an adventurer. We don't know who you are."

"I'm a doctor of medicine," he said. "My father is a clergyman, now retired. We lived in Buffalo and my past is open to investigation. I went to New Haven; afterward I was a Rhodes scholar. My great-grandfather was Governor of North Carolina and I'm a direct descendant of Mad Anthony Wayne."[40]

"Who was Mad Anthony Wayne?" Baby asked suspiciously.

"Mad Anthony Wayne?"

"I think there's enough madness in this affair."

He shook his head hopelessly, just as Nicole came out on the hotel terrace and looked around for them.

"He was too mad to leave as much money as Marshall Field,"[41] he said.

"That's all very well——"

Baby was right and she knew it. Face to face, her father would have it on almost any clergyman. They were an American ducal family without a title—the very name written in a hotel register, signed to an introduction, used in a difficult situation, caused a psychological metamorphosis in people, and in return this change had crystallized her own sense of position. She knew these facts from the English, who had known them for over two hundred years. But she did not know that twice Dick had come close to flinging the marriage in her face. All that saved it this time was Nicole finding their table and glowing away, white and fresh and new in the September afternoon.

How do you do, lawyer. We're going to Como tomorrow for a week and then back to Zurich. That's why I wanted you and sister to settle this, because it doesn't matter to us how much I'm allowed. We're going to live very quietly in Zurich for two years and Dick has enough to take care of us. No, Baby, I'm more practical than you think— It's only for clothes and things I'll need it. . . . Why, that's more than—  *ellipsis*

175

can the estate really afford to give me all that? I know I'll never manage to spend it. Do you have that much? Why do you have more—is it because I'm supposed to be incompetent? All right, let my share pile up then. . . . No, Dick refused to have anything whatever to do with it. I'll have to feel bloated for us both. . . . Baby, you have no more idea of what Dick is like than, than— Now where do I sign? Oh, I'm sorry.

. . . Isn't it funny and lonely being together, Dick. No place to go except close. Shall we just love and love? Ah, but I love the most, and I can tell when you're away from me, even a little. I think it's wonderful to be just like everybody else, to reach out and find you all warm beside me in the bed.

. . . If you will kindly call my husband at the hospital. Yes, the little book is selling everywhere—they want it published in six languages. I was to do the French translation but I'm tired these days—I'm afraid of falling, I'm so heavy and clumsy—like a broken roly-poly that can't stand up straight. The cold stethoscope against my heart and my strongest feeling "Je m'en fiche de tout."—Oh, that poor woman in the hospital with the blue baby, much better dead. Isn't it fine there are three of us now?

. . . That seems unreasonable, Dick—we have every reason for taking the bigger apartment. Why should we penalize ourselves just because there's more Warren money than Diver money. Oh, thank you, cameriere, but we've changed our minds. This English clergyman tells us that your wine here in Orvieto is excellent. It doesn't travel? That must be why we have never heard of it, because we love wine.

The lakes are sunk in the brown clay and the slopes have all the creases of a belly. The photographer gave us the picture of me, my hair limp over the rail on the boat to Capri. "Good-by, Blue Grotte," sang the boatman, "come again soo-oon." And afterward tracing down the hot sinister shin of the Italian boot with the wind soughing around those eerie castles, the dead watching from up on those hills.

. . . This ship is nice, with our heels hitting the deck together. This is the blowy corner and each time we turn it I slant forward against the wind and pull my coat together without losing step with Dick. We are chanting nonsense:

> "Oh—oh—oh—oh
> Other flamingoes than me,
> Oh—oh—oh—oh
> Other flamingoes than me——"

Life is fun with Dick—the people in deck chairs look at us, and a woman is trying to hear what we are singing. Dick is tired of singing it, so go on alone, Dick. You will walk differently alone, dear, through a thicker atmosphere, forcing your way through the shadows of chairs, through the dripping smoke of the funnels. You will feel your own reflection sliding along the eyes of those who look at you. You are no longer insulated; but I suppose you must touch life in order to spring from it.

Sitting on the stanchion of this life-boat I look seaward and let my hair blow and shine. I am motionless against the sky and the boat is made to carry my form onward into the blue obscurity of the future, I am Pallas Athene[42] carved reverently on the front of a galley. The waters are lapping in the public toilets and the agate green foliage of spray changes and complains about the stern.

. . . We travelled a lot that year—from Woolloomooloo Bay to Biskra. On the edge of the Sahara we ran into a plague of locusts and the chauffeur explained kindly that they were bumble-bees. The sky was low at night, full of the presence of a strange and watchful God. Oh, the poor little naked Ouled Naïl;[43] the night was noisy with drums from Senegal and flutes and whining camels, and the natives pattering about in shoes made of old automobile tires.

But I was gone again by that time—trains and beaches they were all one. That was why he took me travelling but after my second child, my little girl, Topsy, was born everything got dark again.

. . . If I could get word to my husband who has seen fit to desert me here, to leave me in the hands of incompetents.

177

You tell me my baby is black—that's farcical, that's very cheap. We went to Africa merely to see Timgad,[44] since my principal interest in life is archeology. I am tired of knowing nothing and being reminded of it all the time.

... When I get well I want to be a fine person like you, Dick—I would study medicine except it's too late. We must spend my money and have a house—I'm tired of apartments and waiting for you. You're bored with Zurich and you can't find time for writing here and you say that it's a confession of weakness for a scientist not to write. And I'll look over the whole field of knowledge and pick out something and really know about it, so I'll have it to hang on to if I go to pieces again. You'll help me, Dick, so I won't feel so guilty. We'll live near a warm beach where we can be brown and young together.

... This is going to be Dick's work house. Oh, the idea came to us both at the same moment. We had passed Tarmes a dozen times and we rode up here and found the houses empty, except two stables. When we bought we acted through a Frenchman but the navy sent spies up here in no time when they found that Americans had bought part of a hill village. They looked for cannons all through the building material, and finally Baby had to twitch wires for us at the Affaires Étrangères in Paris.

No one comes to the Riviera in summer, so we expect to have a few guests and to work. There are some French people here—Mistinguett[45] last week, surprised to find the hotel open, and Picasso and the man who wrote *Pas sur la Bouche*.

... Dick, why did you register Mr. and Mrs. Diver instead of Doctor and Mrs. Diver? I just wondered—it just floated through my mind—you've taught me that work is everything and I believe you. You used to say a man knows things and when he stops knowing things he's like anybody else, and the thing is to get power before he stops knowing things. If you want to turn things topsy-turvy, all right, but must your Nicole follow you walking on her hands, darling?

... Tommy says I am silent. Since I was well the first time I talked a lot to Dick late at night, both of us sitting up in

178

bed and lighting cigarettes, then diving down afterward out of the blue dawn and into the pillows, to keep the light from our eyes. Sometimes I sing, and play with the animals, and I have a few friends too—Mary, for instance. When Mary and I talk neither of us listens to the other. Talk is men. When I talk I say to myself that I am probably Dick. Already I have even been my son, remembering how wise and slow he is. Sometimes I am Doctor Dohmler and one time I may even be an aspect of you, Tommy Barban. Tommy is in love with me, I think, but gently, reassuringly. Enough, though, so that he and Dick have begun to disapprove of each other. All in all, everything has never gone better. I am among friends who like me. I am here on this tranquil beach with my husband and two children. Everything is all right—if I can finish translating this damn recipe for chicken à la Maryland into French. My toes feel warm in the sand.

*Nicole getting better*

"Yes, I'll look. More new people—oh, that girl—yes. Who did you say she looked like. . . . No, I haven't, we don't get much chance to see the new American pictures over here. Rosemary who? Well, we're getting very fashionable for July—seems very peculiar to me. Yes, she's lovely, but there can be too many people."

## XI

DOCTOR RICHARD DIVER and Mrs. Elsie Speers sat in the Café des Alliés in August, under cool and dusty trees. The sparkle of the mica was dulled by the baked ground, and a few gusts of mistral from down the coast seeped through the Esterel and rocked the fishing boats in the harbor, pointing the masts here and there at a featureless sky.

"I had a letter this morning," said Mrs. Speers. "What a terrible time you all must have had with those Negroes! But Rosemary said you were perfectly wonderful to her."

"Rosemary ought to have a service stripe. It was pretty harrowing—the only person it didn't disturb was Abe

North—he flew off to Havre—he probably doesn't know about it yet."

"I'm sorry Mrs. Diver was upset," she said carefully.

Rosemary had written:

"Nicole seemed Out of her Mind. I didn't want to come South with them because I felt Dick had enough on his Hands."

"She's all right now." He spoke almost impatiently. "So you're leaving to-morrow. When will you sail?"

"Right away."

"My God, it's awful to have you go."

"We're glad we came here. We've had a good time, thanks to you. You're the first man Rosemary ever cared for."

Another gust of wind strained around the porphyry hills of la Napoule. There was a hint in the air that the earth was hurrying on toward other weather; the lush midsummer moment outside of time was already over.

"Rosemary's had crushes but sooner or later she always turned the man over to me—" Mrs. Speers laughed, "—for dissection."

"So I was spared."

"There was nothing I could have done. She was in love with you before I ever saw you. I told her to go ahead."

He saw that no provision had been made for him, or for Nicole, in Mrs. Speers' plans—and he saw that her amorality sprang from the conditions of her own withdrawal. It was her right, the pension on which her own emotions had retired. Women are necessarily capable of almost anything in their struggle for survival and can scarcely be convicted of such man-made crimes as "cruelty." So long as the shuffle of love and pain went on within proper walls Mrs. Speers could view it with as much detachment and humor as a eunuch. She had not even allowed for the possibility of Rosemary's being damaged—or was she certain that she couldn't be?

"If what you say is true I don't think it did her any harm." He was keeping up to the end the pretense that he could still think objectively about Rosemary. "She's over it already. Still—so many of the important times in life begin by seeming incidental."

"This wasn't incidental," Mrs. Speers insisted. "You were the first man—you're an ideal to her. In every letter she says that."

"She's so polite."

"You and Rosemary are the politest people I've ever known, but she means this."

"My politeness is a trick of the heart."

This was partly true. From his father Dick had learned the somewhat conscious good manners of the young Southerner coming north after the Civil War. Often he used them and just as often he despised them because they were not a protest against how unpleasant selfishness was but against how unpleasant it looked.

"I'm in love with Rosemary," he told her suddenly. "It's a kind of self-indulgence saying that to you."

It seemed very strange and official to him, as if the very tables and chairs in the Café des Alliés would remember it forever. Already he felt her absence from these skies: on the beach he could only remember the sun-torn flesh of her shoulder; at Tarmes he crushed out her footprints as he crossed the garden; and now the orchestra launching into the "Nice Carnival Song," an echo of last year's vanished gaieties, started the little dance that went on all about her. In a hundred hours she had come to possess all the world's dark magic; the blinding belladonna, the caffein converting physical into nervous energy, the mandragora that imposes harmony.

With an effort he once more accepted the fiction that he shared Mrs. Speers' detachment.

"You and Rosemary aren't really alike," he said. "The wisdom she got from you is all molded up into her persona, into the mask she faces the world with. She doesn't think; her real depths are Irish and romantic and illogical."

Mrs. Speers knew too that Rosemary, for all her delicate surface, was a young mustang, perceptibly by Captain

Doctor Hoyt, U. S. A. Cross-sectioned, Rosemary would have displayed an enormous heart, liver and soul, all crammed close together under the lovely shell.

Saying good-by, Dick was aware of Elsie Speers' full charm, aware that she meant rather more to him than merely a last unwillingly relinquished fragment of Rosemary. He could possibly have made up Rosemary—he could never have made up her mother. If the cloak, spurs and brilliants in which Rosemary had walked off were things with which he had endowed her, it was nice in contrast to watch her mother's grace knowing it was surely something he had not evoked. She had an air of seeming to wait, as if for a man to get through with something more important than herself, a battle or an operation, during which he must not be hurried or interfered with. When the man had finished she would be waiting, without fret or impatience, somewhere on a highstool, turning the pages of a newspaper.

"Good-by—and I want you both to remember always how fond of you Nicole and I have grown."

Back at the Villa Diana, he went to his work-room, and opened the shutters, closed against the mid-day glare. On his two long tables, in ordered confusion, lay the materials of his book. Volume I, concerned with Classification, had achieved some success in a small subsidized edition. He was negotiating for its reissue. Volume II was to be a great amplification of his first little book, *A Psychology for Psychiatrists*. Like so many men he had found that he had only one or two ideas—that his little collection of pamphlets now in its fiftieth German edition contained the germ of all he would ever think or know.

But he was currently uneasy about the whole thing. He resented the wasted years at New Haven, but mostly he felt a discrepancy between the growing luxury in which the Divers lived, and the need for display which apparently went along with it. Remembering his Rumanian friend's story, about the man who had worked for years on the brain of an armadillo, he suspected that patient Germans were sitting close to the libraries of Berlin and Vienna callously anticipating him. He had about decided to brief the work in its present condition and publish it in an undocumented volume of a hundred thousand words as an introduction to more scholarly volumes to follow.

He confirmed this decision walking around the rays of late afternoon in his work-room. With the new plan he could be through by spring. It seemed to him that when a man with his energy was pursued for a year by increasing doubts, it indicated some fault in the plan.

He laid the bars of gilded metal that he used as paper-weights along the sheaves of notes. He swept up, for no servant was allowed in here, treated his washroom sketchily with Bon Ami, repaired a screen and sent off an order to a publishing house in Zurich. Then he drank an ounce of gin with twice as much water. *procrastinating*

He saw Nicole in the garden. Presently he must encounter her and the prospect gave him a leaden feeling. Before her he must keep up a perfect front, now and to-morrow, next week and next year. All night in Paris he had held her in his arms while she slept light under the luminol; in the early morning he broke in upon her confusion before it could form, with words of tenderness and protection, and she slept again with his face against the warm scent of her hair. Before she woke he had arranged everything at the phone in the next room. Rosemary was to move to another hotel. She was to be "Daddy's Girl" and even to give up saying good-by to them. The proprietor of the hotel, Mr. McBeth, was to be the three Chinese monkeys. Packing amid the piled boxes and tissue paper of many purchases, Dick and Nicole left for the Riviera at noon.

Then there was a reaction. As they settled down in the wagon-lit Dick saw that Nicole was waiting for it, and it came quickly and desperately, before the train was out of the ceinture—his only instinct was to step off while the train was still going slow, rush back and see where Rosemary was, what she was doing. He opened a book and bent his pince-nez upon it, aware that Nicole was watching him from her pillow across the compartment. Unable to read, he pretended to be tired and shut his eyes but she was still watching him, and though still she was half asleep from the hangover of the drug, she was relieved and almost happy that he was hers again.

It was worse with his eyes shut for it gave a rhythm of finding and losing, finding and losing; but so as not to appear restless he lay like that until noon. At luncheon things were better—it was always a fine meal; a thousand lunches in inns and restaurants, wagon-lits, buffets, and aeroplanes were a mighty collation to have taken together. The familiar hurry of the train waiters, the little bottles of wine and mineral water, the excellent food of the Paris-Lyons-Méditerranée gave them the illusion that everything was the same as before, but it was almost the first trip he had ever taken with Nicole that was a going away rather than a going toward. He drank a whole bottle of wine save for Nicole's single glass; they talked about the house and the children. But once back in the compartment a silence fell over them like the silence in the restaurant across from the Luxembourg. Receding from a grief, it seems necessary to retrace the same steps that brought us there. An unfamiliar impatience settled on Dick; suddenly Nicole said:

"It seemed too bad to leave Rosemary like that—do you suppose she'll be all right?"

"Of course. She could take care of herself anywhere—" Lest this belittle Nicole's ability to do likewise, he added, "After all, she's an actress, and even though her mother's in the background she *has* to look out for herself."

"She's very attractive."

"She's an infant."

"She's attractive though."

They talked aimlessly back and forth, each speaking for the other.

"She's not as intelligent as I thought," Dick offered.

"She's quite smart."

"Not very, though—there's a persistent aroma of the nursery."

"She's very—very pretty," Nicole said in a detached, emphatic way, "and I thought she was very good in the picture."

"She was well directed. Thinking it over, it wasn't very individual."

"I thought it was. I can see how she'd be very attractive to men."

His heart twisted. To what men? How many men?

—Do you mind if I pull down the curtain?

—Please do, it's too light in here.

Where now? And with whom?

"In a few years she'll look ten years older than you."

"On the contrary. I sketched her one night on a theatre program, I think she'll last."

They were both restless in the night. In a day or two Dick would try to banish the ghost of Rosemary before it became walled up with them, but for the moment he had no force to do it. Sometimes it is harder to deprive oneself of a pain than of a pleasure and the memory so possessed him that for the moment there was nothing to do but to pretend. This was more difficult because he was currently annoyed with Nicole, who, after all these years, should recognize symptoms of strain in herself and guard against them. Twice within a fortnight she had broken up: there had been the night of the dinner at Tarmes when he had found her in her bedroom dissolved in crazy laughter telling Mrs. McKisco she could not go in the bathroom because the key was thrown down the well. Mrs. McKisco was astonished and resentful, baffled and yet in a way comprehending. Dick had not been particularly alarmed then, for afterward Nicole was repentant. She called at Gausse's Hôtel but the McKiscos were gone.

The collapse in Paris was another matter, adding significance to the first one. It prophesied possibly a new cycle, a new pousse of the malady. Having gone through unprofessional agonies during her long relapse following Topsy's birth, he had, perforce, hardened himself about her, making a cleavage between Nicole sick and Nicole well. This made it difficult now to distinguish between his self-protective professional detachment and some new coldness in his heart. As an indifference cherished, or left to atrophy, becomes an emptiness, to this extent he had learned to become empty of

Nicole, serving her against his will with negations and emotional neglect. One writes of scars healed, a loose parallel to the pathology of the skin, but there is no such thing in the life of an individual. There are open wounds, shrunk sometimes to the size of a pin-prick but wounds still. The marks of suffering are more comparable to the loss of a finger, or of the sight of an eye. We may not miss them, either, for one minute in a year, but if we should there is nothing to be done about it.

## XII

HE found Nicole in the garden with her arms folded high on her shoulders. She looked at him with straight gray eyes, with a child's searching wonder.

"I went to Cannes," he said. "I ran into Mrs. Speers. She's leaving to-morrow. She wanted to come up and say good-by to you, but I slew the idea."

"I'm sorry. I'd like to have seen her. I like her."

"Who else do you think I saw—Bartholomew Tailor."

"You didn't."

"I couldn't have missed that face of his, the old experienced weasel. He was looking over the ground for Ciro's menagerie—they'll all be down next year. I suspected Mrs. Abrams was a sort of outpost."

"And Baby was outraged the first summer we came here."

"They don't really give a damn where they are, so I don't see why they don't stay and freeze in Deauville."

"Can't we start rumors about cholera or something?"

"I told Bartholomew that some categories died off like flies here—I told him the life of a suck was as short as the life of a machine-gunner in the war."

"You didn't."

"No, I didn't," he admitted. "He was very pleasant. It was a beautiful sight, he and I shaking hands there on the boulevard. The meeting of Sigmund Freud and Ward McAllister."

Dick didn't want to talk—he wanted to be alone so that his thoughts about work and the future would overpower his thoughts of love and to-day. Nicole knew about it but only darkly and tragically, hating him a little in an animal way, yet wanting to rub against his shoulder.

"The darling," Dick said lightly.

He went into the house, forgetting something he wanted to do there, and then remembering it was the piano. He sat down whistling and played by ear:

> "Just picture you upon my knee
> With tea for two and two for tea
> And me for you and you for me——"

Through the melody flowed a sudden realization that Nicole, hearing it, would guess quickly at a nostalgia for the past fortnight. He broke off with a casual chord and left the piano.

It was hard to know where to go. He glanced about the house that Nicole had made, that Nicole's grandfather had paid for. He owned only his work house and the ground on which it stood. Out of three thousand a year and what dribbled in from his publications he paid for his clothes and personal expenses, for cellar charges, and for Lanier's education, so far confined to a nurse's wage. Never had a move been contemplated without Dick's figuring his share. Living rather ascetically, travelling third-class when he was alone, with the cheapest wine, and good care of his clothes, and penalizing himself for any extravagances, he maintained a qualified financial independence. After a certain point, though, it was difficult—again and again it was necessary to decide together as to the uses to which Nicole's money should be put. Naturally Nicole, wanting to own him, wanting him to stand still forever, encouraged any slackness on his part, and in multiplying ways he was constantly inundated by a trickling of goods and money. The inception of the idea of the cliff villa which they had elaborated as a fantasy one day was a typical example of the forces divorcing them from the first simple arrangements in Zurich.

"Wouldn't it be fun if—" it had been; and then, "Won't it be fun when——"

It was not so much fun. His work became confused with Nicole's problems; in addition, her income had increased so fast of late that it seemed to belittle his work. Also, for the purpose of her cure, he had for many years pretended to a rigid domesticity from which he was drifting away, and this pretense became more arduous in this effortless immobility, in which he was inevitably subjected to microscopic examination. When Dick could no longer play what he wanted to play on the piano, it was an indication that life was being refined down to a point. He stayed in the big room a long time listening to the buzz of the electric clock, listening to time.

In November the waves grew black and dashed over the sea wall onto the shore road—such summer life as had survived disappeared and the beaches were melancholy and desolate under the mistral and rain. Gausse's Hôtel was closed for repairs and enlargement and the scaffolding of the summer Casino at Juan-les-Pins grew larger and more formidable. Going into Cannes or Nice, Dick and Nicole met new people—members of orchestras, restaurateurs, horticultural enthusiasts, ship-builders—for Dick had bought an old dinghy—and members of the Syndicat d'Initiative. They knew their servants well and gave thought to the children's education. In December, Nicole seemed well-knit again; when a month had passed without tension, without the tight mouth, the unmotivated smile, the unfathomable remark, they went to the Swiss Alps for the Christmas holidays.

# XIII

With his cap, Dick slapped the snow from his dark blue ski-suit before going inside. The great hall, its floor pockmarked by two decades of hobnails, was cleared for the tea dance, and four-score young Americans, domiciled in schools near Gstaad, bounced about to the frolic of "Don't Bring Lulu," or exploded violently with the first percussions of the Charleston. It was a colony of the young, simple, and expensive—the Sturmtruppen of the rich were at St. Moritz. Baby Warren felt that she had made a gesture of renunciation in joining the Divers here.

Dick picked out the two sisters easily across the delicately haunted, soft-swaying room—they were poster-like, formidable in their snow costumes, Nicole's of cerulean blue, Baby's of brick red. The young Englishman was talking to them; but they were paying no attention, lulled to the staring point by the adolescent dance.

Nicole's snow-warm face lighted up further as she saw Dick. "Where is he?"

"He missed the train—I'm meeting him later." Dick sat down, swinging a heavy boot over his knee. "You two look very striking together. Every once in a while I forget we're in the same party and get a big shock at seeing you."

Baby was a tall, fine-looking woman, deeply engaged in being almost thirty. Symptomatically she had pulled two men with her from London, one scarcely down from Cambridge, one old and hard with Victorian lecheries. Baby had certain spinsters' characteristics—she was alien from touch, she started if she was touched suddenly, and such lingering touches as kisses and embraces slipped directly through the flesh into the forefront of her consciousness. She made few gestures with her trunk, her body proper—instead, she stamped her foot and tossed her head in almost an old-fashioned way. She relished the foretaste of death, prefigured by the catastrophes of friends—persistently she clung to the idea of Nicole's tragic destiny.

189

Baby's younger Englishman had been chaperoning the women down appropriate inclines and harrowing them on the bob-run. Dick, having turned an ankle in a too ambitious telemark, loafed gratefully about the "nursery slope" with the children or drank kvass with a Russian doctor at the hotel.

"Please be happy, Dick," Nicole urged him. "Why don't you meet some of these ickle durls and dance with them in the afternoon?"

"What would I say to them?"

Her low almost harsh voice rose a few notes, simulating a plaintive coquetry: "Say: 'Ickle durl, oo is de pwettiest sing.' What do you think you say?"

"I don't like ickle durls. They smell of castile soap and peppermint. When I dance with them, I feel as if I'm pushing a baby carriage."

It was a dangerous subject—he was careful, to the point of self-consciousness, to stare far over the heads of young maidens.

"There's a lot of business," said Baby. "First place, there's news from home—the property we used to call the station property. The railroads only bought the centre of it at first. Now they've bought the rest, and it belonged to Mother. It's a question of investing the money."

Pretending to be repelled by this gross turn in the conversation, the Englishman made for a girl on the floor. Following him for an instant with the uncertain eyes of an American girl in the grip of a life-long Anglophilia, Baby continued defiantly:

"It's a lot of money. It's three hundred thousand apiece. I keep an eye on my own investments but Nicole doesn't know anything about securities, and I don't suppose you do either."

"I've got to meet the train," Dick said evasively.

Outside he inhaled damp snowflakes that he could no longer see against the darkening sky. Three children sledding past shouted a warning in some strange language; he heard them yell at the next bend and a little farther on he heard sleigh-bells coming up the hill in the dark. The holiday station glittered with expectancy, boys and girls waiting for new boys and girls, and by the time the train arrived, Dick had caught the rhythm, and pretended to Franz Gregorovious that he was clipping off a half-hour from an endless roll of pleasures. But Franz had some intensity of purpose at the moment that fought through any superimposition of mood on Dick's part. "I may get up to Zurich for a day," Dick had written, "or you can manage to come to Lausanne." Franz had managed to come all the way to Gstaad.

He was forty. Upon his healthy maturity reposed a set of pleasant official manners, but he was most at home in a somewhat stuffy safety from which he could despise the broken rich whom he re-educated. His scientific heredity might have bequeathed him a wider world but he seemed to have deliberately chosen the standpoint of an humbler class, a choice typified by his selection of a wife. At the hotel Baby Warren made a quick examination of him, and failing to find any of the hall-marks she respected, the subtler virtues or courtesies by which the privileged classes recognized one another, treated him thereafter with her second manner. Nicole was always a little afraid of him. Dick liked him, as he liked his friends, without reservations.

For the evening they were sliding down the hill into the village, on those little sleds which serve the same purpose as gondolas do in Venice. Their destination was a hotel with an old-fashioned Swiss tap-room, wooden and resounding, a room of clocks, kegs, steins, and antlers. Many parties at long tables blurred into one great party and ate fondue—a peculiarly indigestible form of Welsh rarebit, mitigated by hot spiced wine.

It was jolly in the big room; the younger Englishman remarked it and Dick conceded that there was no other word. With the pert heady wine he relaxed and pretended that the world was all put together again by the gray-haired men of the golden nineties who shouted old glees at the piano, by the young voices and the bright costumes toned into the room by the swirling smoke. For a moment he felt that they were in a ship with landfall just ahead; in the faces of all the girls was the same innocent expectation of the possibilities inherent in the situation and the night. He looked to see if that special girl was there and got an impression that she was at the table behind them—then he forgot her and invented a rigmarole and tried to make his party have a good time.

"I must talk to you," said Franz in English. "I have only twenty-four hours to spend here."

"I suspected you had something on your mind."

"I have a plan that is—so marvellous." His hand fell upon Dick's knee. "I have a plan that will be the making of us two."

"Well?"

"Dick—there is a clinic we could have together—the old clinic of Braun on the Zugersee. The plant is all modern except for a few points. He is sick—he wants to go up in Austria, to die probably. It is a chance that is just insuperable. You and me—what a pair! Now don't say anything yet until I finish."

From the yellow glint in Baby's eyes, Dick saw she was listening.

"We must undertake it together. It would not bind you too tight—it would give you a base, a laboratory, a centre. You could stay in residence say no more than half the year, when the weather is fine. In winter you could go to France or America and write your texts fresh from clinical experience." He lowered his voice. "And for the convalescence in your family, there are the atmosphere and regularity of the clinic at hand." Dick's expression did not encourage this note so Franz dropped it with the punctuation of his tongue leaving his lip quickly. "We could be partners. I the executive manager, you the theoretician, the brilliant consultant and all that. I know myself—I know I have no genius and you have. But, in my way, I am thought very capable; I am utterly competent at the most modern clinical methods. Sometimes for months I have served as the practical head of the old clinic. The professor says this plan is excellent, he advises me to go ahead. He says he is going to live forever, and work up to the last minute."

Dick formed imaginary pictures of the prospect as a preliminary to any exercise of judgment.

"What's the financial angle?" he asked.

Franz threw up his chin, his eyebrows, the transient wrinkles of his forehead, his hands, his elbows, his shoulders; he strained up the muscles of his legs, so that the cloth of his trousers bulged, pushed up his heart into his throat and his voice into the roof of his mouth.

"There we have it! Money!" he bewailed. "I have little money. The price in American money is two hundred thousand dollars. The innovation—ary—" he tasted the coinage doubtfully, "—steps, that you will agree are necessary, will cost twenty thousand dollars American. But the clinic is a gold mine—I tell you, I have seen the books. For an investment of two hundred and twenty thousand dollars we have an assured income of——"

Baby's curiosity was such that Dick brought her into the conversation.

"In your experience, Baby," he demanded, "have you found that when a European wants to see an American *very* pressingly it is invariably something concerned with money?"

"What is it?" she said innocently.

"This young Privatdocent thinks that he and I ought to launch into big business and try to attract nervous breakdowns from America."

Worried, Franz stared at Baby as Dick continued:

"But who are we, Franz? You bear a big name and I've written two textbooks. Is that enough to attract anybody? And I haven't got that much money—I haven't got a tenth of it." Franz smiled cynically. "Honestly I haven't. Nicole and Baby are rich as Crœsus[46] but I haven't managed to get my hands on any of it yet."

They were all listening now—Dick wondered if the girl at the table behind was listening too. The idea attracted him. He decided to let Baby speak for him, as one often lets women raise their voices over issues that are not in their hands. Baby became suddenly her grandfather, cool and experimental.

"I think it's a suggestion you ought to consider, Dick. I don't know what Doctor Gregory was saying—but it seems to me——"

Behind him the girl had leaned forward into a smoke ring and was picking up something from the floor. Nicole's face, fitted into his own across the table—her beauty, tentatively nesting and posing, flowed into his love, ever braced to protect it.

"Consider it, Dick," Franz urged excitedly. "When one writes on psychiatry, one should have actual clinical contacts. Jung writes, Bleuler writes, Freud writes, Forel writes, Adler writes—also they are in constant contact with mental disorder."

"Dick has me," laughed Nicole. "I should think that'd be enough mental disorder for one man."

"That's different," said Franz cautiously.

Baby was thinking that if Nicole lived beside a clinic she would always feel quite safe about her.

"We must think it over carefully," she said.

Though amused at her insolence, Dick did not encourage it.

"The decision concerns me, Baby," he said gently. "It's nice of you to want to buy me a clinic."

Realizing she had meddled, Baby withdrew hurriedly:

"Of course, it's entirely your affair."

"A thing as important as this will take weeks to decide. I wonder how I like the picture of Nicole and me anchored to Zurich—" He turned to Franz, anticipating: "—I know. Zurich has a gashouse and running water and electric light —I lived there three years."

"I will leave you to think it over," said Franz. "I am confident——"

One hundred pair of five-pound boots had begun to clump toward the door, and they joined the press. Outside in the crisp moonlight, Dick saw the girl tying her sled to one of the sleighs ahead. They piled into their own sleigh and at the crisp-cracking whips the horses strained, breasting the dark air. Past them figures ran and scrambled, the younger ones shoving each other from sleds and runners, landing in the soft snow, then panting after the horses to drop exhausted on a sled or wail that they were abandoned. On either side the fields were beneficently tranquil; the space through which the cavalcade moved was high and limitless. In the country there was less noise as though they were all listening atavistically for wolves in the wide snow.

In Saanen, they poured into the municipal dance, crowded with cow herders, hotel servants, shop-keepers, ski teachers, guides, tourists, peasants. To come into the warm enclosed place after the pantheistic animal feeling without, was to reassume some absurd and impressive knightly name, as thunderous as spurred boots in war, as football cleats on the cement of a locker-room floor. There was conventional yodelling, and the familiar rhythm of it separated Dick from what he had first found romantic in the scene. At first he thought it was because he had hounded the girl out of his consciousness; then it came to him under the form of what Baby had said: "We must think it over carefully—" and the unsaid lines back of that: "We own you, and you'll admit it sooner or later. It is absurd to keep up the pretense of independence."

It had been years since Dick had bottled up malice against a creature—since freshman year at New Haven when he had come upon a popular essay about "mental hygiene." Now he lost his temper at Baby and simultaneously tried to coop it up within him, resenting her cold rich insolence. It would be hundreds of years before any emergent Amazons would ever grasp the fact that a man is vulnerable only in his pride, but delicate as Humpty Dumpty once that is meddled with—though some of them paid the fact a cautious lip-service. Doctor Diver's profession of sorting the broken shells of another sort of egg had given him a dread of breakage. But:

"There's too much good manners," he said on the way back to Gstaad in the smooth sleigh.

"Well, I think that's nice," said Baby.

"No, it isn't," he insisted to the anonymous bundle of fur. "Good manners are an admission that everybody is so tender that they have to be handled with gloves. Now, human respect—you don't call a man a coward or a liar lightly, but if you spend your life sparing people's feelings and feeding their vanity, you get so you can't distinguish what *should* be respected in them."

"I think Americans take their manners rather seriously," said the elder Englishman.

"I guess so," said Dick. "My father had the kind of manners he inherited from the days when you shot first and apologized afterward. Men armed—why, you Europeans haven't carried arms in civil life since the beginning of the eighteenth century——"

"Not actually, perhaps——"

"Not *act*ually. Not really."

"Dick, you've always had such beautiful manners," said Baby conciliatingly.

The women were regarding him across the zoo of robes with some alarm. The younger Englishman did not understand—he was one of the kind who were always jumping around cornices and balconies, as if they thought they were in the rigging of a ship—and filled the ride to the hotel with a preposterous story about a boxing match with his best friend in which they loved and bruised each other for an hour, always with great reserve. Dick became facetious.

"So every time he hit you you considered him an even better friend?"

"I respected him more."

"It's the premise I don't understand. You and your best friend scrap about a trivial matter——"

"If you don't understand, I can't explain it to you," said the young Englishman coldly.

—This is what I'll get if I begin saying what I think, Dick said to himself.

He was ashamed at baiting the man, realizing that the absurdity of the story rested in the immaturity of the attitude combined with the sophisticated method of its narration.

The carnival spirit was strong and they went with the crowd into the grill, where a Tunisian barman manipulated the illumination in a counterpoint, whose other melody was the moon off the ice rink staring in the big windows. In that light, Dick found the girl devitalized, and uninteresting—he turned from her to enjoy the darkness, the cigarette points going green and silver when the lights shone red, the band of white that fell across the dancers as the door to the bar was opened and closed.

"Now tell me, Franz," he demanded, "do you think after sitting up all night drinking beer, you can go back and convince your patients that you have any character? Don't you think they'll see you're a gastropath?"

"I'm going to bed," Nicole announced. Dick accompanied her to the door of the elevator.

"I'd come with you but I must show Franz that I'm not intended for a clinician."

Nicole walked into the elevator.

"Baby has lots of common sense," she said meditatively.

"Baby is one of——"

The door slashed shut—facing a mechanical hum, Dick finished the sentence in his mind, "—Baby is a trivial, selfish woman."

But two days later, sleighing to the station with Franz, Dick admitted that he thought favorably upon the matter.

"We're beginning to turn in a circle," he admitted. "Living on this scale, there's an unavoidable series of strains, and Nicole doesn't survive them. The pastoral quality down on the summer Riviera is all changing anyhow—next year they'll have a Season."

They passed the crisp green rinks where Wiener waltzes blared and the colors of many mountain schools flashed against the pale-blue skies.

"—I hope we'll be able to do it, Franz. There's nobody I'd rather try it with than you——"

"Good-by, Gstaad! Good-by, fresh faces, cold sweet flowers, flakes in the darkness. Good-by, Gstaad, good-by!"

## XIV

DICK awoke at five after a long dream of war, walked to the window and stared out it at the Zugersee. His dream had begun in sombre majesty; navy blue uniforms crossed a dark plaza behind bands playing the second movement of Prokofieff's "Love of Three Oranges." Presently there were fire engines, symbols of disaster, and a ghastly uprising of the mutilated in a dressing station. He turned on his bed-lamp and made a thorough note of it ending with the half-ironic phrase: "Non-combatant's shell-shock."

As he sat on the side of his bed, he felt the room, the house and the night as empty. In the next room Nicole muttered something desolate and he felt sorry for whatever loneliness she was feeling in her sleep. For him time stood still and then every few years accelerated in a rush, like the quick re-wind of a film, but for Nicole the years slipped away by clock and calendar and birthday, with the added poignance of her perishable beauty.

Even this past year and a half on the Zugersee seemed wasted time for her, the seasons marked only by the workmen on the road turning pink in May, brown in July, black in September, white again in Spring. She had come out of her first illness alive with new hopes, expecting so much, yet deprived of any subsistence except Dick, bringing up children she could only pretend gently to love, guided orphans. The people she liked, rebels mostly, disturbed her and were bad for her—she sought in them the vitality that had made them independent or creative or rugged, sought in vain—for their secrets were buried deep in childhood struggles they had forgotten. They were more interested in Nicole's exterior harmony and charm, the other face of her illness. She led a lonely life owning Dick who did not want to be owned.

Many times he had tried unsuccessfully to let go his hold on her. They had many fine times together, fine talks between the loves of the white nights, but always when he turned away from her into himself he left her holding Nothing in her hands and staring at it, calling it many names, but knowing it was only the hope that he would come back soon.

He scrunched his pillow hard, lay down, and put the back of his neck against it as a Japanese does to slow the circulation, and slept again for a time. Later, while he shaved, Nicole awoke and marched around, giving abrupt, succinct orders to children and servants. Lanier came in to watch his father shave—living beside a psychiatric clinic he had developed an extraordinary confidence in and admiration for his father, together with an exaggerated indifference toward most other adults; the patients appeared to him either in their odd aspects, or else as devitalized, over-correct creatures without personality. He was a handsome, promising boy and Dick devoted much 'time to him, in the relationship of a sympathetic but exacting officer and a respectful enlisted man.

"Why," Lanier asked, "do you always leave a little lather on the top of your hair when you shave?"

Cautiously Dick parted soapy lips: "I have never been able to find out. I've often wondered. I think it's because I get the first finger soapy when I make the line of my side-burn, but how it gets up on top of my head I don't know."

"I'm going to watch it all to-morrow."

"That's your only question before breakfast."

"I don't really call it a question."

"That's one on you."

Half an hour later Dick started up to the administration building. He was thirty-eight—still declining a beard he yet had a more medical aura about him than he had worn upon the Riviera. For eighteen months now he had lived at the clinic—certainly one of the best-appointed in Europe. Like Dohmler's it was of the modern type—no longer a single dark and sinister building but a small, scattered, yet deceitfully integrated village—Dick and Nicole had added much in the domain of taste, so that the plant was a thing of beauty, visited by every psychologist passing through Zurich. With the addition of a caddy house it might very well have been a country club. The Eglantine and the Beeches, houses for those sunk into eternal darkness, were screened by little copses from the main building, camouflaged strong-points. Behind was a large truck farm, worked partly by the patients. The workshops for ergo-therapy were three, placed under a single roof, and there Doctor Diver began his morning's inspection. The carpentry shop, full of sunlight, exuded the sweetness of sawdust, of a lost age of wood; always half a dozen men were there, hammering, planing, buzzing—silent men, who lifted solemn eyes from their work as he passed through. Himself a good carpenter, he discussed with them the efficiency of some tools for a moment in a quiet, personal, interested voice. Adjoining was the book-bindery, adapted to the most mobile of patients who were not always, however, those who had the greatest chance for recovery. The last chamber was devoted to beadwork, weaving and work in brass. The faces of the patients here wore the expression of one who has just sighed profoundly, dismissing something insoluble—but their sighs only marked the beginning of another ceaseless round of ratiocination, not in a line as with normal people but in the same circle. Round, round, and round. Around forever. But the bright colors of the stuffs they worked with gave strangers a momentary illusion that all was well, as in a kindergarten. These patients brightened as Doctor Diver came in. Most of them liked him better than they liked Doctor Gregorovious. Those who had once lived in the great world invariably liked him better. There were a few who thought he neglected them, or that he was not simple, or that he posed. Their responses were not dissimilar to those that Dick evoked in non-professional life, but here they were warped and distorted.

One Englishwoman spoke to him always about a subject which she considered her own.

"Have we got music to-night?"

"I don't know," he answered. "I haven't seen Doctor Lladislau. How did you enjoy the music that Mrs. Sachs and Mr. Longstreet gave us last night?"

"It was so-so."

"I thought it was fine—especially the Chopin."

"I thought it was so-so."

"When are you going to play for us yourself?"

She shrugged her shoulders, as pleased at this question as she had been for several years.

"Some time. But I only play so-so."

They knew that she did not play at all—she had had two sisters who were brilliant musicians, but she had never been able to learn the notes when they had been young together.

From the workshop Dick went to visit the Eglantine and the Beeches. Exteriorly these houses were as cheerful as the others; Nicole had designed the decoration and the furniture on a necessary base of concealed grills and bars and immovable furniture. She had worked with so much imagination—the inventive quality, which she lacked, being supplied by the problem itself—that no uninstructed visitor would have dreamed that the light, graceful filagree work at a window was a strong, unyielding end of a tether, that the pieces reflecting modern tubular tendencies were stancher than the massive creations of the Edwardians— even the flowers lay in iron fingers and every casual ornament and fixture was as necessary as a girder in a skyscraper. Her tireless eyes had made each room yield up its greatest usefulness. Complimented, she referred to herself brusquely as a master plumber.

For those whose compasses were not depolarized there seemed many odd things in these houses. Doctor Diver was often amused in the Eglantine, the men's building—here there was a strange little exhibitionist who thought that if he could walk unclothed and unmolested from the Étoile to the Place de la Concorde he would solve many things—and, perhaps, Dick thought, he was quite right.

His most interesting case was in the main building. The patient was a woman of thirty who had been in the clinic six months; she was an American painter who had lived long in Paris. They had no very satisfactory history of her. A cousin had happened upon her all mad and gone and after an unsatisfactory interlude at one of the whoopee cures that fringed the city, dedicated largely to tourist victims of drug and drink, he had managed to get her to Switzerland. On her admittance she had been exceptionally pretty—now she was a living agonizing sore. All blood tests had failed to give a positive reaction and the trouble was unsatisfactorily catalogued as nervous eczema. For two months she had lain under it, as imprisoned in the Iron Maiden. She was co-herent, even brilliant, within the limits of her special hallucinations.

She was particularly his patient. During spells of over-excitement he was the only doctor who could "do anything with her." Several weeks ago, on one of many nights that she had passed in sleepless torture, Franz had succeeded in hypnotizing her into a few hours of needed rest, but he had never again succeeded. Hypnosis was a tool that Dick distrusted and seldom used, for he knew that he could not always summon up the mood in himself—he had once tried it on Nicole and she had scornfully laughed at him.

The woman in room twenty could not see him when he came in—the area about her eyes was too tightly swollen. She spoke in a strong, rich, deep, thrilling voice.

"How long will this last? Is it going to be forever?"

"It's not going to be very long now. Doctor Lladislau tells me there are whole areas cleared up."

"If I knew what I had done to deserve this I could accept it with equanimity."

"It isn't wise to be mystical about it—we recognize it as a nervous phenomenon. It's related to the blush—when you were a girl, did you blush easily?"

She lay with her face turned to the ceiling.

"I have found nothing to blush for since I cut my wisdom teeth."

"Haven't you committed your share of petty sins and mistakes?"

"I have nothing to reproach myself with."

"You're very fortunate."

The woman thought a moment; her voice came up through her bandaged face afflicted with subterranean melodies:

"I'm sharing the fate of the women of my time who challenged men to battle."

"To your vast surprise it was just like all battles," he answered, adopting her formal diction.

"Just like all battles." She thought this over. "You pick a set-up, or else win a Pyrrhic victory, or you're wrecked and ruined—you're a ghostly echo from a broken wall."[47]

"You are neither wrecked nor ruined," he told her. "Are you quite sure you've been in a real battle?"

"Look at me!" she cried furiously.

"You've suffered, but many women suffered before they mistook themselves for men." It was becoming an argument and he retreated. "In any case you mustn't confuse a single failure with a final defeat."

She sneered. "Beautiful words," and the phrase transpiring up through the crust of pain humbled him.

"We would like to go into the true reasons that brought you here—" he began but she interrupted.

"I am here as a symbol of something. I thought perhaps you would know what it was."

"You are sick," he said mechanically.

"Then what was it I had almost found?"

"A greater sickness."

"That's all?"

"That's all." With disgust he heard himself lying, but here and now the vastness of the subject could only be compressed into a lie. "Outside of that there's only confusion and chaos. I won't lecture to you—we have too acute a realization of your physical suffering. But it's only by meeting the problems of every day, no matter how trifling and boring they seem, that you can make things drop back into place again. After that—perhaps you'll be able again to examine——"

He had slowed up to avoid the inevitable end of his thought: "—the frontiers of consciousness." The frontiers that artists must explore were not for her, ever. She was fine-spun, inbred—eventually she might find rest in some quiet mysticism. Exploration was for those with a measure of peasant blood, those with big thighs and thick ankles who could take punishment as they took bread and salt, on every inch of flesh and spirit.

—Not for you, he almost said. It's too tough a game for you.

Yet in the awful majesty of her pain he went out to her unreservedly, almost sexually. He wanted to gather her up in his arms, as he so often had Nicole, and cherish even her mistakes, so deeply were they part of her. The orange light through the drawn blind, the sarcophagus of her figure on the bed, the spot of face, the voice searching the vacuity of her illness and finding only remote abstractions.

As he arose the tears fled lava-like into her bandages.

"That is for something," she whispered. "Something must come out of it."

He stooped and kissed her forehead.

"We must all try to be good," he said.

Leaving her room he sent the nurse in to her. There were other patients to see: an American girl of fifteen who had been brought up on the basis that childhood was intended to be all fun—his visit was provoked by the fact that she had just hacked off all her hair with a nail scissors. There was nothing much to be done for her—a family history of neurosis and nothing stable in her past to build on. The father, normal and conscientious himself, had tried to protect a nervous brood from life's troubles and had succeeded merely in preventing them from developing powers of adjustment to life's inevitable surprises. There was little that Dick could say: "Helen, when you're in doubt you must ask a nurse, you must learn to take advice. Promise me you will."

What was a promise with the head sick? He looked in upon a frail exile from the Caucasus buckled securely in a sort of hammock which in turn was submerged in a warm medical bath, and upon the three daughters of a Portuguese general who slid almost imperceptibly toward paresis. He went into the room next to them and told a collapsed psychiatrist that he was better, always better, and the man tried to read his face for conviction, since he hung on the real world only through such reassurance as he could find in the resonance, or lack of it, in Doctor Diver's voice. After that Dick discharged a shiftless orderly and by then it was the lunch hour.

## XV

MEALS with the patients were a chore he approached with apathy. The gathering, which of course did not include residents at the Eglantine or the Beeches, was conventional enough at first sight, but over it brooded always a heavy melancholy. Such doctors as were present kept up a conversation but most of the patients, as if exhausted by their morning's endeavor, or depressed by the company, spoke little, and ate looking into their plates.

Luncheon over, Dick returned to his villa. Nicole was in the salon wearing a strange expression.

"Read that," she said.

He opened the letter. It was from a woman recently discharged, though with skepticism on the part of the faculty. It accused him in no uncertain terms of having seduced her daughter, who had been at her mother's side during the crucial stage of the illness. It presumed that Mrs. Diver would be glad to have this information and learn what her husband was "really like."

Dick read the letter again. Couched in clear and concise English he yet recognized it as the letter of a manic. Upon a single occasion he had let the girl, a flirtatious little brunette, ride into Zurich with him, upon her request, and in the evening had brought her back to the clinic. In an idle, almost indulgent way, he kissed her. Later, she tried to carry the affair further, but he was not interested and subsequently, probably consequently, the girl had come to dislike him, and taken her mother away.

"This letter is deranged," he said. "I had no relations of any kind with that girl. I didn't even like her."

"Yes, I've tried thinking that," said Nicole.

"Surely you don't believe it?"

"I've been sitting here."

He sank his voice to a reproachful note and sat beside her.

"This is absurd. This is a letter from a mental patient."

"I was a mental patient."

He stood up and spoke more authoritatively.

"Suppose we don't have any nonsense, Nicole. Go and round up the children and we'll start."

In the car, with Dick driving, they followed the little promontories of the lake, catching the burn of light and water in the windshield, tunnelling through cascades of evergreen. It was Dick's car, a Renault so dwarfish that they all stuck out of it except the children, between whom Mademoiselle towered mast-like in the rear seat. They knew every kilometer of the road—where they would smell the pine needles and the black stove smoke. A high sun with a face traced on it beat fierce on the straw hats of the children.

Nicole was silent; Dick was uneasy at her straight hard gaze. Often he felt lonely with her, and frequently she tired him with the short floods of personal revelations that she reserved exclusively for him, "I'm like this—I'm more like that," but this afternoon he would have been glad had she rattled on in staccato for a while and given him glimpses of her thoughts. The situation was always most threatening when she backed up into herself and closed the doors behind her.

At Zug Mademoiselle got out and left them. The Divers approached the Agiri Fair through a menagerie of mammoth steam-rollers that made way for them. Dick parked the car, and as Nicole looked at him without moving, he said: "Come on, darl." Her lips drew apart into a sudden awful smile, and his belly quailed, but as if he hadn't seen it he repeated: "Come on. So the children can get out."

"Oh, I'll come all right," she answered, tearing the words from some story spinning itself out inside her, too fast for him to grasp. "Don't worry about that. I'll come——"

"Then come."

She turned from him as he walked beside her but the smile still flickered across her face, derisive and remote. Only when Lanier spoke to her several times did she manage to fix her attention upon an object, a Punch-and-Judy show, and to orient herself by anchoring to it.

Dick tried to think what to do. The dualism in his views of her—that of the husband, that of the psychiatrist—was increasingly paralyzing his faculties. In these six years she had several times carried him over the line with her, disarming him by exciting emotional pity or by a flow of wit, fantastic and disassociated, so that only after the episode did he realize with the consciousness of his own relaxation from tension, that she had succeeded in getting a point against his better judgment.

A discussion with Topsy about the guignol—as to whether the Punch was the same Punch they had seen last year in Cannes—having been settled, the family walked along again between the booths under the open sky. The women's bonnets, perching over velvet vests, the bright, spreading skirts of many cantons, seemed demure against the blue and orange paint of the wagons and displays. There was the sound of a whining, tinkling hootchy-kootchy show.

Nicole began to run very suddenly, so suddenly that for a moment Dick did not miss her. Far ahead he saw her yellow dress twisting through the crowd, an ochre stitch along the edge of reality and unreality, and started after her. Secretly she ran and secretly he followed. As the hot afternoon went shrill and terrible with her flight he had forgotten the children; then he wheeled and ran back to them, drawing them this way and that by their arms, his eyes jumping from booth to booth.

"Madame," he cried to a young woman behind a white lottery wheel, "Est-ce que je peux laisser ces petits avec vous deux minutes? C'est très urgent—je vous donnerai dix francs."

"Mais oui."

He headed the children into the booth. "Alors—restez avec cette gentille dame."

"Oui, Dick."

He darted off again but he had lost her; he circled the merry-go-round keeping up with it till he realized he was running beside it, staring always at the same horse. He

207

elbowed through the crowd in the buvette; then remembering a predilection of Nicole's he snatched up an edge of a fortune-teller's tent and peered within. A droning voice greeted him: "La septième fille d'une septième fille née sur les rives du Nil—entrez, Monsieur——"

Dropping the flap he ran along toward where the plaisance terminated at the lake and a small ferris wheel revolved slowly against the sky. There he found her.

She was alone in what was momentarily the top boat of the wheel, and as it descended he saw that she was laughing hilariously; he slunk back in the crowd, a crowd which, at the wheel's next revolution, spotted the intensity of Nicole's hysteria.

"Regardez-moi ça!"

"Regarde donc cette Anglaise!"

Down she dropped again—this time the wheel and its music were slowing and a dozen people were around her car, all of them impelled by the quality of her laughter to smile in sympathetic idiocy. But when Nicole saw Dick her laughter died—she made a gesture of slipping by and away from him but he caught her arm and held it as they walked away.

"Why did you lose control of yourself like that?"

"You know very well why."

"No, I don't."

"That's just preposterous—let me loose—that's an insult to my intelligence. Don't you think I saw that girl look at you—that little dark girl. Oh, this is farcical—a child, not more than fifteen. Don't you think I saw?"

"Stop here a minute and quiet down."

They sat at a table, her eyes in a profundity of suspicion, her hand moving across her line of sight as if it were obstructed. "I want a drink—I want a brandy."

"You can't have brandy—you can have a bock if you want it."

"Why can't I have a brandy?"

"We won't go into that. Listen to me—this business about a girl is a delusion, do you understand that word?"

208

"It's always a delusion when I see what you don't want me to see."

He had a sense of guilt as in one of those nightmares where we are accused of a crime which we recognize as something undeniably experienced, but which upon waking we realize we have not committed. His eyes wavered from hers.

"I left the children with a gypsy woman in a booth. We ought to get them."

"Who do you think you are?" she demanded. "Svengali?"[48]

Fifteen minutes ago they had been a family. Now as she was crushed into a corner by his unwilling shoulder, he saw them all, child and man, as a perilous accident.

"We're going home."

"Home!" she roared in a voice so abandoned that its louder tones wavered and cracked. "And sit and think that we're all rotting and the children's ashes are rotting in every box I open? That filth!"

Almost with relief he saw that her words sterilized her, and Nicole, sensitized down to the corium of the skin, saw the withdrawal in his face. Her own face softened and she begged, "Help me, help me, Dick!"

A wave of agony went over him. It was awful that such a fine tower should not be erected, only suspended, suspended from him. Up to a point that was right: men were for that, beam and idea, girder and logarithm; but somehow Dick and Nicole had become one and equal, not apposite and complementary; she was Dick too, the drought in the marrow of his bones. He could not watch her disintegrations without participating in them. His intuition rilled out of him as tenderness and compassion—he could only take the characteristically modern course, to interpose—he would get a nurse from Zurich, to take her over to-night.

"You *can* help me."

Her sweet bullying pulled him forward off his feet. "You've helped me before—you can help me now."

"I can only help you the same old way."

"Some one can help me."

"Maybe so. You can help yourself most. Let's find the children."

There were numerous lottery booths with white wheels— Dick was startled when he inquired at the first and encountered blank disavowals. Evil-eyed, Nicole stood apart, denying the children, resenting them as part of a downright world she sought to make amorphous. Presently Dick found them, surrounded by women who were examining them with delight like fine goods, and by peasant children staring.

"Merci, Monsieur, ah Monsieur est trop généreux. C'était un plaisir, M'sieur, Madame. Au revoir, mes petits."

They started back with a hot sorrow streaming down upon them; the car was weighted with their mutual apprehension and anguish, and the children's mouths were grave with disappointment. Grief presented itself in its terrible, dark unfamiliar color. Somewhere around Zug, Nicole, with a convulsive effort, reiterated a remark she had made before about a misty yellow house set back from the road that looked like a painting not yet dry, but it was just an attempt to catch at a rope that was playing out too swiftly.

Dick tried to rest—the struggle would come presently at home and he might have to sit a long time, restating the universe for her. A "schizophrène" is well named as a split personality—Nicole was alternately a person to whom nothing need be explained and one to whom nothing *could* be explained. It was necessary to treat her with active and affirmative insistence, keeping the road to reality always open, making the road to escape harder going. But the brilliance, the versatility of madness is akin to the resourcefulness of water seeping through, over and around a dike. It requires the united front of many people to work against it. He felt it necessary that this time Nicole cure herself; he wanted to wait until she remembered the other times, and revolted from them. In a tired way, he planned that they would again resume the régime relaxed a year before.

He had turned up a hill that made a short cut to the clinic, and now as he stepped on the accelerator for a short

210

straightaway run parallel to the hillside the car swerved violently left, swerved right, tipped on two wheels and, as Dick, with Nicole's voice screaming in his ear, crushed down the mad hand clutching the steering wheel, righted itself, swerved once more and shot off the road; it tore through low underbrush, tipped again and settled slowly at an angle of ninety degrees against a tree.

The children were screaming and Nicole was screaming and cursing and trying to tear at Dick's face. Thinking first of the list of the car and unable to estimate it Dick bent away Nicole's arm, climbed over the top side and lifted out the children; then he saw the car was in a stable position. Before doing anything else he stood there shaking and panting.

"You—!" he cried.

She was laughing hilariously, unashamed, unafraid, unconcerned. No one coming on the scene would have imagined that she had caused it; she laughed as after some mild escape of childhood. *breakdown*

"You were scared, weren't you?" she accused him. "You wanted to live!"

She spoke with such force that in his shocked state Dick wondered if he had been frightened for himself—but the strained faces of the children, looking from parent to parent, made him want to grind her grinning mask into jelly.

Directly above them, half a kilometer by the winding road but only a hundred yards climbing, was an inn; one of its wings showed through the wooded hill.

"Take Topsy's hand," he said to Lanier, "like that, tight, and climb up that hill—see the little path? When you get to the inn tell them 'La voiture Divare est cassée.' Some one must come right down."

Lanier, not sure what had happened, but suspecting the dark and unprecedented, asked:

"What will you do, Dick?"

"We'll stay here with the car."

Neither of them looked at their mother as they started off. "Be careful crossing the road up there! Look both ways!" Dick shouted after them.

He and Nicole looked at each other directly, their eyes like blazing windows across a court of the same house. Then she took out a compact, looked in its mirror, and smoothed back the temple hair. Dick watched the children climbing for a moment until they disappeared among the pines half way up; then he walked around the car to see the damage and plan how to get it back on the road. In the dirt he could trace the rocking course they had pursued for over a hundred feet; he was filled with a violent disgust that was not like anger.

In a few minutes the proprietor of the inn came running down.

"My God!" he exclaimed. "How did it happen, were you going fast? What luck! Except for that tree you'd have rolled down hill!"

Taking advantage of Émile's reality, the wide black apron, the sweat upon the rolls of his face, Dick signalled to Nicole in a matter-of-fact way to let him help her from the car; whereupon she jumped over the lower side, lost her balance on the slope, fell to her knees and got up again. As she watched the men trying to move the car her expression became defiant. Welcoming even that mood Dick said:

"Go and wait with the children, Nicole."

Only after she had gone did he remember that she had wanted cognac, and that there was cognac available up there—he told Émile never mind about the car; they would wait for the chauffeur and the big car to pull it up onto the road. Together they hurried up to the inn.

## XVI

"I want to go away," he told Franz. "For a month or so, for as long as I can."

"Why not, Dick? That was our original arrangement— it was you who insisted on staying. If you and Nicole——"

"I don't want to go away with Nicole. I want to go away

alone. This last thing knocked me sideways—if I get two hours' sleep in twenty-four, it's one of Zwingli's miracles."

"You wish a real leave of abstinence."

"The word is 'absence.' Look here: if I go to Berlin to the Psychiatric Congress could you manage to keep the peace? For three months she's been all right and she likes her nurse. My God, you're the only human being in this world I can ask this of."

Franz grunted, considering whether or not he could be trusted to think always of his partner's interest.

In Zurich the next week Dick drove to the airport and took the big plane for Munich. Soaring and roaring into the blue he felt numb, realizing how tired he was. A vast persuasive quiet stole over him, and he abandoned sickness to the sick, sound to the motors, direction to the pilot. He had no intention of attending so much as a single session of the Congress—he could imagine it well enough, new pamphlets by Bleuler and the elder Forel[49] that he could much better digest at home, the paper by the American who cured dementia præcox by pulling out his patients' teeth or cauterizing their tonsils, the half-derisive respect with which this idea would be greeted, for no more reason than that America was such a rich and powerful country. The other delegates from America—red-headed Schwartz with his saint's face and his infinite patience in straddling two worlds, as well as dozens of commercial alienists with hangdog faces, who would be present partly to increase their standing, and hence their reach for the big plums of the criminal practice, partly to master novel sophistries that they could weave into their stock in trade, to the infinite confusion of all values. There would be cynical Latins, and some man of Freud's from Vienna. Articulate among them would be the great Jung, bland, super-vigorous, on his rounds between the forests of anthropology and the neuroses of school-boys. At first there would be an American cast to the Congress, almost Rotarian in its forms and ceremonies, then the closer-knit European vitality would fight through, and finally the Americans would play their trump card, the

213

announcement of colossal gifts and endowments, of great new plants and training schools, and in the presence of the figures the Europeans would blanch and walk timidly. But he would not be there to see.

They skirted the Vorarlberg Alps, and Dick felt a pastoral delight in watching the villages. There were always four or five in sight, each one gathered around a church. It was simple looking at the earth from far off, simple as playing grim games with dolls and soldiers. This was the way statesmen and commanders and all retired people looked at things. Anyhow, it was a good draft of relief.

An Englishman spoke to him from across the aisle but he found something antipathetic in the English lately. England was like a rich man after a disastrous orgy who makes up to the household by chatting with them individually, when it is obvious to them that he is only trying to get back his self-respect in order to usurp his former power.

Dick had with him what magazines were available on the station quays: The Century, The Motion Picture, L'Illustration, and the Fliegende Blätter, but it was more fun to descend in his imagination into the villages and shake hands with the rural characters. He sat in the churches as he sat in his father's church in Buffalo, amid the starchy must of Sunday clothes. He listened to the wisdom of the Near East, was Crucified, Died, and was Buried[50] in the cheerful church, and once more worried between five or ten cents for the collection plate, because of the girl who sat in the pew behind.

The Englishman suddenly borrowed his magazines with a little small change of conversation, and Dick, glad to see them go, thought of the voyage ahead of him. Wolf-like under his sheep's clothing of long-staple Australian wool, he considered the world of pleasure—the incorruptible Mediterranean with sweet old dirt caked in the olive trees, the peasant girl near Savona with a face as green and rose as the color of an illuminated missal. He would take her in his hands and snatch her across the border . . .

. . . but there he deserted her—he must press on toward the Isles of Greece, the cloudy waters of unfamiliar ports, the lost girl on shore, the moon of popular songs. A part of

Dick's mind was made up of the tawdry souvenirs of his boyhood. Yet in that somewhat littered Five-and-Ten, he had managed to keep alive the low painful fir e of intelligence.

*[handwritten left margin: mention of Tommy]*

## XVII

*[handwritten right margin: take over D's role (w/ Nicole)]*

TOMMY BARBAN was a ruler, Tommy was a (hero)—Dick happened upon him in the Marienplatz in Munich, in one of those cafés where small gamblers diced on "tapestry" mats. The air was full of politics, and the slap of cards.

Tommy was at a table laughing his martial laugh: "Umbuh—ha-ha! Um-buh—ha-ha!" As a rule, he drank little; courage was his game and his companions were always a little afraid of him. Recently an eighth of the area of his skull had been removed by a Warsaw surgeon and was knitting under his hair, and the weakest person in the café could have killed him with a flip of a knotted napkin.

*[handwritten left margin: description of Tommy]*

"—this is Prince Chillicheff—" a battered, powder-gray Russian of fifty, "—and Mr. McKibben—and Mr. Hannan—" the latter was a lively ball of black eyes and hair, a clown; and he said immediately to Dick:

"The first thing before we shake hands—what do you mean by fooling around with my aunt?"

"Why, I——"

"You heard me. What are you doing here in Munich anyhow?"

"Um-bah—ha-ha!" laughed Tommy.

"Haven't you got aunts of your own? Why don't you fool with them?"

Dick laughed, whereupon the man shifted his attack:

"Now let's not have any more talk about aunts. How do I know you didn't make up the whole thing? Here you are a complete stranger with an acquaintance of less than half an hour, and you come up to me with a cock-and-bull story about your aunts. How do I know what you have concealed about you?"

Tommy laughed again, then he said good-naturedly, but

215

firmly, "That's enough, Carly. Sit down, Dick—how're you? How's Nicole?"

He did not like any man very much nor feel their presence with much intensity—he was all relaxed for combat; as a fine athlete playing secondary defense in any sport is really resting much of the time, while a lesser man only pretends to rest and is at a continual and self-destroying nervous tension.

Hannan, not entirely suppressed, moved to an adjoining piano, and with recurring resentment on his face whenever he looked at Dick, played chords, from time to time muttering, "Your aunts," and, in a dying cadence, "I didn't say aunts anyhow. I said pants."

"Well, how're you?" repeated Tommy. "You don't look so—" he fought for a word, "—so jaunty as you used to, so spruce, you know what I mean."

The remark sounded too much like one of those irritating accusations of waning vitality and Dick w as about to retort by commenting on the extraordinary suits worn by Tommy and Prince Chillicheff, suits of a cut and pattern fantastic enough to have sauntered down Beale Street on a Sunday—when an explanation was forthcoming.

"I see you are regarding our clothes," said the Prince. "We have just come out of Russia."

"These were made in Poland by the court tailor," said Tommy. "That's a fact—Pilsudski's own tailor."

"You've been touring?" Dick asked.

They laughed, the Prince inordinately and meanwhile clapping Tommy on the back.

"Yes, we have been touring. That's it, touring. We have made the Grand Tour of all the Russias. In state."

Dick waited for an explanation. It came from Mr. McKibben in two words.

"They escaped."

"Have you been prisoners in Russia?"

"It was I," explained Prince Chillicheff, his dead yellow eyes staring at Dick. "Not a prisoner but in hiding."

"Did you have much trouble getting out?"

"Some trouble. We left three Red Guards dead at the

border. Tommy left two—" He held up two fingers like a Frenchman—"I left one."

"That's the part I don't understand," said Mr. McKibben. "Why they should have objected to your leaving."

Hannan turned from the piano and said, winking at the others: "Mac thinks a Marxian is somebody who went to St. Mark's school."

It was an escape story in the best tradition—an aristocrat hiding nine years with a former servant and working in a government bakery; the eighteen-year-old daughter in Paris who knew Tommy Barban. . . . During the narrative Dick decided that this parched papier mâché relic of the past was scarcely worth the lives of three young men. The question arose as to whether Tommy and Chillicheff had been frightened.

"When I was cold," Tommy said. "I always get scared when I'm cold. During the war I was always frightened when I was cold."

McKibben stood up.

"I must leave. To-morrow morning I'm going to Innsbruck by car with my wife and children—and the governess."

"I'm going there to-morrow, too," said Dick.

"Oh, are you?" exclaimed McKibben. "Why not come with us? It's a big Packard and there's only my wife and my children and myself—and the governess——"

"I can't possibly——"

"Of course she's not really a governess," McKibben concluded, looking rather pathetically at Dick. "As a matter of fact my wife knows your sister-in-law, Baby Warren."

But Dick was not to be drawn in a blind contract.

"I've promised to travel with two men."

"Oh," McKibben's face fell. "Well, I'll say good-by." He unscrewed two blooded wire-hairs from a nearby table and stood ready to depart; Dick pictured the jammed Packard pounding toward Innsbruck with the McKibbens and their children and their baggage and yapping dogs—and the governess.

"The paper says they know the man who killed him,"

said Tommy. "But his cousins did not want it in the papers, because it happened in a speakeasy. What do you think of that?"

"It's what's known as family pride."

Hannan played a loud chord on the piano to attract attention to himself.

"I don't believe his first stuff holds up," he said. "Even barring the Europeans there are a dozen Americans can do what North did."

It was the first indication Dick had had that they were talking about Abe North.

"The only difference is that Abe did it first," said Tommy.

"I don't agree," persisted Hannan. "He got the reputation for being a good musician because he drank so much that his friends had to explain him away somehow——"

"What's this about Abe North? What about him? Is he in a jam?"

"Didn't you read The Herald this morning?"

"No."

"He's dead. He was beaten to death in a speakeasy in New York. He just managed to crawl home to the Racquet Club to die——"

"*Abe North?*"

"Yes, sure, they——"

"*Abe North?*" Dick stood up. "Are you sure he's dead?"

Hannan turned around to McKibben: "It wasn't the Racquet Club he crawled to—it was the Harvard Club. I'm sure he didn't belong to the Racquet."

"The paper said so," McKibben insisted.

"It must have been a mistake. I'm quite sure."

"*Beaten to death in a speakeasy.*"

"But I happen to know most of the members of the Racquet Club," said Hannan. "It *must* have been the Harvard Club."

Dick got up, Tommy too. Prince Chillicheff started out of a wan study of nothing, perhaps of his chances of ever getting out of Russia, a study that had occupied him so long that it was doubtful if he could give it up immediately, and joined them in leaving.

*"Abe North beaten to death."*

On the way to the hotel, a journey of which Dick was scarcely aware, Tommy said:

"We're waiting for a tailor to finish some suits so we can get to Paris. I'm going into stock-broking and they wouldn't take me if I showed up like this. Everybody in your country is making millions. Are you really leaving to-morrow? We can't even have dinner with you. It seems the Prince had an old girl in Munich. He called her up but she'd been dead five years and we're having dinner with the two daughters."

The Prince nodded.

"Perhaps I could have arranged for Doctor Diver."

"No, no," said Dick hastily.

He slept deep and awoke to a slow mournful march passing his window. It was a long column of men in uniform, wearing the familiar helmet of 1914, thick men in frock coats and silk hats, burghers, aristocrats, plain men. It was a society of veterans going to lay wreaths on the tombs of the dead. The column marched slowly with a sort of swagger for a lost magnificence, a past effort, a forgotten sorrow. The faces were only formally sad but Dick's lungs burst for a moment with regret for Abe's death, and his own youth of ten years ago.

# XVIII

HE reached Innsbruck at dusk, sent his bags up to a hotel and walked into town. In the sunset the Emperor Maximilian knelt in prayer above his bronze mourners; a quartet of Jesuit novices paced and read in the university garden. The marble souvenirs of old sieges, marriages, anniversaries, faded quickly when the sun was down, and he had Erbsensuppe with Würstchen cut up in it, drank four Pilsener and refused a formidable dessert known as "Kaiserschmarren."

Despite the overhanging mountains Switzerland was far away, Nicole was far away. Walking in the garden later when it was quite dark he thought about her with detachment, loving her for her best self. He remembered once when the grass was damp and she came to him on hurried feet, her thin slippers drenched with dew. She stood upon his shoes nestling close and held up her face, showing it as a book open at a page.

"Think how you love me," she whispered. "I don't ask you to love me always like this, but I ask you to remember. Somewhere inside me there'll always be the person I am to-night."

But Dick had come away for his soul's sake, and he began thinking about that. He had lost himself—he could not tell the hour when, or the day or the week, the month or the year. Once he had cut through things, solving the most complicated equations as the simplest problems of his simplest patients. Between the time he found Nicole flowering under a stone on the Zürichsee and the moment of his meeting with Rosemary the spear had been blunted.

Watching his father's struggles in poor parishes had wedded a desire for money to an essentially unacquisitive nature. It was not a healthy necessity for security—he had never felt more sure of himself, more thoroughly his own man, than at the time of his marriage to Nicole. Yet he had been swallowed up like a gigolo, and somehow permitted his arsenal to be locked up in the Warren safety-deposit vaults.

 *Dick's reflection*

"There should have been a settlement in the Continental style; but it isn't over yet. I've wasted eight years teaching the rich the ABC's of human decency, but I'm not done. I've got too many unplayed trumps in my hand."

He loitered among the fallow rose bushes and the beds of damp sweet indistinguishable fern. It was warm for October but cool enough to wear a heavy tweed coat buttoned by a little elastic tape at the neck. A figure detached itself from the black shape of a tree and he knew it was the woman whom he had passed in the lobby coming out. He was in love with every pretty woman he saw now, their forms at a distance, their shadows on a wall.

Her back was toward him as she faced the lights of the town. He scratched a match that she must have heard, but she remained motionless.

—Was it an invitation? Or an indication of obliviousness? He had long been outside of the world of simple desires and their fulfillments, and he was inept and uncertain. For all he knew there might be some code among the wanderers of obscure spas by which they found each other quickly.

—Perhaps the next gesture was his. Strange children should smile at each other and say, "Let's play."

He moved closer, the shadow moved sideways. Possibly he would be snubbed like the scapegrace drummers he had heard of in youth. His heart beat loud in contact with the unprobed, undissected, unanalyzed, unaccounted for. Suddenly he turned away, and, as he did, the girl, too, broke the black frieze she made with the foliage, rounded a bench at a moderate but determined pace and took the path back to the hotel.

With a guide and two other men, Dick started up the Birkkarspitze next morning. It was a fine feeling once they were above the cowbells of the highest pastures—Dick looked forward to the night in the shack, enjoying his own fatigue, enjoying the captaincy of the guide, feeling a delight in his own anonymity. But at mid-day the weather changed to black sleet and hail and mountain thunder. Dick and one of the other climbers wanted to go on but the guide refused. Regretfully they struggled back to Innsbruck to start again to-morrow.

After dinner and a bottle of heavy local wine in the deserted dining-room, he felt excited, without knowing why, until he began thinking of the garden. He had passed the girl in the lobby before supper and this time she had looked at him and approved of him, but it kept worrying him: Why? When I could have had a good share of the pretty women of my time for the asking, why start that now? With a wraith, with a fragment of my desire? Why?

His imagination pushed ahead—the old asceticism, the actual unfamiliarity, triumphed: God, I might as well go back to the Riviera and sleep with Janice Caricamento or the Wilburhazy girl. To belittle all these years with something cheap and easy?

He was still excited, though, and he turned from the veranda and went up to his room to think. Being alone in body and spirit begets loneliness, and loneliness begets more loneliness.

Upstairs he walked around thinking of the matter and laying out his climbing clothes advantageously on the faint heater; he again encountered Nicole's telegram, still unopened, with which diurnally she accompanied his itinerary. He had delayed opening it before supper—perhaps because of the garden. It was a cablegram from Buffalo, forwarded through Zurich.

"Your father died peacefully tonight HOLMES"

He felt a sharp wince at the shock, a gathering of the forces of resistance; then it rolled up through his loins and stomach and throat.

He read the message again. He sat down on the bed, breathing and staring; thinking first the old selfish child's thought that comes with the death of a parent, how will it affect me now that this earliest and strongest of protections is gone?

The atavism passed and he walked the room still, stopping from time to time to look at the telegram. Holmes was formally his father's curate but actually, and for a decade, rector of the church. How did he die? Of old age—he was seventy-five. He had lived a long time.

Dick felt sad that he had died alone—he had survived his wife, and his brothers and sisters; there were cousins in Virginia but they were poor and not able to come North, and Holmes had had to sign the telegram. Dick loved his father—again and again he referred judgments to what his father would probably have thought or done. Dick was born several months after the death of two young sisters and his father, guessing what would be the effect on Dick's mother, had saved him from a spoiling by becoming his moral guide. He was of tired stock yet he raised himself to that effort.

In the summer father and son walked downtown together to have their shoes shined—Dick in his starched duck sailor suit, his father always in beautifully cut clerical clothes—and the father was very proud of his handsome little boy. He told Dick all he knew about life, not much but most of it true, simple things, matters of behavior that came within his clergyman's range. "Once in a strange town when I was first ordained, I went into a crowded room and was confused as to who was my hostess. Several people I knew came toward me, but I disregarded them because I had seen a gray-haired woman sitting by a window far across the room. I went over to her and introduced myself. After that I made many friends in that town."

His father had done that from a good heart—his father had been sure of what he was, with a deep pride of the two proud widows who had raised him to believe that nothing could be superior to "good instincts," honor, courtesy, and courage.

The father always considered that his wife's small fortune belonged to his son, and in college and in medical school sent him a check for all of it four times a year. He was one of those about whom it was said with smug finality in the gilded age: "very much the gentleman, but not much get-up-and-go about him."

. . . Dick sent down for a newspaper. Still pacing to and from the telegram open on his bureau, he chose a ship to go to America. Then he put in a call for Nicole in Zurich, remembering so many things as he waited, and wishing he had always been as good as he had intended to be.

# XIX

For an hour, tied up with his profound reaction to his father's death, the magnificent façade of the homeland, the harbor of New York, seemed all sad and glorious to Dick, but once ashore the feeling vanished, nor did he find it again in the streets or the hotels or the trains that bore him first to Buffalo, and then south to Virginia with his father's body. Only as the local train shambled into the lowforested clayland of Westmoreland County did he feel once more identified with his surroundings; at the station he saw a star he knew, and a cold moon bright over Chesapeake Bay; he heard the rasping wheels of buckboards turning, the lovely fatuous voices, the sound of sluggish primeval rivers flowing softly under soft Indian names.

Next day at the churchyard his father was laid among a hundred Divers, Dorseys, and Hunters. It was very friendly leaving him there with all his relations around him. Flowers were scattered on the brown unsettled earth. Dick had no more ties here now and did not believe he would come back. He knelt on the hard soil. These dead, he knew them all, their weather-beaten faces with blue flashing eyes, the spare violent bodies, the souls made of new earth in the forest-heavy darkness of the seventeenth century.

"Good-by, my father—good-by, all my fathers."

On the long-roofed steamship piers one is in a country that is no longer here and not yet there. The hazy yellow vault is full of echoing shouts. There are the rumble of trucks and the clump of trunks, the strident chatter of cranes, the first salt smell of the sea. One hurries through, even though there's time; the past, the continent, is behind; the future is the glowing mouth in the side of the ship; the dim, turbulent alley is too confusedly the present.

Up the gangplank and the vision of the world adjusts itself, narrows. One is a citizen of a commonwealth smaller than Andorra, no longer sure of anything. The men at the purser's desk are as oddly shaped as the cabins; disdainful are the eyes of voyagers and their friends. Next the loud mournful whistles, the portentous vibration and the boat, the human idea—is in motion. The pier and its faces slide by and for a moment the boat is a piece accidentally split off from them; the faces become remote, voiceless, the pier is one of many blurs along the water front. The harbor flows swiftly toward the sea.

With it flowed Albert McKisco, labelled by the newspapers as its most precious cargo. McKisco was having a vogue. His novels were pastiches of the work of the best

Mr. McKisco

— combining characteristics of popular authors
— imitation of popular styles + combining (Ulysses)

people of his time, a feat not to be disparaged, and in
addition he possessed a gift for softening and debasing what
he borrowed, so that many readers were charmed by the
ease with which they could follow him. Success had im-
proved him and humbled him. He was no fool about his
capacities—he realized that he possessed more vitality than
many men of superior talent, and he was resolved to enjoy
the success he had earned. "I've done nothing yet," he
would say. "I don't think I've got any real genius. But if I
keep trying I may write a good book." Fine dives have been
made from flimsier spring-boards. The innumerable snubs
of the past were forgotten. Indeed, his success was founded
psychologically upon his duel with Tommy Barban, upon
the basis of which, as it withered in his memory, he had
created, afresh, a new self-respect.

Spotting Dick Diver the second day out, he eyed him
tentatively, then introduced himself in a friendly way and
sat down. Dick laid aside his reading and, after the few
minutes that it took to realize the change in McKisco, the
disappearance of the man's annoying sense of inferiority,
found himself pleased to talk to him. McKisco was "well-
informed" on a range of subjects wider than Goethe's—it
was interesting to listen to the innumerable facile combinations that he referred to as his opinions. They struck up an
acquaintance, and Dick had several meals with them. The
McKiscos had been invited to sit at the captain's table but
with nascent snobbery they told Dick that they "couldn't
stand that bunch."

Violet was very grand now, decked out by the grand
couturières, charmed about the little discoveries that well-
bred girls make in their teens. She could, indeed, have
learned them from her mother in Boise but her soul was
born dismally in the small movie houses of Idaho, and she
had had no time for her mother. Now she "belonged"—
together with several million other people—and she was
happy, though her husband still shushed her when she grew
violently naïve.

The McKiscos got off at Gibraltar. Next evening in
Naples Dick picked up a lost and miserable family of two

girls and their mother in the bus from the hotel to the station. He had seen them on the ship. An overwhelming desire to help, or to be admired, came over him: he showed them fragments of gaiety; tentatively he bought them wine, with pleasure saw them begin to regain their proper egotism. He pretended they were this and that, falling in with his own plot, and drinking too much to sustain the illusion, and all this time the women thought only that this was a windfall from heaven. He withdrew from them as the night waned and the train rocked and snorted at Cassino and Frosinone. After weird American partings in the station at Rome, Dick went to the Hotel Quirinal, somewhat exhausted.

At the desk he suddenly stared and upped his head. As if a drink were acting on him, warming the lining of his stomach, throwing a flush up into his brain, he saw the person he had come to see, the person for whom he had made the Mediterranean crossing.

Simultaneously Rosemary saw him, acknowledging him before placing him; she looked back startled, and, leaving the girl she was with, she hurried over. Holding himself erect, holding his breath, Dick turned to her. As she came across the lobby, her beauty all groomed, like a young horse dosed with black-seed oil and hoofs varnished, shocked him awake; but it all came too quick for him to do anything except conceal his fatigue as best he could. To meet her starry-eyed confidence he mustered an insincere pantomime implying, "You *would* turn up here—of all the people in the world."

Her gloved hands closed over his on the desk; "Dick— we're making 'The Grandeur that was Rome'—at least we think we are; we may quit any day."

He looked at her hard, trying to make her a little self-conscious, so that she would observe less closely his unshaven face, his crumpled and slept-in collar. Fortunately, she was in a hurry.

"We begin early because the mists rise at eleven—phone me at two."

In his room Dick collected his faculties. He left a call for

226

noon, stripped off his clothes and dove literally into a heavy sleep.

He slept over the phone call but awoke at two, refreshed. Unpacking his bag, he sent out suits and laundry. He shaved, lay for half an hour in a warm bath and had breakfast. The sun had dipped into the Via Nazionale and he let it through the portières with a jingling of old brass rings. Waiting for a suit to be pressed, he discovered from the Corriere della Sera that "una novella di Sainclair Lewis 'Wall Street'[51] nella quale l'autore analizza la vita sociale di una piccola città Americana." Then he tried to think about Rosemary.

At first he thought nothing. She was young and magnetic, but so was Topsy. He guessed that she had had lovers and had loved them in the last four years. Well, you never knew exactly how much space you occupied in people's lives. Yet from this fog his affection emerged—the best contacts are when one knows the obstacles and still wants to preserve a relation. The past drifted back and he wanted to hold her eloquent giving-of-herself in its precious shell, till he enclosed it, till it no longer existed outside him. He tried to collect all that might attract her—it was less than it had been four years ago. Eighteen might look at thirty-four through a rising mist of adolescence; but twenty-two would see thirty-eight with discerning clarity. Moreover, Dick had been at an emotional peak at the time of the previous encounter; since then there had been a lesion of enthusiasm.

When the valet returned he put on a white shirt and collar and a black tie with a pearl; the cords of his reading-glasses passed through another pearl of the same size that swung a casual inch below. After sleep, his face had resumed the ruddy brown of many Riviera summers, and to limber himself up he stood on his hands on a chair until his fountain pen and coins fell out. At three he called Rosemary and was bidden to come up. Momentarily dizzy from his acrobatics, he stopped in the bar for a gin-and-tonic.

"Hi, Doctor Diver!"

Only because of Rosemary's presence in the hotel did

227

Dick place the man immediately as Collis Clay. He had his old confidence and an air of prosperity and big sudden jowls.

"Do you know Rosemary's here?" Collis asked.

"I ran into her."

"I was in Florence and I heard she was here so I came down last week. You'd never know Mama's little girl." He modified the remark, "I mean she was so carefully brought up and now she's a woman of the world—if you know what I mean. Believe me, has she got some of these Roman boys tied up in bags! And how!"

"You studying in Florence?"

"Me? Sure, I'm studying architecture there. I go back Sunday—I'm staying for the races."

With difficulty Dick restrained him from adding the drink to the account he carried in the bar, like a stock-market report.

## XX

When Dick got out of the elevator he followed a tortuous corridor and turned at length toward a distant voice outside a lighted door. Rosemary was in black pajamas; a luncheon table was still in the room; she was having coffee.

"You're still beautiful," he said. "A little more beautiful than ever."

"Do you want coffee, youngster?"

"I'm sorry I was so unpresentable this morning."

"You didn't look well—you all right now? Want coffee?"

"No, thanks."

"You're fine again. I was scared this morning. Mother's coming over next month, if the company stays. She always asks me if I've seen you over here, as if she thought we were living next door. Mother always liked you—she always felt you were someone I ought to know."

"Well, I'm glad she still thinks of me."

"Oh, she does," Rosemary reassured him. "A very great deal."

"I've seen you here and there in pictures," said Dick. "Once I had 'Daddy's Girl' run off just for myself!"

"I have a good part in this one if it isn't cut."

She crossed behind him, touching his shoulder as she passed. She phoned for the table to be taken away and settled in a big chair.

"I was just a little girl when I met you, Dick. Now I'm a woman."

"I want to hear everything about you."

"How is Nicole—and Lanier and Topsy?"

"They're fine. They often speak of you——"

The phone rang. While she answered it Dick examined two novels—one by Edna Ferber,[52] one by Albert McKisco.  The waiter came for the table; bereft of its presence Rosemary seemed more alone in her black pajamas.

" . . . I have a caller. . . . No, not very well. I've got to go to the costumer's for a long fitting. . . . No, not now. . . ."

As though with the disappearance of the table she felt released, Rosemary smiled at Dick—that smile as if they two together had managed to get rid of all the trouble in the world and were now at peace in their own heaven. . . .

"That's done," she said. "Do you realize I've spent the last hour getting ready for you?"

But again the phone called her. Dick got up to change his hat from the bed to the luggage stand, and in alarm Rosemary put her hand over the mouthpiece of the phone. "You're not going!"

"No."

When the communication was over he tried to drag the afternoon together saying: "I expect some nourishment from people now."

"Me too," Rosemary agreed. "The man that just phoned me once knew a second cousin of mine. Imagine calling anybody up for a reason like that!"

Now she lowered the lights for love. Why else should she want to shut off his view of her? He sent his words to her

229

like letters, as though they left him some time before they reached her.

"Hard to sit here and be close to you, and not kiss you." Then they kissed passionately in the centre of the floor. She pressed against him, and went back to her chair.

It could not go on being merely pleasant in the room. Forward or backward; when the phone rang once more he strolled into the bedchamber and lay down on her bed, opening Albert McKisco's novel. Presently Rosemary came in and sat beside him.

"You have the longest eyelashes," she remarked.

"We are now back at the Junior Prom. Among those present are Miss Rosemary Hoyt, the eyelash fancier——"

She kissed him and he pulled her down so that they lay side by side, and then they kissed till they were both breathless. Her breathing was young and eager and exciting. Her lips were faintly chapped but soft in the corners.

When they were still limbs and feet and clothes, struggles of his arms and back, and her throat and breasts, she whispered, "No, not now—those things are rhythmic."

Disciplined he crushed his passion into a corner of his mind, but bearing up her fragility on his arm until she was poised half a foot above him, he said lightly:

"Darling—that doesn't matter."

Her face had changed with his looking up at it; there was the eternal moonlight in it.

"That would be poetic justice if it should be you," she said. She twisted away from him, walked to the mirror, and boxed her disarranged hair with her hands. Presently she drew a chair close to the bed and stroked his cheek.

"Tell me the truth about you," he demanded.

"I always have."

"In a way—but nothing hangs together."

They both laughed but he pursued.

"Are you actually a virgin?"

"No-o-o!" she sang. "I've slept with six hundred and forty men—if that's the answer you want."

"It's none of my business."

"Do you want me for a case in psychology?"

230

"Looking at you as a perfectly normal girl of twenty-two, living in the year nineteen twenty-eight, I guess you've taken a few shots at love."

"It's all been—abortive," she said.

Dick couldn't believe her. He could not decide whether she was deliberately building a barrier between them or whether this was intended to make an eventual surrender more significant.

"Let's go walk in the Pincio," he suggested.

He shook himself straight in his clothes and smoothed his hair. A moment had come and somehow passed. For three years Dick had been the ideal by which Rosemary measured other men and inevitably his stature had increased to heroic size. She did not want him to be like other men, yet here were the same exigent demands, as if he wanted to take some of herself away, carry it off in his pocket.

Walking on the greensward between cherubs and philosophers, fauns and falling water, she took his arm snugly, settling into it with a series of little readjustments, as if she wanted it to be right because it was going to be there forever. She plucked a twig and broke it, but she found no spring in it. Suddenly seeing what she wanted in Dick's face she took his gloved hand and kissed it. Then she cavorted childishly for him until he smiled and she laughed and they began having a good time.

"I can't go out with you to-night, darling, because I promised some people a long time ago. But if you'll get up early I'll take you out to the set to-morrow."

He dined alone at the hotel, went to bed early, and met Rosemary in the lobby at half-past six. Beside him in the car she glowed away fresh and new in the morning sunshine. They went out through the Porta San Sebastiano and along the Appian Way until they came to the huge set of the Forum, larger than the Forum itself. Rosemary turned him over to a man who led him about the great props: the arches and tiers of seats and the sanded arena. She was working on a stage which represented a guard-room for Christian prisoners, and presently they went there and watched Nicotera, one of many hopeful Valentinos, strut and pose before a dozen female "captives," their eyes melancholy and startling with mascara.

Rosemary appeared in a knee-length tunic.

"Watch this," she whispered to Dick. "I want your opinion. Everybody that's seen the rushes says——"

"What are the rushes?"

"When they run off what they took the day before. They say it's the first thing I've had sex appeal in."

"I don't notice it."

"You wouldn't! But I have."

Nicotera in his leopard skin talked attentively to Rosemary while the electrician discussed something with the director, meanwhile leaning on him. Finally the director pushed his hand off roughly and wiped a sweating forehead, and Dick's guide remarked: "He's on the hop again, and how!"

"Who?" asked Dick, but before the man could answer the director walked swiftly over to them.

"Who's on the hop—you're on the hop yourself." He spoke vehemently to Dick, as if to a jury. "When he's on the hop he always thinks everybody else is, and how!" He glared at the guide a moment longer, then he clapped his hands: "All right—everybody on the set."

It was like visiting a great turbulent family. An actress approached Dick and talked to him for five minutes under the impression that he was an actor recently arrived from London. Discovering her mistake she scuttled away in panic. The majority of the company felt either sharply superior or sharply inferior to the world outside, but the former feeling prevailed. They were people of bravery and industry; they were risen to a position of prominence in a nation that for a decade had wanted only to be entertained.

The session ended as the light grew misty—a fine light for painters, but, for the camera, not to be compared with the clear California air. Nicotera followed Rosemary to the car and whispered something to her—she looked at him without smiling as she said good-by.

Dick and Rosemary had luncheon at the Castelli dei Caesari, a splendid restaurant in a high-terraced villa overlooking the ruined forum of an undetermined period of the decadence. Rosemary took a cocktail and a little wine, and Dick took enough so that his feeling of dissatisfaction left him. Afterward they drove back to the hotel, all flushed and happy, in a sort of exalted quiet. She wanted to be taken and she was, and what had begun with a childish infatuation on a beach was accomplished at last.

## XXI

ROSEMARY had another dinner date, a birthday party for a member of the company. Dick ran into Collis Clay in the lobby, but he wanted to dine alone, and pretended an engagement at the Excelsior. He drank a cocktail with Collis and his vague dissatisfaction crystallized as impatience—he no longer had an excuse for playing truant to the clinic. This was less an infatuation than a romantic memory. Nicole was his girl—too often he was sick at heart about her, yet she was his girl. Time with Rosemary was self-indulgence—time with Collis was nothing plus nothing.

In the doorway of the Excelsior he ran into Baby Warren. Her large beautiful eyes, looking precisely like marbles, stared at him with surprise and curiosity. "I thought you were in America, Dick! Is Nicole with you?"

"I came back by way of Naples."

The black band on his arm reminded her to say: "I'm so sorry to hear of your trouble."

Inevitably they dined together. "Tell me about everything," she demanded.

Dick gave her a version of the facts, and Baby frowned. She found it necessary to blame someone for the catastrophe in her sister's life.

"Do you think Doctor Dohmler took the right course with her from the first?"

"There's not much variety in treatment any more—of course you try to find the right personality to handle a particular case."

233

"Dick, I don't pretend to advise you or to know much about it but don't you think a change might be good for her—to get out of that atmosphere of sickness and live in the world like other people?"

"But you were keen for the clinic," he reminded her. "You told me you'd never feel really safe about her——"

"That was when you were leading that hermit's life on the Riviera, up on a hill way off from anybody. I didn't mean to go back to that life. I meant, for instance, London. The English are the best-balanced race in the world."

"They are not," he disagreed.

"They are. I know them, you see. I meant it might be nice for you to take a house in London for the spring season—I know a dove of a house in Talbot Square you could get, furnished. I mean, living with sane, well-balanced English people."

She would have gone on to tell him all the old propaganda stories of 1914 if he had not laughed and said:

"I've been reading a book by Michael Arlen[53] and if that's——"

She ruined Michael Arlen with a wave of her salad spoon.

"He only writes about degenerates. I mean the worth-while English."

As she thus dismissed her friends they were replaced in Dick's mind only by a picture of the alien, unresponsive faces that peopled the small hotels of Europe.

"Of course it's none of my business," Baby repeated, as a preliminary to a further plunge, "but to leave her alone in an atmosphere like that——"

"I went to America because my father died."

"I understand that, I told you how sorry I was." She fiddled with the glass grapes on her necklace. "But there's so *much* money now. Plenty for everything, and it ought to be used to get Nicole well."

"For one thing I can't see myself in London."

"Why not? I should think you could work there as well as anywhere else."

He sat back and looked at her. If she had ever suspected the rotted old truth, the real reason for Nicole's illness, she

234

had certainly determined to deny it to herself, shoving it back in a dusty closet like one of the paintings she bought by mistake.

They continued the conversation in the Ulpia, where Collis Clay came over to their table and sat down, and a gifted guitar player thrummed and rumbled "Suona Fanfara Mia" in the cellar piled with wine casks.

"It's possible that I was the wrong person for Nicole," *second thoughts* Dick said. "Still she would probably have married someone of my type, someone she thought she could rely on—indefinitely."

"You think she'd be happier with somebody else?" Baby thought aloud suddenly. "Of course it could be arranged."

Only as she saw Dick bend forward with helpless laughter did she realize the preposterousness of her remark.

*Baby thinks he doesn't love Nicole*

"Oh, you understand," she assured him. "Don't think for a moment that we're not grateful for all you've done. And we know you've had a hard time——"

"For God's sake," he protested. "If I didn't love Nicole it might be different."

"But you do love Nicole?" she demanded in alarm. *surprised to learn he does*

Collis was catching up with the conversation now and Dick switched it quickly: "Suppose we talk about something else—about you, for instance. Why don't you get married? We heard you were engaged to Lord Paley, the cousin of the——"

"Oh, no." She became coy and elusive. "That was last year."

"Why don't you marry?" Dick insisted stubbornly.

"I don't know. One of the men I loved was killed in the war, and the other one threw me over."

"Tell me about it. Tell me about your private life, Baby, and your opinions. You never do—we always talk about Nicole."

"Both of them were Englishmen. I don't think there's any higher type in the world than a first-rate Englishman, do you? If there is I haven't met him. This man—oh, it's a long story. I hate long stories, don't you?"

"And how!" said Collis.

"Why, no—I like them if they're good."

"That's something you do so well, Dick. You can keep a party moving by just a little sentence or a saying here and there. I think that's a wonderful talent."

"It's a trick," he said gently. That made three of her opinions he disagreed with.

"Of course I like formality—I like things to be just so, and on the grand scale. I know you probably don't but you must admit it's a sign of solidity in me."

Dick did not even bother to dissent from this.

"Of course I know people say, Baby Warren is racing around over Europe, chasing one novelty after another, and missing the best things in life, but I think on the contrary that I'm one of the few people who really go after the best things. I've known the most interesting people of my time." Her voice blurred with the tinny drumming of another guitar number, but she called over it, "I've made very few big mistakes——"

—Only the very big ones, Baby.

She had caught something facetious in his eye and she changed the subject. It seemed impossible for them to hold anything in common. But he admired something in her, and he deposited her at the Excelsior with a series of compliments that left her shimmering.

Rosemary insisted on treating Dick to lunch next day. They went to a little trattoria kept by an Italian who had worked in America, and ate ham and eggs and waffles. Afterward, they went to the hotel. Dick's discovery that he was not in love with her, nor she with him, had add ed to rather than diminished his passion for her. Now that he knew he would not enter further into her life, she became the strange woman for him. He supposed many men meant no more than that when they said they were in love—not a wild submergence of soul, a dipping of all colors into an obscuring dye, such as his love for Nicole had been. Certain thoughts about Nicole, that she should die, sink into mental darkness, love another man, made him physically sick.

Nicotera was in Rosemary's sitting-room, chattering about a professional matter. When Rosemary gave him his cue to go, he left with humorous protests and a rather insolent wink at Dick. As usual the phone clamored and Rosemary was engaged at it for ten minutes, to Dick's increasing impatience.

"Let's go up to my room," he suggested, and she agreed.

She lay across his knees on a big sofa; he ran his fingers through the lovely forelocks of her hair.

"Let me be curious about you again?" he asked.

"What do you want to know?"

"About men. I'm curious, not to say prurient."

"You mean how long after I met you?"

"Or before."

"Oh, no." She was shocked. "There was nothing before. You were the first man I cared about. You're still the only man I really care about." She considered. "It was about a year, I think."

"Who was it?"

"Oh, a man."

He closed in on her evasion.

"I'll bet I can tell you about it: the first affair was unsatisfactory and after that there was a long gap. The second was better, but you hadn't been in love with the man in the first place. The third was all right——"

Torturing himself he ran on. "Then you had one real affair that fell of its own weight, and by that time you were getting afraid that you wouldn't have anything to give to the man you finally loved." He felt increasingly Victorian. "Afterwards there were half a dozen just episodic affairs, right up to the present. Is that close?"

She laughed between amusement and tears.

"It's about as wrong as it could be," she said, to Dick's relief. "But some day I'm going to find somebody and love him and love him and never let him go."

Now his phone rang and Dick recognized Nicotera's voice, asking for Rosemary. He put his palm over the transmitter.

237

"Do you want to talk to him?"

She went to the phone and jabbered in a rapid Italian Dick could not understand.

"This telephoning takes time," he said. "It's after four and I have an engagement at five. You better go play with Signor Nicotera."

"Don't be silly."

"Then I think that while I'm here you ought to count him out."

"It's difficult." She was suddenly crying. "Dick, I do love you, never anybody like you. But what have you got for me?"

"What has Nicotera got for anybody?"

"That's different."

—Because youth called to youth.

"He's a spic!" he said. He was frantic with jealousy, he didn't want to be hurt again.

"He's only a baby," she said, sniffing. "You know I'm yours first."

In reaction he put his arms about her but she relaxed wearily backward; he held her like that for a moment as in the end of an adagio, her eyes closed, her hair falling straight back like that of a girl drowned.

"Dick, let me go. I never felt so mixed up in my life."

He was a gruff red bird and instinctively she drew away from him as his unjustified jealousy began to snow over the qualities of consideration and understanding with which she felt at home.

"I want to know the truth," he said.

"Yes, then. We're a lot together, he wants to marry me, but I don't want to. What of it? What do you expect me to do? You never asked me to marry you. Do you want me to play around forever with half-wits like Collis Clay?"

"You were with Nicotera last night?"

"That's none of your business," she sobbed. "Excuse me, Dick, it is your business. You and Mother are the only two people in the world I care about."

"How about Nicotera?"

"How do I know?"

238

She had achieved the elusiveness that gives hidden significance to the least significant remarks.

"Is it like you felt toward me in Paris?"

"I feel comfortable and happy when I'm with you. In Paris it was different. But you never know how you once felt. Do you?"

He got up and began collecting his evening clothes— if he had to bring all the bitterness and hatred of the world into his heart, he was not going to be in love with her again.

"I don't care about Nicotera!" she declared. "But I've got to go to Livorno with the company to-morrow. Oh, why did this have to happen?" There was a new flood of tears. "It's such a shame. Why did you come here? Why couldn't we just have the memory anyhow? I feel as if I'd quarrelled with Mother."

As he began to dress, she got up and went to the door.

"I won't go to the party to-night." It was her last effort. "I'll stay with you. I don't want to go anyhow."

The tide began to flow again, but he retreated from it.

"I'll be in my room," she said. "Good-by, Dick."

"Good-by."

"Oh, such a shame, such a shame. Oh, such a shame. What's it all about anyhow?"

"I've wondered for a long time."

"But why bring it to me?"

"I guess I'm the Black Death," he said slowly. "I don't seem to bring people happiness any more."

## XXII

THERE were five people in the Quirinal bar after dinner, a high-class Italian frail who sat on a stool making persistent conversation against the bartender's bored: "Si . . . Si . . . Si," a light, snobbish Egyptian who was lonely but chary of the woman, and the two Americans.

Dick was always vividly conscious of his surroundings,

239

while Collis Clay lived vaguely, the sharpest impressions dissolving upon a recording apparatus that had early atrophied, so the former talked and the latter listened, like a man sitting in a breeze.

Dick, worn away by the events of the afternoon, was taking it out on the inhabitants of Italy. He looked around the bar as if he hoped an Italian had heard him and would resent his words.

"This afternoon I had tea with my sister-in-law at the Excelsior. We got the last table and two men came up and looked around for a table and couldn't find one. So one of them came up to us and said, 'Isn't this table reserved for the Princess Orsini?' and I said: 'There was no sign on it,' and he said: 'But I think it's reserved for the Princess Orsini.' I couldn't even answer him."

"What'd he do?"

"He retired." Dick switched around in his chair. "I don't like these people. The other day I left Rosemary for two minutes in front of a store and an officer started walking up and down in front of her, tipping his hat."

"I don't know," said Collis after a moment. "I'd rather be here than up in Paris with somebody picking your pocket every minute."

He had been enjoying himself, and he held out against anything that threatened to dull his pleasure.

"I don't know," he persisted. "I don't mind it here."

Dick evoked the picture that the few days had imprinted on his mind, and stared at it. The walk toward the American Express past the odorous confectioneries of the Via Nazionale, through the foul tunnel up to the Spanish Steps, where his spirit soared before the flower stalls and the house where Keats had died. He cared only about people; he was scarcely conscious of places except for their weather, until they had been invested with color by tangible events. Rome was the end of his dream of Rosemary.

A bell-boy came in and gave him a note.

"*I did not go to the party,*" it said. "*I am in my room. We leave for Livorno early in the morning.*"

Dick handed the note and a tip to the boy.

"Tell Miss Hoyt you couldn't find me." Turning to Collis he suggested the Bonbonieri.

They inspected the tart at the bar, granting her the minimum of interest exacted by her profession, and she stared back with bright boldness; they went through the deserted lobby oppressed by draperies holding Victorian dust in stuffy folds, and they nodded at the night concierge who returned the gesture with the bitter servility peculiar to night servants. Then in a taxi they rode along cheerless streets through a dank November night. There were no women in the streets, only pale men with dark coats buttoned to the neck, who stood in groups beside shoulders of cold stone.

"My God!" Dick sighed.

"What's a matter?"

"I was thinking of that man this afternoon: 'This table is reserved for the Princess Orsini.' Do you know what these old Roman families are? They're bandits, they're the ones who got possession of the temples and palaces after Rome went to pieces and preyed on the people."

"I like Rome," insisted Collis. "Why won't you try the races?"

"I don't like races."

"But all the women turn out——"

"I know I wouldn't like anything here. I like France, where everybody thinks he's Napoleon—down here everybody thinks he's Christ."

At the Bonbonieri they descended to a panelled cabaret, hopelessly impermanent amid the cold stone. A listless band played a tango and a dozen couples covered the wide floor with those elaborate and dainty steps so offensive to the American eye. A surplus of waiters precluded the stir and bustle that even a few busy men can create; over the scene as its form of animation brooded an air of waiting for something, for the dance, the night, the balance of forces which kept it stable, to cease. It assured the impressionable guest that whatever he was seeking he would not find it here.

This was plain as plain to Dick. He looked around, hoping his eye would catch on something, so that spirit instead of imagination could carry on for an hour. But there was nothing and after a moment he turned back to Collis. He had told Collis some of his current notions, and he was bored with his audience's short memory and lack of response. After half an hour of Collis he felt a distinct lesion of his own vitality.

They drank a bottle of Italian mousseux, and Dick became pale and somewhat noisy. He called the orchestra leader over to their table; this was a Bahama Negro, conceited and unpleasant, and in a few minutes there was a row.

"You asked me to sit down."

"All right. And I gave you fifty lire, didn't I?"

"All right. All right. All right."

"All right, I gave you fifty lire, didn't I? Then you come up and asked me to put some more in the horn!"

"You asked me to sit down, didn't you? Didn't you?"

"I asked you to sit down but I gave you fifty lire, didn't I?"

"All right. All right."

The Negro got up sourly and went away, leaving Dick in a still more evil humor. But he saw a girl smiling at him from across the room and immediately the pale Roman shapes around him receded into decent, humble perspective. She was a young English girl, with blonde hair and a healthy, pretty English face and she smiled at him again with an invitation he understood, that denied the flesh even in the act of tendering it.

"There's a quick trick or else I don't know bridge," said Collis.

Dick got up and walked to her across the room.

"Won't you dance?"

The middle-aged Englishman with whom she was sitting said, almost apologetically: "I'm going out soon."

Sobered by excitement Dick danced. He found in the girl a suggestion of all the pleasanter English things; the story of safe gardens ringed around by the sea was implicit in her bright voice and as he leaned back to look at her, he meant what he said to her so sincerely that his voice trembled. When her current escort should leave, she promised to come

242

and sit with them. The Englishman accepted her return with repeated apologies and smiles.

Back at his table Dick ordered another bottle of spumante. "She looks like somebody in the movies," he said. "I can't think who." He glanced impatiently over his shoulder. "Wonder what's keeping her?"

"I'd like to get in the movies," said Collis thoughtfully. "I'm supposed to go into my father's business but it doesn't appeal to me much. Sit in an office in Birmingham for twenty years——"

His voice resisted the pressure of materialistic civilization.

"Too good for it?" suggested Dick.

"No, I don't mean that."

"Yes, you do."

"How do you know what I mean? Why don't you practise as a doctor, if you like to work so much?"

Dick had made them both wretched by this time, but simultaneously they had become vague with drink and in a moment they forgot; Collis left, and they shook hands warmly.

"Think it over," said Dick sagely.

"Think what over?"

"You know." It had been something about Collis going into his father's business—good sound advice.

Clay walked off into space. Dick finished his bottle and then danced with the English girl again, conquering his unwilling body with bold revolutions and stern determined marches down the floor. The most remarkable thing suddenly happened. He was dancing with the girl, the music stopped—and she had disappeared.

"Have you seen her?"

"Seen who?"

"The girl I was dancing with. Su'nly disappeared. Must be in the building."

"No! No! That's the ladies' room."

He stood up by the bar. There were two other men there, but he could think of no way of starting a conversation. He could have told them all about Rome and the violent origins of the Colonna and Gaetani families but he realized

243

that as a beginning that would be somewhat abrupt. A row of Yenci dolls on the cigar counter fell suddenly to the floor; there was a subsequent confusion and he had a sense of having been the cause of it, so he went back to the cabaret and drank a cup of black coffee. Collis was gone and the English girl was gone and there seemed nothing to do but go back to the hotel and lie down with his black heart. He paid his check and got his hat and coat.

There was dirty water in the gutters and between the rough cobblestones; a marshy vapor from the Campagna, a sweat of exhausted cultures tainted the morning air. A quartet of taxi-drivers, their little eyes bobbing in dark pouches, surrounded him. One who leaned insistently in his face he pushed harshly away.

"Quanto a Hotel Quirinal?"

"Cento lire."

Six dollars. He shook his head and offered thirty lire which was twice the day-time fare, but they shrugged their shoulders as one pair, and moved off.

"Trente-cinque lire e mancie," he said firmly.

"Cento lire."

He broke into English.

"To go half a mile? You'll take me for forty lire."

"Oh, no."

He was very tired. He pulled open the door of a cab and got in.

"Hotel Quirinal!" he said to the driver who stood obstinately outside the window. "Wipe that sneer off your face and take me to the Quirinal."

"Ah, no."

Dick got out. By the door of the Bonbonieri some one was arguing with the taxi-drivers, some one who now tried to explain their attitude to Dick; again one of the men pressed close, insisting and gesticulating and Dick shoved him away.

"I want to go the Quirinal Hotel."

"He says wan huner lire," explained the interpreter.

"I understand. I'll give him fif'y lire. Go on away." This last to the insistent man who had edged up once more. The man looked at him and spat contemptuously.

The passionate impatience of the week leaped up in Dick and clothed itself like a flash in violence, the honorable, the traditional resource of his land; he stepped forward and clapped the man's face.

They surged about him, threatening, waving their arms, trying ineffectually to close in on him—with his back against the wall Dick hit out clumsily, laughing a little and for a few minutes the mock fight, an affair of foiled rushes and padded, glancing blows, swayed back and forth in front of the door. Then Dick tripped and fell; he was hurt somewhere but he struggled up again wrestling in arms that suddenly broke apart. There was a new voice and a new argument but he leaned against the wall, panting and furious at the indignity of his position. He saw there was no sympathy for him but he was unable to believe that he was wrong.

*fight*

They were going to the police station and settle it there. His hat was retrieved and handed to him, and with some one holding his arm lightly he strode around the corner with the taxi-men and entered a bare barrack where carabinieri lounged under a single dim light.

At a desk sat a captain, to whom the officious individual who had stopped the battle spoke at length in Italian, at times pointing at Dick, and letting himself be interrupted by the taxi-men who delivered short bursts of invective and denunciation. The captain began to nod impatiently. He held up his hand and the hydra-headed address, with a few parting exclamations, died away. Then he turned to Dick.

"Spick Italiano?" he asked.

"No."

"Spick Français?"

"Oui," said Dick, glowering.

"Alors. Écoute. Va au Quirinal. Espèce d'endormi. Écoute: vous êtes soûl. Payez ce que le chauffeur demande. Comprenez-vous?"

Diver shook his head.

"Non, je ne veux pas."

*"Come?"*

"Je paierai quarante lires. C'est bien assez."

The captain stood up.

"Écoute!" he cried portentously, "Vous êtes soûl. Vous avez battu le chauffeur. Comme ci, comme ça." He struck the air excitedly with right hand and left, "C'est bon que je vous donne la liberté. Payez ce qu'il a dit—cento lire. Va au Quirinal."

Raging with humiliation, Dick stared back at him.

"All right." He turned blindly to the door—before him, leering and nodding, was the man who had brought him to the police station. "I'll go home," he shouted, "but first I'll fix this baby."

He walked past the staring carabinieri and up to the grinning face, hit it with a smashing left beside the jaw. The man dropped to the floor.

For a moment he stood over him in savage triumph—but even as a first pang of doubt shot through him the world reeled; he was clubbed down, and fists and boots beat on him in a savage tattoo. He felt his nose break like a shingle and his eyes jerk as if they had snapped back on a rubber band into his head. A rib splintered under a stamping heel. Momentarily he lost consciousness, regained it as he was raised to a sitting position and his wrists jerked together with handcuffs. He struggled automatically. The plain-clothes lieutenant whom he had knocked down stood dabbing his jaw with a handkerchief and looking into it for blood; he came over to Dick, poised himself, drew back his arm and smashed him to the floor.

When Doctor Diver lay quite still a pail of water was sloshed over him. One of his eyes opened dimly as he was being dragged along by the wrists through a bloody haze, and he made out the human and ghastly face of one of the taxi-drivers.

"Go to the Excelsior hotel," he cried faintly. "Tell Miss Warren. Two hundred lire! Miss Warren. Due centi lire! Oh, you dirty—you God——"

Still he was dragged along through the bloody haze, choking and sobbing, over vague irregular surfaces into some small place where he was dropped upon a stone floor. The men went out, a door clanged, he was alone.

# XXIII

UNTIL one o'clock Baby Warren lay in bed, reading one of Marion Crawford's curiously inanimate Roman stories; then she went to a window and looked down into the street. Across from the hotel two carabinieri, grotesque in swaddling capes and harlequin hats, swung voluminously from this side and that, like mains'ls coming about, and watching them she thought of the guards' officer who had stared at her so intensely at lunch. He had possessed the arrogance of a tall member of a short race, with no obligation save to be tall. Had he come up to her and said: "Let's go along, you and I," she would have answered: "Why not?"—at least it seemed so now, for she was still disembodied by an unfamiliar background.

Her thoughts drifted back slowly through the guardsman to the two carabinieri, to Dick—she got into bed and turned out the light.

A little before four she was awakened by a brusque knocking.

"Yes—what is it?"

"It's the concierge, Madame."

She pulled on her kimono and faced him sleepily.

"Your friend name Deever he's in a trouble. He had trouble with the police, and they have him in the jail. He sent a taxi up to tell, the driver says that he promised him two hundred lire." He paused cautiously for this to be approved. "The driver says Mr. Deever in the bad trouble. He had a fight with the police and is terribly bad hurt."

"I'll be right down."

She dressed to an accompaniment of anxious heartbeats and ten minutes later stepped out of the elevator into the dark lobby. The chauffeur who brought the message was gone; the concierge hailed another one and told him the location of the jail. As they rode, the darkness lifted and thinned outside and Baby's nerves, scarcely awake, cringed faintly at the unstable balance between night and day. She began to race against the day; sometimes on the broad avenues she gained but whenever the thing that was pushing up paused for a moment, gusts of wind blew here and there impatiently and the slow creep of light began once more. The cab went past a loud fountain splashing in a voluminous shadow, turned into an alley so curved that the buildings were warped and strained following it, bumped and rattled over cobblestones, and stopped with a jerk where two sentry boxes were bright against a wall of green damp. Suddenly from the violet darkness of an archway came Dick's voice, shouting and screaming.

"Are there any English? Are there any Americans? Are there any English? Are there any—oh, my God! You dirty Wops!"

His voice died away and she heard a dull sound of beating on the door. Then the voice began again.

"Are there any Americans? Are there any English?"

Following the voice she ran through the arch into a court, whirled about in momentary confusion and located the small guard-room whence the cries came. Two carabinieri started to their feet, but Baby brushed past them to the door of the cell.

"Dick!" she called. "What's the trouble?"

"They've put out my eye," he cried. "They handcuffed me and then they beat me, the goddamn—the——"

Flashing around Baby took a step toward the two carabinieri.

"What have you done to him?" she whispered so fiercely that they flinched before her gathering fury.

"Non capisco inglese."

In French she execrated them; her wild, confident rage filled the room, enveloped them until they shrank and wriggled from the garments of blame with which she invested them. "Do something! Do something!"

"We can do nothing until we are ordered."

"Bene. *Bay-nay! Bene!*"

Once more Baby let her passion scorch around them until they sweated out apologies for their impotence, looking at each other with the sense that something had after all gone terribly wrong. Baby went to the cell door, leaned against it, almost caressing it, as if that could make Dick feel her presence and power, and cried: "I'm going to the Embassy, I'll be back." Throwing a last glance of infinite menace at the carabinieri she ran out.

She drove to the American Embassy where she paid off the taxi-driver upon his insistence. It was still dark when she ran up the steps and pressed the bell. She had pressed it three times before a sleepy English porter opened the door to her.

"I want to see some one," she said. "Any one—but right away."

"No one's awake, Madame. We don't open until nine o'clock."

Impatiently she waved the hour away.

"This is important. A man—an American has been terribly beaten. He's in an Italian jail."

"No one's awake now. At nine o'clock——"

"I can't wait. They've put out a man's eye—my brother-in-law, and they won't let him out of jail. I must talk to some one—can't you see? Are you crazy? Are you an idiot, you stand there with that look in your face?"

"Hime unable to do anything, Madame."

"You've got to wake some one up!" She seized him by the shoulders and jerked him violently. "It's a matter of life and death. If you won't wake someone a terrible thing will happen to you——"

"Kindly don't lay hands on me, Madame."

From above and behind the porter floated down a weary Groton voice.[54]

"What is it there?"

The porter answered with relief.

"It's a lady, sir, and she has shook me." He had stepped back to speak and Baby pushed forward into the hall. On an upper landing, just aroused from sleep and wrapped in a white embroidered Persian robe, stood a singular young man. His face was of a monstrous and unnatural pink, vivid

249

yet dead, and over his mouth was fastened what appeared to be a gag. When he saw Baby he moved his head back into a shadow.

"What is it?" he repeated.

Baby told him, in her agitation edging forward to the stairs. In the course of her story she realized that the gag was in reality a mustache bandage and that the man's face was covered with pink cold cream, but the fact fitted quietly into the nightmare. The thing to do, she cried passionately, was for him to come to the jail with her at once and get Dick out.

"It's a bad business," he said.

"Yes," she agreed conciliatingly. "Yes?"

"This trying to fight the police." A note of personal affront crept into his voice. "I'm afraid there's nothing to be done until nine o'clock."

"Till nine o'clock," she repeated aghast. "But you can do something, certainly! You can come to the jail with me and see that they don't hurt him any more."

"We aren't permitted to do anything like that. The Consulate handles these things. The Consulate will be open at nine."

His face, constrained to impassivity by the binding strap, infuriated Baby.

"I can't wait until nine. My brother-in-law says they've put his eye out—he's seriously hurt! I have to get to him. I have to find a doctor." She let herself go and began to cry angrily as she talked, for she knew that he would respond to her agitation rather than her words. "You've got to do something about this. It's your business to protect American citizens in trouble."

But he was of the Eastern seaboard and too hard for her. Shaking his head patiently at her failure to understand his position he drew the Persian robe closer about him and came down a few steps.

"Write down the address of the Consulate for this lady," he said to the porter, "and look up Doctor Colazzo's address and telephone number and write that down too." He turned to Baby, with the expression of an exasperated

Christ. "My dear lady, the diplomatic corps represents the Government of the United States to the Government of Italy. It has nothing to do with the protection of citizens, except under specific instructions from the State Department. Your brother-in-law has broken the laws of this country and been put in jail, just as an Italian might be put in jail in New York. The only people who can let him go are the Italian courts and if your brother-in-law has a case you can get aid and advice from the Consulate, which protects the rights of American citizens. The Consulate does not open until nine o'clock. Even if it were my brother I couldn't do anything——"

"Can you phone the Consulate?" she broke in. *stubborn*

"We can't interfere with the Consulate. When the Consul gets there at nine——"

"Can you give me his home address?" *stubborn*

After a fractional pause the man shook his head. He took the memorandum from the porter and gave it to her.

"Now I'll ask you to excuse me."

He had manœuvred her to the door: for an instant the violet dawn fell shrilly upon his pink mask and upon the linen sack that supported his mustache; then Baby was standing on the front steps alone. She had been in the Embassy ten minutes.

The piazza whereon it faced was empty save for an old man gathering cigarette butts with a spiked stick. Baby caught a taxi presently and went to the Consulate but there was no one there save a trio of wretched women scrubbing the stairs. She could not make them understand that she wanted the Consul's home address—in a sudden resurgence of anxiety she rushed out and told the chauffeur to take her to the jail. He did not know where it was, but by the use of the words *semper dritte, dextra* and *sinestra* she manœuvred him to its approximate locality, where she dismounted and explored a labyrinth of familiar alleys. But the buildings and the alleys all looked alike. Emerging from one trail into the Piazza di Spagna she saw the American Express Company and her heart lifted at the word "American" on the sign. There was a light in the window and hurrying across the square she tried the door, but it was locked, and inside the clock stood at seven. Then she thought of Collis Clay.

She remembered the name of his hotel, a stuffy villa sealed in red plush across from the Excelsior. The woman on duty at the office was not disposed to help her—she had no authority to disturb Mr. Clay, and refused to let Miss Warren go up to his room alone; convinced finally that this was not an affair of passion she accompanied her.

Collis lay naked upon his bed. He had come in tight and, awakening, it took him some moments to realize his nudity. He atoned for it by an excess of modesty. Taking his clothes into the bathroom he dressed in haste, muttering to himself "Gosh. She certainly musta got a good look at me." After some telephoning, he and Baby found the jail and went to it.

The cell door was open and Dick was slumped on a chair in the guard-room. The carabiniere had washed some of the blood from his face, brushed him and set his hat concealingly upon his head. Baby stood in the doorway trembling.

"Mr. Clay will stay with you," she said. "I want to get the Consul and a doctor."

"All right."

"Just stay quiet."

"All right."

"I'll be back."

She drove to the Consulate; it was after eight now, and she was permitted to sit in the ante-room. Toward nine the Consul came in and Baby, hysterical with impotence and exhaustion, repeated her story. The Consul was disturbed. He warned her against getting into brawls in strange cities, but he was chiefly concerned that she should wait outside—with despair she read in his elderly eye that he wanted to be mixed up as little as possible in this catastrophe. Waiting on his action, she passed the minutes by phoning a doctor to go to Dick. There were other people in the ante-room and several were admitted to the Consul's office. After half an hour she chose the moment of some one's coming out and pushed past the secretary into the room.

"This is outrageous! An American has been beaten half

to death and thrown into prison and you make no move to help."

"Just a minute, Mrs.——"

*persistant* "I've waited long enough. You come right down to the jail and get him out!"

"Mrs.——"

"We're people of considerable standing in America—" Her mouth hardened as she continued. "If it wasn't for the scandal we can—I shall see that your indifference to this matter is reported in the proper quarter. If my brother-in-

*Stubborn* law were a British citizen he'd have been free hours ago, but you're more concerned with what the police will think than about what you're here for."

"Mrs.——"

"You put on your hat and come with me right away."

The mention of his hat alarmed the Consul who began to clean his spectacles hurriedly and to ruffle his papers. This proved of no avail: the American Woman, aroused, stood over him; the clean-sweeping irrational temper that had broken the moral back of a race and made a nursery out of a continent, was too much for him. He rang for the Vice-consul—Baby had won.

Dick sat in the sunshine that fell profusely through the guard-room window. Collis was with him and two cara-binieri, and they were waiting for something to happen. With the narrowed vision of his one eye Dick could see the carabinieri; they were Tuscan peasants with short upper lips and he found it difficult to associate them with the brutality of last night. He sent one of them to fetch him a *drinking* glass of beer.

The beer made him light-headed and the episode was momentarily illumined by a ray of sardonic humor. Collis was under the impression that the English girl had some-thing to do with the catastrophe, but Dick was sure she had disappeared long before it happened. Collis was still absorbed by the fact that Miss Warren had found him naked on his bed.

Dick's rage had retreated into him a little and he felt a

253

vast criminal irresponsibility. What had happened to him was so awful that nothing could make any difference unless he could choke it to death, and, as this was unlikely, he was hopeless. He would be a different person henceforward, and in his raw state he had bizarre feelings of what the new self would be. The matter had about it the impersonal quality of an act of God. No mature Aryan is able to profit by a humiliation; when he forgives it has become part of his life, he has identified himself with the thing which has humiliated him—an upshot that in this case was impossible.

When Collis spoke of retribution, Dick shook his head and was silent. A lieutenant of carabinieri, pressed, burnished, vital, came into the room like three men and the guards jumped to attention. He seized the empty beer bottle and directed a stream of scolding at his men. The new spirit was in him, and the first thing was to get the beer bottle out of the guard-room. Dick looked at Collis and laughed.

The Vice-consul, an over-worked young man named Swanson, arrived, and they started to the court; Collis and Swanson on either side of Dick and the two carabinieri close behind. It was a yellow, hazy morning; the squares and arcades were crowded and Dick, pulling his hat low over his head, walked fast, setting the pace, until one of the short-legged carabinieri ran alongside and protested. Swanson arranged matters.

"I've disgraced you, haven't I?" said Dick jovially.

"You're liable to get killed fighting Italians," replied Swanson sheepishly. "They'll probably let you go this time but if you were an Italian you'd get a couple of months in prison. And how!"

"Have you ever been in prison?"

Swanson laughed.

"I like him," announced Dick to Clay. "He's a very likeable young man and he gives people excellent advice, but I'll bet he's been to jail himself. Probably spent weeks at a time in jail."

Swanson laughed.

"I mean you want to be careful. You don't know how these people are."

"Oh, I know how they are," broke out Dick, irritably. "They're god damn stinkers." He turned around to the carabinieri: "Did you get that?"

"I'm leaving you here," Swanson said quickly. "I told your sister-in-law I would—our lawyer will meet you upstairs in the court-room. You want to be careful."

"Good-by." Dick shook hands politely. "Thank you very much. I feel you have a future——"

With another smile Swanson hurried away, resuming his official expression of disapproval.

Now they came into a courtyard on all four sides of which outer stairways mounted to the chambers above. As they crossed the flags a groaning, hissing, booing sound went up from the loiterers in the courtyard, voices full of fury and scorn. Dick stared about.

"What's that?" he demanded, aghast.

One of the carabinieri spoke to a group of men and the sound died away.

They came into the court-room. A shabby Italian lawyer from the Consulate spoke at length to the judge while Dick and Collis waited aside. Some one who knew English turned from the window that gave on the yard and explained the sound that had accompanied their passage through. A native of Frascati had raped and slain a five-year-old child and was to be brought in that morning—the crowd had assumed it was Dick.

In a few minutes the lawyer told Dick that he was freed— *Dick freed* the court considered him punished enough.

"Enough!" Dick cried. "Punished for what?"

"Come along," said Collis. "You can't do anything now."

"But what did I do, except get into a fight with some taxi men?"

"They claim you went up to a detective as if you were going to shake hands with him and hit him——"

"That's not true! I told him I was going to hit him—I didn't know he was a detective."

"You better go along," urged the lawyer.

"Come along." Collis took his arm and they descended the steps.

"I want to make a speech," Dick cried. "I want to explain to these people how I raped a five-year-old girl. Maybe I did——"

"Come along."

Baby was waiting with a doctor in a taxi-cab. Dick did not want to look at her and he disliked the doctor, whose stern manner revealed him as one of that least palpable of European types, the Latin moralist. Dick summed up his conception of the disaster, but no one had much to say. In his room in the Quirinal the doctor washed off the rest of the blood and the oily sweat, set his nose, his fractured ribs and fingers, disinfected the smaller wounds and put a hopeful dressing on the eye. Dick asked for a quarter of a grain of morphine, for he was still wide awake and full of nervous energy. With the morphine he fell asleep; the doctor and Collis left and Baby waited with him until a woman could arrive from the English nursing home. It had been a hard night but she had the satisfaction of feeling that, whatever Dick's previous record was, they now possessed a moral superiority over him for as long as he proved of any use.

own Dick

# BOOK III

*Nicole's point of view privileged.*

Dick
Nicole

toward end.

Nicole waits for message that her marriage
is disintigrating before she gets
involved w/ Tommy.

Boat = end of relationship btw.
          Nicole + Dick

# I

FRAU KAETHE GREGOROVIOUS overtook her husband on the path of their villa.

"How was Nicole?" she asked mildly; but she spoke out of breath, giving away the fact that she had held the question in her mind during her run.

Franz looked at her in surprise.

"Nicole's not sick. What makes you ask, dearest one?"

"You see her so much—I thought she must be sick."

"We will talk of this in the house."

Kaethe agreed meekly. His study was over in the administration building and the children were with their tutor in the living-room; they went up to the bedroom.

"Excuse me, Franz," said Kaethe before he could speak. "Excuse me, dear, I had no right to say that. I know my obligations and I am proud of them. But there is a bad feeling between Nicole and me."

"Birds in their little nests agree," Franz thundered. Finding the tone inappropriate to the sentiment he repeated his command in the spaced and considered rhythm with which his old master, Doctor Dohmler, could cast significance on the tritest platitude. "Birds—in—their—nests—*agree!*"

"I realize that. You haven't seen me fail in courtesy toward Nicole."

"I see you failing in common sense. Nicole is half a patient —she will possibly remain something of a patient all her life. In the absence of Dick I am responsible." He hesitated; sometimes as a quiet joke he tried to keep news from Kaethe. "There was a cable from Rome this morning. Dick has had grippe and is starting home to-morrow."

Relieved, Kaethe pursued her course in a less personal tone:

*acting*

"I think Nicole is less sick than any one thinks—she only cherishes her illness as an instrument of power. She ought to be in the cinema, like your Norma Talmadge[55]—that's where all American women would be happy."

259

"Are you jealous of Norma Talmadge, on a film?"

"I don't like Americans. They're selfish, *self*ish!"

"You like Dick?"

"I like him," she admitted. "He's different, he thinks of others."

—And so does Norma Talmadge, Franz said to himself. Norma Talmadge must be a fine, noble woman beyond her loveliness. They must compel her to play foolish rôles; Norma Talmadge must be a woman whom it would be a great privilege to know.

Kaethe had forgotten about Norma Talmadge, a vivid shadow that she had fretted bitterly upon one night as they were driving home from the movies in Zurich.

*[handwritten: Dick marrying for $]*

"—Dick married Nicole for her money," she said. "That was his weakness—you hinted as much yourself one night."

"You're being malicious."

"I shouldn't have said that," she retracted. "We must all live together like birds, as you say. But it's difficult when Nicole acts as—when Nicole pulls herself back a little, as if she were holding her breath—as if I *smelt* bad!"

Kaethe had touched a material truth. She did most of her work herself, and, frugal, she bought few clothes. An American shop-girl, laundering two changes of underwear every night, would have noticed a hint of yesterday's reawakened sweat about Kaethe's person, less a smell than an ammoniacal reminder of the eternity of toil and decay. To Franz this was as natural as the thick dark scent of Kaethe's hair, and he would have missed it equally; but to Nicole, born hating the smell of a nurse's fingers dressing her, it was an offense only to be endured.

*[handwritten: Nicole thinks she is better than Kaethe b/c she has more $]*

"And the children," Kaethe continued. "She doesn't like them to play with our children—" but Franz had heard enough:

"Hold your tongue—that kind of talk can hurt me professionally, since we owe this clinic to Nicole's money. Let us have lunch."

Kaethe realized that her outburst had been ill-advised, but Franz's last remark reminded her that other Americans *[handwritten: rich]*

260

had money, and a week later she put her dislike of Nicole into new words.

The occasion was the dinner they tendered the Divers upon Dick's return. Hardly had their footfalls ceased on the path when she shut the door and said to Franz:

"Did you see around his eyes? He's been on a debauch!" *morally corrupt*

"Go gently," Franz requested. "Dick told me about that as soon as he came home. He was boxing on the trans-Atlantic ship. The American passengers box a lot on these trans-Atlantic ships."

"I believe that?" she scoffed. "It hurts him to move one of his arms and he has an unhealed scar on his temple—you can see where the hair's been cut away."

Franz had not noticed these details.

"But what?" Kaethe demanded. "Do you think that sort of thing does the clinic any good? The liquor I smelt on him *drinking too much* to-night, and several other times since he's been back."

She slowed her voice to fit the gravity of what she was about to say: "Dick is no longer a serious man." *not taking his work seriously*

Franz rocked his shoulders up the stairs, shaking off her persistence. In their bedroom he turned on her.

"He is most certainly a serious man and a brilliant man. Of all the men who have recently taken their degrees in neuro-pathology in Zurich, Dick has been regarded as the most brilliant—more brilliant than I could ever be."

"For shame!"

"It's the truth—the shame would be not to admit it. I turn to Dick when cases are highly involved. His publications are still standard in their line—go into any medical library and ask. Most students think he's an Englishman—they don't believe that such thoroughness could come out of America." He groaned domestically, taking his pajamas from under the pillow, "I can't understand why you talk this way, Kaethe—I thought you liked him."

"For shame!" Kaethe said. "You're the solid one, you do the work. It's a case of hare and tortoise—and in my opinion the hare's race is almost done."

"Tch! Tch!"

"Very well, then. It's true."

With his open hand he pushed down air briskly.

"Stop!"

The upshot was that they had exchanged viewpoints like debaters. Kaethe admitted to herself that she had been too hard on Dick, whom she admired and of whom she stood in awe, who had been so appreciative and understanding of herself. As for Franz, once Kaethe's idea had had time to sink in, he never after believed that Dick was a serious person. And as time went on he convinced himself that he had never thought so.

## II

*lying to his wife*

DICK told Nicole an expurgated version of the catastrophe in Rome—in his version he had gone philanthropically to the rescue of a drunken friend. He could trust Baby Warren to hold her tongue, since he had painted the disastrous effect of the truth upon Nicole. All this, however, was a low hurdle compared to the lingering effect of the episode upon him.

In reaction he took himself for an intensified beating in his work, so that Franz, trying to break with him, could find no basis on which to begin a disagreement. No friendship worth the name was ever destroyed in an hour without some painful flesh being torn—so Franz let himself believe with ever-increasing conviction that Dick travelled intellectually and emotionally at such a rate of speed that the vibrations jarred him—this was a contrast that had previously been considered a virtue in their relation. So, for the shoddiness of needs, are shoes made out of last year's hide.

Yet it was May before Franz found an opportunity to insert the first wedge. Dick came into his office white and tired one noon and sat down, saying:

"Well, she's gone."

"She's dead?"

"The heart quit."

Dick sat exhausted in the chair nearest the door. During three nights he had remained with the scabbed anonymous woman-artist he had come to love, formally to portion out the adrenalin, but really to throw as much wan light as he could into the darkness ahead.

Half appreciating his feeling, Franz travelled quickly over an opinion:

"It was neuro-syphilis. All the Wassermanns we took won't tell me differently. The spinal fluid——"

"Never mind," said Dick. "Oh, God, never mind! If she cared enough about her secret to take it away with her, let it go at that."

"You better lay off for a day." _getting Dick to leave the clinic_

"Don't worry, I'm going to."

Franz had his wedge; looking up from the telegram that he was writing to the woman's brother he inquired: "Or do you want to take a little trip?" _leave the clinic_

"Not now."

"I don't mean a vacation. There's a case in Lausanne. I've been on the phone with a Chilian all morning——"

"She was so damn brave," said Dick. "And it took her so long." Franz shook his head sympathetically and Dick got himself together. "Excuse me for interrupting you."

"This is just a change—the situation is a father's problem with his son—the father can't get the son up here. He wants somebody to come down there."

"What is it? Alcoholism? Homosexuality? When you say Lausanne——"

"A little of everything."

"I'll go down. Is there any money in it?"

"Quite a lot, I'd say. Count on staying two or three days, and get the boy up here if he needs to be watched. In any case take your time, take your ease; combine business with pleasure." _leave clinic_

After two hours' train sleep Dick felt renewed, and he approached the interview with Señor Pardo y Cuidad Real in good spirits.

These interviews were much of a type. Often the sheer hysteria of the family representative was as interesting psychologically as the condition of the patient. This one was no exception: Señor Pardo y Cuidad Real, a handsome iron-gray Spaniard, noble of carriage, with all the appurtenances of wealth and power, raged up and down his suite in the Hôtel des Trois Mondes and told the story of his son with no more self-control than a drunken woman.

"I am at the end of my invention. My son is corrupt. He was corrupt at Harrow, he was corrupt at King's College, Cambridge. He's incorrigibly corrupt. Now that there is this drinking it is more and more obvious how he is, and there is continual scandal. I have tried everything—I worked out a plan with a doctor friend of mine, sent them together for a tour of Spain. Every evening Francisco had an injection of cantharides[56] and then the two went together to a reputable bordello—for a week or so it seemed to work but the result was nothing. Finally last week in this very room, rather in that bathroom—" he pointed at it, "—I made Francisco strip to the waist and lashed him with a whip——"

Exhausted with his emotion he sat down and Dick spoke:

"That was foolish—the trip to Spain was futile also—" He struggled against an upsurging hilarity—that any reputable medical man should have lent himself to such an amateurish experiment! "—Señor, I must tell you that in these cases we can promise nothing. In the case of the drinking we can often accomplish something—with proper co-operation. The first thing is to see the boy and get enough of his confidence to find whether he has any insight into the matter."

—The boy, with whom he sat on the terrace, was about twenty, handsome and alert.

"I'd like to know your attitude," Dick said. "Do you feel that the situation is getting worse? And do you want to do anything about it?"

"I suppose I do," said Francisco, "I am very unhappy."

"Do you think it's from the drinking or from the abnormality?"

"I think the drinking is caused by the other." He was serious for a while—suddenly an irrepressible facetiousness broke through and he laughed, saying, "It's hopeless. At King's I was known as the Queen of Chile. That trip to

Spain—all it did was to make me nauseated by the sight of a woman."

Dick caught him up sharply.

"If you're happy in this mess, then I can't help you and I'm wasting my time."

"No, let's talk—I despise most of the others so." There was some manliness in the boy, perverted now into an active resistance to his father. But he had that typically roguish look in his eyes that homosexuals assume in discussing the subject.

"It's a hole-and-corner business at best," Dick told him. "You'll spend your life on it, and its consequences, and you won't have time or energy for any other decent or social act. If you want to face the world you'll have to begin by controlling your sensuality—and, first of all, the drinking that provokes it——"

He talked automatically, having abandoned the case ten minutes before. They talked pleasantly through another hour about the boy's home in Chile and about his ambitions. It was as close as Dick had ever come to comprehending such a character from any but the pathological angle—he gathered that this very charm made it possible for Francisco to perpetrate his outrages, and, for Dick, charm always had an independent existence, whether it was the mad gallantry of the wretch who had died in the clinic this morning, or the courageous grace which this lost young man brought to a drab old story. Dick tried to dissect it into pieces small enough to store away—realizing that the totality of a life may be different in quality from its segments, and also that life during the forties seemed capable of being observed only in segments. His love for Nicole and Rosemary, his friendship with Abe North, with Tommy Barban in the broken universe of the war's ending—in such contacts the personalities had seemed to press up so close to him that he became the personality itself—there seemed some necessity of taking all or nothing; it was as if for the remainder of his life he was condemned to carry with him the egos of certain people, early met and early loved, and to be only as complete as they were complete themselves. There was some element of loneliness involved—so easy to be loved—so hard to love.

As he sat on the veranda with young Francisco, a ghost of the past swam into his ken. A tall, singularly swaying male detached himself from the shrubbery and approached Dick and Francisco with feeble resolution. For a moment he formed such an apologetic part of the vibrant landscape that Dick scarcely remarked him—then Dick was on his feet, shaking hands with an abstracted air, thinking, "My God, I've stirred up a nest!" and trying to collect the man's name.

"This is Doctor Diver, isn't it?"

"Well, well—Mr. Dumphry, isn't it?"

"Royal Dumphry. I had the pleasure of having dinner one night in that lovely garden of yours."

"Of course." Trying to dampen Mr. Dumphry's enthusiasm, Dick went into impersonal chronology. "It was in nineteen—twenty four—or twenty-five——"

He had remained standing, but Royal Dumphry, shy as he had seemed at first, was no laggard with his pick and spade; he spoke to Francisco in a flip, intimate manner, but the latter, ashamed of him, joined Dick in trying to freeze him away.

"Doctor Diver—one thing I want to say before you go. I've never forgotten that evening in your garden—how nice you and your wife were. To me it's one of the finest memories in my life, one of the happiest ones. I've always thought of it as the most civilized gathering of people that I have ever known."

Dick continued a crab-like retreat toward the nearest door of the hotel.

"I'm glad you remembered it so pleasantly. Now I've got to see——"

"I understand," Royal Dumphry pursued sympathetically. "I hear he's dying."

"Who's dying?"

"Perhaps I shouldn't have said that—but we have the same physician."

Dick paused, regarding him in astonishment. "Who're you talking about?"

"Why, your wife's father—perhaps I——"

266

"My *what?*"

"I suppose—you mean I'm the first person——"

"You mean my wife's father is here, in Lausanne?"

"Why, I thought you knew—I thought that was why you were here."

"What doctor is taking care of him?"

Dick scrawled the name in a notebook, excused himself, and hurried to a telephone booth.

It was convenient for Doctor Dangeu to see Doctor Diver at his house immediately.

Doctor Dangeu was a young Genevois; for a moment he was afraid that he was going to lose a profitable patient, but, when Dick reassured him, he divulged the fact that Mr. Warren was indeed dying.

"He is only fifty but the liver has stopped restoring itself; the precipitating factor is alcoholism." —warning for Dick?

"Doesn't respond?"

"The man can take nothing except liquids—I give him three days, or at most, a week."

"Does his elder daughter, Miss Warren, know his condition?"

"By his own wish no one knows except the man-servant. It was only this morning I felt I had to tell him—he took it excitedly, although he has been in a very religious and resigned mood from the beginning of his illness."

Dick considered: "Well—" he decided slowly, "in any case I'll take care of the family angle. But I imagine they would want a consultation."

"As you like."

"I know I speak for them when I ask you to call in one of the best-known internal medicine men around the lake—Herbrugge, from Geneva."

"I was thinking of Herbrugge."

"Meanwhile I'm here for a day at least and I'll keep in touch with you."

That evening Dick went to Señor Pardo y Cuidad Real and they talked.

"We have large estates in Chile—" said the old man. "My son could well be taking care of them. Or I can get

him in any one of a dozen enterprises in Paris—" He shook
his head and paced across the windows against a spring rain
so cheerful that it didn't even drive the swans to cover.
"My only son! Can't you take him with you?"

The Spaniard knelt suddenly at Dick's feet.

"Can't you cure my only son? I believe in you—you can
take him with you, cure him."

"It's impossible to commit a person on such grounds. I
wouldn't if I could."

The Spaniard got up from his knees.

"I have been hasty—I have been driven——"

Descending to the lobby Dick met Doctor Dangeu in the
elevator.

"I was about to call your room," the latter said. "Can we
speak out on the terrace?"

"Is Mr. Warren dead?" Dick demanded.

"He is the same—the consultation is in the morning.
Meanwhile he wants to see his daughter—your wife—with
the greatest fervor. It seems there was some quarrel——"

"I know all about that."

The doctors looked at each other, thinking.

"Why don't you talk to him before you make up your
mind?" Dangeu suggested. "His death will be graceful—
merely a weakening and sinking."

With an effort Dick consented.

"All right."

The suite in which Devereux Warren was gracefully
weakening and sinking was of the same size as that of the
Señor Pardo y Cuidad Real—throughout this hotel there
were many chambers wherein rich ruins, fugitives from
justice, claimants to the thrones of mediatized principali-
ties, lived on the derivatives of opium or barbitol listening
eternally as to an inescapable radio, to the coarse melodies
of old sins. This corner of Europe does not so much draw
people as accept them without inconvenient questions.
Routes cross here—people bound for private sanitariums or
tuberculosis resorts in the mountains, people who are no
longer persona grata in France or Italy.

The suite was darkened. A nun with a holy face was

nursing the man whose emaciated fingers stirred a rosary on the white sheet. He was still handsome and his voice summoned up a thick burr of individuality as he spoke to Dick, after Dangeu had left them together.

"We get a lot of understanding at the end of life. Only now, Doctor Diver, do I realize what it was all about."

Dick waited.

"I've been a bad man. You must know how little right I have to see Nicole again, yet a Bigger Man than either of us says to forgive and to pity." The rosary slipped from his weak hands and slid off the smooth bed covers. Dick picked it up for him. "If I could see Nicole for ten minutes I would go happy out of the world."

"It's not a decision I can make for myself," said Dick. "Nicole is not strong." He made his decision but pretended to hesitate. "I can put it up to my professional associate."

"What your associate says goes with me—very well, Doctor. Let me tell you my debt to you is so large——"

Dick stood up quickly.

"I'll let you know the result through Doctor Dangeu."

In his room he called the clinic on the Zugersee. After a long time Kaethe answered from her own house.

"I want to get in touch with Franz."

"Franz is up on the mountain. I'm going up myself—is it something I can tell him, Dick?"

"It's about Nicole—her father is dying here in Lausanne. Tell Franz that, to show him it's important; and ask him to phone me from up there."

"I will."

"Tell him I'll be in my room here at the hotel from three to five, and again from seven to eight, and after that to page me in the dining-room."

In plotting these hours he forgot to add that Nicole was not to be told; when he remembered it he was talking into a dead telephone. Certainly Kaethe should realize.

. . . Kaethe had no exact intention of telling Nicole about the call when she rode up the deserted hill of mountain wild flowers and secret winds, where the patients were taken to ski in winter and to climb in spring. Getting off the train she

269

saw Nicole shepherding the children through some organized romp. Approaching, she drew her arm gently along Nicole's shoulder, saying: "You are clever with children—you must teach them more about swimming in the summer."

In the play they had grown hot, and Nicole's reflex in drawing away from Kaethe's arm was automatic to the point of rudeness. Kaethe's hand fell awkwardly into space, and then she too reacted, verbally, and deplorably.

*thinks she is better than Kaethe*

"Did you think I was going to embrace you?" she demanded sharply. "It was only about Dick, I talked on the phone to him and I was sorry——"

"Is anything the matter with Dick?"

Kaethe suddenly realized her error, but she had taken a tactless course and there was no choice but to answer as Nicole pursued her with reiterated questions: ". . . then *why* were you sorry?"

"Nothing about Dick. I must talk to Franz."

"It *is* about Dick."

There was terror in her face and collaborating alarm in the faces of the Diver children, near at hand. Kaethe collapsed with: "Your father is ill in Lausanne—Dick wants to talk to Franz about it."

*Kaethe tells Nicole*

"Is he very sick?" Nicole demanded—just as Franz came up with his hearty hospital manner. Gratefully Kaethe passed the remnant of the buck to him—but the damage was done.

"I'm going to Lausanne," announced Nicole.

"One minute," said Franz. "I'm not sure it's advisable. I must first talk on the phone to Dick."

"Then I'll miss the train down," Nicole protested, "and then I'll miss the three o'clock from Zurich! If my father is dying I must—" She left this in the air, afraid to formulate it. "I *must* go. I'll have to run for the train." She was running even as she spoke toward the sequence of flat cars that crowned the bare hill with bursting steam and sound. Over her shoulder she called back, "If you phone Dick tell him I'm coming, Franz!" . . .

. . . Dick was in his own room in the hotel reading The

New York Herald when the swallow-like nun rushed in—simultaneously the phone rang.

"Is he dead?" Dick demanded of the nun, hopefully.

"Monsieur, il est parti—he has gone away."

"*Comment?*"

"Il est parti—his man and his baggage have gone away too!"

It was incredible. A man in that condition to arise and depart.

Dick answered the phone-call from Franz. "You shouldn't have told Nicole," he protested.

"Kaethe told her, very unwisely."

"I suppose it was my fault. Never tell a thing to a woman till it's done. However, I'll meet Nicole . . . say, Franz, the craziest thing has happened down here—the old boy took up his bed and walked. . . ."

"At what? What did you say?"

"I say he walked, old Warren—he walked!"

"But why not?"

"He was supposed to be dying of general collapse . . . he got up and walked away, back to Chicago, I guess. . . . I don't know, the nurse is here now. . . . I don't know, Franz —I've just heard about it. . . . Call me later."

He spent the better part of two hours tracing Warren's movements. The patient had found an opportunity between the change of day and night nurses to resort to the bar where he had gulped down four whiskeys; he paid his hotel bill with a thousand dollar note, instructing the desk that the change should be sent after him, and departed, presumably for America. A last-minute dash by Dick and Dangeu to overtake him at the station resulted only in Dick's failing to meet Nicole; when they did meet in the lobby of the hotel she seemed suddenly tired, and there was a tight purse to her lips that disquieted him.

"How's father?" she demanded.

"He's much better. He seemed to have a good deal of reserve energy after all." He hesitated, breaking it to her easy. "In fact he got up and went away."

~~Wanting a drink~~, for the chase had occupied the dinner hour, he led her, puzzled, toward the grill, and continued as they occupied two leather easy-chairs and ordered a high-ball and a glass of beer: "The man who was taking care of him made a wrong prognosis or something—wait a minute, I've hardly had time to think the thing out myself."

"He's *gone?*"

"He got the evening train for Paris."

They sat silent. From Nicole flowed a vast tragic apathy.

"It was instinct," Dick said, finally. "He was really dying, but he tried to get a resumption of rhythm—he's not the first person that ever walked off his death-bed—like an old clock—you know, you shake it and somehow from sheer habit it gets going again. Now your father——"

"Oh, don't tell me," she said.

"His principal fuel was fear," he continued. "He got afraid, and off he went. He'll probably live till ninety——"

"Please don't tell me any more," she said. "Please don't— I couldn't stand any more."

"All right. The little devil I came down to see is hopeless. We may as well go back to-morrow."

"I don't see why you have to—come in contact with all this," she burst forth.

"Oh, don't you? Sometimes I don't either."

She put her hand on his.

"Oh, I'm sorry I said that, Dick."

Some one had brought a phonograph into the bar and they sat listening to "The Wedding of the Painted Doll."

## III

ONE morning a week later, stopping at the desk for his mail, Dick became aware of some extra commotion out-side: patient Von Cohn Morris was going away. His parents, Australians, were putting his baggage vehemently into a large limousine, and beside them stood Doctor Lladis-lau protesting with ineffectual attitudes against the violent gesturings of Morris, senior. The young man was regarding his embarkation with aloof cynicism as Doctor Diver approached.

"Isn't this a little sudden, Mr. Morris?"

Mr. Morris started as he saw Dick—his florid face and the large checks on his suit seemed to turn off and on like electric lights. He approached Dick as though to strike him.

"High time we left, we and those who have come with us," he began, and paused for breath. "It is high time, Doctor Diver. High time."

"Will you come in my office?" Dick suggested.

"Not I! I'll talk to you, but I'm washing my hands of you and your place."

"I'm sorry about that."

He shook his finger at Dick. "I was just telling this doctor here. We've wasted our time and our money."

Doctor Lladislau stirred in a feeble negative, signalling up a vague Slavic evasiveness. Dick had never liked Lladislau. He managed to walk the excited Australian along the path in the direction of his office, trying to persuade him to enter; but the man shook his head.

"It's *you*, Doctor Diver, *you*, the very man. I went to Doctor Lladislau because you were not to be found, Doctor Diver, and because Doctor Gregorovious is not expected until the nightfall, and I would not wait. No, sir! I would not wait a minute after my son told me the truth."

He came up menacingly to Dick, who kept his hands loose enough to drop him if it seemed necessary. "My son is here for alcoholism, and he told us he smelt liquor on your breath. Yes, sir!" He made a quick, apparently unsuccessful sniff. "Not once, but twice Von Cohn says he has smelt liquor on your breath. I and my lady have never touched a drop of it in our lives. We hand Von Cohn to you to be cured, and within a month he twice smells liquor on your breath! What kind of cure is that there?"

Dick hesitated; Mr. Morris was quite capable of making a scene on the clinic drive.

"After all, Mr. Morris, some people are not going to give up what they regard as food because of your son——"

273

"But you're a doctor, man!" cried Morris furiously. "When the workmen drink their beer that's bad cess to them—but you're here supposing to cure——"

"This has gone too far. Your son came to us because of kleptomania."

"What was behind it?" The man was almost shrieking. "Drink—black drink. Do you know what color black is? It's black! My own uncle was hung by the neck because of it, you hear! My son comes to a sanitarium, and a doctor reeks of it!"

"I must ask you to leave."

"You *ask* me! We *are* leaving!"

"If you could be a little temperate we could tell you the results of the treatment to date. Naturally, since you feel as you do, we would not want your son as a patient——"

"You dare to use the word temperate to me?"

Dick called to Doctor Lladislau and as he approached, said: "Will you represent us in saying good-by to the patient and to his family?"

He bowed slightly to Morris and went into his office, and stood rigid for a moment just inside the door. He watched until they drove away, the gross parents, the bland, degenerate offspring: it was easy to prophesy the family's swing around Europe, bullying their betters with hard ignorance and hard money. But what absorbed Dick after the disappearance of the caravan was the question as to what extent he had provoked this. He drank claret with each meal, took a night-cap, generally in the form of hot rum, and sometimes he tippled with gin in the afternoons—gin was the most difficult to detect on the breath. He was averaging a half-pint of alcohol a day, too much for his system to burn up.

Dismissing a tendency to justify himself, he sat down at his desk and wrote out, like a prescription, a régime that would cut his liquor in half. Doctors, chauffeurs, and Protestant clergymen could never smell of liquor, as could painters, brokers, cavalry leaders; Dick blamed himself only for indiscretion. But the matter was by no means clarified half an hour later when Franz, revivified by an Alpine fort-

274

night, rolled up the drive, so eager to resume work that he was plunged in it before he reached his office. Dick met him there.

"How was Mount Everest?"

"We could very well have done Mount Everest the rate we were doing. We thought of it. How goes it all? How is my Kaethe, how is your Nicole?"

"All goes smooth domestically. But my God, Franz, we had a rotten scene this morning."

"How? What was it?"

Dick walked around the room while Franz got in touch with his villa by telephone. After the family exchange was over, Dick said: "The Morris boy was taken away—there was a row."

Franz's buoyant face fell.

"I knew he'd left. I met Lladislau on the veranda."

"What did Lladislau say?"

"Just that young Morris had gone—that you'd tell me about it. What about it?"

"The usual incoherent reasons."

"He was a devil, that boy."

"He was a case for anesthesia," Dick agreed. "Anyhow, the father had beaten Lladislau into a colonial subject by the time I came along. What about Lladislau? Do we keep him? I say no—he's not much of a man, he can't seem to cope with anything." Dick hesitated on the verge of the truth, swung away to give himself space within which to recapitulate. Franz perched on the edge of a desk, still in his linen duster and travelling gloves. Dick said:

"One of the remarks the boy made to his father was that your distinguished collaborator was a drunkard. The man is a fanatic, and the descendant seems to have caught traces of vin-du-pays on me."

Franz sat down, musing on his lower lip. "You can tell me at length," he said finally.

"Why not now?" Dick suggested. "You must know I'm the last man to abuse liquor." His eyes and Franz's glinted on each other, pair on pair. Lladislau let the man get so worked up that I was on the defensive. It might have hap-

275

pened in front of patients, and you can imagine how hard it could be to defend yourself in a situation like that!"

Franz took off his gloves and coat. He went to the door and told the secretary, "Don't disturb us." Coming back into the room he flung himself at the long table and fooled with his mail, reasoning as little as is characteristic of people in such postures, rather summoning up a suitable mask for what he had to say.

"Dick, I know well that you are a temperate, well-balanced man, even though we do not entirely agree on the subject of alcohol. But a time has come—Dick, I must say frankly that I have been aware several times that you have had a drink when it was not the moment to have one. There is some reason. Why not try another leave of abstinence?"

*—alcoholic —leave Clinic*

"Absence," Dick corrected him automatically. "It's no solution for me to go away."

They were both chafed, Franz at having his return marred and blurred.

"Sometimes you don't use your common sense, Dick."

"I never understood what common sense meant applied to complicated problems—unless it means that a general practitioner can perform a better operation than a specialist."

He was seized by an overwhelming disgust for the situation. To explain, to patch—these were not natural functions at their age—better to continue with the cracked echo of an old truth in the ears.

"This is no go," he said suddenly.

"Well, that's occurred to me," Franz admitted. "Your heart isn't in this project any more, Dick."

*doesn't enjoy his work anymore*

"I know. I want to leave—we could strike some arrangement about taking Nicole's money out gradually."

"I have thought about that too, Dick—I have seen this coming. I am able to arrange other backing, and it will be possible to take all your money out by the end of the year."

Dick had not intended to come to a decision so quickly, nor was he prepared for Franz's so ready acquiescence in the break, yet he was relieved. Not without desperation he had long felt the ethics of his profession dissolving into a lifeless mass.

*doesn't enjoy his work anymore*

276

# IV

THE Divers would return to the Riviera, which was home. The Villa Diana had been rented again for the summer, so they divided the intervening time between German spas and French cathedral towns where they were always happy for a few days. Dick wrote a little with no particular method; it was one of those parts of life that are an awaiting; not upon Nicole's health, which seemed to thrive on travel, nor upon work, but simply an awaiting. The factor that gave purposefulness to the period was the children.

Dick's interest in them increased with their ages, now eleven and nine. He managed to reach them over the heads of employees on the principle that both the forcing of children and the fear of forcing them were inadequate substitutes for the long, careful watchfulness, the checking and balancing and reckoning of accounts, to the end that there should be no slip below a certain level of duty. He came to know them much better than Nicole did, and in expansive moods over the wines of several countries he talked and played with them at length. They had that wistful charm, almost sadness, peculiar to children who have learned early not to cry or laugh with abandon; they were apparently moved to no extremes of emotion, but content with a simple regimentation and the simple pleasures allowed them. They lived on the even tenor found advisable in the experience of old families of the Western world, brought up rather than brought out. Dick thought, for example, that nothing was more conducive to the development of observation than compulsory silence.

Lanier was an unpredictable boy with an inhuman curiosity. "Well, how many Pomeranians would it take to lick a lion, father?" was typical of the questions with which he harassed Dick. Topsy was easier. She was nine and very fair and exquisitely made like Nicole, and in the past Dick had worried about that. Lately she had become as robust as any American child. He was satisfied with them both, but conveyed the fact to them only in a tacit way. They were

277

not let off breaches of good conduct—"Either one learns politeness at home," Dick said, "or the world teaches it to you with a whip and you may get hurt in the process. What do I care whether Topsy 'adores' me or not? I'm not bringing her up to be my wife."

Another element that distinguished this summer and autumn for the Divers was a plenitude of money. Due to the sale of their interest in the clinic, and to developments in America, there was now so much that the mere spending of it, the care of goods, was an absorption in itself. The style in which they travelled seemed fabulous.

*Self-indulgent*

Regard them, for example, as the train slows up at Boyen where they are to spend a fortnight visiting. The shifting from the wagon-lit has begun at the Italian frontier. The governess's maid and Madame Diver's maid have come up from second class to help with the baggage and the dogs. Mlle. Bellois will superintend the hand-luggage, leaving the Sealyhams to one maid and the pair of Pekinese to the other. It is not necessarily poverty of spirit that makes a woman surround herself with life—it can be a superabundance of interest, and, except during her flashes of illness. Nicole was capable of being curator of it all. For example with the great quantity of heavy baggage—presently from the van would be unloaded four wardrobe trunks, a shoe trunk, three hat trunks and two hat boxes, a chest of servants' trunks, a portable filing-cabinet, a medicine case, a spirit lamp container, a picnic set, four tennis rackets in presses and cases, a phonograph, a typewriter. Distributed among the spaces reserved for family and entourage were two dozen supplementary grips, satchels and packages, each one numbered, down to the tag on the cane case. Thus all of it could be checked up in two minutes on any station platform, some for storage, some for accompaniment from the "light trip list" or the "heavy trip list," constantly revised, and carried on metal-edged plaques in Nicole's purse. She had devised the system as a child when travelling with her failing mother. It was equivalent to the system of a regimental supply officer who must think of the bellies and equipment of three thousand men.

*excess*

278

The Divers flocked from the train into the early gathered twilight of the valley. The village people watched the debarkation with an awe akin to that which followed the Italian pilgrimages of Lord Byron a century before. Their hostess was the Contessa di Minghetti, lately Mary North. The journey that had begun in a room over the shop of a paperhanger in Newark had ended in an extraordinary marriage.

"Conte di Minghetti" was merely a papal title—the wealth of Mary's husband flowed from his being ruler-owner of manganese deposits in southwestern Asia. He was not quite light enough to travel in a Pullman south of Mason-Dixon; he was of the Kabyle-Berber-Sabaean-Hindu strain that belts across north Africa and Asia, more sympathetic to the European than the mongrel faces of the ports.

When these princely households, one of the East, one of the West, faced each other on the station platform, the splendor of the Divers seemed pioneer simplicity by comparison. Their hosts were accompanied by an Italian major-domo carrying a staff, by a quartet of turbaned retainers on motorcycles, and by two half-veiled females who stood respectfully a little behind Mary and salaamed at Nicole, making her jump with the gesture.

To Mary as well as to the Divers the greeting was faintly comic; Mary gave an apologetic, belittling giggle; yet her voice, as she introduced her husband by his Asiatic title, flew proud and high.

In their rooms as they dressed for dinner, Dick and Nicole grimaced at each other in an awed way: such rich as want to be thought democratic pretend in private to be swept off their feet by swank.

"Little Mary North knows what she wants," Dick muttered through his shaving cream. "Abe educated her, and now she's married to a Buddha. If Europe ever goes Bolshevik she'll turn up as the bride of Stalin."

Nicole looked around from her dressing-case. "Watch your tongue, Dick, will you?" But she laughed. "They're very swell. The warships all fire at them or salute them or something. Mary rides in the royal bus in London."

279

"All right," he agreed. As he heard Nicole at the door asking for pins, he called, "I wonder if I could have some whiskey; I feel the mountain air!"

*drinking*

"She'll see to it," presently Nicole called through the bathroom door. "It was one of those women who were at the station. She has her veil off."

"What did Mary tell you about life?" he asked.

"She didn't say so much—she was interested in high life—she asked me a lot of questions about my genealogy and all that sort of thing, as if I knew anything about it. But it seems the bridegroom has two very tan children by another marriage—one of them ill with some Asiatic thing they can't diagnose. I've got to warn the children. Sounds very peculiar to me. Mary will see how we'd feel about it." She stood worrying a minute.

"She'll understand," Dick reassured her. "Probably the child's in bed."

At dinner Dick talked to Hosain, who had been at an English public school. Hosain wanted to know about stocks and about Hollywood and Dick, whipping up his imagination with champagne, told him preposterous tales.

*drinking*

"Billions?" Hosain demanded.

"Trillions," Dick assured him.

"I didn't truly realize——"

"Well, perhaps millions," Dick conceded. "Every hotel guest is assigned a harem—or what amounts to a harem."

"Other than the actors and directors?"

"Every hotel guest—even travelling salesmen. Why, they tried to send me up a dozen candidates, but Nicole wouldn't stand for it."

Nicole reproved him when they were in their room alone. "Why so many highballs? Why did you use your word spic in front of him?"

"Excuse me, I meant smoke. The tongue slipped."

"Dick, this isn't faintly like you."

"Excuse me again. I'm not much like myself any more."

That night Dick opened a bathroom window, giving on a narrow and tubular court of the château, gray as rats but echoing at the moment to plaintive and peculiar music, sad as a flute. Two men were chanting in an Eastern language or dialect full of k's and l's—he leaned out but he could not see them; there was obviously a religious significance in the sounds, and tired and emotionless he let them pray for him too, but what for, save that he should not lose himself in his increasing melancholy, he did not know.

Next day, over a thinly wooded hillside they shot scrawny birds, distant poor relations to the partridge. It was done in a vague imitation of the English manner, with a corps of inexperienced beaters whom Dick managed to miss by firing only directly overhead.

On their return Lanier was waiting in their suite.

"Father, you said tell you immediately if we were near the sick boy."

Nicole whirled about, immediately on guard.

"—so, Mother," Lanier continued, turning to her, "the boy takes a bath every evening and to-night he took his bath just before mine and I had to take mine in his water, and it was dirty."

"What? Now what?"

"I saw them take Tony out of it, and then they called me into it and the water was dirty."

"But—did you take it?"

"Yes, Mother."

"Heavens!" she exclaimed to Dick.

He demanded: "Why didn't Lucienne draw your bath?"

"Lucienne can't. It's a funny heater—it reached out of herself and burned her arm last night and she's afraid of it, so one of those two women——"

"You go in this bathroom and take a bath now."

"Don't say *I* told you," said Lanier from the doorway.

Dick went in and sprinkled the tub with sulphur; closing the door he said to Nicole:

"Either we speak to Mary or we'd better get out."

She agreed and he continued: "People think their children are constitutionally cleaner than other people's, and their diseases are less contagious."

Dick came in and helped himself from the decanter, chewing a biscuit savagely in the rhythm of the pouring water in the bathroom.

"Tell Lucienne that she's got to learn about the heater—" he suggested. At that moment the Asiatic woman came in person to the door.

"El Contessa——"

Dick beckoned her inside and closed the door.

"Is the little sick boy better?" he inquired pleasantly.

"Better, yes, but he still has the eruptions frequently."

"That's too bad—I'm very sorry. But you see our children mustn't be bathed in his water. That's out of the question— I'm sure your mistress would be furious if she had known you had done a thing like that."

"I?" She seemed thunderstruck. "Why, I merely saw your maid had difficulty with the heater—I told her about it and started the water."

"But with a sick person you must empty the bathwater entirely out, and clean the tub."

"I?"

Chokingly the woman drew a long breath, uttered a convulsed sob and rushed from the room.

"She mustn't get up on western civilization at our expense," he said grimly.

At dinner that night he decided that it must inevitably be a truncated visit: about his own country Hosain seemed to have observed only that there were many mountains and some goats and herders of goats. He was a reserved young man—to draw him out would have required the sincere effort that Dick now reserved for his family. Soon after dinner Hosain left Mary and the Divers to themselves, but the old unity was split—between them lay the restless social fields that Mary was about to conquer. Dick was relieved when, at nine-thirty, Mary received and read a note and got up.

"You'll have to excuse me. My husband is leaving on a short trip—and I must be with him."

Next morning, hard on the heels of the servant bringing coffee, Mary entered their room. She was dressed and they

282

were not dressed, and she had the air of having been up for some time. Her face was toughened with quiet jerky fury

"What is this story about Lanier having been bathed in a dirty bath?"

Dick began to protest, but she cut through:

"*What* is this story that you commanded my husband's sister to clean Lanier's tub?"

She remained on her feet staring at them, as they sat impotent as idols in their beds, weighted by their trays. Together they exclaimed: "His *sister!*"

"That you ordered one of his sisters to clean out a tub!"

"We didn't—" their voices rang together saying the same thing, "—I spoke to the native servant——"

"You spoke to Hosain's sister."

Dick could only say: "I supposed they were two maids."

"You were told they were Himadoun."

"What?" Dick got out of bed and into a robe.

"I explained it to you at the piano night before last. Don't tell me you were too merry to understand."

"Was that what you said? I didn't hear the beginning. I didn't connect the—we didn't make any connection, Mary. Well, all we can do is see her and apologize."

"See her and apologize! I explained to you that when the oldest member of the family—when the oldest one marries, well, the two oldest sisters consecrate themselves to being Himadoun, to being his wife's ladies-in-waiting."

"Was that why Hosain left the house last night?"

Mary hesitated; then nodded.

"He had to—they all left. His honor makes it necessary."

Now both the Divers were up and dressing; Mary went on:

"And what's all that about the bathwater. As if a thing like that could happen in this house! We'll ask Lanier about it."

Dick sat on the bedside indicating in a private gesture to Nicole that she should take over. Meanwhile Mary went to the door and spoke to an attendant in Italian.

"Wait a minute," Nicole said. "I won't have that."

283

"You accused us," answered Mary, in a tone she had never used to Nicole before. "Now I have a right to see."

"I won't have the child brought in." Nicole threw on her clothes as though they were chain mail.

"That's all right," said Dick. "Bring Lanier in. We'll settle this bathtub matter—fact or myth."

Lanier, half clothed mentally and physically, gazed at the angered faces of the adults.

"Listen, Lanier," Mary demanded, "how did you come to think you were bathed in water that had been used before?"

"Speak up," Dick added.

"It was just dirty, that was all."

"Couldn't you hear the new water running, from your room, next door?"

Lanier admitted the possibility but reiterated his point—the water was dirty. He was a little awed; he tried to see ahead:

"It couldn't have been running, because——"

They pinned him down.

"Why not?"

He stood in his little kimono arousing the sympathy of his parents and further arousing Mary's impatience—then he said:

"The water was dirty, it was full of soap-suds."

"When you're not sure what you're saying——" Mary began, but Nicole interrupted.

"Stop it, Mary. If there were dirty suds in the water it was logical to think it was dirty. His father told him to come——"

"There couldn't have been dirty suds in the water."

Lanier looked reproachfully at his father, who had betrayed him. Nicole turned him about by the shoulders and sent him out of the room; Dick broke the tensity with a laugh.

Then, as if the sound recalled the past, the old friendship, Mary guessed how far away from them she had gone and said in a mollifying tone: "It's always like that with children."

Her uneasiness grew as she remembered the past. "You'd be silly to go—Hosain wanted to make this trip anyhow. After all, you're my guests and you just blundered into the thing." But Dick, made more angry by this obliqueness and the use of the word blunder, turned away and began arranging his effects, saying:

"It's too bad about the young women. I'd like to apologize to the one who came in here."

"If you'd only listened on the piano seat!"

"But you've gotten so damned dull, Mary. I listened as long as I could."

"Be quiet!" Nicole advised him.

"I return his compliment," said Mary bitterly. "Goodby, Nicole." She went out.

After all that there was no question of her coming to see them off; the major-domo arranged the departure. Dick left formal notes for Hosain and the sisters. There was nothing to do except to go, but all of them, especially Lanier, felt bad about it.

"I insist," insisted Lanier on the train, "that it was dirty bathwater."

"That'll do," his father said. "You better forget it—unless you want me to divorce you. Did you know there was a new law in France that you can divorce a child?"

Lanier roared with delight and the Divers were unified again—Dick wondered how many more times it could be done.

V

NICOLE went to the window and bent over the sill to take a look at the rising altercation on the terrace; the April sun shone pink on the saintly face of Augustine, the cook, and blue on the butcher's knife she waved in her drunken hand. She had been with them since their return to Villa Diana in February.

Because of an obstruction of an awning she could see only

Dick's head and his hand holding one of his heavy canes with a bronze knob on it. The knife and the cane, menacing each other, were like tripos and short sword in a gladiatorial combat. Dick's words reached her first:

"—care how much kitchen wine you drink but when I find you digging into a bottle of Chablis Mouton——"

"You talk about drinking!" Augustine cried, flourishing her sabre. "You drink—all the time!"

*drinking*

Nicole called over the awning: "What's the matter, Dick?" and he answered in English:

"The old girl has been polishing off the vintage wines. I'm firing her—at least I'm trying to."

"Heavens! Well, don't let her reach you with that knife."

Augustine shook her knife up at Nicole. Her old mouth was made of two small intersecting cherries.

"I would like to say, Madame, if you knew that your husband drinks over at his bastide⁵⁷ comparatively as a day-laborer——"

"Shut up and get out!" interrupted Nicole. "We'll get the gendarmes."

"*You'll* get the gendarmes! With my brother in the corps! You—a disgusting American?"

In English Dick called up to Nicole:

"Get the children away from the house till I settle this."

"—disgusting Americans who come here and drink up our finest wines," screamed Augustine with the voice of the commune.

Dick mastered a firmer tone.

"You must leave now! I'll pay you what we owe you."

"Very sure you'll pay me! And let me tell you—" she came close and waved the knife so furiously that Dick raised his stick, whereupon she rushed into the kitchen and returned with the carving knife reinforced by a hatchet.

The situation was not prepossessing—Augustine was a strong woman and could be disarmed only at the risk of serious results to herself—and severe legal complications which were the lot of one who molested a French citizen. Trying a bluff Dick called up to Nicole:

"Phone the poste de police." Then to Augustine, indicating her armament, "This means arrest for you."

"Ha-*ha!*" she laughed demoniacally; nevertheless she came no nearer. Nicole phoned the police but was answered with what was almost an echo of Augustine's laugh. She heard mumbles and passings of the word around—the connection was suddenly broken.

Returning to the window she called down to Dick: "Give her something extra!"

"If I could get to that phone!" As this seemed impracticable, Dick capitulated. For fifty francs, increased to a hundred as he succumbed to the idea of getting her out hastily, Augustine yielded her fortress, covering the retreat with stormy grenades of "Salaud!" She would leave only when her nephew could come for her baggage. Waiting cautiously in the neighborhood of the kitchen Dick heard a cork pop, but he yielded the point. There was no further trouble—when the nephew arrived, all apologetic, Augustine bade Dick a cheerful, convivial good-by and called up "Au revoir, Madame! Bonne chance!" to Nicole's window.

The Divers went to Nice and dined on a bouillabaisse, which is a stew of rock fish and small lobsters, highly seasoned with saffron, and a bottle of cold Chablis. He expressed pity for Augustine.

"I'm not sorry a bit," said Nicole.

"I'm sorry—and yet I wish I'd shoved her over the cliff."

There was little they dared talk about in these days; seldom did they find the right word when it counted, it arrived always a moment too late when one could not reach the other any more. To-night Augustine's outburst had shaken them from their separate reveries; with the burn and chill of the spiced broth and the parching wine they talked.

"We can't go on like this," Nicole suggested. "Or can we?—what do you think?" Startled that for the moment Dick did not deny it, she continued, "Some of the time I think it's my fault—I've ruined you."

"So I'm ruined, am I?" he inquired pleasantly.

"I didn't mean that. But you used to want to create things—now you seem to want to smash them up."

287

She trembled at criticizing him in these broad terms—but his enlarging silence frightened her even more. She guessed that something was developing behind the silence, behind the hard, blue eyes, the almost unnatural interest in the children. Uncharacteristic bursts of temper surprised her—he would suddenly unroll a long scroll of contempt for some person, race, class, way of life, way of thinking. It was as though an incalculable story was telling itself inside him, about which she could only guess at in the moments when it broke through the surface.

"After all, what do you get out of this?" she demanded.

"Knowing you're stronger every day. Knowing that your illness follows the law of diminishing returns."

His voice came to her from far off, as though he were speaking of something remote and academic; her alarm made her exclaim, "Dick!" and she thrust her hand forward to his across the table. A reflex pulled Dick's hand back and he added: "There's the whole situation to think of, isn't there? There's not just you." He covered her hand with his and said in the old pleasant voice of a conspirator for pleasure, mischief, profit, and delight:

"See that boat out there?"

It was the motor yacht of T. F. Golding lying placid among the little swells of the Nicean bay, constantly bound upon a romantic voyage that was not dependent upon actual motion. "We'll go out there now and ask the people on board what's the matter with them. We'll find out if they're happy."

"We hardly know him," Nicole objected.

"He urged us. Besides, Baby knows him—she practically married him, doesn't she—didn't she?"

When they put out from the port in a hired launch it was already summer dusk and lights were breaking out in spasms along the rigging of the Margin. As they drew up alongside, Nicole's doubts reasserted themselves.

"He's having a party——"

"It's only a radio," he guessed.

They were hailed—a huge white-haired man in a white suit looked down at them, calling:

"Do I recognize the Divers?"

"Boat ahoy, Margin!"

Their boat moved under the companionway; as they mounted Golding doubled his huge frame to give Nicole a hand.

"Just in time for dinner."

A small orchestra was playing astern.

"I'm yours for the asking—but till then
You can't ask me to behave——"

And as Golding's cyclonic arms blew them aft without touching them, Nicole was sorrier they had come, and more impatient at Dick. Having taken up an attitude of aloofness from the gay people here, at the time when Dick's work and her health were incompatible with going about, they had a reputation as refusers. Riviera replacements during the ensuing years interpreted this as a vague unpopularity. Nevertheless, having taken such a stand, Nicole felt it should not be cheaply compromised for a momentary self-indulgence.

As they passed through the principal salon they saw ahead of them figures that seemed to dance in the half light of the circular stern. This was an illusion made by the enchantment of the music, the unfamiliar lighting, and the surrounding presence of water. Actually, save for some busy stewards, the guests loafed on a wide divan that followed the curve of the deck. There were a white, a red, a blurred dress, the laundered chests of several men, <u>of whom one</u>, detaching <u>and identifying himself, brought from Nicole a rare little</u> <u>cry of delight.</u>

"Tommy!"

Brushing aside the Gallicism of his formal dip at her hand, Nicole pressed her face against his. They sat, or rather lay down together on the Antoninian bench. His handsome face was so dark as to have lost the pleasantness of deep tan, without attaining the blue beauty of negroes—it was just worn leather. The foreignness of his depigmentation by unknown suns, his nourishment by strange soils, his tongue awkward with the curl of many dialects, his reactions attuned to odd alarms—these things fascinated and rested Nicole—in the moment of meeting she lay on his bosom, spiritually, going out and out. ... Then self-preservation reasserted itself and retiring to her own world she spoke lightly.

"You look just like all the adventurers in the movies— but why do you have to stay away so long?"

Tommy Barban looked at her, uncomprehending but alert; the pupils of his eyes flashed.

"Five years," she continued, in throaty mimicry of nothing. "*Much* too long. Couldn't you only slaughter a certain number of creatures and then come back, and breathe our air for a while?"

In her cherished presence Tommy Europeanized himself quickly.

"Mais pour nous héros," he said, "il nous faut du temps, Nicole. Nous ne pouvons pas faire de petits exercices d'héroïsme—il faut faire les grandes compositions."

"Talk English to me, Tommy."

"Parlez français avec moi, Nicole."

"But the meanings are different—in French you can be heroic and gallant with dignity, and you know it. But in English you can't be heroic and gallant without being a little absurd, and you know that too. That gives me an advantage."

"But after all—" He chuckled suddenly. "Even in English I'm brave, heroic and all that."

She pretended to be groggy with wonderment but he was not abashed.

"I only know what I see in the cinema," he said.

"Is it all like the movies?"

"The movies aren't so bad—now this Ronald Colman— have you seen his pictures about the Corps d'Afrique du Nord? They're not bad at all."

"Very well, whenever I go to the movies I'll know you're going through just that sort of thing at that moment."

As she spoke, Nicole was aware of a small, pale, pretty young woman with lovely metallic hair, almost green in the deck lights, who had been sitting on the other side of Tommy and might have been part either of their conversation or of the one next to them. She had obviously had a monopoly of Tommy, for now she abandoned hope of his attention with what was once called ill grace, and petulantly crossed the crescent of the deck.

"After all, I am a hero," Tommy said calmly, only half joking. "I have ferocious courage, *usually*, something like a lion, something like a drunken man."

Nicole waited until the echo of his boast had died away in his mind—she knew he had probably never made such a statement before. Then she looked among the strangers, and found as usual the fierce neurotics, pretending calm, liking the country only in horror of the city, of the sound of their own voices which had set the tone and pitch. . . . She asked:

"Who is the woman in white?"

"The one who was beside me? Lady Caroline Sibly-Biers."[58] They listened for a moment to her voice across the way:

*"The man's a scoundrel, but he's a cat of the stripe. We sat up all night playing two-handed chemin-de-fer, and he owes me a mille Swiss."*

Tommy laughed and said: "She is now the wickedest woman in London—whenever I come back to Europe there is a new crop of the wickedest women from London. She's the very latest—though I believe there is now one other who's considered almost as wicked."

Nicole glanced again at the woman across the deck—she was fragile, tubercular—it was incredible that such narrow shoulders, such puny arms could bear aloft the pennon of decadence, last ensign of the fading empire. Her resemblance was rather to one of John Held's[59] flat-chested flappers than to the hierarchy of tall languid blondes who had posed for painters and novelists since before the war.

Golding approached, fighting down the resonance of his huge bulk, which transmitted his will as through a gargantuan amplifier, and Nicole, still reluctant, yielded to his reiterated points: that the Margin was starting for Cannes immediately after dinner; that they could always pack in some caviare and champagne, even though they had dined; that in any case Dick was now on the phone, telling their chauffeur in Nice to drive their car back to Cannes and leave it in front of the Café des Alliés where the Divers could retrieve it.

They moved into the dining salon and Dick was placed next to Lady Caroline. Nicole saw that his usually ruddy face was drained of blood; he talked in a dogmatic voice, of which only snatches reached Nicole:

". . . It's all right for you English, you're doing a dance of death. . . . Sepoys in the ruined fort, I mean Sepoys at the gate and gaiety in the fort and all that. The green hat, the crushed hat, no future."

Lady Caroline answered him in short sentences spotted with the terminal "What?" the double-edged "Quite!" the depressing "Cheerio!" that always had a connotation of imminent peril, but Dick appeared oblivious to the warning signals. Suddenly he made a particularly vehement pronouncement, the purport of which eluded Nicole, but she saw the young woman turn dark and sinewy, and heard her answer sharply:

"After all a chep's a chep and a chum's a chum."

Again he had offended some one—couldn't he hold his tongue a little longer? How long? To death then.

At the piano, a fair-haired young Scotsman from the orchestra (entitled by its drum "The Ragtime College Jazzes of Edinboro") had begun singing in a Danny Deever[60] monotone, accompanying himself with low chords on the piano. He pronounced his words with great precision, as though they impressed him almost intolerably.

> *There was a young lady from hell,*
> *Who jumped at the sound of a bell,*
> *Because she was bad—bad—bad,*
> *She jumped at the sound of a bell,*
> *From hell* (BOOMBOOM)
> *From hell* (TOOTTOOT)
> *There was a young lady from hell——*"

"What is all this?" whispered Tommy to Nicole.

The girl on the other side of him supplied the answer:

"Caroline Sibly-Biers wrote the words. He wrote the music."

"Quelle enfanterie!" Tommy murmured as the next verse began, hinting at the jumpy lady's further predilections. "On dirait qu'il récite Racine!"

On the surface at least, Lady Caroline was paying no attention to the performance of her work. Glancing at her again Nicole found herself impressed, neither with the character nor the personality, but with the sheer strength derived from an attitude; Nicole thought that she was formidable, and she was confirmed in this point of view as the party rose from table. Dick remained in his seat wearing an odd expression; then he crashed into words with a harsh ineptness.

"I don't like innuendo in these deafening English whispers."

Already half-way out of the room Lady Caroline turned and walked back to him; she spoke in a low clipped voice purposely audible to the whole company.

"You came to me asking for it—disparaging my countrymen, disparaging my friend, Mary Minghetti. I simply said you were observed associating with a questionable crowd in Lausanne. Is that a deafening whisper? Or does it simply deafen *you?*"

"It's still not loud enough," said Dick, a little too late. "So I am actually a notorious——"

Golding crushed out the phrase with his voice saying:

"What! What!" and moved his guests on out, with the threat of his powerful body. Turning the corner of the door Nicole saw that Dick was still sitting at the table. She was furious at the woman for her preposterous statement, equally furious at Dick for having brought them here, for having become fuddled, for having untipped the capped barbs of his irony, for having come off humiliated—she was a little more annoyed because she knew that her taking possession of Tommy Barban on their arrival had first irritated the Englishwoman.

A moment later she saw Dick standing in the gangway, apparently in complete control of himself as he talked with

Golding; then for half an hour she did not see him anywhere about the deck and she broke out of an intricate Malay game, played with string and coffee beans, and said to Tommy:

"I've got to find Dick."

Since dinner the yacht had been in motion westward. The fine night streamed away on either side, the Diesel engines pounded softly, there was a spring wind that blew Nicole's hair abruptly when she reached the bow, and she had a sharp lesion of anxiety at seeing Dick standing in the angle by the flagstaff. His voice was serene as he recognized her.

"It's a nice night."

"I was worried."

"Oh, you were worried?"

"Oh, don't talk that way. It would give me so much pleasure to think of a little something I could do for you, Dick."

He turned away from her, toward the veil of starlight over Africa.

"I believe that's true, Nicole. And sometimes I believe that the littler it was, the more pleasure it would give you."

"Don't talk like that—don't say such things."

His face, wan in the light that the white spray caught and tossed back to the brilliant sky had none of the lines of annoyance she had expected. It was even detached; his eyes focussed upon her gradually as upon a chessman to be moved; in the same slow manner he caught her wrist and drew her near.

"You ruined me, did you?" he inquired blandly. "Then we're both ruined. So——"

Cold with terror she put her other wrist into his grip. All right, she would go with him—again she felt the beauty of the night vividly in one moment of complete response and abnegation—all right, then——

—But now she was unexpectedly free and Dick turned his back sighing: "Tch! tch!"

Tears streamed down Nicole's face—in a moment she heard some one approaching; it was Tommy.

"You found him! Nicole thought maybe you jumped overboard, Dick," he said, "because that little English poule slanged you."

"It'd be a good setting to jump overboard," said Dick mildly.

"Wouldn't it?" agreed Nicole hastily. "Let's borrow life-preservers and jump over. I think we should do something spectacular. I feel that all our lives have been too restrained."

Tommy sniffed from one to the other trying to breathe in the situation with the night. "We'll go ask the Lady Beer-and-Ale what to do—she should know the latest things. And we should memorize her song 'There was a young lady from l'enfer.' I shall translate it, and make a fortune from its success at the Casino."

"Are you rich, Tommy?" Dick asked him, as they retraced the length of the boat.

"Not as things go now. I got tired of the brokerage business and went away. But I have good stocks in the hands of friends who are holding it for me. All goes well."

"Dick's getting rich," Nicole said. In reaction her voice had begun to tremble.

On the after deck Golding had fanned three pairs of dancers into action with his colossal paws. Nicole and Tommy joined them and Tommy remarked: "Dick seems to be drinking."

"Only moderately," she said loyally.

"There are those who can drink and those who can't. Obviously Dick can't. You ought to tell him not to."

"I!" she exclaimed in amazement. "*I* tell Dick what he should do or shouldn't do!"

But in a reticent way Dick was still vague and sleepy when they reached the pier at Cannes. Golding buoyed him down into the launch of the Margin whereupon Lady Caroline shifted her place conspicuously. On the dock he bowed good-by with exaggerated formality, and for a moment he seemed about to speed her with a salty epigram, but the bone of Tommy's arm went into the soft part of his and they walked to the attendant car.

"I'll drive you home," Tommy suggested.

"Don't bother—we can get a cab."

"I'd like to, if you can put me up."

On the back seat of the car Dick remained quiescent until the yellow monolith of Golfe-Juan was passed, and then the constant carnival at Juan-les-Pins where the night was musical and strident in many languages. When the car turned up the hill toward Tarmes, he sat up suddenly, prompted by the tilt of the vehicle, and delivered a peroration:

"A charming representative of the—" he stumbled momentarily, "—a firm of—bring me brains addled à l'Anglaise." Then he went into an appeased sleep, belching now and then contentedly into the soft warm darkness.

# VI

NEXT morning Dick came early into Nicole's room. "I waited till I heard you up. Needless to say I feel badly about the evening—but how about no post-mortems?"

"I'm agreed," she answered coolly, carrying her face to the mirror.

"Tommy drove us home? Or did I dream it?"

"You know he did."

"Seems probable," he admitted, "since I just heard him coughing. I think I'll call on him."

She was glad when he left her, for almost the first time in her life—his awful faculty of being right seemed to have deserted him at last.

Tommy was stirring in his bed, waiting for café au lait.

"Feel all right?" Dick asked.

When Tommy complained of a sore throat he seized at a professional attitude.

"Better have a gargle or something."

"You have one?"

"Oddly enough I haven't—probably Nicole has."

"Don't disturb her."

"She's up."

"How is she?"

Dick turned around slowly. "Did you expect her to be dead because I was tight?" His tone was pleasant. "Nicole is now made of—of Georgia pine, which is the hardest wood known, except lignum vitæ from New Zealand——"

Nicole, going downstairs, heard the end of the conversation. She knew, as she had always known, that Tommy loved her; she knew he had come to dislike Dick, and that Dick had realized it before he did, and would react in some positive way to the man's lonely passion. This thought was succeeded by a moment of sheerly feminine satisfaction. She leaned over her children's breakfast table and told off instructions to the governess, while upstairs two men were concerned about her. *Tommy Loves Nicole*

Later in the garden she was happy; she did not want anything to happen, but only for the situation to remain in suspension as the two men tossed her from one mind to another; she had not existed for a long time, even as a ball.

"Nice, rabbits, isn't it—Or is it? Hey, rabbit—hey you! Is it nice?—hey? Or does it sound very peculiar to you?"

The rabbit, after an experience of practically nothing else and cabbage leaves, agreed after a few tentative shiftings of the nose.

Nicole went on through her garden routine. She left the flowers she cut in designated spots to be brought to the house later by the gardener. Reaching the sea wall she fell into a communicative mood and no one to communicate with; so she stopped and deliberated. She was somewhat shocked at the idea of being interested in another man—but other women have lovers—why not me? In the fine spring morning the inhibitions of the male world disappeared and she reasoned as gaily as a flower, while the wind blew her hair until her head moved with it. Other women have had lovers —the same forces that last night had made her yield to Dick up to the point of death, now kept her head nodding to the wind, content and happy with the logic of, Why shouldn't I? *morally corrupt*

She sat upon the low wall and looked down upon the sea. But from another sea, the wide swell of fantasy, she had fished out something tangible to lay beside the rest of her

297

loot. If she need not, in her spirit, be forever one with Dick as he had appeared last night, she must be something in addition, not just an image on his mind, condemned to endless parades around the circumference of a medal.

Nicole had chosen this part of the wall on which to sit, because the cliff shaded to a slanting meadow with a cultivated vegetable garden. Through a cluster of boughs she saw two men carrying rakes and spades and talking in a counterpoint of Niçois and Provençal. Attracted by their words and gestures she caught the sense:

"I laid her down here."

"I took her behind the vines there."

"She doesn't care—neither does he. It was that sacred dog. Well, I laid her down here——"

"You got the rake?"

"You got it yourself, you clown."

"Well, I don't care where you laid her down. Until that night I never even felt a woman's breast against my chest since I married—twelve years ago. And now you tell me——"

"But listen about the dog——"

Nicole watched them through the boughs; it seemed all right what they were saying—one thing was good for one person, another for another. Yet it was a man's world she had overheard; going back to the house she became doubtful again.

Dick and Tommy were on the terrace. She walked through them and into the house, brought out a sketch pad and began a head of Tommy.

"Hands never idle—distaff flying," Dick said lightly. How could he talk so trivially with the blood still drained down from his cheeks so that the auburn lather of beard showed red as his eyes? She turned to Tommy saying:

"I can always do something. I used to have a nice active little Polynesian ape and juggle him around for hours till people began to make the most dismal rough jokes——"

She kept her eyes resolutely away from Dick. Presently he excused himself and went inside—she saw him pour himself two glasses of water, and she hardened further.

"Nicole—" Tommy began but interrupted himself to clear the harshness from his throat.

"I'm going to get you some special camphor rub," she suggested. "It's American—Dick believes in it. I'll be just a minute."

"I must go really."

Dick came out and sat down. "Believes in what?" When she returned with the jar neither of the men had moved, though she gathered they had had some sort of excited conversation about nothing.

The chauffeur was at the door, with a bag containing Tommy's clothes of the night before. The sight of Tommy in clothes borrowed from Dick moved her sadly, falsely, as though Tommy were not able to afford such clothes.

"When you get to the hotel rub this into your throat and chest and then inhale it," she said.

"Say, there," Dick murmured as Tommy went down the steps, "don't give Tommy the whole jar—it has to be ordered from Paris—it's out of stock down here."

Tommy came back within hearing and the three of them stood in the sunshine, Tommy squarely before the car so that it seemed by leaning forward he would tip it upon his back.

Nicole stepped down to the path.

"Now catch it," she advised him. "It's extremely rare." _cares more about Tommy than Dick by giving the jar away_

She heard Dick grow silent at her side; she took a step off from him and waved as the car drove off with Tommy and the special camphor rub. Then she turned to take her own medicine.

"There was no necessity for that gesture," Dick said. "There are four of us here—and for years whenever there's a cough——"

They looked at each other.

"We can always get another jar—" then she lost her nerve and presently followed him upstairs where he lay down on his own bed and said nothing.

"Do you want lunch to be brought up to you?" she asked.

He nodded and continued to lie quiescent, staring at the

299

ceiling. Doubtfully she went to give the order. Upstairs
again she looked into his room—the blue eyes, like searchlights, played on a dark sky. She stood a minute in the doorway, aware of the sin she had committed against him, half
afraid to come in. . . . She put out her hand as if to rub his
head, but he turned away like a suspicious animal. Nicole
could stand the situation no longer; in a kitchen-maid's
panic she ran downstairs, afraid of what the stricken man
above would feed on while she must still continue her dry
suckling at his lean chest.

In a week Nicole forgot her flash about Tommy—she had
not much memory for people and forgot them easily. But
in the first hot blast of June she heard he was in Nice. He
wrote a little note to them both—and she opened it under
the parasol, together with other mail they had brought from
the house. After reading it she tossed it over to Dick, and in
exchange he threw a telegram into the lap of her beach
pajamas:

"Dears will be at Gausses tomorrow unfortunately without
mother am counting on seeing you.

ROSEMARY"

"I'll be glad to see her," said Nicole, grimly.

## VII

BUT she went to the beach with Dick next morning with
a renewal of her apprehension that Dick was contriving at
some desperate solution. Since the evening on Golding's
yacht she had sensed what was going on. So delicately
balanced was she between an old foothold that had always
guaranteed her security, and the imminence of a leap from
which she must alight changed in the very chemistry of
blood and muscle, that she did not dare bring the matter
into the true forefront of consciousness. The figures of Dick
and herself, mutating, undefined, appeared as spooks

300

caught up into a fantastic dance. For months every word had seemed to have an overtone of some other meaning, soon to be resolved under circumstances that Dick would determine. Though this state of mind was perhaps more hopeful—the long years of sheer being had had an enlivening effect on the parts of her nature that early illness had killed, that Dick had not reached, through no fault of his but simply because no one nature can extend entirely inside another—it was still disquieting. The most unhappy aspect of their relations was Dick's growing indifference, at present personified by too much drink; Nicole did not know whether she was to be crushed or spared—Dick's voice, throbbing with insincerity, confused the issue; she couldn't guess how he was going to behave next upon the tortuously slow unrolling of the carpet, nor what would happen at the end, at the moment of the leap.

For what might occur thereafter she had no anxiety—she suspected that that would be the lifting of a burden, an unblinding of eyes. Nicole had been designed for change, for flight, with money as fins and wings. The new state of things would be no more than if a racing chassis, concealed for years under the body of a family limousine, should be stripped to its original self. Nicole could feel the fresh breeze already—the wrench it was she feared, and the dark manner of its coming.

The Divers went out on the beach with her white suit and his white trunks very white against the color of their bodies. Nicole saw Dick peer about for the children among the confused shapes and shadows of many umbrellas, and as his mind temporarily left her, ceasing to grip her, she looked at him with detachment, and decided that he was seeking his children, not protectively but for protection. Probably it was the beach he feared, like a deposed ruler secretly visiting an old court. She had come to hate his world with its delicate jokes and politenesses, forgetting that for many years it was the only world open to her. Let him look at it—his beach, perverted now to the tastes of the tasteless; he could search it for a day and find no stone of the Chinese Wall he had once erected around it, no footprint of an old friend.

For a moment Nicole was sorry it was so; remembering the glass he had raked out of the old trash heap, remembering the sailor trunks and sweaters they had bought in a Nice back street—garments that afterward ran through a vogue in silk among the Paris couturiers, remembering the simple little French girls climbing on the breakwaters crying "Dites donc! Dites donc!" like birds, and the ritual of the morning time, the quiet restful extraversion toward sea and sun—many inventions of his, buried deeper than the sand under the span of so few years. . . .

Now the swimming place was a "club," though, like the international society it represented, it would be hard to say who was not admitted.

Nicole hardened again as Dick knelt on the straw mat and looked about for Rosemary. Her eyes followed his, searching among the new paraphernalia, the trapezes over the water, the swinging rings, the portable bathhouses, the floating towers, the searchlights from last night's fêtes, the modernistic buffet, white with a hackneyed motif of endless handlebars.

The water was almost the last place he looked for Rosemary, because few people swam any more in that blue paradise, children and one exhibitionistic valet who punctuated the morning with spectacular dives from a fifty-foot rock—most of Gausse's guests stripped the concealing pajamas from their flabbiness only for a short hangover dip at one o'clock.

"There she is," Nicole remarked.

She watched Dick's eyes following Rosemary's track from raft to raft; but the sigh that rocked out of her bosom was something left over from five years ago.

"Let's swim out and speak to Rosemary," he suggested.

"You go."

"We'll both go." She struggled a moment against his pronouncement, but eventually they swam out together, tracing Rosemary by the school of little fish who followed her, taking their dazzle from her, the shining spoon of a trout hook.

Nicole stayed in the water while Dick hoisted himself up

beside Rosemary, and the two sat dripping and talking, exactly as if they had never loved or touched each other. Rosemary was beautiful—her youth was a shock to Nicole, who rejoiced, however, that the young girl was less slender by a hairline than herself. Nicole swam around in little rings, listening to Rosemary who was acting amusement, joy, and expectation—more confident than she had been five years ago.

"I miss Mother so, but she's meeting me in Paris, Monday."

"Five years ago you came here," said Dick. "And what a funny little thing you were, in one of those hotel peignoirs!"

"How you remember things! You always did—and always the nice things."

Nicole saw the old game of flattery beginning again and she dove under water, coming up again to hear:

"I'm going to pretend it's five years ago and I'm a girl of eighteen again. You could always make me feel some you know, kind of, you know, kind of happy way—you and Nicole. I feel as if you're still on the beach there, under one of those umbrellas—the nicest people I'd ever known, maybe ever will."

Swimming away, Nicole saw that the cloud of Dick's heartsickness had lifted a little as he began to play with Rosemary, bringing out his old expertness with people, a tarnished object of art; she guessed that with a drink or so he would have done his stunts on the swinging rings for her, fumbling through stunts he had once done with ease. She noticed that this summer, for the first time, he avoided high diving.

Later, as she dodged her way from raft to raft, Dick overtook her.

"Some of Rosemary's friends have a speed boat, the one out there. Do you want to aquaplane? I think it would be amusing."

Remembering that once he could stand on his hands on a chair at the end of a board, she indulged him as she might have indulged Lanier. Last summer on the Zugersee they had played at that pleasant water game, and Dick had lifted

303

a two-hundred-pound man from the board onto his shoulders and stood up. But women marry all their husbands' talents and naturally, afterwards, are not so impressed with them as they may keep up the pretense of being. Nicole had not even pretended to be impressed, though she had said "Yes" to him, and "Yes, I thought so too."

She knew, though, that he was somewhat tired, that it was only the closeness of Rosemary's exciting youth that prompted the impending effort—she had seen him draw the same inspiration from the new bodies of her children and she wondered coldly if he would make a spectacle of himself. The Divers were older than the others in the boat—the young people were polite, deferential, but Nicole felt an undercurrent of "Who are these Numbers anyhow?" and she missed Dick's easy talent of taking control of situations and making them all right—he had concentrated on what he was going to try to do.

The motor throttled down two hundred yards from shore and one of the young men dove flat over the edge. He swam at the aimless twisting board, steadied it, climbed slowly to his knees on it—then got on his feet as the boat accelerated. Leaning back he swung his light vehicle ponderously from side to side in slow, breathless arcs that rode the trailing side-swell at the end of each swing. In the direct wake of the boat he let go his rope, balanced for a moment, then back-flipped into the water, disappearing like a statue of glory, and reappearing as an insignificant head while the boat made the circle back to him.

Nicole refused her turn; then Rosemary rode the board neatly and conservatively, with facetious cheers from her admirers. Three of them scrambled egotistically for the honor of pulling her into the boat, managing, among them, to bruise her knee and hip against the side.

"Now you, Doctor," said the Mexican at the wheel.

Dick and the last young man dove over the side and swam to the board. Dick was going to try his lifting trick and Nicole began to watch with smiling scorn. This physical showing-off for Rosemary irritated her most of all.

When the men had ridden long enough to find their balance, Dick knelt, and putting the back of his neck in the other man's crotch, found the rope through his legs, and slowly began to rise.

The people in the boat, watching closely, saw that he was having difficulties. He was on one knee; the trick was to straighten all the way up in the same motion with which he left his kneeling position. He rested for a moment, then his face contracted as he put his heart into the strain, and lifted.

The board was narrow, the man, though weighing less than a hundred and fifty, was awkward with his weight and grabbed clumsily at Dick's head. When, with a last wrenching effort of his back, Dick stood upright, the board slid sidewise and the pair toppled into the sea.

In the boat Rosemary exclaimed: "Wonderful! They almost had it."

But as they came back to the swimmers Nicole watched for a sight of Dick's face. It was full of annoyance as she expected, because he had done the thing with ease only two years ago.

The second time he was more careful. He rose a little, testing the balance of his burden, settled down again on his knee; then, grunting "Alley oop!" began to rise—but before he could really straighten out, his legs suddenly buckled and he shoved the board away with his feet to avoid being struck as they fell off.

This time when the Baby Gar came back it was apparent to all the passengers that he was angry.

"Do you mind if I try that once more?" he called, treading water. "We almost had it then."

"Sure. Go ahead."

To Nicole he looked white-around-the-gills, and she cautioned him:

"Don't you think that's enough for now?"

He didn't answer. The first partner had had plenty and was hauled over the side, the Mexican driving the motor boat obligingly took his place.

He was heavier than the first man. As the boat gathered

305

motion, Dick rested for a moment, belly-down on the board. Then he got beneath the man and took the rope, and his muscles flexed as he tried to rise.

He could not rise. Nicole saw him shift his position and strain upward again but at the instant when the weight of his partner was full upon his shoulders he became immovable. He tried again—lifting an inch, two inches—Nicole felt the sweat glands of her forehead open as she strained with him—then he was simply holding his ground, then he collapsed back down on his knees with a smack, and they went over, Dick's head barely missing a kick of the board.

"Hurry back!" Nicole called to the driver; even as she spoke she saw him slide under water and she gave a little cry; but he came up again and turned on his back, and the Mexican swam near to help. It seemed forever till the boat reached them but when they came alongside at last and Nicole saw Dick floating exhausted and expressionless, alone with the water and the sky, her panic changed suddenly to contempt.

"We'll help you up, Doctor. . . . Get his foot . . . all right . . . now altogether. . . ."

Dick sat panting and looking at nothing.

"I knew you shouldn't have tried it," Nicole could not help saying.

"He'd tired himself the first two times," said the Mexican.

"It was a foolish thing," Nicole insisted. Rosemary tactfully said nothing.

After a minute Dick got his breath, panting, "I couldn't have lifted a paper doll that time."

An explosive little laugh relieved the tension caused by his failure. They were all attentive to Dick as he disembarked at the dock. But Nicole was annoyed—everything he did annoyed her now.

She sat with Rosemary under an umbrella while Dick went to the buffet for a drink—he returned presently with some sherry for them.

"The first drink I ever had was with you," Rosemary said, and with a spurt of enthusiasm she added, "Oh, I'm so glad to see you and *know* you're all right. I was worried—"

Her sentence broke as she changed direction "that maybe you wouldn't be."

"Did you hear I'd gone into a process of deterioration?"

"Oh, no. I simply—just heard you'd changed. And I'm glad to see with my own eyes it isn't true."

"It is true," Dick answered, sitting down with them. "The change came a long way back—but at first it didn't show. The manner remains intact for some time after the morale cracks."

"Do you practise on the Riviera?" Rosemary demanded hastily.

"It'd be a good ground to find likely specimens." He nodded here and there at the people milling about in the golden sand. "Great candidates. Notice our old friend, Mrs. Abrams, playing duchess to Mary North's queen? Don't get jealous about it—think of Mrs. Abrams' long climb up the back stairs of the Ritz on her hands and knees and all the carpet dust she had to inhale."

Rosemary interrupted him. "But is that really Mary North?" She was regarding a woman sauntering in their direction followed by a small group who behaved as if they were accustomed to being looked at. When they were ten feet away, Mary's glance flickered fractionally over the Divers, one of those unfortunate glances that indicate to the glanced-upon that they have been observed but are to be overlooked, the sort of glance that neither the Divers nor Rosemary Hoyt had ever permitted themselves to throw at any one in their lives. Dick was amused when Mary perceived Rosemary, changed her plans and came over. She spoke to Nicole with pleasant heartiness, nodded unsmilingly to Dick as if he were somewhat contagious—whereupon he bowed in ironic respect—as she greeted Rosemary.

"I heard you were here. For how long?"

"Until to-morrow," Rosemary answered.

She, too, saw how Mary had walked through the Divers to talk to her, and a sense of obligation kept her unenthusiastic. No, she could not dine to-night.

Mary turned to Nicole, her manner indicating affection blended with pity.

"How are the children?" she asked.

They came up at the moment, and Nicole gave ear to a request that she overrule the governess on a swimming point.

"No," Dick answered for her. "What Mademoiselle says must go."

Agreeing that one must support delegated authority, Nicole refused their request, whereupon Mary—who in the manner of an Anita Loos heroine had dealings only with Faits Accomplis, who indeed could not have house-broken a French poodle puppy—regarded Dick as though he were guilty of a most flagrant bullying. Dick, chafed by the tiresome performance, inquired with mock solicitude:

"How are your children—and their aunts?"

Mary did not answer; she left them, first draping a sympathetic hand over Lanier's reluctant head. After she had gone Dick said: "When I think of the time I spent working over her."

"I like her," said Nicole.

Dick's bitterness had surprised Rosemary, who had thought of him as all-forgiving, all-comprehending. Suddenly she recalled what it was she had heard about him. In conversation with some State Department people on the boat—Europeanized Americans who had reached a position where they could scarcely have been said to belong to any nation at all, at least not to any great power though perhaps to a Balkan-like state composed of similar citizens— the name of the ubiquitously renowned Baby Warren had occurred and it was remarked that Baby's younger sister had thrown herself away on a dissipated doctor. "He's not received anywhere any more," the woman said.

The phrase disturbed Rosemary, though she could not place the Divers as living in any relation to society where such a fact, if fact it was, could have any meaning, yet the hint of a hostile and organized public opinion rang in her ears. "He's not received anywhere any more." She pictured Dick climbing the steps of a mansion, presenting cards and being told by a butler: "We're not receiving you any more"; then proceeding down an avenue only to be told the same

*change in personality*

thing by the countless other butlers of countless Ambassadors, Ministers, Chargés d'Affaires. . . .

Nicole wondered how she could get away. She guessed that Dick, stung into alertness, would grow charming and would make Rosemary respond to him. Sure enough, in a moment his voice managed to qualify everything unpleasant he had said:

"Mary's all right—she's done very well. But it's hard to go on liking people who don't like you."

Rosemary, falling into line, swayed toward Dick and crooned:

"Oh, you're so nice. I can't imagine anybody not forgiving you anything, no matter what you did to them." Then feeling that her exuberance had transgressed on Nicole's rights, she looked at the sand exactly between them: "I wanted to ask you both what you thought of my latest pictures—if you saw them."

Nicole said nothing, having seen one of them and thought little about it.

"It'll take a few minutes to tell you," Dick said. "Let's suppose that Nicole says to you that Lanier is ill. What do you do in life? What does anyone do? They *act*—face, voice, words—the face shows sorrow, the voice shows shock, the words show sympathy."

"Yes—I understand."

"But, in the theatre, No. In the theatre all the best comédiennes have built up their reputations by bur*les*quing the correct emotional responses—fear and love and sympathy."

"I see." Yet she did not quite see.

Losing the thread of it, Nicole's impatience increased as Dick continued:

"The danger to an actress is in responding. Again, let's suppose that somebody told you, 'Your lover is dead.' In life you'd probably go to pieces. But on the stage you're trying to entertain—the audience can do the 'responding' for themselves. First the actress has lines to follow, then she has to get the audience's attention back on herself, away from the murdered Chinese or whatever the thing is. So she must do something unexpected. If the audience thinks the character is hard she goes soft on them—if they think she's soft she goes hard. You go all *out* of character—you understand?"

"I don't quite," admitted Rosemary. "How do you mean out of character?"

"You do the unexpected thing until you've manœuvred the audience back from the objective fact to yourself. *Then* you slide into character again."

Nicole could stand no more. She stood up sharply, making no attempt to conceal her impatience. Rosemary, who had been for a few minutes half-conscious of this, turned in a conciliatory way to Topsy.

"Would you like to be an actress when you grow up? I think you'd make a fine actress."

Nicole stared at her deliberately and in her grandfather's voice said, slow and distinct:

"It's absolutely *out* to put such ideas in the heads of other people's children. Remember, we may have quite different plans for them." She turned sharply to Dick. "I'm going to take the car home. I'll send Michelle for you and the children."

"You haven't driven for months," he protested.

"I haven't forgotten how."

Without a glance at Rosemary whose face was "responding" violently, Nicole left the umbrella.

In the bathhouse, she changed to pajamas, her expression still hard as a plaque. But as she turned into the road of arched pines and the atmosphere changed—with a squirrel's flight on a branch, a wind nudging at the leaves, a cock splitting distant air, with a creep of sunlight transpiring through the immobility, then the voices of the beach receded—Nicole relaxed and felt new and happy; her thoughts were clear as good bells—she had a sense of being cured and in a new way. Her ego began blooming like a great rich rose as she scrambled back along the labyrinths in which she had wandered for years. She hated the beach, resented the places where she had played planet to Dick's sun.

310

"Why, I'm almost complete," she thought. "I'm practically standing alone, without him." And like a happy child, wanting the completion as soon as possible, and knowing vaguely that Dick had planned for her to have it, she lay on her bed as soon as she got home and wrote Tommy Barban in Nice a short provocative letter.

*letter to Tommy*

But that was for the daytime—toward evening with the inevitable diminution of nervous energy, her spirits flagged, and the arrows flew a little in the twilight. She was afraid of what was in Dick's mind; again she felt that a plan underlay his current actions and she was afraid of his plans—they worked well and they had an all-inclusive logic about them which Nicole was not able to command. She had somehow given over the thinking to him, and in his absences her every action seemed automatically governed by what he would like, so that now she felt inadequate to match her intentions against his. Yet think she must; she knew at last the number on the dreadful door of fantasy, the threshold to the escape that was no escape; she knew that for her the greatest sin now and in the future was to delude herself. It had been a long lesson but she had learned it. Either you think—or else others have to think for you and take power from you, pervert and discipline your natural tastes, civilize and sterilize you.

*afraid of Dick*

*Nicole's resolve*

They had a tranquil supper with Dick drinking much beer and being cheerful with the children in the dusky room. Afterward he played some Schubert songs and some new jazz from America that Nicole hummed in her harsh, sweet contralto over his shoulder.

*drinking*

> "Thank y' father-r
> Thank y' mother-r
> Thanks for meetingup with one another——"

"I don't like that one," Dick said, starting to turn the page.
"Oh, play it!" she exclaimed. "Am I going through the rest of life flinching at the word 'father'?"

> "—Thank the horse that pulled the buggy that night!
> Thank you both for being justabit tight——"

Later they sat with the children on the Moorish roof and watched the fireworks of two casinos, far apart, far down on the shore. It was lonely and sad to be so empty-hearted toward each other.

Next morning, back from shopping in Cannes, Nicole found a note saying that Dick had taken the small car and gone up into Provence for a few days by himself. Even as she read it the phone rang—it was Tommy Barban from Monte Carlo, saying that he had received her letter and was driving over. She felt her lips' warmth in the receiver as she welcomed his coming.

## VIII

SHE bathed and anointed herself and covered her body with a layer of powder, while her toes crunched another pile on a bath towel. She looked microscopically at the lines of her flanks, wondering how soon the fine, slim edifice would begin to sink squat and earthward. In about six years, but now I'll do—in fact I'll do as well as any one I know.

She was not exaggerating. The only physical disparity between Nicole at present and the Nicole of five years before was simply that she was no longer a young girl. But she was enough ridden by the current youth worship, the moving pictures with their myriad faces of girl-children, blandly represented as carrying on the work and wisdom of the world, to feel a jealousy of youth.

She put on the first ankle-length day dress that she had owned for many years, and crossed herself reverently with *priest* Chanel Sixteen. When Tommy drove up at one o'clock she had made her person into the trimmest of gardens.

*Affair?* How good to have things like this, to be worshipped again, to pretend to have a mystery! She had lost two of the great arrogant years in the life of a pretty girl—now she felt like making up for them; she greeted Tommy as if he were one of many men at her feet, walking ahead of him instead of beside him as they crossed the garden toward the market umbrella. Attractive women of nineteen and of twenty-nine are alike in their breezy confidence; on the contrary, the exigent womb of the twenties does not pull the outside world centripetally around itself. The former are ages of insolence, comparable the one to a young cadet, the other to a fighter strutting after combat.

But whereas a girl of nineteen draws her confidence from a surfeit of attention, a woman of twenty-nine is nourished on subtler stuff. Desirous, she chooses her apéritifs wisely, or, content, she enjoys the caviare of potential power. Happily she does not seem, in either case, to anticipate the subsequent years when her insight will often be blurred by panic, by the fear of stopping or the fear of going on. But on the landings of nineteen or twenty-nine she is pretty sure that there are no bears in the hall.

Nicole did not want any vague spiritual romance—she wanted an "affair"; she wanted a change. She realized, thinking with Dick's thoughts, that from a superficial view it was a vulgar business to enter, without emotion, into an indulgence that menaced all of them. On the other hand, she blamed Dick for the immediate situation, and honestly thought that such an experiment might have a therapeutic value. All summer she had been stimulated by watching people do exactly what they were tempted to do and pay no penalty for it—moreover, in spite of her intention of no longer lying to herself, she preferred to consider that she was merely feeling her way and that at any moment she could withdraw. . . .

In the light shade Tommy caught her up in his white-duck arms and pulled her around to him, looking at her eyes.

"Don't move," he said. "I'm going to look at you a great deal from now on."

There was some scent on his hair, a faint aura of soap from his white clothes. Her lips were tight, not smiling and they both simply looked for a moment.

"Do you like what you see?" she murmured.

"Parle français."

313

"Very well," and she asked again in French. "Do you like what you see?"

He pulled her closer.

"I like whatever I see about you." He hesitated. "I thought I knew your face but it seems there are some things I didn't know about it. When did you begin to have white crook's eyes?"

She broke away, shocked and indignant, and cried in English:

"Is that why you wanted to talk French?" Her voice quieted as the butler came with sherry. "So you could be offensive more accurately?"

She parked her small seat violently on the cloth-of-silver chair cushion.

"I have no mirror here," she said, again in French, but decisively, "but if my eyes have changed it's because I'm well again. And being well perhaps I've gone back to my true self—I suppose my grandfather was a crook and I'm a crook by heritage, so there we are. Does that satisfy your logical mind?"

He scarcely seemed to know what she was talking about.

"Where's Dick—is he lunching with us?"

Seeing that his remark had meant comparatively little to him she suddenly laughed away its effect.

"Dick's on a tour," she said. "Rosemary Hoyt turned up, and either they're together or she upset him so much that he wants to go away and dream about her."

"You know, you're a little complicated after all."

"Oh no," she assured him hastily. "No, I'm not really—I'm just a—I'm just a whole lot of different simple people."

Marius brought out melon and an ice pail, and Nicole, thinking irresistibly about her crook's eyes, did not answer; he gave one an entire nut to crack, this man, instead of giving it in fragments to pick at for meat.

"Why didn't they leave you in your natural state?" Tommy demanded presently. "You are the most dramatic person I have known."

She had no answer.

314

_affair_

"All this taming of women!" he scoffed.

"In any society there are certain—" She felt Dick's ghost prompting at her elbow but she subsided at Tommy's overtone:

"I've brutalized many men into shape but I wouldn't take a chance on half the number of women. Especially this 'kind' bullying—what good does it do anybody?—you or him or anybody?"

Her heart leaped and then sank faintly with a sense of what she owed Dick

"I suppose I've got——"

"You've got too much money," he said impatiently. "That's the crux of the matter. Dick can't beat that."

She considered while the melons were removed.

"What do you think I ought to do?"

For the first time in ten years she was under the sway of a personality other than her husband's. Everything Tommy said to her became part of her forever.

They drank the bottle of wine while a faint wind rocked the pine needles and the sensuous heat of early afternoon made blinding freckles on the checkered luncheon cloth. Tommy came over behind her and laid his arms along hers, clasping her hands. Their cheeks touched and then their lips and she gasped half with passion for him, half with the sudden surprise of its force. . . .

"Can't you send the governess and the children away for the afternoon?"

"They have a piano lesson. Anyhow I don't want to stay here."

"Kiss me again."

A little later, riding toward Nice, she thought: So I have white crook's eyes, have I? Very well then, better a sane crook than a mad puritan.

His assertion seemed to absolve her from all blame or responsibility and she had a thrill of delight in thinking of herself in a new way. New vistas appeared ahead, peopled with the faces of many men, none of whom she need obey or even love. She drew in her breath, hunched her shoulders with a wriggle and turned to Tommy.

"Have we *got* to go all the way to your hotel at Monte Carlo?"

He brought the car to a stop with a squeak of tires.

"No!" he answered. "And, my God, I have never been so happy as I am this minute."

They had passed through Nice following the blue coast and begun to mount to the middling-high Corniche. Now Tommy turned sharply down to the shore, ran out a blunt peninsula, and stopped in the rear of a small shore hotel.

Its tangibility frightened Nicole for a moment. At the desk an American was arguing interminably with the clerk about the rate of exchange. She hovered, outwardly tranquil but inwardly miserable, as Tommy filled out the police blanks—his real, hers false. Their room was a Mediterranean room, almost ascetic, almost clean, darkened to the glare of the sea. Simplest of pleasures—simplest of places. Tommy ordered two cognacs, and when the door closed behind the waiter, he sat in the only chair, dark, scarred and handsome, his eyebrows arched and upcurling, a fighting Puck, an earnest ?
Satan.

Before they had finished the brandy they suddenly moved together and met standing up; then they were sitting on the bed and he kissed her hardy knees. Struggling a little still, like a decapitated animal, she forgot about Dick and her new white eyes, forgot Tommy himself and sank deeper and deeper into the minutes and the moment.

. . . When he got up to open a shutter and find out what caused the increasing clamor below their windows, his figure was darker and stronger than Dick's, with high lights along the rope-twists of muscle. Momentarily he had forgotten her too—almost in the second of his flesh breaking from hers she had a foretaste that things were going to be different than she had expected. She felt the nameless fear which precedes all emotions, joyous or sorrowful, inevitably as a hum of thunder precedes a storm.

Tommy peered cautiously from the balcony and reported.

"All I can see is two women on the balcony below this. They're talking about weather and tipping back and forth in American rocking-chairs."

"Making all that noise?"

"The noise is coming from somewhere below them. Listen."

> "Oh, way down South in the land of cotton
> Hotels bum and business rotten
> Look away——"

"It's Americans."

Nicole flung her arms wide on the bed and stared at the ceiling; the powder had dampened on her to make a milky surface. She liked the bareness of the room, the sound of the single fly navigating overhead. Tommy brought the chair over to the bed and swept the clothes off it to sit down; she liked the economy of the weightless dress and espadrilles that mingled with his ducks upon the floor.

He inspected the oblong white torso joined abruptly to the brown limbs and head, and said, laughing gravely:

"You are all new like a baby." —∆ *ref. to young?*

"With white eyes."

"I'll take care of that."

"It's very hard taking care of white eyes—especially the ones made in Chicago."

"I know all the old Languedoc peasant remedies."[61]

"Kiss me, on the lips, Tommy."

"That's so American," he said, kissing her nevertheless. "When I was in America last there were girls who would tear you apart with their lips, tear themselves too, until their faces were scarlet with the blood around the lips all brought out in a patch—but nothing further."

Nicole leaned up on one elbow.

"I like this room," she said.

He looked around.

"I find it somewhat meagre. Darling, I'm glad you wouldn't wait until we got to Monte Carlo."

"Why only meagre? Why, this is a wonderful room, Tommy—like the bare tables in so many Cézannes and Picassos."

"I don't know." He did not try to understand her.

317

"There's that noise again. My God, has there been a murder?"

He went to the window and reported once more:

"It seems to be two American sailors fighting and a lot more cheering them on. They are from your battleship off shore." He wrapped a towel around himself and went farther out on the balcony. "They have poules with them. I have heard about this now—the women follow them from place to place wherever the ship goes. But what women! One would think with their pay they could find better women! Why the women who followed Korniloff! Why we never looked at anything less than a ballerina!"

Nicole was glad he had known so many women, so that the word itself meant nothing to him; she would be able to hold him so long as the person in her transcended the universals of her body.

"Hit him where it hurts!"

"Yah-h-h-h!"

"Hey, what I tell you get inside that right!"

"Come on, Dulschmit, you son!"

"*Yaa-Yaa!*"

"*YA-YEH-YAH!*"

Tommy turned away.

"This place seems to have outlived its usefulness, you agree?"

She agreed, but they clung together for a moment before dressing, and then for a while longer it seemed as good enough a palace as any. . . .

Dressing at last Tommy exclaimed:

"*My God*, those two women in the rocking-chairs on the balcony below us haven't moved. They're trying to talk this matter out of existence. They're here on an economical holiday, and all the American navy and all the whores in Europe couldn't spoil it."

He came over gently and surrounded her, pulling the shoulder strap of her slip into place with his teeth; then a sound split the air outside: Cr-ACK—BOOM-M-m-*m!* It was the battleship sounding a recall.

Now, down below their window, it was pandemonium

318

indeed—for the boat was moving to shores as yet unannounced. Waiters called accounts and demanded settlements in impassioned voices, there were oaths and denials; the tossing of bills too large and change too small; passouts were assisted to the boats, and the voices of the naval police chopped with quick commands through all voices. There were cries, tears, shrieks, promises as the first launch shoved off and the women crowded forward on the wharf, screaming and waving.

Tommy saw a girl rush out upon the balcony below waving a napkin, and before he could see whether or not the rocking Englishwomen gave in at last and acknowledged her presence, there was a knock at their own door. Outside, excited female voices made them agree to unlock it, disclosing two girls, young, thin and barbaric, unfound rather than lost, in the hall. One of them wept chokingly.

"Kwee wave off your porch?" implored the other in passionate American. "Kwee please? Wave at the boy friends? Kwee, please. The other rooms is all locked."

"With pleasure," Tommy said.

The girls rushed out on the balcony and presently their voices struck a loud treble over the din.

" 'By, Charlie! Charlie, look *up!*"

"Send a wire gen'al alivery Nice!"

"Charlie! He don't see me."

One of the girls hoisted her skirt suddenly, pulled and ripped at her pink step-ins and tore them to a sizable flag; then, screaming "Ben! Ben!" she waved it wildly. As Tommy and Nicole left the room it still fluttered against the blue sky. Oh, say can you see the tender color of remembered flesh?—while at the stern of the battleship arose in rivalry the Star-Spangled Banner.

They dined at the new Beach Casino at Monte Carlo . . . much later they swam in Beaulieu in a roofless cavern of white moonlight formed by a circlet of pale boulders about a cup of phosphorescent water, facing Monaco and the blur of Menton. She liked his bringing her there to the eastward vision and the novel tricks of wind and water; it was all as new as they were to each other. Symbolically she lay across his saddle-bow as surely as if he had wolfed her away from Damascus and they had come out upon the Mongolian plain. Moment by moment all that Dick had taught her fell away and she was ever nearer to what she had been in the beginning, prototype of that obscure yielding up of swords that was going in the world about her. Tangled with love in the moonlight she welcomed the anarchy of her lover.

They awoke together finding the moon gone down and the air cool. She struggled up demanding the time and Tommy called it roughly at three.

"I've got to go home then."

"I thought we'd sleep in Monte Carlo."

"No. There's a governess and the children. I've got to roll in before daylight."

"As you like."

They dipped for a second, and when he saw her shivering he rubbed her briskly with a towel. As they got into the car with their heads still damp, their skins fresh and glowing, they were loath to start back. It was very bright where they were and as Tommy kissed her she felt him losing himself in the whiteness of her cheeks and her white teeth and her cool brow and the hand that touched his face. Still attuned to Dick, she waited for interpretation or qualification; but none was forthcoming. Reassured sleepily and happily that none would be, she sank low in the seat and drowsed until the sound of the motor changed and she felt them climbing toward Villa Diana. At the gate she kissed him an almost automatic good-by. The sound of her feet on the walk was changed, the night noises of the garden were suddenly in the past but she was glad, none the less, to be back. The day had progressed at a staccato rate, and in spite of its satisfactions she was not habituated to such strain.

# IX

AT four o'clock next afternoon a station taxi stopped at the gate and Dick got out. Suddenly off balance, Nicole ran from the terrace to meet him, breathless with her effort at self-control.

"Where's the car?" she asked.

"I left it in Arles. I didn't feel like driving any more."

"I thought from your note that you'd be several days."

"I ran into a mistral and some rain."

"Did you have fun?"

"Just as much fun as anybody has running away from things. I drove Rosemary as far as Avignon and put her on her train there." They walked toward the terrace together, where he deposited his bag. "I didn't tell you in the note because I thought you'd imagine a lot of things."

"That was very considerate of you." Nicole felt surer of herself now.

"I wanted to find out if she had anything to offer—the only way was to see her alone."

"Did she have—anything to offer?"

"Rosemary didn't grow up," he answered. "It's probably better that way. What have you been doing?"

She felt her face quiver like a rabbit's.

"I went dancing last night—with Tommy Barban. We went——"

He winced, interrupting her.

"Don't tell me about it. It doesn't matter what you do, only I don't want to know anything definitely."

"There isn't anything to know."

"All right, all right." Then as if he had been away a week: "How are the children?"

The phone rang in the house.

"If it's for me I'm not home," said Dick turning away quickly. "I've got some things to do over in the work-room."

Nicole waited till he was out of sight behind the well; then she went into the house and took up the phone.

"Nicole, comment vas-tu?"

"Dick's home."

He groaned.

"Met me here in Cannes," he suggested. "I've got to talk to you."

"I can't."

"Tell me you love me." Without speaking she nodded at the receiver; he repeated, "Tell me you love me."

"Oh, I do," she assured him. "But there's nothing to be done right now."

"Of course there is," he said impatiently. "Dick sees it's over between you two—it's obvious he has quit. What does he expect you to do?"

"I don't know. I'll have to—" She stopped herself from saying "—to wait until I can ask Dick," and instead finished with: "I'll write and I'll phone you to-morrow."

She wandered about the house rather contentedly, resting on her achievement. She was a mischief, and that was a satisfaction; no longer was she a huntress of corralled game. Yesterday came back to her now in innumerable detail—detail that began to overlay her memory of similar moments when her love for Dick was fresh and intact. She began to slight that love, so that it seemed to have been tinged with sentimental habit from the first. With the opportunistic memory of women she scarcely recalled how she had felt when she and Dick had possessed each other in secret places around the corners of the world, during the month before they were married. Just so had she lied to Tommy last night, swearing to him that never before had she so entirely, so completely, so utterly. . . .

. . . then remorse for this moment of betrayal, which so cavalierly belittled a decade of her life, turned her walk toward Dick's sanctuary.

Approaching noiselessly she saw him behind his cottage, sitting in a steamer chair by the cliff wall, and for a moment she regarded him silently. He was thinking, he was living a world completely his own and in the small motions of his face, the brow raised or lowered, the eyes narrowed or widened, the lips set and reset, the play of his hands, she

322

saw him progress from phase to phase of his own story spinning out inside him, his own, not hers. Once he clenched his fists and leaned forward, once it brought into his face an expression of torment and despair—when this passed its stamp lingered in his eyes. For almost the first time in her life she was sorry for him—it is hard for those who have once been mentally afflicted to be sorry for those who are well, and though Nicole often paid lip service to the fact that he had led her back to the world she had forfeited, she had thought of him really as an inexhaustible energy, incapable of fatigue—she forgot the troubles she caused him at the moment when she forgot the troubles of her own that had prompted her. That he no longer controlled her—did he know that? Had he willed it all?—she felt as sorry for him as she had sometimes felt for Abe North and his ignoble destiny, sorry as for the helplessness of infants and the old.

*feels sorry for Dick*

She went up putting her arm around his shoulder and touching their heads together said:

"Don't be sad."

He looked at her coldly.

*isolated from Nicole*

"Don't touch me!" he said.

Confused she moved a few feet away.

"Excuse me," he continued abstractedly. "I was just thinking what I thought of you——"

"Why not add the new classification to your book?"

"I have thought of it—'Furthermore and beyond the psychoses and the neuroses——' "

"I didn't come over here to be disagreeable."

"Then why *did* you come, Nicole? I can't do anything for you any more. I'm trying to save myself."

"From my contamination?"

"Profession throws me in contact with questionable company sometimes."

She wept with anger at the abuse.

*fighting*

"You're a coward! You've made a failure of your life, and you want to blame it on me."

*strength*

While he did not answer she began to feel the old hypnotism of his intelligence, sometimes exercised without power but always with substrata of truth under truth which she

323

could not break or even crack. Again she struggled with it, fighting him with her small, fine eyes, with the plush arrogance of a top dog, with her nascent transference to another man, with the accumulated resentment of years; she fought him with her money and her faith that her sister disliked him and was behind her now; with the thought of the new enemies he was making with his bitterness, with her quick guile against his wine-ing and dine-ing slowness, her health and beauty against his physical deterioration, her unscrupulousness against his moralities—for this inner battle she used even her weaknesses—fighting bravely and courageously with the old cans and crockery and bottles, empty receptacles of her expiated sins, outrages, mistakes. And suddenly, in the space of two minutes she achieved her victory and justified herself to herself without lie or subterfuge, cut the cord forever. Then she walked, weak in the legs, and sobbing coolly, toward the household that was hers at last.

Dick waited until she was out of sight. Then he leaned his head forward on the parapet. The case was finished. Doctor Diver was at liberty.

X

At two o'clock that night the phone woke Nicole and she heard Dick answer it from what they called the restless bed, in the next room.

"Oui, oui . . . mais à qui est-ce que je parle? . . . Oui. . . ." His voice woke up with surprise. "But can I speak to one of the ladies, Sir the Officer? They are both ladies of the very highest prominence, ladies of connections that might cause political complications of the most serious. . . . It is a fact, I swear to you. . . . Very well, you will see."

He got up and, as he absorbed the situation, his self-knowledge assured him that he would undertake to deal with it—the old fatal pleasingness, the old forceful charm, swept back with its cry of "Use me!" He would have to go fix this thing that he didn't care a damn about, because it had early become a habit to be loved, perhaps from the moment when he had realized that he was the last hope of a decaying clan. On an almost parallel occasion, back in Dohmler's clinic on the Zürichsee, realizing this power, he had made his choice, chosen Ophelia, chosen the sweet poison and drunk it. Wanting above all to be brave and kind, he had wanted, even more than that, to be loved. So it had been. So it would ever be, he saw, simultaneously with the slow archaic tinkle from the phone box as he rang off.

*Hamlet*

*= p. 149*

There was a long pause. Nicole called, "What is it? Who is it?"

Dick had begun to dress even as he hung up the phone.

"It's the poste de police in Antibes—they're holding Mary North and that Sibly-Biers. It's something serious—the agent wouldn't tell me; he kept saying 'pas de mortes—pas d'automobiles' but he implied it was just about everything else."

"Why on earth did they call on *you?* It sounds very peculiar to me."

"They've got to get out on bail to save their faces; and only some property owner in the Alpes-Maritimes can give bail."

"They had their nerve."

"I don't mind. However I'll pick up Gausse at the hotel——"

Nicole stayed awake after he had departed wondering what offense they could have committed; then she slept. A little after three when Dick came in she sat up stark awake saying, "What?" as if to a character in her dream.

"It was an extraordinary story—" Dick said. He sat on the foot of her bed, telling her how he had roused old Gausse from an Alsatian coma, told him to clean out his cash drawer, and driven with him to the police station.

"I don't like to do something for that Anglaise," Gausse grumbled.

Mary North and Lady Caroline, dressed in the costume of French sailors, lounged on a bench outside the two dingy cells. The latter had the outraged air of a Briton who momentarily expected the Mediterranean fleet to steam up to her assistance. Mary Minghetti was in a condition of panic and collapse—she literally flung herself at Dick's stomach as though that were the point of greatest association, imploring him to do something. Meanwhile the chief of police explained the matter to Gausse who listened to each word with reluctance, divided between being properly appreciative of the officer's narrative gift and showing that, as the perfect servant, the story had no shocking effect on him.

"It was merely a lark," said Lady Caroline with scorn. "We were pretending to be sailors on leave, and we picked up two silly girls. They got the wind up and made a rotten scene in a lodging house."

Dick nodded gravely, looking at the stone floor, like a priest in the confessional—he was torn between a tendency to ironic laughter and another tendency to order fifty stripes of the cat and a fortnight of bread and water. The lack, in Lady Caroline's face, of any sense of evil, except the evil wrought by cowardly Provençal girls and stupid police, confounded him; yet he had long concluded that certain classes of English people lived upon a concentrated essence of the anti-social that, in comparison, reduced the gorgings of New York to something like a child contracting indigestion from ice cream.

"I've got to get out before Hosain hears about this," Mary pleaded. "Dick, you can always arrange things—you always could. Tell 'em we'll go right home, tell 'em we'll pay anything."

"I shall not," said Lady Caroline disdainfully. "Not a shilling. But I shall jolly well find out what the Consulate in Cannes has to say about this."

"No, no!" insisted Mary. "We've got to get out tonight."

"I'll see what I can do," said Dick, and added, "but money will certainly have to change hands." Looking at them as though they were the innocents that he knew they were not, he shook his head: "Of all the crazy stunts!"

Lady Caroline smiled complacently.

"You're an insanity doctor, aren't you? You ought to be able to help us—and Gausse has *got* to!"

At this point Dick went aside with Gausse and talked over the old man's findings. The affair was more serious than had been indicated—one of the girls whom they had picked up was of a respectable family. The family were furious, or pretended to be; a settlement would have to be made with them. The other one, a girl of the port, could be more easily dealt with. There were French statutes that would make conviction punishable by imprisonment or, at the very least, public expulsion from the country. In addition to the difficulties, there was a growing difference in tolerance between such townspeople as benefited by the foreign colony and the ones who were annoyed by the consequent rise of prices. Gausse, having summarized the situation, turned it over to Dick. Dick called the chief of police into conference.

"Now you know that the French government wants to encourage American touring—so much so that in Paris this summer there's an order that Americans can't be arrested except for the most serious offenses."

"This is serious enough, my God."

"But look now—you have their Cartes d'Identité?"

"They had none. They had nothing—two hundred francs and some rings. Not even shoe-laces that they could have hung themselves with!"

Relieved that there had been no Cartes d'Identité Dick continued.

"The Italian Countess is still an American citizen. She is the grand-daughter—" he told a string of lies slowly and portentously, "of John D. Rockefeller Mellon. You have heard of him?"

"Yes, oh heavens, yes. You mistake me for a nobody?"

"In addition she is the niece of Lord Henry Ford and so connected with the Renault and Citroën companies—" He thought he had better stop here. However the sincerity of his voice had begun to affect the officer, so he continued: "To arrest her is just as if you arrested a great royalty of England. It might mean—War!"

"But how about the Englishwoman?"

"I'm coming to that. She is affianced to the brother of the Prince of Wales—the Duke of Buckingham."

"She will be an exquisite bride for him."

"Now we are prepared to give—" Dick calculated quickly, "one thousand francs to each of the girls—and an additional thousand to the father of the 'serious' one. Also two thousand in addition, for you to distribute as you think best—" he shrugged his shoulders, "—among the men who made the arrest, the lodging-house keeper and so forth. I shall hand you the five thousand and expect you to do the negotiating immediately. Then they can be released on bail on some charge like disturbing the peace, and whatever fine there is will be paid before the magistrate to-morrow—by messenger."

Before the officer spoke Dick saw by his expression that it would be all right. The man said hesitantly, "I have made no entry because they have no Cartes d'Identité. I must see —give me the money."

An hour later Dick and M. Gausse dropped the women by the Majestic Hotel, where Lady Caroline's chauffeur slept in her landaulet.

"Remember," said Dick, "you owe Monsieur Gausse a hundred dollars apiece."

"All right," Mary agreed, "I'll give him a check to-morrow—and something more."

"Not I!" Startled, they all turned to Lady Caroline, who, now entirely recovered, was swollen with righteousness. "The whole thing was an outrage. By no means did I authorize you to give a hundred dollars to those people."

Little Gausse stood beside the car, his eyes blazing suddenly.

"You won't pay me?"

"Of course she will," said Dick.

Suddenly the abuse that Gausse had once endured as a bus boy in London flamed up and he walked through the moonlight up to Lady Caroline.

He whipped a string of condemnatory words about her, and as she turned away with a frozen laugh, he took a step after her and swiftly planted his little foot in the most celebrated of targets. Lady Caroline, taken by surprise, flung up her hands like a person shot as her sailor-clad form sprawled forward on the sidewalk.

Dick's voice cut across her raging: "Mary, you quiet her down! or you'll both be in leg-irons in ten minutes!"

On the way back to the hotel old Gausse said not a word, until they passed the Juan-les-Pins Casino, still sobbing and coughing with jazz; then he sighed forth:

"I have never seen women like this sort of women. I have known many of the great courtesans of the world, and for them I have much respect often, but women like these women I have never seen before."

## XI

DICK and Nicole were accustomed to go together to the barber, and have haircuts and shampoos in adjoining rooms. From Dick's side Nicole could hear the snip of shears, the count of changes, the Voilàs and Pardons. The day after his return they went down to be shorn and washed in the perfumed breeze of the fans.

In front of the Carleton Hotel, its windows as stubbornly blank to the summer as so many cellar doors, a car passed them and Tommy Barban was in it. Nicole's momentary glimpse of his expression, taciturn and thoughtful and, in the second of seeing her, wide-eyed and alert, disturbed her. She wanted to be going where he was going. The hour with the hair-dresser seemed one of the wasteful intervals that composed her life, another little prison. The coiffeuse in her white uniform, faintly sweating lip-rouge and cologne reminded her of many nurses.

In the next room Dick dozed under an apron and a lather of soap. The mirror in front of Nicole reflected the passage between the men's side and the women's, and Nicole started up at the sight of Tommy entering and wheeling sharply into the men's shop. She knew with a flush of joy that there was going to be some sort of showdown.

She heard fragments of its beginning.

"Hello, I want to see you."

". . . serious."

". . . serious."

". . . perfectly agreeable."

In a minute Dick came into Nicole's booth, his expression emerging annoyed from behind the towel of his hastily rinsed face.

"Your friend has worked himself up into a state. He wants to see us together, so I agreed to have it over with. Come along!"

"But my hair—it's half cut."

"Never mind—come along!"

Resentfully she had the staring coiffeuse remove the towels.

Feeling messy and unadorned she followed Dick from the hotel. Outside Tommy bent over her hand.

"We'll go to the Café des Alliés," said Dick.

"Wherever we can be alone," Tommy agreed.

Under the arching trees, central in summer, Dick asked: "Will you take anything, Nicole?"

"A citron pressé."

"For me a demi," said Tommy.

"The Blackenwite with siphon," said Dick.

"Il n'y a plus de Blackenwite. Nous n'avons que le Johnny Walkair."

"Ça va."

> "She's—not—wired for sound
> but on the quiet
> you ought to try it——"

"Your wife does not love you," said Tommy suddenly. "She loves me."

The two men regarded each other with a curious impotence of expression. There can be little communication between men in that position, for their relation is indirect, and consists of how much each of them has possessed or will possess of the woman in question, so that their emotions pass

330

through her divided self as through a bad telephone connection.

"Wait a minute," Dick said. "Donnez moi du gin et du siphon."

"Bien, Monsieur."

"All right, go on, Tommy." *marriage finished*

"It's very plain to me that your marriage to Nicole has run its course. She is through. I've waited five years for that to be so."

"What does Nicole say?"

They both looked at her.

"I've gotten very fond of Tommy, Dick." *loves Tommy*

He nodded.

*Rosemary*

"You don't care for me any more," she continued. "It's all just habit. Things were never the same after Rosemary."

Unattracted to this angle, Tommy broke in sharply with: *verbal attack on Dick*

"You don't understand Nicole. You treat her always like a patient because she was once sick."

They were suddenly interrupted by an insistent American, of sinister aspect, vending copies of The Herald and of The Times fresh from New York.

"Got everything here, buddies," he announced. "Been here long?"

"Cessez cela! Allez ouste!" Tommy cried and then to Dick, "Now no woman would stand such——"

"Buddies," interrupted the American again. "You think I'm wasting my time—but lots of others don't." He brought a gray clipping from his purse—and Dick recognized it as he saw it. It cartooned millions of Americans pouring from liners with bags of gold. "You think I'm not going to get part of that? Well, I am. I'm just over from Nice for the Tour de France."

As Tommy got him off with a fierce "allez-vous-en," Dick identified him as the man who had once hailed him in the rue des Saints Anges, five years before.

"When does the Tour de France get here?" he called after him.

"Any minute now, Buddy."

He departed at last with a cheery wave and Tommy returned to Dick.

"Elle doit avoir plus avec moi qu'avec vous."

"Speak English! What do you mean 'doit avoir'?"

" 'Doit avoir?' Would have more happiness with me."

"You'd be new to each other. But Nicole and I have had much happiness together, Tommy."

"L'amour de famille," Tommy said, scoffing.

"If you and Nicole married won't that be 'l'amour de famille'?" The increasing commotion made him break off; presently it came to a serpentine head on the promenade and a group, presently a crowd, of people sprung from hidden siestas, lined the curbstone.

Boys sprinted past on bicycles, automobiles jammed with elaborate betasselled sportsmen slid up the street, high horns tooted to announce the approach of the race, and unsuspected cooks in undershirts appeared at restaurant doors as around a bend a procession came into sight. First was a lone cyclist in a red jersey, toiling intent and confident out of the westering sun, passing to the melody of a high chattering cheer. Then three together in a harlequinade of faded color, legs caked yellow with dust and sweat, faces expressionless, eyes heavy and endlessly tired.

Tommy faced Dick, saying: "I think Nicole wants a divorce—I suppose you'll make no obstacles?"

A troupe of fifty more swarmed after the first bicycle racers, strung out over two hundred yards; a few were smiling and self-conscious, a few obviously exhausted, most of them indifferent and weary. A retinue of small boys passed, a few defiant stragglers, a light truck carried the dupes of accident and defeat. They were back at the table. Nicole wanted Dick to take the initiative, but he seemed content to sit with his face half-shaved matching her hair half-washed.

"Isn't it true you're not happy with me any more?" Nicole continued. "Without me you could get to your work again—you could work better if you didn't worry about me."

Tommy moved impatiently.

*Tommy +*
*Nicole*

"That is so useless. Nicole and I love each other, that's all
there is to it."

"Well, then," said the Doctor, "since it's all settled, suppose we go back to the barber shop."

*Dick*
*agrees to*
*divorce*

Tommy wanted a row: "There are several points——"

"Nicole and I will talk things over," said Dick equitably.
"Don't worry—I agree in principle, and Nicole and I understand each other. There's less chance of unpleasantness
if we avoid a three-cornered discussion."

Unwillingly acknowledging Dick's logic, Tommy was
moved by an irresistible racial tendency to chisel for an
advantage.

"Let it be understood that from this moment," he said,
"I stand in the position of Nicole's protector until details
can be arranged. And I shall hold you strictly accountable
for any abuse of the fact that you continue to inhabit the
same house."

*Tommy*
*is N's*
*protector*

"I never did go in for making love to dry loins," said
Dick.

He nodded, and walked off toward the hotel with Nicole's
whitest eyes following him.

"He was fair enough," Tommy conceded. "Darling, will
we be together to-night?"

"I suppose so."

So it had happened—and with a minimum of drama;
Nicole felt outguessed, realizing that from the episode of the
camphor-rub, Dick had anticipated everything. But also
she felt happy and excited, and the odd little wish that she
could tell Dick all about it faded quickly. But her eyes followed his figure until it became a dot and mingled with the
other dots in the summer crowd.

# XII

THE day before Doctor Diver left the Riviera he spent all his time with his children. He was not young any more with a lot of nice thoughts and dreams to have about himself, so he wanted to remember them well. The children had been told that this winter they would be with their aunt in London and that soon they were going to come and see him in America. Fräulein was not to be discharged without his consent.

He was glad he had given so much to the little girl—about the boy he was more uncertain—always he had been uneasy about what he had to give to the ever-climbing, ever-clinging, breast-searching young. But, when he said good-by to them, he wanted to lift their beautiful heads off their necks and hold them close for hours.

He embraced the old gardener who had made the first garden at Villa Diana six years ago; he kissed the Provençal girl who helped with the children. She had been with them for almost a decade and she fell on her knees and cried until Dick jerked her to her feet and gave her three hundred francs. Nicole was sleeping late, as had been agreed upon— he left a note for her, and one for Baby Warren who was just back from Sardinia and staying at the house. Dick took a big drink from a bottle of brandy three feet high, holding ten quarts, that some one had presented them with.

Then he decided to leave his bags by the station in Cannes and take a last look at Gausse's beach.

The beach was peopled with only an advance guard of children when Nicole and her sister arrived that morning. A white sun, chivied of outline by a white sky, boomed over a windless day. Waiters were putting extra ice into the bar; an American photographer from the A.P.[62] worked with his equipment in a precarious shade and looked up quickly at every footfall descending the stone steps. At the hotel his

334

prospective subjects slept late in darkened rooms upon their recent opiate of dawn.

When Nicole started out on the beach she saw Dick, not dressed for swimming, sitting on a rock above. She shrank back in the shadow of her dressing-tent. In a minute Baby joined her, saying:

"Dick's still there."

"I saw him."

"I think he might have the delicacy to go."

"This is his place—in a way, he discovered it. Old Gausse always says he owes everything to Dick."

Baby looked calmly at her sister.

"We should have let him confine himself to his bicycle excursions," she remarked. "When people are taken out of their depths they lose their heads, no matter how charming a bluff they put up."

"Dick was a good husband to me for six years," Nicole said. "All that time I never suffered a minute's pain because of him, and he always did his best never to let anything hurt me."

Baby's lower jaw projected slightly as she said:

"That's what he was educated for."

The sisters sat in silence; Nicole wondering in a tired way about things; Baby considering whether or not to marry the latest candidate for her hand and money, an authenticated Hapsburg. She was not quite *think*ing about it. Her affairs had long shared such a sameness, that, as she dried out, they were more important for their conversational value than for themselves. Her emotions had their truest existence in the telling of them.

"Is he gone?" Nicole asked after a while. "I think his train leaves at noon."

Baby looked.

"No. He's moved up higher on the terrace and he's talking to some women. Anyhow there are so many people now that he doesn't *have* to see us."

He had seen them though, as they left their pavilion, and he followed them with his eyes until they disappeared again. He sat with Mary Minghetti, drinking anisette.

335

"You were like you used to be the night you helped us," she was saying, "except at the end, when you were horrid about Caroline. Why aren't you nice like that always? You can be."

It seemed fantastic to Dick to be in a position where Mary North could tell him about things.

"Your friends still like you, Dick. But you say awful things to people when you've been drinking. I've spent most of my time defending you this summer."

"That remark is one of Doctor Eliot's classics."

"It's true. Nobody cares whether you drink or not—" She hesitated, "even when Abe drank hardest, he never offended people like you do."

"You're all so dull," he said.

"But we're all there is!" cried Mary. "If you don't like nice people, try the ones who aren't nice, and see how you like that! All people want is to have a good time and if you make them unhappy you cut yourself off from nourishment."

"Have I been nourished?" he asked.

Mary was having a good time, though she did not know it, as she had sat down with him only out of fear. Again she refused a drink and said: "Self-indulgence is back of it. Of course, after Abe you can imagine how I feel about it—since I watched the progress of a good man toward alcoholism——"

Down the steps tripped Lady Caroline Sibly-Biers with blithe theatricality.

Dick felt fine—he was already well in advance of the day; arrived at where a man should be at the end of a good dinner, yet he showed only a fine, considered, restrained interest in Mary. His eyes, for the moment clear as a child's, asked her sympathy and stealing over him he felt the old necessity of convincing her that he was the last man in the world and she was the last woman.

. . . Then he would not have to look at those two other figures, a man and a woman, black and white and metallic against the sky. . . .

"You once liked me, didn't you?" he asked.

336

"*Liked* you—I *loved* you. Everybody loved you. You could've had anybody you wanted for the asking——"

"There has always been something between you and me." She bit eagerly. "Has there, Dick?"

"Always—I knew your troubles and how brave you were about them." But the old interior laughter had begun inside him and he knew he couldn't keep it up much longer.

"I always thought you knew a lot," Mary said enthusiastically. "More about me than any one has ever known. Perhaps that's why I was so afraid of you when we didn't get along so well."

His glance fell soft and kind upon hers, suggesting an emotion underneath; their glances married suddenly, bedded, strained together. Then, as the laughter inside of him became so loud that it seemed as if Mary must hear it, Dick switched off the light and they were back in the Riviera sun.

"I must go," he said. As he stood up he swayed a little; he did not feel well any more—his blood raced slow. He raised his right hand and with a papal cross he blessed the beach from the high terrace. Faces turned upward from several umbrellas.

"I'm going to him." Nicole got to her knees.

"No, you're not," said Tommy, pulling her down firmly. "Let well enough alone."


# XIII

NICOLE kept in touch with Dick after her new marriage; there were letters on business matters, and about the children. When she said, as she often did, "I loved Dick and I'll never forget him," Tommy answered, "Of course not—why should you?"

Dick opened an office in Buffalo, but evidently without success. Nicole did not find what the trouble was, but she heard a few months later that he was in a little town named Batavia, N.Y., practising general medicine, and later that he was in Lockport, doing the same thing. By accident she heard more about his life there than anywhere: that he bicycled a lot, was much admired by the ladies, and always had a big stack of papers on his desk that were known to be an important treatise on some medical subject, almost in process of completion. He was considered to have fine manners and once made a good speech at a public health meeting on the subject of drugs; but he became entangled with a girl who worked in a grocery store, and he was also involved in a lawsuit about some medical question; so he left Lockport.

After that he didn't ask for the children to be sent to America and didn't answer when Nicole wrote asking him if he needed money. In the last letter she had from him he told her that he was practising in Geneva, N.Y., and she got the impression that he had settled down with some one to keep house for him. She looked up Geneva in an atlas and found it was in the heart of the Finger Lakes section and considered a pleasant place. Perhaps, so she liked to think, his career was biding its time, again like Grant's in Galena; his latest note was post-marked from Hornell, N.Y., which is some distance from Geneva and a very small town; in any case he is almost certainly in that section of the country, in one town or another.

*Tender is the Night* was first published in 1934, by Charles Scribner's Sons in New York and Chatto & Windus in London. In 1951 a revised version was published, edited by Malcolm Cowley from a copy of the novel which Fitzgerald had reorganized and in which he had made corrections. Penguin Books began reprinting this revised version in 1955.

Scholarly opinion, both textual and critical, has come, however, to regard the Cowley version with disfavour. Fitzgerald had clearly not completed his revision project and he may have abandoned it as not worth carrying out. His basic idea was to reconstruct the novel into chronological order, placing the 'flashback' chapters (Book II, I to X) at the begining of the book. Fitzgerald's workng copy contains a few alterations which he thought required by the 'new' order and some others, but Cowley made hundreds more (of both kinds), and there is no way in which a reader of the revised version can tell without research whether Fitzgerald actually wrote what he is reading.

This new Penguin Books text returns to the first edition, and is the first UK paperback to be based upon it. Where there seemed any need for change, however small, all Fitzgerald's manuscripts, typescripts and surviving proof-sheets were consulted to determine whether a preferable reading might have been lost in transmission. (In the late stages of composition and proof-reading, Fitzgerald was very hard-pressed for deadlines and his health was poor. His attention to textual accuracy was subordinated to other matters.) The serial publication of the novel in *Scribner's Magazine* has also been consulted, as have almost all subsequent reprints of the novel and the textual work of Matthew J. Bruccoli cited in the List of Variants: each has provided suggestions in particular difficult cases. But every alteration from the first edition (US) has been itemized in the List of Variants, and readers of the Penguin Books text may thus know at a glance whether any change has been made, where the reading in the text originates, and what the first edition read. It is hoped by this means to present the best modern reprint available.

ARNOLD GOLDMAN

# NOTES

## BOOK I

**1** *. . . and Cannes, five miles away*: As the first paragraph indicates, the time scheme of the novel is complex. The time span runs from June 1925 in Book I to summer 1929 in Book III. However, Book II (chs. I–IX) returns to 1917–19. For a detailed outline and commentary, see Parkinson, ch. 3.

**2** *'Antheil's my man'*: George Antheil (1900–59). An avant-garde American composer, living in Paris during the early 1920s, who sought to represent contemporary life by producing music 'like an incredibly beautiful machine'. His *Ballet mécanique* (1926) was scored for anvils, aeroplane propellers, electric bells, motor horns, pieces of tin and steel and sixteen player-pianos.

**3** *'McKisco?'*: Nicole is hunting for the brand-name Crisco, which would link the pasticheur McKisco to a butter substitute. See Cummings, p. 261.

**4** *'. . . since Connie Talmadge was a kid'*: Connie Talmadge (1893–1973). A Hollywood comedienne during the 1920s, whose sophisticated comedies were nearly as popular as her sister Norma's dramas. Brady's reference to 'kid' links Talmadge to the work of D. W. Griffiths (a director Fitzgerald admired and for whom Talmadge performed in *Intolerance* (1916)). Griffiths' pre-war films often involved 'child-women' as stars (Mae Marsh, Blanche Sweet, Lilian Gish, Mary Pickford). See Prigozy.

**5** *apostolic gesture*: One of several clerical allusions (see also 'chasuble' (48), 'sacred' (53), 'Vêtements Ecclésiastiques' (103)), culminating in Dick's papal blessing of the beach (337). In his 'General Plan' for the novel (1932), Fitzgerald spoke of Diver as 'a natural idealist, a spoiled priest.' Quoted in Bruccoli, *Some Sort of Epic Grandeur*, p. 335.

**6** *Villa Diana*: Diana is the goddess of hunting, patroness of woodlands and chastity. She had an aversion to marriage and obtained from her father (Jupiter) permission to live in perpetual celibacy and to preside over the travails of women. Her destruction of Actaeon (turned to a stag and torn to pieces by her dogs) for penetrating her private groves suggests her resentment of intrusion. The Villa is very much of Nicole's design, and its name alludes richly both to her gardening and to her desires.

**7** *Mrs. Burnett*: Frances Burnett (1849–1924). Author of romantic stories and novels, many of them for children, of which the most famous are *Little Lord Fauntleroy* (1886) and *The Secret Garden* (1911). Allusions to writing for children (see also Lewis Carroll and Jules Verne (67), and *Daddy-Long-Legs* and *Molly-Make-Believe* (135)) are part of a more general associative network concerned with the provision of coercive entertainment for children. The 'tensile strength' of Dick's 'social' and 'psychiatric balance' (76) is often ghosted by the language of toy-making (132, 133, 153, 176, 207, 272). Dick's skills as a socialite and psychiatrist are synonymous, depending on a capacity to reconstruct the mental interiors of others in forms that would have been understandable to pedagogues in Victorian nurseries.

**8** *the Riff*: A traditionally warlike tribe, of Berber extraction, living in the mountains of Northern Morocco. In 1922 they defeated Spanish occupiers to found the Republic of the Riff, but Spanish and French forces subdued the rebellion in 1926.

**9** *who would not be pleased at carrying lamps helpfully through the darkness?*: echoes Claudius' cry at the close of 'The Mouse-Trap' (*Hamlet* V. 2); Hamlet's 'Give me some light' is taken up by All as 'Lights, lights, lights!' Fitzgerald alludes to *Hamlet* to suggest the enormity of the disruption just witnessed by Mrs McKisco in the Diver bathroom.

**10** *'Plagued by the nightingale'*: Doherty argues that the novel deals with characters variously enamoured of romantic allusion and, more particularly, that Nicole functions as a Keatsian nightingale, drawing Dick towards ecstatic union and subsequent oblivion and self-loss. The novel is subtitled 'A Romance', and takes its title from Keats' 'Ode to a Nightingale', a poem which Fitzgerald said he could never read without tears. See the epigraph and Doherty.

**11** *President Tyler*: President John Tyler (1790–1862). Tenth president of the US (1841–5) an aristocratic Virginian Republican, possibly cited by Fitzgerald because he was noted as 'approachable, courteous' and conciliatory. Such a lineage links Mary North to Dick in the matter of well-mannered Southern patriarchs.

**12** *'I'll be at the hotel at four'*: Recalls 'And if it rains, a closed car at four.' ('A Game of Chess', T. S. Eliot, *The Waste Land*). Fitzgerald admired T. S. Eliot and met him in 1932. He knew *The Waste Land* extremely well. See Vot, p. 271.

**13** *... and three yards of new cloth the colour of prawns*: The account of the Parisian shopping spree may well have been suggested by stanzas XIV and XV of Keats' 'Isabella; or, The Pot of Basil'. See Swann, p. 437.

**14** *Hermès*: Well-known purveyor of luxury goods to the wealthy. Also the Greek name for Mercury, the messenger of the gods, the patron of travellers and also the god of thieves and pickpockets: an apt presence in a passage concerned jointly with production as an errand run for the wealthy and with property as theft. Fitzgerald intimates that the errand will culminate in a train wreck, an allusion to the stock market crash of October 1929. In the final chapters Tommy Barban states that his stocks are doing well (295), and the lives of the wealthy on the beach appear untouched by financial crisis – details which indicate that the novel closes in the summer of 1929 and prior to the crash.

15 *Beaumont-Hamel . . . Thiepval . . . Marne*: Sites significant for the 1916 British offensive against the Germans, known by the troops as the Great Fuck-Up. Paul Fussell describes it as 'the largest engagement fought since the beginnings of civilization' (p. 12). Abe North challenges Dick's seriousness by pointing out that large-scale modern warfare was invented at Petersburg, an American Civil War siege (1864/5). He adds that Dick's account of the Western front as a 'love battle' derives from D. H. Lawrence. Fitzgerald read Lawrence's *Fantasia of the Unconscious* around May 1930 with some enthusiasm. On the same subject, Lawrence notes: 'There we leave humanity, encamped in an appalling mess beside the railway-smash of love . . . But never any more will there be enough love-steam to get the system properly running. It is done.' Quoted in Wexelblatt, *American Literature*, pp. 377–88.

16 *Undine*: A fairy romance by Baron de la Motte Fouqué, written in 1811. Undine, a water nymph reared as human, marries a knight but is snatched by her watery kin; she returns to prevent her husband's remarriage with a fatal kiss. Dick will first meet Nicole on 'a damp April day, with . . . water inert in the low places' (132). The allusion is not simply to T. S. Eliot's 'April is the cruellest month' ('The Burial of the Dead', *The Waste Land*), but is one of a network of references linking sexual love to water and things watery, and so – as with *Undine* – to dissolution and to death. (See, for example, 160 and 171.)

17 '*The silver cord is cut and the golden bowl is broken*': Echoes the prefiguration of last days in *Ecclesiastes*, xii.6.

18 *Cardinal de Retz*: (1614–79). Archbishop of Paris (1653–62), but he lacked all ecclesiastical vocation and energetically pursued cabals and conspiracies as a minister to Louis XIV. Fitzgerald may intend some allusion to Dr Diver's role as a 'spoiled priest' ministering to a competitive social set with the graces of a religious father. See note 5.

19 *Louisa M. Alcott or Madame de Ségur*: Louisa May Alcott (1832–88). A writer most noted for *Little Women* (1868–9). Since Sophie Rostopchine, Comtesse de Ségur (1799–1874) wrote children's books with titles like *Nouveaux contes de fées pour les petits enfants* (1858) and *Les petites filles modèles* (1858), it is to be assumed that the women in question are allusively numbered among the numerous 'child-women' who populate the novel.

**20** *General Pershing*: John Joseph Pershing (1860–1948). The American general who commanded the US Expeditionary Force in Europe during the First World War.

**21** *a Goldberg cartoon*: Rube Goldberg (1883–1970) drew machines and contraptions of great complexity whose function was to perform easy tasks. By 1928 his cartoons were nationally syndicated.

**22** *Tarkington*: Booth Tarkington (1869–1948). Author of a series of novels about life in the Midwest, most notably *The Magnificent Ambersons* (1918) and *Alice Adams* (1921).

**23** *a church in Ferrara*: Fitzgerald may be confusing Ferrara with Canossa, scene of Henry IV's humiliating penance before Pope Gregory in 1077.

**24** *Tad*: Thomas A. Dorgan (1875–1928). His work for the New York *Journal* and *American* was both popular and acerbic. One of a group of cartoonists who, in the 1900s, introduced strip cartoons into the dailies, he was also noted for his political images, particularly for attacks on the power of the Trusts.

**25** *Cheyne-Stokes tendencies*: A cyclical respiratory pattern characterized by slowing down, stopping for a number of seconds, and then speeding up.

**26** *Teput Dome*: i.e. Teapot dome, the popular name for a scandal during the presidency of Warren Harding. The scandal broke in 1924 and became synonymous with government corruption. See note 36.

**27** *Mosby*: John Singleton Mosby (1833–1916). A Confederate Ranger based in Virginia during the Civil War. He started with nine men but by 1865 had eight well-equipped companies; indeed, he was so successful that between 1864 and 1865 he acted as judge and administrator in the north of the state, which became known popularly as 'Mosby's Confederacy'. As cavalry officer, Mosby is the stuff of legend and as such doubtless appealed to the Reverend Diver (also from Virginia, 222).

**28** *'Miss Television'*: Demonstrations of various kinds of experimental television were made in the late 1920s. NBC and CBS opened television stations in New York (1930 and 1931), but to little effect, since pictures were fuzzy, screens tiny and costs enormous. Dick's remark suggests just how far Fitzgerald associates Rosemary with future social and cultural forms.

**29** *Grant*: Ulysses S. Grant (1822–85). The most capable of the Union generals during the Civil War and eighteenth President of the US. The first of three references (see also 132 and 338). The sustained analogy between Diver and Grant rests on three points of contact: both men drank too much; both presided over corrupt administrations but did not lose their personal integrity, and both experienced cultural periods (the Gilded Age and the Jazz Age) which were characterized by post-war boom and collapse. See Wexelblatt, *Notes on Modern Literature*, 16.

**30** *Arbuckle case*: Roscoe 'Fatty' Arbuckle (1887–1933). One of the silent screen's major stars, mainly remembered for his role in a notorious Hollywood scandal. In 1921, after initial accusations of rape and murder, he was charged with the manslaughter (during a wild party) of Virginia Rappe. Tried three times, he was acquitted in 1922, but his career was ruined.

**31** *'McBeth?'*: Fitzgerald's hotelier shares the name of Shakespeare's Scottish king perhaps because Lady Macbeth is driven to self-destruction by her inability to erase images of Duncan's blood from her person (Macbeth V.1).

## BOOK II

**32** *Fairy Blackstick*: Named for 'the ebony wand or crutch' she carries, Thackeray's fairy offers 'misfortune' as a christening gift and, on being refused entry to a later royal christening, turns a porter into a metal door knocker, whose nose and parts are subsequently much abused. In the context of 'big stiff' (130) and Dick's thought that it might be 'nice' to be 'less intact' in order to 'build out some broken side' (131), Blackstick adds ethnic coloration to the emergent pattern of phallic instability which attends Dr Diver's name and desires.

**33** *Kraepelin*: Emil Kraepelin (1856–1926). German pioneer in experimental psychopathology who formulated a highly influential system for classifying psychosis (162) and helped initiate the discipline of abnormal psychology.

**34** *transference*: A psychoanalytic term referring to a process, during analysis, whereby a patient 'actualizes' unconscious wishes by 'transferring' them on to the analyst. In the transference, infantile prototypes re-emerge and are experienced with a strong sensation of immediacy.

**35** *Daddy-Long-Legs and Molly-Make-Believe*: *Daddy-Long-Legs*: Jean Webster's work of 1912 features a heroine who rises from orphanage to college by way of the generosity of an unknown patron, whom she nicknames Daddy-Long-Legs. The denouement has the college girl discover that her young man is, in fact, he whom she has called 'Daddy'. *Molly Make-Believe*: Eleanore Abbott's bestseller of 1910 is a fairy story of convalescence, whose innocent and manipulative heroine contrives to cure and marry an arthritic and despairing young man.

**36** *Devereux Warren*: The sources of the name are probably several: the initials may recall Daddy Warbucks, whose little girl, Orphan Annie, first captivated America as a comic strip in 1924; while Warren possibly derives from President Warren Harding, whose daughter, born to his mistress

Nan Britton, wrote a bestselling memoir, *The President's Daughter*, in 1927. See Prigozy.

**37** ... *a pantheon of heroes*: Franz's view of Zurich garners a Who's Who of its more notable citizens. Johann Kaspar Lavater (1741–1801), an antagonist of rationalism and writer on physiognomy whose work influenced Heinrich Pestalozzi (1746–1827), the educationalist, who through Fröbel, his most influential disciple, became grandfather of the Kindergarten; Alfred Escher (1819–82) a Zurich-based banker, industrialist and railway baron, and Zwingli (1484–1531), the protestant reformer who made the city the second centre of the Reformation.

**38** *'G't night—g't night'*: Joins Dick's departure from Gstaad, 'Good-by, Gstaad, good-by!' (197) and his lament over his father's grave 'Good-by, my father—good-by, all my fathers' (224), as a running allusion to the litany of 'Goonight[s]' and 'good nights' at the close of T. S. Eliot's 'A Game of Chess', *The Waste Land*.

**39** *absent himself from felicity a while*: An allusion to Hamlet's dying instruction to Horatio, 'Absent thee from felicity awhile ... To tell my story' (V.2). 'Felicity', in Fitzgerald's usage, is synonymous with Nicole; but for Hamlet it is coterminous with 'death' – an intertextual conjunction which intimates that Dick and Nicole's liaison is fatal from the first.

**40** *Mad Anthony Wayne*: (1745–96). Gained his epithet for his style of command during the Revolutionary War. In 1791 Washington appointed him Major-General to the rehabilitated American Army for a 'successful' campaign against the Northwestern Indians.

**41** *Marshall Field*: (1834–1906). Chicago-based founder of the Marshall Field retail company, and of one of the city's 'great feudal families' of whom Dohmler has read (142).

**42** *Pallas Athene*: Nicole's allusion to the Greek goddess of war, wisdom and the liberal arts may tacitly refer to Athena's birth, full grown and armed, from the split head of her father, Zeus.

**43** *Ouled Naïl*: An Algerian tribe who were not poor, little or customarily naked. If Nicole were in Algeria she could not hear drums 1,500 miles away, in Senegal. Fitzgerald drew on his short story, 'One Trip Abroad' (1930) for several of the details of the North African trip. See also Natterman.

**44** *Timgad*: The largest remains of any imperial city outside Italy, located in North-East Algeria. Biskra (177) is also an archaeological site.

**45** *Mistinguett*: (1875–1956). The stage name of Jeanne Bourgeois, a French music-hall performer, noted for her performances at the *Folies-Bergère*, the Casino de Paris and the Moulin Rouge.

**46** *Crœsus*: Last of the Lydian kings (sixth century BC), who introduced the coining of gold and whose wealth was proverbial.

**47** '. . . *a ghostly echo from a broken wall*': The American artist, enclosed in an 'Iron Maiden' formed by her own sores, is attended by tangential references to Eliot's work. The 'subterranean melodies' which afflict her bandaged face owe something to the 'sea girl[s']' voices at the close of 'The Love Song of J. Alfred Prufrock', while her account of herself as 'a ghostly echo from a broken wall' alludes to the bats who 'crawled head downward down a blackened wall' and to 'voices singing out of empty cisterns and exhausted wells' ('What the Thunder Said', *The Waste Land*). Since these references serve to link the artist, to whom Dick 'went out . . . almost sexually', with deathly or poisonous waters, they are part of a systematic network forming between female sexuality and male dissolution.

**48** *Svengali*: A character in George du Maurier's novel *Trilby* (1894) who, through hypnotic power, transforms the heroine Trilby into a great singer. Nicole's deranged question appears to confuse the hypnotized subject with the hypnotist.

**49** *Bleuler and the elder Forel*: Eugen Bleuler (1857–1939): The Zurich-based physician and psychiatrist who introduced the term 'schizophrenia', and resisted the notion that schizophrenics could not be successfully treated. Or, Manfred Bleuler (1903–), who continued his father's work and introduced the principle of an active community into the relief of mental disorders. Both careers are of relevance to Dr Diver's treatment of Nicole. Auguste Forel (1848–1931): A Swiss psychologist, teaching at the University of Zurich, who used and wrote on hypnosis, but is probably best known for *The Sexual Problem* (1905).

**50** *was Crucified, Died and was Buried*: The 'wisdom' to which Dick listens is drawn from the Creed to the Holy Communion (*The Book of Common Prayer*). Christ 'suffered, and was buried, and the third day he rose again according to the Scriptures, and ascended into heaven, and sitteth on the right hand of the Father'. The Reverend Diver having died, Dick's capacity for resurrection is to be doubted.

**51** '*Wall Street*': Sinclair Lewis (1885–1951) published *Main Street* (1920). Fitzgerald includes an Italian misappropration of Lewis' title in 1928 to ensure that the shadow of the Crash falls across events towards the close of his own novel.

**52** *Edna Ferber*: (1887–1968). A Michigan-born novelist and playwright who resided in New York and is perhaps best known for *Showboat* (1926), which was made into an operetta by Kern and Hammerstein (1927).

**53** *Michael Arlen*: Author of *The Green Hat* (1925), a popular writer whom Fitzgerald considered 'dead' and 'second rate' (by 1930), an example of what he too might have become had he gone for 'half-baked books', rather than struggling with *Tender is the Night.* See Bruccoli, *Some Sort of Epic Grandeur,* 294–5.

**54** *Groton voice:* Groton is a famous American private school, whose pupils' voices are necessarily aristocratic.


## BOOK III

**55** *Norma Talmadge:* (1897–1957). The oldest and most successful of the three Talmadge sisters. Having been in movies since 1911, her career ended with the coming of sound. In 1917 she formed a successful production company with her husband Joseph Schenck, whom she called 'Daddy'.

**56** *cantharides:* A preparation of dried beetles (or Spanish flies) traditionally believed to be an aphrodisiac.

**57** *bastide:* A small country house in the south of France.

**58** *Lady Caroline Sibly-Biers:* Milton Stern annotates her name, 'she is sibling to all the girlboybabies, and her life is the bier of all the broken decalogues.' See Stern, p. 72.

**59** *John Held:* (1889–1958). Both as an artist and an author, in such books as *Grim Youth* (1930) and *The Flesh is Weak* (1931), Held was considered a leading interpreter of the younger generation of the Jazz Age.

**60** *Danny Deever:* The allusion is to Kipling's poem of the same name (*Rudyard Kipling's Verse* (New York: Doubleday, 1940), 395–6). Since 'they're hangin' Danny Deever in the mornin',' the piano player's voice provides an apt accompaniment to Dick's social demise.

**61** *Languedoc peasant remedies:* Southern France. A play on 'long dick', indicating that Tommy Barban is equipped to replace Dick, 'the big stiff' (130), who goes limp in the water after failing to stand upright on the surf board (306).

**62** *A.P.:* Associated Press.

# LIST OF VARIANTS

Key to editions cited:

P      Penguin Books edition, Harmondsworth, 1982, 1986

I      First American edition: Charles Scribner's Sons, New York, 1934 (fourth printing 1951)

S      Serial publication: *Scribner's Magazine*, January–April 1934; book galleys were set from S

I–B      First British edition: Chatto & Windus, London, 1934

F      Fitzgerald's copy (Princeton University Library); annotated *c.* 1938

POR      *The Portable Scott Fitzgerald*: Viking Press, New York, 1945

C      ed. Malcolm Cowley: Charles Scribner's Sons, New York, 1951 ('With the Author's Final Revisions')

BH      The Bodley Head, London, 1959

M      Matthew J. Bruccoli, "Materials for a Centenary Edition of *Tender is the Night*" *Studies in Bibliography*, XVII (1964), pp. 177–93

Manuscript material from the Princeton University Library is identified by a B followed by a number. This gives the 'key number' of the manuscript according to Matthew J. Bruccoli, *The Composition of 'Tender is the Night'* (University of Pittsburgh Press, 1963), followed by the page or galley number.

g      galley
rbg      revised book galley
urbg      unrevised book galley
cts      carbon typescript

E.g., B183: urbg101 is unrevised book galley numbered 101 in the group of manuscripts designated key number 183 by Bruccoli. B137:282 is page 282 of the manuscript in the group with the key number 137.

The variant in the Penguin Books edition is here followed by its latest mss and/or earliest printed location(s), by the rejected reading of the first American edition (I), and by any other significant variant forms.

| Epig. 1 | *night,* C; *night* ... I |
| Epig. 5 | "Ode ... Nightingale" B130; Ode ... Nightingale. I |
| 11.30 | Hôtel I–B; Hotel I |
| 13.30 | Golfe-Juan P; Golfe Juan I |
| 18.14 | Antheil B140:9; Anthiel I |
| 18.16 | *Ulysses* S; Ulysses I |
| 19.6 | *Ulysses* S; Ulysses I |
| 21.20 | was C; were I |
| 22.22 | the Pont I–B; The Pont I |
| 22.23 | Amphitheatre S, I–B; Ampitheatre I |
| 23. 15–16 | "Nice Carnival Song" M; Nice Carnival Song I |
| 23.18 | citronnade P; citronade I |
| 23.29 | Hôtel I–B; Hotel I |
| 23.32 | valuation P; valuations I |
| 23.34 | czar C; Czar I |
| 24. 3–4 | bookshops I–B; book shops I |
| 24.16 | Hôtel I–B; Hotel I |
| 24.27 | that S; the I |
| 25.14 | was C; were I |
| 25.25 | character, C; character I |
| 26.2 | swimming. I–B; swimming, I |
| 28.27 | head, P; head I |
| 28.30 | Señor C; Signor I |
| 29.13 | umbrella, C; umbrella. I |
| 31.13 | as nearly sulky S; nearly as sulkily I |
| 31.14 | la P; La I |
| 31.22 | dwarf P; dwarfed I |
| 35.2 | Siena C; Sienna I |
| 42.8 | Divers' S, I–B; Diver's I |
| 43.16 | Viking madonna P; viking Madonna I; viking madonna C |
| 44.20 | sentiment was I–B; sentiment, was I |
| 47.10 | Iles de Lérins C; Isles des Lerins I |
| 49.14 | Hôtel I–B; hotel I |
| 53.31 | cavalry: I–B; cavalry. I |
| 58.36 | Juan-les-Pins P; Juan les Pins I |
| 62.18 | chair.... P O R; chair ... I |
| 64.1 | Saints P; Saintes I |
| 64.1, 78.25, 79.11, 82.27, 104.19, 110.2, 116.26, 117.8 | rue P; Rue I |

| 178.24 | Affaires Étrangères  POR;  *Affaires Etrangères*  I |
|---|---|

178.24  Affaires Étrangères  POR;  *Affaires Etrangères*  I
178.27  Mistinguett  P;  Mistinguet  I
178.32  mind—you've  P;  mind. You've  I
179.24  Alliés  S, I–B;  Alliées  I
180.5  "Nicole  C;  Nicole  I;  "*Nicole*  S
180.6  Hands  P;  hands  I;  *Hands*  S
181.20  Alliés  S, I–B;  Alliées  I
181.25  "Nice Carnival Song,"  C;  Nice Carnival Song,  I
183.27  McBeth  I–B;  MacBeth  I
185.28  Hôtel  I–B;  Hotel  I
186.21  menagerie  C;  Menagerie  I
188.20  Juan-les-Pins  P;  Juan les Pins  I
189.8  Sturmtruppen  C;  *Sturmtruppen*  I
191.4  Gregorovious  I–B;  Gregorovius  I
193.14  have  B143:218;  haven't  I
193.24  Privatdocent  S;  Privat docent  I
195. 29–30  Humpty Dumpty  C;  Humpty-Dumpty  I
198.7  his bed-lamp  C;  his bed-lamp light  I;  the light  S
200.6  roof,  POR;  roof  I
201.17  uninstructed  M;  instructed  I
202.13  torture,  C;  torture  I
205.23  manic  S;  maniac  I, B184:cts;  manic (depressive: crossed out)  B143:237
210.25  schizophrène  P;  schizophrène  I
212.16  Émile's  C;  Emile's  I
212.27  Émile  C;  Emile  I
213.17, 36  Congress  P;  congress  I
213.20  patients'  S;  patient's  I
215.6  cafés  POR;  cafés,  I
215.15  a  C;  A  I
216.28  inordinately and meanwhile  S;  inordinately meanwhile  I
216.21  Grand  S;  grand  I
217.35  stood ready to depart  S;  departed  I
219.29–30  Erbsensuppe  M;  erbsen-suppe  I
219.30  Würstchen  C;  würstchen  I;  *Würstchen*  POR
219.30  four Pilsener  P;  four helles of Pilsener  I;  four seidels of Pilsener  C;  four hellas of Pilsener  S

| 297.18 | rabbit P; Rabbit. I |
| 298.9 | Niçois C; Niçoise I |
| 300. 19–21 | "Dears...ROSEMARY" P; Dears... ROSEMARY. I |
| 300.19 | tomorrow S; to-morrow I |
| 300.20 | you S; you. I |
| 301.5 | hopeful— I–B; hopeful,— I |
| 301.7 | reached, C; reached— I |
| 302.38 | hook S, B183:urbg95, B184:cts; nook I |
| 306.14–15 | the Mexican C; "Château" I; the South American B155:g18 |
| 307.16 | Abrams' I–B; Abram's I; Abrams's S |
| 308.9 | Loos S; Loos' I |
| 308.24 | boat— C; boat,— I |
| 310.29 | changed— B148:376, I–B; changed,— I |
| 314.33 | eyes, C; eyes I |
| 316.24 | animal, she I–B; animal she I |
| after 319.32 | (extra space between lines) S, B183:urbg101; (no extra space, being bottom and top of pages) I |
| 319.37 | Menton P; Mentone I |
| 324.24 | est-ce que S; est-ce-que I |
| 324.24 | Oui...." B183:urbg102; Oui..." I |
| 325.15 | Sibly-Biers S; Sibley-Biers I |
| 325.22 | Alpes-Maritimes I–B; Alpes Maritimes I |
| 330.18 | Alliés S, I–B; Alliées I |
| 331.22 | buddies P; Buddies I |
| 331.24 | ouste P O R; Ouste I |
| 331.33 | "allez-vous-en," S, I–B; "allez-vous-en." I (stop is probably broken type) |
| 331.35 | rue des P; Due de I |
| 333.7 | principle S, I–B; principal I |
| 334.32 | A.P. B155:g28; A. and P. I |
| after 337.22 | (no space between lines) S, B183:urbg 106; (extra space between lines) I |
| 338.14, 21 | N.Y., S. B183:urbg106; New York, I |
| 338.18 | section B146:411; Section I |

Readings from Fitzgerald's copy of *Tender is the Night* (F), have been accepted only where they appear to be corrections, independent of his proposed structural alterations, and not stylistic alterations.

357

End-of-line hyphenations in the first American edition have been treated in this edition according to their earlier appearances in serial or manuscript.

Arnold Goldman
July 1980, November 1985